March ,

Dear Katie & Jim,
Here is a story about your beloved home - away - from home.

RIPE BREADFRUIT

Much Aloha,

Heather + Rik
Keokea

RIPE BREADFRUIT

By

ARMINE VON TEMPSKI

OX BOW PRESS
WOODBRIDGE, CONNECTICUT

Copyright 1935, copyright renewed 1962

1992 reprint by
Ox Bow Press
P.O. Box 4045
Woodbridge, CT 06525

Paperback cover painting by Cecelia Rodriquez

Library of Congress Cataloging-in-Publication Data
Von Tempski, Armine, 1892–1943.
Ripe breadfruit / by Armine von Tempski.
p.   cm.
Originally published: New York : Dodd, Mead & Co., 1935.
ISBN 0–918024–98–6 (acid-free)
1. Hawaii—History—Fiction. 1. Title.
PS3543.O647R55   1992
813'.52—dc20   92–33054
                                                    CIP

The paper used in this book meets the guidelines for permanence
and durability of the Committee on Production Guidelines for
Book Longevity of the Council on Library Resources.

Printed in the United States of America

To

MY DAD,
LOUIS VON TEMPSKI

and to

MY HUSBAND,
ALFRED LATHROP BALL

CONTENTS

PART I

TREVELLYAN

CHAPTER 1

WALTER HAMILTON reluctantly slowed down his heated horse. Beyond the bulge of the cinder cone ahead lay the estate of Lani-o-akua, famed throughout the Pacific. Despite the fact that he had been born on Maui he had never visited it. From the front veranda of his home in Waikapu, at the base of the West Maui mountains—facing the peninsula sweeping eastward into the mass of Haleakala—he could see the stately groves of trees Hi-ball Trevellyan had planted, mounting toward the summit year by year.

At sunset and dawn, when contours were distinct, he could distinguish the white stack of Trevellyan's sugar mill, and above it terraced gardens hanging on the steep slopes of vivid hills. Below the mill, wedged in between black lava flows, fields of pale green cane grew triumphantly out of volcanic cinder which the ages had transformed into rich soil. He was curious to visit the locality and meet the man who owned it, a man about whom incredible stories circulated.

As owner and manager of the Waikapu sugar plantation Hamilton was prominent on Maui. He was practical and efficient but he was Island born and from long association with Polynesians had unconsciously absorbed many of their characteristics.

Like the majority of children born in Hawaii, each day when his nurse had fed and dressed him he had been placed in the care of a Hawaiian cowboy, appointed to teach him to ride, rope, and swim. From the age of four he had been in the saddle all day, riding with his guardian and the other *paniolos* as they went about their work. The impressionable and formative years of his childhood had been largely spent in the company of a race keenly attuned to nature. His ears had been trained to hear the minute sounds of rocks and earth worked on by changes of the atmosphere, his nostrils caught scents as unerringly as an animal's, his eyes distinguished shadings of color in clouds, sea, and vegetation invisible to the average Aryan. He could lie in bed at night and name the direction of the wind by its sound, he could anticipate the movements of animals, and divine the imperceptible change of one season slipping into another; a sort of vast rustle or stir in earth, sky, and sea, an instant of altered vibrations, then a great peace, like a sigh, when the transition had been completed.

His nature, developed to a point where it was aware of hidden forces working behind and through tangible objects, grasped the fact that the district through which he was riding possessed a peculiar quality. There was prodigal abundance in the damp, dark soil, warm as a cow's flank, breathing softly. Strange vibrations emanated from the trees. Vagrant airs, coming from distant islands, suggested ghostly fingers running idly over a harp. Across the wild wastes of lava below, spilling to the sea, the majestic dissonances of the Pacific, mingling with the rhythm of the universe, invested the afternoon with an extra dimension.

His horse climbed the first short, steep slope, then walked easily along the narrow path curving around the swell of the tree-covered cone. An occasional break in the groves surrounding him revealed glimpses of buildings and gardens lying in a wide, sun-drenched depression some hundreds of feet below. A long, tree-shaded avenue threaded the slightly seaward sloping valley clinging to the steep flank of Haleakala which filled the east with its fire-scorched summit.

In the Polynesian language the name Lani-o-akua had immense significance; Lani-o-akua, heaven of the gods, meaning wealth and profusion bordering on the supernatural. The soil, richest on the island, black, close, deep, holding unending life, was mysterious and insistent, friend and enemy, distracting men from their heritage of things spiritual to things earthly.

He hoped that Hi-ball Trevellyan would be at home when he called. He was eager to see the old man about whom he had heard so many contradictory stories. Trevellyan's origin was shrouded in mystery; it was known that in the early days, before buying Lani-o-akua, he had captained a whaling ship which anchored each winter with the rest of the fleet opposite Lahaina. Those who had met him declared that a sort of ruthless force thrust through his brutal exterior. It was said that the first time Trevellyan had seen the southwestern slope of Haleakala from the bridge of his ship, he had banged his fist against the railing and sworn he would never rest until he owned it.

The abundant slopes, like vast thighs, the hills, like

sumptuous breasts, stirred the extravagant fibre of Trevellyan's soul. He had boldly sailed his ship to Makena, the then uncharted bay at the base of the mountain, and anchored in the shadow of a purple cone, known to the natives as Puu-olai, hill of earthquakes. Lava flows, sufficiently recent to be ink-black, streamed down the slopes of the mountain through light green groves of *kukui* trees; cones and contorted ridges contributed toward the feeling of unrest pervading the locality, but far above shining hills, golden-green forests and grassy swales beckoned.

Leaving his ship in charge of the first mate, Trevellyan had tramped through wastes of cactus and over lava beds until he reached the verdant slopes he had seen. The region, beautiful beyond anything on Maui, took possession of his imagination. It was hinted that he smuggled opium for the Chinese who were being imported to Hawaii, and hunted whales as well. Eventually, he made sufficient money to buy Lani-o-akua. He had beautified the land, he had built greatly, but the Hawaiians declared that no good would ever come to an estate whose trees and crops had been watered with sweat and tears.

With magnificent disregard of everything save the goal he had in view—to make Lani-o-akua the most beautiful as well as the most profitable estate in Hawaii—Trevellyan had cheated and bullied Hawaiian families out of inherited holdings, then had retained them as cowboys in his employ, as though trying to make restitution for the wrong he had done them. He had planted the first successful sugar cane, built the first mill in the Islands, laid out gardens whose loveliness was broadcast over half the world.

Finding the natives too easy-going for the furthering of his titanic plans, he relegated them to work the cattle ranch adjunct to almost every Island plantation, and imported Chinese contract labor to plant cane, construct reservoirs, and work in the gardens. He drove them unmercifully. They swarmed over Lani-o-akua in hundreds, patient, weary figures in faded blue denim, toiling like ants.

It was common knowledge that every morning Trevellyan stamped down to the barracks where his Orientals were housed to assure himself that every man was out. If some unfortunate, prostrated with weariness or heavy with opium—temporarily dulling the misery of his lot—ventured to huddle in a bunk, Trevellyan seized the limp black queue and with a bellow and a wrench had the fellow on the floor, hurrying him out with well-aimed kicks from the heavy top boots he always wore and, gossip had it, slept in.

He carried a blacksnake * when he walked and as he rode it lay in a coil about the pommel of his saddle waiting until some trifling incident loosed his always-ready wrath. Then it sang and whined among cringing yellow bodies, cutting neat strips out of faded cloth, and leaving long red welts on bony backs.

Trevellyan's oaths, his black beard, his eyes like coals burning under ragged brows had become an Island legend. When he entertained, no local people, save King Kalakaua and his special favorites, Old Man Calhoun of Hana, and one or two others were invited. But occasionally a British warship was seen to anchor at Makena and lines of horses plodded up the long slopes carrying

* blacksnake-whip.

officers and crew to the spacious gardens for feasts that lasted for days and which, from reports, were bacchanalian orgies that made the birds rise screaming from the trees.

Trevellyan. Trevellyan was this and that; he was the bastard son of a prince; he was gutter scum; he kept apart because he felt that no one in the Islands, save King Kalakaua and Old Man Calhoun, were good enough for him to know; he dared not contact people for fear they might discover what he really was.

Hamilton looking up, realized he had been so lost in thought that he had arrived in Lani-o-akua before he realized it. A majestic garden, speared by slanting shafts of late sunlight, waited above the road. Leading through it was a sloped walk of flat stones, finished by a wide picket gate. Towering camphor, breadfruit, *kukui* and Norfolk Island pine-trees stood above vivid lawns that rose gently to a long, low-lying house banked with tropical shrubs and flowers.

A cold little breeze came down from the summit of Haleakala, hinting at approaching evening. Through massed tree trunks Hamilton got glimpses of flower beds flaunting lawless symphonies of color. Seeing a watering trough near the steps leading into the garden, he headed his horse for it. Dropping the reins on the animal's neck he was about to dismount when he saw a girl standing in the garden.

Her attitude suggested that she was expecting someone. Warmth and richness enveloped her as if she had been born in summer. In her was lodged the abundance of the earth. Her hair was the color of ripe corn, her mouth was sultry, and her eyes, set strangely in her face, affected him oddly. Their expression suggested that she could be completely indifferent to anything which did not directly concern her, that she could even watch, without emotion, mankind's slow, painful ascent toward God. Somewhere in the hills a wild peacock screamed, "Who cares! Who cares!" like a voice mocking humanity. The sound chilled Hamilton, but lifting his hat, he dismounted and walked to the bottom of the steps.

"Could you tell me if Mr. Trevellyan is at home?" he asked.

The girl did not reply immediately. Her eyes, grave and unfathomable, were fixed upon him and he divined in her, despite her quietness, the abandon he had seen in lava flows racing down mountain slopes to reach the sea. After a few instants she replied.

"Father's in Honolulu. I don't know when he will be back."

Her low, rich voice had the cadences of a wide, deep river flowing strongly and quietly between its banks. Hamilton tried to imagine her in another setting but could not. In her flowing white *holoku* * with the tall trees behind her, she seemed an integral part of the landscape. Her personality, like the district, had an inevitable quality.

"I'm sorry Mr. Trevellyan is away. I had hoped he might be in. My name is Walter Hamilton. I live at Waikapu. I feel, not knowing your father, that I should explain my presence in Lani-o-akua."

The girl waited.

* *holoku*—glorified version of the Mother Hubbard, worn by white women in Hawaii until about 1900.

"I was riding around the island with a party of main-land friends when word reached me in Kaupo, that one of the rollers in my mill had jammed. As it is grind-ing season it is imperative for me to get back. I sent my guests on with a guide and returned this way, as it's shorter and being so close—"

"Come in. I'll send one of the Chinese to get Ka-aina to take your horse."

"It's getting late. I have a twenty-five mile ride ahead of me and should get along," Hamilton said, glancing at the falling sun blazing a path of splendor over the sea. "My horse was thirsty," he glanced at the animal which had lifted its head from the water and stood with pricked ears, gazing toward some invisible object, "and I was curi-ous. I thought," he hastily corrected himself, "that it would hardly be neighborly to be so close and not call on your father."

The girl regarded him briefly from under her thick lashes, then with a strong, white hand gathered up the train of her *holoku*. "Stay for dinner," she urged. "There's a new moon, and after food and a rest your horse will make better time."

Hamilton hesitated. Behind him, between the tree tops, the ghost of a new moon showed like a fine, white feather in the sky. Late sunlight touched the bright, brown hair covering his well-modelled head, and out-lined his profile with its wide brow and kind, strong chin.

In the hills the peacock screamed again, harshly and shrilly.

"It's kind of you to invite me, but I think I'll push along," Hamilton said, lifting his hat and mounting.

The girl gazed at him and laughed oddly. Hamilton realized that, without uttering a word, she was saying everything a woman could say to a man. Silence, deepened and intensified by the remote echo of the sea encompassed them. He hesitated, reluctant to hurt her, but the isolation of Lani-o-akua was a menace, subconsciously brewing the perilous knowledge that in such a spot a man was beyond the censorship of his fellows. Raising his hat, he wheeled his horse and started down the avenue which the hurried twilight of the tropics was already filling with gloom.

He rode lost in thought. Darkness enfolded him and occasionally his horse started at some imagined terror lurking among the trees. Soothing it, he rode on. The dim procession of years which had marched over Lani-o-akua quickened to life in his mind. He regretted that Trevellyan had been away. It would have been illuminating to meet the man who was responsible for building such a place and who had fathered such a daughter. He felt her mind pulling him back and commended himself for his wisdom in refusing her invitation to dinner.

The atmosphere emanating from the locality went hand in hand with its name, Lani-o-akua, which implied it was the abode of supernatural forces. An extra quality was lodged in the soil and growth about him. Stones had distinct vibrations and a collective and individual presence lodged in the tall trees clustering the hills. He felt defrauded in not having had the chance to meet Trevellyan and, perhaps, get a glimpse of the real story behind the fabrications of Island gossip.

His horse shied sharply. When he got it quieted and

started on he realized that it was limping. Dismounting, he inspected the inside of its hoof and, finding a nail imbedded to the head, he got out his pocket knife and gently worked it out. He led the animal a few yards, then saw that it was out of the question to ride it the twenty-five miles to Waikapu.

Drawing a cigar from his pocket, he lighted it. The tiny flare of the sulphur match, which he detached from the cluster he carried, made a pool of light in the dark. The stark, white trunk of a dead eucalyptus stood out for an instant. He started leading his horse, watching to see if the lameness might wear off, but the limp increased. He smiled. If he had been a Hawaiian, he would have concluded that Trevellyan's daughter had *kahuna'd* * him.

Recollecting that he had seen corrals and a long stable on the lower side of the road, he headed for them. As he drew nearer he saw light spilling from the many windows of the house, withdrawn in its stately setting. The night was quiet, but the dark was filled with the muted protestations of the sea, forever fraying its edges against rough lava promontories.

Arriving at the corrals he turned in an open gate. An elderly Hawaiian, carrying a lantern, came out of the stable and, seeing him, halted.

"Aloha," he said, then in a concerned voice, "Horse *pilikea?*" †

Hamilton explained what had happened. The man nodded and led the way into the stable. Thoroughbreds reached lean heads over the doors of their loose-boxes

---

* *kahuna*—to put a spell on a person or situation.
† *pilikea*—in trouble.

and, smelling a stranger, whistled warningly. A mare with a gleam of white in her eye snapped at Hamilton's arm as he passed.

"Sha!" the cowboy cried, gesturing indignantly. "Typhoon, all the time make like this. No use!" He spoke apologetically, as if he felt the hospitality of the place had been betrayed.

"It doesn't matter," Hamilton laughed.

He noted the man's patient face, beautified by gentle, brown eyes. He was beginning to be bowed, but his figure was lean and hard from years of riding.

"What name you?" the Hawaiian asked, as he busied himself unsaddling the horse.

"Walter Hamilton."

"Which place you stop?"

"Waikapu."

"Too far. No use go back tonight. More better stop Lani-o-akua. I fix horse, then find Mr. David."

"Mr. David?" Hamilton asked, puzzled.

"Mr. David English fella. Come last year. When Mr. Hi-ball no stop Mr. David boss."

Hamilton saw that the Hawaiian was studying him while he filled a bucket with water and poured a disinfectant into it. The scrutiny made Hamilton vaguely uncomfortable, and, as if suspecting it, the old man occupied himself with the horse's hoof.

"Me Ka-aina," he announced in conversational tones. "Little more thirty year now I work for Mr. Hi-ball. You come Lani-o-akua before?"

"No. This is my first visit."

"Before missionaries came to Hawaii," Ka-aina said in his own tongue, "the gods walked on earth. When the missionaries came, the gods went away," He paused, an attentive expression on his face. "But at Lani-o-akua the gods are stronger than the missionaries. Listen. You can hear them, gods, going everywhere."

From the steeply rising hills behind the stables, the infinitesimal rustlings and whisperings of vegetation settling to sleep filled the night with a deep, solemn murmur, creating the illusion of unseen bodies moving through the foliage. Hamilton smiled.

"All right, laugh," Ka-aina said, with the tolerant good humor of a Polynesian. "Missionary laugh too, but Lani-o-akua not missionary place. This the *akuas* * place."

"So you're not a Christian?" Hamilton said.

The man looked up indignantly. "Sure I Christian. I go church with other Kanakas for sing, but Christian God he big *Akua*. He no bother about other *akuas* like the missionaries do. He understand about them. He the *Alii* † and the other *akuas* like the common people."

"Perhaps you're right," Hamilton said.

"Three, four day, foot all right," Ka-aina announced, turning the horse into an empty loose-box. Shaking a bucket of grain into the manger, he latched the door.

"Already you see Patricia?" he asked, without looking at Hamilton.

"Miss Trevellyan?"

"*Ae*." ‡

"Yes, she was in the garden when I stopped to water my horse."

"The *akuas* said you would come today," Ka-aina

* *akua*—god.
† *Alii*—chief.
‡ *Ae*—yes.

announced with satisfaction. "You stop here and I find Mr. David."

Hamilton smiled and settled his back against the stable door. Above the dim, gray shape of the sugar mill, the new moon hung like a slice of apricot in the sky. Everywhere were fine, noble shadows and the great, strong shapes of trees. The dark was stabbed by the distance-muted throbbing of a guitar, played by some Hawaiian, and through the beauty of the night, Chinese voices came like far-off gongs.

A firm footfall and the faint ring of Ka-aina's spurs roused him. A slim, erect young man materialized out of the dark and came to the stable door.

"Good evening. I'm Birthwood. Ka-aina told me about your horse. Mrs. Trevellyan insists that you stay the night. I will see that your animal is cared for and that you have a mount tomorrow."

Hamilton liked the young fellow. He had quality and reserve, but his mouth, despite its firm curves, was still unfinished.

"I'm sorry to inconvenience you by this mishap," Hamilton remarked as they started for the garden.

"Lani-o-akua has unlimited accommodations for guests," Birthwood said in his crisp, English voice.

"Been here long?" Hamilton asked.

"Eighteen months."

"Like it?"

"It's interesting."

Hamilton glanced at Birthwood's expressionless face. Crossing the road, they went up the steps into the garden. Light pouring from open windows showed sweeps of lawn and huge urns, holding century plants, effectively placed to silhouette their fantastic outlines against the faint silver of the sea. When they reached the veranda, Birthwood called out and a woman appeared.

"Mrs. Trevellyan, Mr. Hamilton," Birthwood said, and stepped back.

Hamilton was confused. It seemed impossible that this woman, who smacked of an English servant, was the mother of the girl he had seen in the garden. She fluttered into foolish speech, retreated into apprehensive silences, and he suspected the habit was fear of the headlong man she had married. There was only one conclusion to be drawn; a youthful indiscretion had compelled Trevellyan to marry beneath him and the marriage had outlawed him from his own class and kind.

"David, show Mr. Hamilton to one of the cottages," Mrs. Trevellyan said when greetings were over. "I insisted upon your staying, Mr. Hamilton, when David told me about your horse," she put up a hand to her dull, elaborately curled hair. "Hi-ball doesn't like people to visit here—when he's not home. Sometimes Patricia, David, and I are alone for weeks."

Hamilton flushed. "If Mr. Trevellyan prefers no guests when he's absent, I'll go on."

"He makes exceptions for people who only stay the night," Mrs. Trevellyan announced. Smiling foolishly, she started indoors.

Birthwood led the way toward the cottages nestling among orange and breadfruit trees. Hamilton was amazed at the extent of the place; Lani-o-akua could easily shelter fifty guests. Walking to the nearest cottage, Birthwood opened the door and showed Hamilton in to a low-ceilinged room furnished with a gigantic four-poster, washstand, chair, and bureau.

"This is King Kalakaua's cottage," Birthwood said, a faint smile lighting his eyes. "In order to reach the other bedrooms guests must enter and exit through this door. Mr. Trevellyan had the place constructed for His Majesty's convenience. With this arrangement King Kalakaua can, when the fancy seizes him to play cards, which is often, make his companions' escape impossible."

Hamilton laughed. Birthwood showed him the bathroom and left. While Hamilton washed up, he thought of stories told about Kalakaua. It was at Lani-o-akua that the King, having lost the sum allotted him annually by his subjects for gambling, with complete disregard for the responsibilities of his position, was said to have put the island of Kahoolawe into the pot as his stake— and lost it. He glanced at an oil painting on the wall, depicting five men seated about a table littered with cards and poker chips. Kalakaua occupied the center of the canvas, stripped of his insignias of royalty. In shirt sleeves, the high light of excitement in his eyes, he faced his companions, one hand resting on four kings, face upward on the table, and the other placed aggressively on his breast. Directly facing him sat a small, sandy man with his clenched fist on four aces. The other players watched, apprehension and amusement on their faces. Recalling the tale, told with gusto from Shanghai to New York, Hamilton chuckled.

For once in his life Kalakaua, with his passion for poker and his notorious bad luck at it, won a pot sufficiently large to satisfy even his extravagant spirit. Having come to Lani-o-akua with the four men with whom he habitually played poker, a game was started and continued without cessation for seventy-two hours. Then, after a deal, an excited expression leaped to his eyes. Through narrowed lids he had studied the sugar baron, who openly boasted that the wide lands he had planted in cane had all been won from Kalakaua at poker. The baron had smiled, raised Kalakaua, and waited. The King raised him in turn. The pot assumed immense proportions. Kalakaua and the baron continued to raise one another, and one by one the other players dropped out. At last, the baron called for a showdown.

"It's a shame to rob you like this, Kalakaua," he had remarked. "You can't beat me, you never have."

The King gave him a quick, curious look, laughed, and laid down four kings. Triumphantly, the baron laid down four aces. Kalakaua reached out a strong brown arm and jovially swept the mountain of gold dollars and bills toward him.

"Hold on!" the baron protested. "Four aces beat four kings."

"But five kings are better than four aces," Kalakaua announced, laughing uproariously, and striking the cards before him with the palm of one hand while he thumped himself on the chest with the other. There was no questioning his kingship. He took the pot, but from that day the sugar baron never spoke to him.

When he was washed up, Hamilton strolled on to the veranda. Beyond the brief circle of light from within the cottage, there was nothing but the night, waiting behind a throbbing curtain of darkness. "Lani-o-akua." He repeated the syllables thoughtfully. It was a name with which to conjure. Here a king gambled with islands for stakes and used himself as a trump card.

Here warships visited an individual. Here, the natives declared, gods still walked on earth. Here a girl, glamorous as a princess in a fairy tale, wandered in gardens made famous by Stevenson, Stoddard, and Mark Twain. From within the big house came the sound of a harp softly played. The music, like water rippling against dark shores, was disturbing. Around him the land of Lani-o-akua crouched, forging eerie spells. He was aware of the stir in the vegetation about him, busy with growth even in sleep. He felt the presence of Haleakala sleeping under the stars and of lava working secretly in the vitals of the island. An awareness in the night seemed to stoop closer, blind, impassive—as though some listening, unseen being was imposing, in an effortless and inevitable way its veiled purpose.

CHAPTER II

When he reached the house Hamilton entered the drawing room. It was long and lofty. Spreading silver candelabra shed soft light on polished tables. Flowers breathed from alabaster and crystal bowls. An air of luxury and extravagance, foreign to Hawaii, pervaded everything. Costly oils hung on the walls, rich rugs lay on the floor. Hamilton went forward and saw Patricia seated at her harp. The instrument curved above her like a lifted arm of gold, casting a faint reflection on her white dress.

"I did not expect to have the pleasure of seeing you so soon again," he said in conversational tones.

She gazed at him without replying, and he wondered what thoughts peopled the silences of her mind. A gust of wind coming down from the cold, blue rim of Haleakala streamed through the garden shaking the tree tops as though the night wanted to rid itself of something. Patricia touched the strings of her harp with a thoughtful stroke, then glanced up.

"Ka-aina said you would come," she announced. "So I knew when you left that something would happen to make you come back."

"Ka-aina?" Hamilton said, looking incredulous. "That's the old Hawaiian, who took care of my horse. How could he possibly—?"

"Ka-aina knows when things are going to happen before they do," the girl announced.

The gravity of her face made Hamilton smile. Her eyes, which had been profound and veiled, lighted, and tilting up her chin she laughed like an impudent child.

"You don't believe that?" she accused.

He shook his head. A Chinese boy appeared in the doorway and announced dinner. Patricia gave Hamilton a curious sidelong glance and rose. She stood beside him for an instant, sweet-scented, slender, but her head was above his shoulder, and the way she held herself and moved suggested the prow of a white-winged ship lifting above the sea.

"Do you go to Honolulu often?" Hamilton asked as they walked toward the dining room.

"I've never been away from Lani-o-akua," the girl replied. "Daddy imported governesses from England to teach me, but they never stayed long. You've never met him, but you've heard about him, haven't you?"

"Yes."

Patricia glanced at him, started to speak, then decided against it, and Hamilton suspected that her silences might be more dangerous than another woman's speech.

During dinner, in an effort to counteract the effect of his environment, Hamilton reviewed facts. Actually, everything was quite usual. He was dining on a vast estate, one of many in the Islands, with two women and a silent young man.

He studied the appointments of the table; costly crystal, heavy silver, damask with the finish of satin. Probably Trevellyan had brought it all from England. The food was the best the Islands had to offer, supplemented with caviar and French champagne. Silent Chinese boys served efficiently, but he noted that the girl, not the mother, sat at the head of the table.

Hamilton wished for the dozenth time that Trevellyan had been present. His curiosity to meet him had increased. His spirit dominated the house and gardens, landscaped so lavishly on the volcanic flanks of Haleakala. A man other than Trevellyan would have planted every acre in cane to swell his fortune and because Trevellyan sacrificed wealth in order to create beauty, it proved that he had that splash of splendor in his make-up which often redeems otherwise impossible men and women.

He attempted to visualize him opposite Patricia; black browed, choleric, truculent as a wild boar. The table was built to seat fifty guests. Kalakaua would be on Trevellyan's right, courtly, gay, his broad chest covered with decorations, and a wreath of flowers poised like a rakish crown on his curly head. The favorites with whom the King played poker, a cabinet minister, a butcher, a lawyer, and, until recently, a sugar baron, would be scattered among lean-flanked British naval officers, absurdly conscious of the garlands around their necks. There would be wine, music, Hawaiian hula girls, gayly lighted gardens, bursts of boisterous mirth, and then, according to gossip, the stately entertainment would degenerate into an orgy.

Hamilton was too intelligent to presume to judge

his fellow men, but he was high minded and recoiled from anything unbeautiful. While appreciating that all men, more or less, were victims of lesser moments, the knowledge that at Lani-o-akua such moments were catered to, tainted the beauty of the place.

He saw Patricia watching him. Undoubtedly Trevellyan saw to it that his daughter was kept in the background when he staged the orgies that relieved his savage and festering soul, but it was impossible for anyone as highly organized as Patricia to be unaffected by the vibrations thrown off by people who, secure in the knowledge of complete isolation, gave rein to their lesser natures in a wholesale way.

"I hope," Mrs. Trevellyan's voice roused him and he realized the heavy silence that brooded over the table, "that now you're here, you'll spend a day or so with us."

"Nothing would give me greater pleasure, but it's out of the question," Hamilton replied.

"If you leave without seeing Daddy's garden, he'll be insulted, for he loves it better than anything on earth," Patricia said. "Stay tomorrow, anyway, till after lunch."

She spoke carelessly, but her eyes were fixed commandingly upon him, reminding Hamilton of a child plotting to hold a coveted toy an instant longer.

"I'm sorry, it's impossible. I must leave early."

"David, tell Ka-aina to saddle my mare, Typhoon, for Mr. Hamilton at five o'clock."

"Of course I'll not take your mare," Hamilton retorted, slow anger creeping through him. He realized that more was passing between them than the actual words. Their glances met like crossing swords and their

spirits clashed. Patricia watched him, and Birthwood
glanced at her apprehensively, lips set in a hard line.
His expression made Hamilton wonder what unleashed
emotions the young man had been compelled to watch
at Lani-o-akua.

"I'm sending boys out at three tomorrow morning
to bring in extra mounts," Birthwood said. "They should
be back about eleven. Perhaps—"

"Thanks, Birthwood, I can stay till then."

Hamilton appreciated that the young Englishman had
come to his rescue as though the pair of them, representa-
tives of a normal, well-behaved world, were leagued together to withstand the Trevellyans and Lani-o-akua.

He covertly studied the aloof young fellow and concluded he must be related to the family. Patricia's attitude toward him was a sort of casual friendliness, in
which liking and indifference mingled. Suspecting her
potentialities, it seemed odd that Trevellyan was satisfied
to leave her and Birthwood alone in such a place, but
Birthwood's character was apparent in the way he held
himself, as though while knowing he was part of Lani-
o-akua, he was, at the same time, in spirit forever apart
from it.

The memory of that evening haunted Hamilton the
rest of his life. Dinner done, they adjourned to the
drawing room. He attempted to make conversation,
tried to discover common friends, spoke of celebrities
who had visited the Islands, but his efforts were fruitless.

Patricia sat pressed into the corner of a deep couch,
her eyes unfathomable. Birthwood was withdrawn, Mrs.

Trevellyan tittered, spoke, then hastily retreated into uneasy silences. In desperation Hamilton asked Patricia to play the harp. She rose indifferently, but when she sat down beside the instrument, her eyes seized his and deliberately, with a gesture of a woman embracing a lover, took the towering harp into her arms.

Hair pricked on Hamilton's scalp. Through the contagious impurities of life, through disillusionment, he had remained loyal to his ideal of love, and it seemed as if Patricia were looking into his heart and mocking it. He had married a woman, fancying her beautiful exterior was a reflection of her soul, only to discover that she was incapable of loving in the way he loved, but despite the fact he had remained loyal.

At times he felt more solitary and abandoned than anyone he knew, and yet his boyhood dream of love, exalted and complete, refused to die. Real love had little of the flesh in it. It was the pulse of the world, the heart beat of the universe, the answer to the great homesickness in humanity for contact with God. Only love in its highest form could lift a human being into regions beyond self to touch the divine source behind everything. And this girl, almost a child, was deliberately trying to distract him from concepts which kept him sensitized to rare forces in life, attempting to barter things of the spirit for things of the flesh.

He looked at her condemningly, and she smiled back. He was instantly shamed, realizing that the desire in her waking being to possess him was as old as the earth. The cry in her for a mate, for completion, had been planted there in the dim beginnings of time.

Thrusting back his chair, he focussed his attention on

the music that her fingers drew from the resounding strings. In it was the joy that tingles along the keel of a ship cutting blue waters, the zest of wind blowing over forested ranges, and the thrill in dewdrops clinging to the trembling edges of young, green leaves.

She sat like an image carved in stone, only her arms and fingers moving, suggesting a weary swimmer trying to reach a far-off shore. The tragedy of her life, of all life, stole into Hamilton's mind, weighting it. He contrasted this girl's fate with his own; she was the victim of inheritance and environment, he of intangible ideals. More than likely life would trick them both.

The supposition made him feel kin to her. They were both atoms projected to the earth from space. They would go from the earth—where? An inarticulate rebellion against everything swept him, and at that instant Patricia stopped playing. Her white arms fell slowly from the instrument and her hands landed like winged birds in her lap, creating the impression of a person defenceless against the assaults of life. Before he knew what he was doing, he crossed the room to her.

"Thank you, that was masterly," he said.

She smiled like a pleased child. Her hair smelled as sweet as dry grass under a hot sun. Light from a tall lamp behind her glanced off her chin, and the hush of her waiting breathing sent a pang through Hamilton. He tried to comprehend her, to realize her. She seemed a dozen different women in one and that, probably, was her fascination.

"Before we retire, Patricia," Mrs. Trevellyan said, nervously folding and unfolding her hands, "take Mr. Hamilton into the garden to see the moonlight."

The girl gave the woman a look of complete scorn. "The moon has probably set. It's less than a week old." Admiration filled Hamilton for the loophole she offered him, and for the shield she held up to defend herself in case he might refuse. This was no ordinary girl, she was a supreme achievement. There was no reason to wound her vanity. He was stronger than Lani-o-akua, stronger than Patricia, who was the reflection of its strange, deep soul.

"Moon or no moon the garden will be beautiful," he said rising. "Let's go outside for a few minutes."

A faint color rose into Patricia's cheeks. Her lashes fell, veiling her eyes, then swept upward. In an instant, without speaking, without moving, she bestowed upon him the glory of her headlong love. He was shaken. Kingdoms had been overthrown, the course of history altered by passion such as blazed from this girl's eyes. He felt Birthwood watching them, and wondered if, perhaps, he had had to combat it.

Rising, Patricia thrust her arm through his with a warm, nestling movement. In the effort to assemble his faculties, Hamilton's arm tensed under Patricia's. Color flamed into her cheeks, but with an effort she thrust it back and waited beside him, outwardly cool and indifferent. The incident revealed, as nothing else could have, the force housed in her.

They started for the veranda, and he was only conscious of her arm locked through his, an arm filled with magnetism. They halted before going down the steps, and it seemed as if they were the only two people in the world.

In the dark Patricia's eyes were compelling and unscrupulous. He surmised the wild tides surging through her. Her face suggested a person listening to the whispers of her waking body, and he divined again the fatal abandon in her.

They walked, without speaking, to the gate. Through spaces between gigantic breadfruit and camphor trees, the distant sea shone like hammered silver, with here and there cloud shadows lying on it like sunken islands. A hand's space above Kahoolawe the moon lay like a gold leaf in the sky. Everywhere was unbroken solitude, yet on all sides the ceaseless stir of minute and vital things.

Reaching the gate, Hamilton disengaged himself and leaned upon the pickets.

"Tell me what you've heard about Lani-o-akua and— us," Patricia commanded.

Hamilton was taken aback. For an instant he did not know what to answer.

"I've heard a great deal, Patricia," he said, finally.

"What sort of things?"

When he hesitated to reply, she laced her fingers together. "You don't have to tell me. I know, though I've never been away from here. I can guess the things that people feel, think, and say about us. We're outlaws and outlawed. The Hawaiians say that no luck can ever come to Lani-o-akua until the gods, that Daddy's outraged, have a proper sacrifice."

"What has your father done that other men haven't done before him?" Hamilton asked. "How could he outrage gods?" his voice mocked her gently. "There is only one—"

"God?" she took the word off his lips.

"Yes."

"He isn't here," she asserted.

The locality and the night, combined with Patricia's words, created the illusion that their surroundings were a colossal bowl filled with the black smoke of burning worlds ascending upwards in a titanic conflagration.

"If God isn't here, Patricia, He will come," Hamilton insisted gently. "You are fanciful, you've lived too much alone. You should have had companions of your own age to play with as you grew up. Tell me about yourself."

"There isn't anything to tell. Ka-aina's taken care of me since I was a baby," her expression softened. "Ka-aina is the only person I love. Daddy," she caught her breath, "I love-and-hate him."

"I'm sorry he's away."

"Can't you feel him even though he's gone?" she asked.

"Yes, strongly."

"Daddy's wonderful and terrible. His spirit never leaves Lani-o-akua. It's his mistress."

"That's an astounding statement."

"Men do fall in love with localities," Patricia insisted. "Lani-o-akua got hold of Daddy's soul the first time he ever saw it."

"I've heard the story."

She glanced at him. "He wanted it and he got it. He's determined to make it the most beautiful place in the world."

"I can't see how a man who is responsible for such beauty—" Hamilton indicated their surroundings.

"Could be cursed?" the girl interrupted.

"Yes."

"Because he drove the Hawaiians from their homes and tore down the great fishing temple to build his sugar mill. And somewhere, deep inside him, I think he's sorry and afraid."

"But you hear of great entertainments here, lasting days, of—"

"Every so often something inside Daddy tears loose and he goes sort of crazy. Everyone around him goes crazy too, as if the feeling were in the air."

"And you?" Hamilton inquired after a silence.

"When Daddy 'gives his devil a run' Ka-aina takes me to Kanaio, where his wife lives. I stay there with them until the *luau* is done. But inside I feel wild like Daddy does."

"Mrs. Trevellyan?"

"She locks herself into her wing of the house and cries." The girl's voice was scornful. "She's scared of Lani-o-akua. She hates it. When Dad's home she's so frightened she's foolish. I'm not afraid of him. He makes me mad, but he's grand in a dreadful way."

"Patricia," Hamilton placed his hand compassionately over her laced fingers. "You should get away from here."

She caught her breath with an excited gasp.

"Take me!" Beautiful, imperious, she stood beside him. A truant thought stabbed Hamilton. What this girl could give to a man she loved. She was a white flame.

"I'm married, Patricia."

She stared at him as if she could not credit it.

"You belong to me. Ka-aina said you would come. I loved you from the instant I saw you riding up the road."

Fear ran through Hamilton's mind. He knew what

her father must have looked like when he saw the slopes of Lani-o-akua from his ship.

"Patricia, please—" he said, managing his voice with difficulty.

"I will have you. The gods of Lani-o-akua brought you to me."

"You mustn't—"

"Say such things?" she asked.

Hamilton nodded.

"If I don't say them with my lips, I'm saying them to you inside, and have been since I first saw you. And I'll keep on saying them till you—"

"That's why I went away."

"But you came back."

"My lame horse compelled me to."

She looked affronted.

"Forgive me. It hurts unspeakably to wound you. I'm human. You have a body made for love, you're too beautiful for your own good. Don't make it difficult. There's something about you, about this place—"

"That makes you want to let go your blouse, as the Hawaiians say?"

"Yes. But I won't."

She gave a high laugh, then without warning, like a wave rushing into a bay, she was in his arms. He tried to free himself, gently at first, then fiercely. He stripped himself of her clinging arms, but the muffled beating of her heart, like a distant surf assaulting barrier reefs, upset him.

"Hold me tight, for just an instant. I'm like Daddy! I want you, as he wanted Lani-o-akua. He had to have it or—burst."

Hamilton looked into her eyes. Behind them fires raged.

"Patricia, I'm almost old enough to be your father. If you knew men of your own age, you wouldn't look at me. It's love you want, not me. It'll come."

The last tip of the moon vanished behind the humped-backed island in the southwest, and it seemed as if the light of the stars lessened. From a distant camp came a snatch of Hawaiian music, the outpourings of the sad, confused hearts of a destroyed people. Breathlessly, terrifyingly, it swept Hamilton and Patricia together.

"We must go in," Hamilton said unsteadily, when he freed himself from the embrace.

"But you haven't kissed me yet," she whispered, thrusting back into his arms.

He realized, with astonishment, he hadn't kissed her. They had just clung together like drowning people, blindly, instinctively.

"My dear," he hesitated, then looking into her upturned face said slowly, "I'll kiss you. Once. I can't send you from me in this state." Slowly, gravely, he pressed his lips to hers.

When he released her, she held herself proudly, and taking hold of his arm, started up the dim walk leading to the house.

CHAPTER III

FROM habit Hamilton woke before dawn. Like every
other rancher and sugar planter in Hawaii, he was always in the saddle and riding over his estate by five. It
was stimulating to see laborers trooping through the
fields, to listen to harness clanking on mule teams trotting along ginger-banked roads, to watch wooden
flumes, choked with water, rushing cane to the mill.

For an instant he thought he was at home. An aroma
of coffee permeated the air, birds were singing, men
calling to one another. Sitting up he looked around and
realized he was at Lani-o-akua. Thrusting his fingers
through his hair, he stared out of the window. An unpleasant conviction that some untoward happening had
overtaken him lingered in the back of his mind. Then
he recalled what had transpired in the garden. Hell, he
thought, and getting up walked into the bathroom. The
icy plunge and vigorous rubbing with rough towels
seemed to restore him to the well-ordered round of
yesterday's life.

He listened to the Chinamen talking as they raked up
the lawn, to horses trotting by, to the faint, persistent
rumbling of the sugar mill. It was easy in the fresh,

bright morning to argue that the night before had not
been out of order, although a trifle astounding. He had
kissed a girl other than his wife, but had not prolonged
it more than necessary. To have sent a girl of Patricia's
type to bed aching would have been inhuman. Kissed,
she would sleep. Compassion filled him. What an inheritance she had to combat.

Perhaps sometime during the forenoon there would
be an opportunity to talk to her alone. Could he make
her understand that people who attempted to plunder
life usually, in the end, got plundered by it?

He went out to the veranda and looked at the garden.
To come to Lani-o-akua again would be unwise. He
might as well see all of it. A person gained nothing
from association with people like the Trevellyans, who
were pirates in spirit. But the place was worth knowing.
It had a definite place in the history of Hawaii, for it was
at Lani-o-akua that sugar cane had first been commer-
cially successful.

He studied the garden. Stone walks, flanked by beds
of flowers, led off in half a dozen directions. Closer
scrutiny made him realize that all the walks were for use
as well as for beauty, since each one drained into a
reservoir. The southwestern end of Haleakala, being of
recent volcanic formation, had no forested valleys to
retain moisture, and every drop of rainfall must be
hoarded. Contrasting Trevellyan's water system with
that of other planters he mentally saluted him. There
was something impressive in his consistent worship of
beauty.

Strolling over, he inspected the nearest reservoir.
Against the concrete coping, violets and forget-me-nots

were crowded, tall *kukui* trees with stag-horn ferns hanging from their trunks led away in a little secret walk. Pink begonias, taller than a man, Easter lilies, plumaria, gardenias, agapantha, and tiger lilies fought for supremacy in well-cared-for beds. The old house thrust back into crowding trees as if trying to get a longer perspective on everything. Behind it, hills completely covered with eucalyptus, cypresses, and *kukuis* rose into the mass of Haleakala. Sunlight glinted along the edges of leaves, dew winked between spears of grass. A peacock stepped haughtily out of a mass of shrubs, then shrieked as if a demon had tweaked its tail feathers. Cowboys with flower-wreathed hats jogged down the avenue, bullock carts bumped past the mill. From the stable came the imperious whinny of thoroughbreds, impatient to be led out for their morning canter.

Hamilton started for the gate and just as he reached it, the horses began emerging from the stable, snorting, plunging, shaking their heads. Hawaiians on sober work horses laughed as they wrestled with their charges, fighting to get free of leading reins.

He watched the line of restive animals vanish down the avenue leaving a fine dust in their wake which hung for a while in the still air. Descending the steps he started for the stable. As he neared it he breathed deeply, enjoying the smell of grain and hay. Entering the wide doorway he saw Ka-aina squatting beside his horse, examining its lame leg.

"Fine. One week more can ride again," he announced, looking up. Rising, he patted the horse's shoulder, headed it into the loose-box, and dropped the latch in place.

"Go today?" he inquired, glancing at Hamilton.

"After lunch."

"What for so quick? More better stop two, three day."

"No can," Hamilton answered, falling into the jargon of the many races in Hawaii. "Too much *hana-hana*." *

"What for all time *haole* † mans like get rich? You got nice plantation, plenty horses, good house."

"We confuse riches with happiness I suppose," Hamilton replied.

Ka-aina nodded and busied himself coiling a rope which he hung carefully on a nail hammered into the side of the stall. When it was placed to his satisfaction, he asked over his shoulder:

"You like see mausoleum?"

"What mausoleum?" Hamilton asked.

"Mr. Hi-ball make swell bury place for when he *maké.*‡ Come, I show you."

Hamilton knew Polynesians sufficiently well to appreciate that they were jealous and secretive about places of burial. The fact that Ka-aina wished him to see the one Trevellyan had built for himself was astounding for it invested him with rights belonging only to the immediate members of the family.

"Perhaps Mr. Trevellyan would not like me to see it," he protested.

Ka-aina gestured, brushing the words aside. Hamilton's curiosity was aroused. There was something impressive in the fact that Trevellyan, like the Pharaohs,

---

* *hana-hana*—work.
† *haole*—white man.
‡ *maké*—die.

built a tomb for himself while he lived. It set him apart
from ordinary human beings.

Ka-aina started through the field. To the left the
sugar mill quivered and rumbled like an angry beast. In
its shadow, blue coated coolies toiled, and lumbering
oxen pulled high-wheeled wagons, loaded with cane,
over fragments of lava. Walking past the mill Ka-aina
swerved to avoid a reservoir and started climbing the
flank of a steep, tree-planted hill.

A peacock flew up screeching, little high-backed pigs
scampered into the underbrush. The air was laden with
fragrances from earth, trees, flowers, and the sea.

A long walk, planted with Italian cypresses, led along
the back of the hill that ended in a steep rise. Upon it
a huge urn of yellowish marble was silhouetted against
the sky. Directly below, to the left, on a terrace cut
into the volcanic rock and cinder, the mass of the mausoleum, weathered to tones of pink and ochre, faced the
sweep of the plains. A level space planted with vivid
turf and banked with lilies suggested a great step giving off into space. The hill fell precipitously to the plains
below and looking through the tree tops, one experienced a sensation of gazing down at the earth from another planet.

Green gloom crouched among the trees shading the
mausoleum, ahead blue reaches swept into infinity. There
was a murmur of many small voices, careless under the
sun, a sense of solitude, peace, and detachment. Ka-aina
glanced at Hamilton looking pleased and doubtful at
the same time. After an instant he removed his hat and
held it between his brown hands. Hamilton was bareheaded but signified that he was uncovering himself.

Standing in the sunlight he experienced a sensation dim, yet vivid. For the first time he was conscious of the pulse of the universe, an enduring, persistent heartbeat, muffled but strong, with a mystical regularity in its stroke, steady, unaltered through millions of years.

Living silence flowed above and around him in mute, invisible waves; peace, rest, widening like circles in a pool. His brain, endlessly at work since birth; his heart, a commotion of desires; his soul, eternally fluttering anxious and passionate wings—seemed to merge into each other and be at rest. He was barely conscious of breathing for he seemed to have absorbed all life, and all life to have absorbed him.

He tried to realize the experience, marvelous beyond anything he had known, but as he tried to grasp it, it vanished and he felt like a ship-wrecked person washed up on a desolate shore. A gusty breeze shook the tree tops and they seemed to consult hurriedly together.

"You like?" Ka-aina asked, anxiously.

"It's very fine," Hamilton answered, studying the buttressed lines of the mausoleum. It was evident that Trevellyan had selected the spot carefully. It commanded a view of Lani-o-akua and the entire island, yet was completely concealed. When the old man slept his last sleep, he would still dominate garden and plain, blue sky and distant mountain. His presence would linger among the things he loved. Everything might crumble and pass with the centuries, but in the trees he had planted, and in their uncounted millions of seedlings, atoms of his indomitable spirit would persist. Because of the splendid growth he had given to the southwestern end of Haleakala, the island would remember him when he was gone. Like an army swarming toward the summit, the trees rose, potential forests that would conserve moisture, prevent erosion, and add to the beauty of the island.

"Well, you old pirate," Hamilton thought, "you may be an outlaw, a sinner, and a tyrant, but you're grand."

He laid his hand on a wide iron door, studded with bolts, and Ka-aina moved his hat uneasily between his gnarled fingers.

"No can go inside. Lock," he said, his forehead gathered into working furrows. He swallowed, then rushed a mental ditch. "Patricia Mama stop inside," he indicated the masonry reverently.

"Patricia's mother! I thought—"

"That woman," Ka-aina said in Hawaiian, "is not Patricia's mother. She had a girl by Mr. Hi-ball, but he sent the child to England when it was small. Nobody knows about it but me. After Mr. Hi-ball got Lani-o-akua he worked day and night for ten years to make it beautiful. He built this," the man signed at the tomb. "When everything was finished, he told me he was going to England. He stayed over a year and returned by Inter-Island steamer early one morning—with Patricia. Everyone was frightened for his eyes were those of a madman. He sent for me and told me to hitch up a wagon as there was something at Makena he wanted to bring to Lani-o-akua. I was afraid. We went down to the sea. Inside an empty house was a new and fine coffin. It was heavy and there were only the pair of us to lift it. We brought it here. When it was inside the mausoleum, he told me to pick all the lilies on this hill."

Stopping, Ka-aina wiped his face.

"When the coffin was covered with flowers, Mr. Hi-ball told me he was a chief in his own land, but had loved a girl higher born than he was. Her people forbid her to marry Mr. Hi-ball so he left England and hunted whales for many years. He got money, built Lani-o-akua, because his sweetheart had promised to run away when he had a place for her. When everything was finished Mr. Hi-ball went for her. He was afraid for her to have a baby in Hawaii because there were no good doctors. They went to France for a year. But Mr. Hi-ball and his wife were both a little old and when Patricia was born her mother died. For Mr. Hi-ball everything was finished. He married his wife's maid so Patricia would have an English nurse. When he told me tears ran from my eyes. He said, 'God damn you, don't cry. I had her, she loved me, Patricia is our child!' He walked around, then said, 'The work must go on. Patricia's mother was of royal birth, and her daughter must have a royal estate, even if it's in the middle of the Pacific. And by God, when Patricia grows up, I'll marry her to one of her own class and kind, if I have to shanghai him!' Then he pushed me out of the door and locked it. He never told me I must not speak of it. He knew I would keep his secret, and now I have told it to you."

"Everything I've heard is forgotten."

"Thank you," the man said in Hawaiian, studying the wide, blue stretches of the sea. "I'm getting old. Mr. Hi-ball is a hard man, but he trusts me. Everyone thinks he's in Honolulu, but he's gone to England to get a husband for Patricia. He is afraid that if the Chinamen know he's so far away they will not work hard enough to suit him. He likes them to think he may come back at

any minute. Many time when you think he is in Honolulu, you look up and there he is. He is like a god. He
seems to be here when you can't see him. Perhaps he's
behind one of those trees at this moment." Ka-aina shivered. "If he knew I had told you all this he would
kill me."

"Why did you?"

"You don't know?" Ka-aina asked, as if he could not
credit his ears.

"I haven't the faintest notion," Hamilton replied in
Hawaiian.

"The gods told me that yesterday a man would come
whose fate was bound up with this family's."

"There are no gods, there is only one God and—"

"He doesn't stop at Lani-o-akua," the man interrupted.

Hamilton felt curiously upset. Patricia had said that
also. He studied the sun-bathed trees, thinking deeply.

"Perhaps you will be angry at what I'm going to say,"
the Hawaiian announced, staring at the turf, "but I
think very good if you and Patricia—"

"I'm married."

The man looked unbelieving, then shrugged his shoulders as if abandoning the future to the gods.

"Perhaps, Patricia," Mrs. Trevellyan said, as they rose
from the breakfast table, "Mr. Hamilton would be interested in seeing the big pool. Of course," the woman
turned with one of her simpers, "you've heard the story
about it."

Hamilton shook his head.

"The Hawaiians call it *Ku-Ka-Huelo*, but," Mrs.

Trevellyan fluttered, "Patricia will tell you about it."

"Mr. Hamilton may not be interested in either the pool or the story," Patricia announced, making the words into bits of iron.

"On the contrary," Hamilton said.

Patricia looked at him, then walked slowly to the veranda. Hamilton followed. He had wanted an opportunity to talk to her and here it was. She waited by the railing and he took hold of her arm.

"Pat—"

"No one has ever called me that but you. It makes me feel like a little girl."

"That's what you are."

"But I couldn't feel about you as I do if I were little," she protested. "All full of fire that runs through me in streams."

"Steady," Hamilton cautioned.

Her hand stole to her throat. "I feel like Daddy does sometimes, as if things were tearing loose inside me."

Hamilton shook her arm gently.

"When we get to the pool I want to talk to you."

She gazed at the trees, then started along the walk running parallel to the house, and halted beside a giant cactus. With a gesture she indicated innumerable names carved into the fleshy meat. Names cut into hearts, names pierced with arrows, true lovers' knots, and wreaths framing still other signatures. Hamilton started reading them and desisted. The report that no Island people, save the King and one or two others, visited Lani-o-akua was untrue. On the cactus were the signatures of some of the most highly respected men in Hawaii, and their names were linked with those of women other than their wives.

"Daddy calls this tree the Family Skeleton of Hawaii," the girl said, laughing.

Hamilton gestured protestingly.

"Dad thinks it's funny. He's real anyway. He doesn't pretend to be good like these men do. When they meet here at Dad's *luaus* * they say, 'You here! Good God!' and they laugh and say things like, 'Trevellyan's got the right idea; after you give your devil a run it goes to sleep for a while.' And stuff like that. The cowboys joke about it."

She broke off as though the subject had lost interest and watched Hamilton, a strange smile hovering about her lips. She started up a path between beds of Easter lilies that led toward the trees hiding the hill. Mimosa bushes in flower filled the air with spice. Bees swarmed over them, sunshine catching in their transparent wings.

"It's hot," Patricia said, looking back.

Hamilton nodded, and she started on. He watched her go up the steep slope, moving with the superb ease of a thoroughbred horse. Trees closed in about them, and presently great trunks shut off everything but little patches of sunshine and shadow. Hamilton was always conscious of peace when he walked among trees. The familiar, pleasant sense of their strength lulled the increasing unrest filling him. Overhead, the sun sat lightly among their green tops which moved to an occasional breeze.

Patricia paused for breath. "We're nearly there," she announced, pushing a strand of hair off her cheek.

* *luau*—feast.

With a gay scramble she went up a bank, Hamilton at her heels. Then he saw the pool, *Ku-Ka-Huelo*. He estimated that the reservoir must hold half a million gallons of water. A paved walk, banked with forget-me-nots and frail, pink Castilian roses, surrounded the inner edge of the pool like a great, living wreath. Urns, grouped against a ring of cypresses, cast long reflections over the water.

Overhead was a circle of blue, enclosed by trees that looked solidly carved into the sky. Hamilton had never realized how strangely and strongly color can, at moments, appeal to the imagination. In this pageant of green, gold, and blue he seemed to see the naked soul of the Islands, bold and gorgeous, like a great trumpet sounding a reveille. He stared at the circle of blue overhead. The sun tore a hole in it, dazzling his eyes. For an instant he continued to look upward, trying to realize the magnitude of ether going into infinitude. His soul seemed to be snatched upward by a great magnet and he looked down hurriedly, then saw, reflected in the still pool, the compliment of the blue world overhead, seemingly receding from his feet into the vitals of the earth. World overhead and world underneath met like answers; two gigantic bowls set lip to lip forming a hollow sphere.

"Let's go to the seat by the god," Patricia said, indicating an odd stone that vaguely suggested a human head half turned around. A sense of depression descended on Hamilton, but he nodded. They reached a stone bench beneath over-hanging ferns. Behind it water fell into a shallow marble bowl and trickled across stones to the reservoir.

"Well, Pat," he said when they were seated, "suppose

you tell me the story."

"I might as well get it over. You know what *Ku-Ka-Huelo* means?"

" 'The tail goes up,' like a racehorse's does when it's been pushed too fast and suddenly comes to the end of it's endurance?"

She nodded.

"It's another story of Daddy. All the stories of Lani-o-akua are really about Daddy. One day he decided he wanted a half million gallon reservoir on top of this hill. By noon he had seven hundred Chinamen digging. In a week it was finished and cemented. He worked the men so hard that two of them died. Because the *akuas* had sacrifices, rain came and filled it."

Hamilton studied her; her voice, her expression were unmoved. Despite his advantage in years he felt inadequate to deal with her. He had better talk to her as he had intended, make her see. What did he want to make her see anyway? Oh, yes, that people who tried to plunder life usually got plundered by it.

"I'm going to talk to you," he announced gravely.

"What about?"

"I want to talk to you about yourself."

Slipping off the bench, she seated herself at his feet, then, watching him, laid an arm across his knees.

"Go on, I'm listening."

"And while you listen you'll think your own thoughts."

"Probably," she replied, watching him.

"I hope I won't hurt your feelings."

"Go on," she laughed. "I'm curious."

"It has to do with what you told me last night, about

wanting things—anyhow."

"That's in the very fabric of Daddy and me. You can't get it out of us."

"You can build against it."

"Why?"

"Because it destroys."

"It doesn't. Look at Daddy. He goes through life like a wild bull, charging everything that stands in his way, and he gets what he wants. If he didn't, he'd burst. I'm like Daddy."

"You're too beautiful to plan calmly to be ruthless. In the end—"

"I shall get everything I want from life," she interrupted. "I know it. I've always known it. Ever since I was little," she looked into the blue above them like a person challenging the universe. "Sometimes I almost explode because I want everything at once."

She sat, the epitome of chained force. Then her expression altered. Her face, the way she held herself, leaning a little backward, breast and neck exposed, suggested that she was offering herself, her life, and all the mysteries in her to some imagined being who dominated her savage and ecstatic soul. She incarnated passion by suggesting the two halves of it. Her parted lips seemed to be receiving the fiery touch of another mouth upon them. Suddenly she grasped Hamilton's arms.

"I'm bursting," she said in a hard, dry voice. "You must love me."

"Steady, Pat. You're making the profound error of mistaking passion for love."

She shook her head indignantly.

"Pat, you're tragic, and don't know it. When I think

about you growing up in this atmosphere, my soul aches
for you."

"I'm aching for you. If you hadn't kissed me last
night—" she caught her breath with a gasp. "Love me—
quickly!"

"Pat, you don't know—"

"What I'm asking for?" her voice mocked him. "I
do." Scrambling to her knees, her arms went about him.
"Pat, please!"

He took violent hold of her arms. Her pale, passionate
face was lifted beseechingly. A sort of savage rage tore
him. He had read somewhere, that to know woman
through the senses was wisdom. Humanity had been
shaped through her and through her it must be saved.
But he had clung to the ideal of another sort of love and
in return had had nothing. The love this girl was thrusting at him might be, after all, the only love possible on
earth. The other higher kind was, perhaps, a delusion.
He had searched to find it in vain. Did it exist?

"Kiss me, and you'll forget everything," she whispered.

"I won't, Pat, not the way you want me to."

"Why?"

"In the first place I'm married—"

"So are the other men who come to Daddy's *luaus*."

"I'm not like them, and I'll be damned if I'll behave
as they do."

With a sudden, fierce movement the girl thrust into
his arms. About her was a powerful aura that made the
blood leap and aroused longing for violence. Her nature
was eternally afire.

"Love me just once," she commanded, "then if you

want to you can go."

Hamilton partially freed himself of her.

"I could not love a woman and go," he exclaimed indignantly.

"You mean if you loved me the way I want you to, you would not walk out of the picture?"

"It would be contemptible."

She gazed at him. "If you won't love me," she allowed each word its full weight, "I'll drown myself in this pool tonight. I love you. I can't breathe. I won't stand this hell!" She beat her head against his shoulder.

Hamilton caught it with one arm, holding it fast.

"Pat, for God's sake—"

She looked into his eyes.

"We better go down. It must be lunch time."

Hamilton started at Patricia's voice and passed a hand dully over his face. It was almost a blasphemy for her to look so lovely, to sit in such ordered beauty, her dress in correct folds, her hair pinned tidily at the nape of her neck. She was untouched, unsoiled by what she had done. Impregnable. Leaning over the water, she calmly considered her reflection. He wondered what she would say. Words were on her lips. Taking one of his hands between both of hers, she looked at it, then gazed into his eyes.

"It's a shame," she whispered softly. "You're unhappy."

"How can I help being, Pat?"

"Don't look like that, don't let your voice sound like that, as if you'd killed something. I'm happy and you must be too. When will you come again?"

He did not answer. Rising to her knees, she wound her arms about him.

"I've got to see you every day."

It was an ultimatum. Behind her, trees stood like the army of Lani-o-akua, supporting her. The fight ebbed out of Hamilton.

"Very well. I'll see you every day."

"On your honor."

"On my dishonor," he exclaimed, and moved as if trying to shake off a distasteful garment. "But I won't see you here, at Lani-o-akua!"

"I'll ride down every day and meet you at—" she whispered the name of a red blowhole, lost in the wastes of *ilima* * and cactus covering the plains of the isthmus, that joined the two halves of the island.

* *ilima*—flowering shrub.

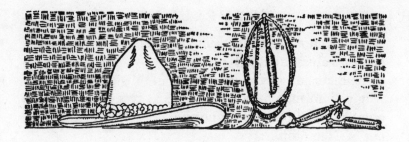

CHAPTER IV

"Ka-aina, when you've unsaddled Typhoon, I want to talk to you," Patricia said as she dismounted.

He nodded and took the mare by the bridle, making no comment upon her overheated condition. Patricia crossed her arms on the top rail of the corral, thoughtfully considering a heavy ring, set with a square ruby, which hung on her left hand.

Ka-aina walked the mare until she cooled off, then led her into the stable. He wondered, apprehensively, what was coming. He knew Patricia had a lover and suspected it was Hamilton. For months he had followed her at a distance when she rode to her trysting place below the red blowhole. He had no wish to pry into her affairs, but she had been his charge since infancy and he wanted to assure himself that her secret was safeguarded from any chance of discovery. To his way of thinking there was nothing wrong in the girl having a lover. She was full-grown, with every right to a man, but it was imperative that Trevellyan get no wind of it when he came home.

Ka-aina blanketed the mare and put her back in the loose-box. After the dim light in the stable, the sunshine blinded him. When his eyes had become adjusted, he saw Patricia leaning on the fence in the same attitude as when he had left her. Behind her, dusty shrubs drooped at the feet of tall eucalyptus. Oranges and figs, a lone pomegranate, and a mango tree strung along a path that went toward the mill. Patricia straightened up.

"When is Father coming home?"

"Only he knows that."

The girl laced her fingers together and tore them apart.

"What is he doing in Honolulu? He's been away seven months."

"I no know what kind things he is making."

Mynah birds consulted noisily in the trees, doves cooed. The afternoon was dry and warm, the air scented with blossoming *Inia*,* but a sense of trouble and tragedy crept over Ka-aina. He looked uneasily over his shoulder, as a little pig scampered through the weeds and dodged under a gate. Patricia gestured in a nervous way.

"Is something the matter, Patricia?" Ka-aina asked gently in Hawaiian.

"I have had a lover, and I'm going to have a child."

The old man looked at her, then remarked:

"When gods love, their children are beautiful."

The girl thrust her elbows over the rail and put her weight upon them. Her attitude suggested the child of long ago whom he had worshipped. That little girl had been lost in the woman before him, a woman who was, he suspected, at heart a replica of Trevellyan.

"How long have you known you were going to have a baby?"

* *Inia*—Pride-of-India tree.

"About six, almost seven months."

"Your lover?"

"He left four months ago for America."

"And did not take you?" Ka-aina cried, as if such a thing could not be credited. Then a thought came to him and an expression of anger and grief contorted his features. "Patricia!"

"What?" she demanded.

"You say your lover left four months ago and yet every day you still go to *Puu-ula.** You—you have a new lover already!" Ka-aina's face screwed up like that of a child about to burst into tears. "You—Trevellyans!"

Patricia lifted her arm to strike him, then noting the grief in his eyes, desisted.

"I go there every day so I can be where we used to meet," she said unsteadily.

Ka-aina caught her hand between his. Perhaps this girl was not like her father, perhaps true love had claimed her in time to save her.

"Oh, Patricia, I too glad, I too glad!"

"He's gone to get a divorce so he can marry me. He gave me this ring." She held out her hand.

"Good, good. I too much like you marry with Mr. Walter."

The girl looked at him with a startled glance.

"No scare. Never I tell anybody," he took her hand between his rough ones. "Mr. Walter glad when he know about the baby?"

"I didn't tell him. I was afraid he might not go for his divorce. Now I'm afraid Father may come back before he does." Breaking off she stared at the sea.

* *Puu-ula*—red hill.

Ka-aina looked at her carefully.

"You look all the same before, Patricia, only more pretty. When girl got sweetheart, always look more nice. Mr. Walter fine. I like very much. I think that time when he coming to Lani-o-akua sure you two fellas—" he laughed indulgently, feeling invested with importance, then his forehead gathered into knots. "Lucky Mr. Hi-ball no stop."

"Do you think anyone suspects my condition?" Patricia asked.

"No can tell unless look very hard in *holoku*," he indicated the loose graceful garment she wore.

"Did you?"

"No, Patricia," he answered truthfully.

She looked relieved, and stared at the tree tops gilded with sunlight.

"If Daddy ever finds out you've protected us—"

"Maybe he kill me. No matter. I'm old, life belongs to the young."

Patricia put out her hand impulsively. "Besides Walter, you are the only person I love," she said.

Ka-aina kissed her hand.

"You were given to me to take care of when you were a small baby," he said in Hawaiian. "To me you are that baby still. When yours comes," his face lighted, "I take care for you."

"I shall have to go away," Patricia said, looking at the highly colored gardens. "Daddy will never forgive me. But someone has to inherit Lani-o-akua and I would like it to be my child. I thought I hated this place but now I must leave, I realize I love it."

Ka-aina dug tears out of his eyes with the backs of

his hands.

"No speak this kind, Patricia. Sure, Papa mad. But after by and by he forget. Young time mans hard, but when you get old—" he gestured eloquently. "Sure you come Lani-o-akua again. Sure when Mr. Hi-ball *maké*, you and Mr. Walter stop here."

"Maybe," Patricia said, and walked away.

Ka-aina watched her go into the garden. When the house engulfed her, he took a cigarette out of his blue cotton jacket, lighted it, and squatted on his hams. Picking up a twig, he stuck the cigarette into one corner of his mouth and squinted to keep the levelling rays of the falling sun out of his eyes. Smoothing the dust with his palm, he made a succession of tiny strokes in it with the twig. Seven—that made two more months to go. Trevellyan had stated, definitely, that he would be gone at least a year. By then the baby would be born and Patricia and her lover gone.

A spasm crossed his face. Memories of Patricia as a baby flitted through his mind. His neck remembered the tickle of her golden fluff, his chest the warmth of her small, limp body against it. He had carried her on a pillow in front of his saddle, undressed her when she bathed in the sea, protected her from punishment when she did wrong. If only she would arrange to leave her child with him, life would be rich. Children were the compensation of age, for only in old age had one sufficient leisure to enjoy them.

Rising, he looked around, then started along a weed-grown trail that led past the mill. Occasionally he glanced over his shoulder to make sure he was not observed. Entering the garden through a side gate, he started for the great pool. When he reached it, he halted, and stared thoughtfully at the glassy water which reflected flowers and the long shadows of trees. Removing the wreath from his hat, he held it reverently in one hand. Circling the reservoir, he paused before the twisted, gray rock. Placing the wreath upon it, he retreated a step and with his hat in his hands, began praying;

"Gods of Lani-o-akua, keep the child here. I will guard it, care for it, love it, keep it safe for this place."

He waited while shadows stretched across the island and twilight gathered at the edge of the sea. The sun was near its setting. Small, fiery clouds floated above Kahoolawe, lying like a red wound in the sea. Mystery was gathering over everything.

A small bird fell with a quick, darting flight and landed on the rock encircled by his wreath. There was something fairy-like in its quick, dainty movements. It ruffled its plumage and with minute, friendly chirpings picked at fern seeds behind a curled frond sticking up between two faded, red roses. It whisked about fearless, inquiring, then whistling flew joyously away. Ka-aina scratched his head, puzzled.

"Linnet. Linnet," he said. Linnets were not native to Hawaii. Linnets came from countries at the end of the long, blue road of the sea.

Ka-aina awakened, his heart beating unevenly. A lantern, turned low, spread a circle of light in his room. Outside the night was still and dark, but by the smell in the air he knew morning was approaching. Sounds of Lani-o-akua came faintly; a stray gust of wind prowling down from Haleakala, a mango falling, the complaints and whisperings of shrubs. But he was convinced that some untoward noise had awakened him.

Putting his feet carefully over the side of his bed, he stood up. Except on Saturdays when he went home, he slept in a small shack adjoining the stable. He listened for a commotion among the horses, but everything was quiet. Pulling on his breeches, he buttoned them with unsteady hands and opened the door cautiously. Leaves rustled in the tree-tops with an expostulatory sound. The soft voices of the earth, worked on by changes of atmosphere, melted into the faint, regular respiration of the sea, muted by distance to a whisper. He strained his ears fancying he heard a step on the path leading down past the mill. Nothing. His imagination was tricking him. After standing for several minutes facing the black curtain of darkness spread over the sea and islands, he stepped back, closing the door tightly.

There was comfort in the little, rough room lighted by the dim, hot lantern. His slicker hung from its accustomed nail in the wall, his carefully coiled lasso beside it. By his saddle, his mighty rowelled spurs lay neatly together ready to buckle on in the morning. Going back he sat down on the edge of the untidy bed and smoked a cigarette. The fragrant smoke caught pleasantly in his lungs. When it was finished, he ground it out with his heel and rolled up in his blankets. He listened to the wind, breathed deeply of the clean night, and pillowed his head on his arm. Two hours until dawn. Sleep; sleep was drink and love to the old.

He was dropping off with a long sigh when a familiar tramp sounded outside. The door flung open and a great, black figure filled the opening.

"Ka-aina!"

"*Auwe! Auwe!*" *

"Don't yell, I'm no *akua!*" Trevellyan bawled. "Here, get up, you old *molowaa!* † Wake David and send him to the office. Assemble the men. There is much to be done during the next few days," he slapped his thigh. "Gad, it's great to be back." He lingered in the doorway taking greedy gulps of the night air. "Lani-o-akua," he uttered the sonorous syllables affectionately, giving them a grand roll. "There's nothing like it in the world. How's my girl? How's everything? How are you, old man?"

Swaggering across the room, he smacked Ka-aina on the back with rough fondness. Ka-aina scrambled hurriedly out of bed and Trevellyan seated himself upon it.

Ka-aina looked with mingled fear and affection at Trevellyan looming up like a gigantic headland from the flatness of the bed. There was a heroic quality in the magnificent hewing of his body and the bold moulding of his head. His shoulders were heavy, his arms long and powerful, but his hands those of a courtier. The breeding of centuries had given the turn to his wrists, steel-strong, slender, but marred by a black mat of wiry hair completely encircling them. His fingers tapered like a woman's; fingers that would have been white had a courtier owned them, but that were tanned the clear, deep brown of a pirate's. You could vision them, had they been white, handling a rapier, but you saw a cutlass grasped in them instead.

Tousled, black hair with a fine, living gleam to it

---

* *auwe*—alas, woe is me!
† *molowaa*—lazy bones.

rushed down over his forehead, swelling boldly at the brows, black beard leaped up, and between them a tanned space showed, lighted by the blackness of his eyes. All the force of the world seemed to crouch in his body, the upper part clad in a fine white silk shirt, the lower part breeched in black cloth that seemed part of the high, black boots casing his powerful legs.

"Here, Ka-aina, dig up a drink. I've walked all the way from Makena."

With unsteady hands the old man drew a bottle from behind a soiled quilt thrown in a corner. Trevellyan pulled out the cork and swallowed a third of the contents, wiped his mouth, and handed the bottle back to Ka-aina. "Take some. You'll need it before the day's done," he said with a great, boisterous laugh.

Trevellyan was happy and excited. Something was afoot. Ka-aina drank deeply. Yes, he would need the drink, many drinks, before the day was done. They all would. He shivered with pleasure as the liquor charged through his system. For an instant its fire warmed him, then cold numbed his body. He simply dared not . . . think!

After a while they went out. A deep mystery was abroad, the unending mystery of day creeping up over the curve of the earth. It was still dark, save where a ghostly radiance showed in the east above Haleakala. A sacred presence seemed to have come nearer to the earth and grazing animals lifted their heads as if saluting it.

Trevellyan walked strongly, peering at passing objects that loomed up in the dark and vanished. Ka-aina followed at his heels. Occasionally Trevellyan threw remarks over his shoulder or asked questions. As they approached the house, he grunted in a satisfied manner. "Coffee," he said in a great voice, "coffee off my own trees, not the filthy muck that masquerades for coffee in England. Hawaii! Nothing can touch it. Lani-o-akua! The greatest place on earth!" he threw out his right arm in a gesture of salute.

He walked into the lighted kitchen, connected to the main house by a long, latticed runway. The Chinese cook was busy at the stove. Hearing steps he turned. His yellow face blanched and Trevellyan laughed, pulled a chair out with a loud, scraping noise, and sat down.

"Well, Chong, I'm back! Coffee for two. Ka-aina, come in. I want to talk to you."

Ka-aina left the veranda where he had halted and Trevellyan jerked out a chair, slewing it around in order to have his man face him.

He sat down without embarrassment, but with apprehension. Island etiquette, strange and involved, made it permissible for man and master to meet as equals when the occasion demanded it. Pulling one of the cups of steaming coffee toward him, he heaped four tablespoonfuls of sugar into it, and gulped it down. Trevellyan watched him for an instant, then leaned back in his chair. A curious, affectionate smile lighted the black depths of his eyes, making them splendid.

"Ka-aina," he said, nursing his cup between his hands, "I've found the man I want for Patricia. He will be here in three days. In three days Lani-o-akua must wear the face of a bride waiting for her groom."

Nausea hit the pit of Ka-aina's stomach, and his ears

roared with the sound of gods crashing from their thrones.

"After we've had coffee, send David to the office. The mill will have to be closed. I know we're grinding," he said, in answer to some expression in the Hawaiian's eyes, "but to hell with money and everything else, until this business is finished. It's got to be done right! Brandy, Chong! I must be getting old," he laughed, boisterously. "The walk up from Makena has tired me a little."

Pouring a generous measure of the liquor into his coffee, he drained it off.

"Ha!" he exclaimed. "Now for the day's work." Pushing back his chair he sat lost in thought, then signed to the cook. "Chong, tell Mrs. Trevellyan to come here."

The man murmured an answer and slid away like an uneasy shadow.

Ka-aina sat, his arms resting heavily on the table. Footsteps roused him. Mrs. Trevellyan entered, saw her husband and scattered, mentally and physically. She was wearing a soiled, silk wrapper. Out of it peeped the neck of a high, tightly-fastened night-dress. Hair, which had been hastily taken down from curling pins and left in fantastic ringlets that needed combing, trailed down the lean stalk of her neck.

"How *did* you get here? When the cook said you wanted me, I told him he *must* be dreaming."

Trevellyan let out a bellow of laughter, threw out a careless arm, and drawing his wife to him, kissed her indifferently. Then two devils popped up in the liquid, black depths of his eyes and he began looking her over.

"I know I look a fright, Hi-ball, but you took me completely by surprise. I . . . oh . . ." She looked too stupid for speech and too frightened to chase a chicken away.

"I don't give a hang how you look," Trevellyan said, not unkindly. "How is Patricia?"

"Well, Hi-ball, well," his wife answered, uttering his name with reluctance, as if outraged by its levity.

"When she wakes, tell her I'm home and want to see her in the office."

"I'll wake her," Mrs. Trevellyan drew the wrapper closer across her flat breast.

"Let her sleep," Trevellyan commanded. "She better get all the sleep she can while she can," he winked at Ka-aina.

The old man averted his eyes. Light had come suddenly, dimming the lamps in the kitchen. Bravely, beautifully the new day walked over the island, edging it with gold. Trevellyan thrust back his chair, then seeing his daughter's tall figure walking hurriedly through the garden, he shouted:

"Patricia!"

She halted, hesitated, then turned. As she crossed the threshold her eyes met Ka-aina's carefully, commanding him to see her later.

"Well," Trevellyan cried, "glad to see your old Dad home?"

She kissed him.

"What have you been doing while I was away?"

"Nothing," she answered, calmly.

Trevellyan pinched her cheek. "You look ripping. Sit down. I want to see you in the office presently."

The girl seated herself. Outside mynah birds scolded

noisily in the trees.

"Hand me the brandy, Patricia."

The girl obeyed. Ka-aina rubbed his hand unhappily along the seam of his breeches and looked to see if she had removed her ring. It was gone.

After some talk, Patricia got up and strolled out of the room. Trevellyan watched her.

"Gad, what a filly! I've found the man for her. A man her equal in beauty and birth."

"What do you mean?" Mrs. Trevellyan asked, her eyes fixed on Patricia's departing figure. From the expression on her face, Ka-aina knew that, for the first time, she realized Patricia's condition.

"I went to England on purpose to arrange a suitable match for my girl. Admiral Hawke has reached Honolulu. In three days he'll be here." Trevellyan slapped his thigh. "He's well-born and handsome enough even to suit her."

Mrs. Trevellyan sat, nervously fingering the cuffs of her wrapper, but made no reply. Seeing the expression in her eyes, Trevellyan banged his fist on the table.

"Do you think I'd let my girl throw herself away on Island scum?" he shouted, glaring at the woman before him. "She'll mate with her own kind!"

"But supposing she doesn't . . ."

"Patricia'll do as I say," Trevellyan roared. "All women, when it comes to marriage, are not the poor, shrinking thing you are. When she sees Hawke . . ." He laughed and got to his feet. "Ka-aina, send David to the office."

"*Ae*," the man answered.

Trevellyan vanished and his wife signed to Ka-aina

to wait. Her dry, meager body shook, then her head thumped down into her arms and she wept weakly. The Chinese cook glanced at her, his expression implying that Trevellyan troubles were not his concern; his business was to keep in the good graces of his master. Ka-aina patted the woman awkwardly on the back, attempting to steady her.

Patricia appeared in the doorway. Ka-aina started and Mrs. Trevellyan looked up. The eyes of the two women met, locked, and clashed.

"He'll blame me for not watching you better!" Fear and fury transformed Mrs. Trevellyan from a weak, cringing creature into a lap-dog yapping impotently. "As if I could control you!" she gulped. "Who is the man? You . . . slut!"

Patricia's eyes blazed.

"Hold your tongue! Ka-aina."

"Yes, child?"

"I've got to see you some time today. We must plan . . ." She looked at him commandingly.

She was harassed and uneasy, but not frightened, and the man admired her courage. He looked at the green and gold slope of the hill glimpsed through the kitchen door, like a person expecting a blow that cannot be avoided. If she knew the absolute awfulness of what was in store for her! He doubled up his right hand so tightly that the muscles of his palm cramped. Pain shot up his arm and he had to use his left hand to force the fingers open. When he looked up, Patricia had gone. He hurried out in search of Birthwood, and heard Trevellyan instructing him in the office.

Ka-aina attempted to pass across the lawn beneath the

window without being seen. He must talk to Patricia, warn her of what was in store for her. Spying him, Trevellyan shouted for him to come in and he edged through the door and waited, hat in hand. Young Birthwood watched with an expressionless face.

"Listen closely, David," Trevellyan ordered. "In three days I'm expecting Admiral Hawke here in his warship. Have a hundred saddle horses ready to go to Makena on Thursday morning. Close the mill. Set the coolies to cleaning up the gardens and hoeing the roadsides. Everything has got to be ship-shape. That beggar, Hawke, must be impressed," he laughed and winked at Ka-aina. "Dispatch ten of the cowboys into the mountain with pack-horses to get ferns and *maile* * for *luau* tables. Send others down to the beach for sea-food. Ka-aina'll arrange for hula girls and wreaths. There must be music, drinks, entertainment. We'll feast Hawke, his officers, and men royally. Drive the fact home to them that Lani-o-akua . . ." Trevellyan desisted, meditated, then told Birthwood the reason for Hawke's visit. Birthwood inclined his head and made no comment, but Ka-aina fancied he looked disturbed.

"I've things to straighten out, David; Patricia's dowery for instance. You're connected with the family and should have pride in having things as I want them. Pity your father got into that scrape that put him out of his regiment, but it's no fault of yours. I'm glad to have you here. I know you're faithful to my interests. If I didn't trust you absolutely, I'd not dare to leave you alone here with such a temptation as Patricia handy,"

* *maile*—sweet vine.

Trevellyan remarked, as he went through the papers littering his desk.

Birthwood's reserved young face grew white and strained. Ka-aina glanced at him, and knew he had seen that Patricia was going to have a child, and was afraid, when Trevellyan discovered it, he might be suspected. It was enough to daunt anyone. Steps sounded on the walk.

"Go out and see who wants me, Ka-aina," Trevellyan ordered.

He obeyed. A Chinaman came up the steps carrying a stone idol in his arms. Ka-aina looked at it and recoiled.

"What does that fool want?" Trevellyan shouted.

The Chinaman's eyes met Ka-aina's carefully, then crossing the narrow veranda, he stepped into the office. He explained that he had been plowing below the mill and had turned up a god. Trevellyan glanced at the image carelessly, impatient of the interruption, but the men had orders to bring anything discovered on the place to him at once. Then an expression of deepened interest, mixed with curiosity, showed in his eyes. He ordered the man to set the idol on the desk. Birthwood pushed aside the papers and the coolie set the dusty piece of stone down gingerly.

"Well, Ka-aina," Trevellyan said, after he had examined it, "what sort of god is this? I've never seen one like it. David," he addressed Birthwood, "it's Janus-faced." He indicated the flattened features, the cruel, slanting eyes, and the small, wedge-shaped mouth. Both faces were identical.

Ka-aina was paralyzed. He was afraid of offending the deity by explaining it was a Shark god of the most malignant kind. It had power over the past and future. It looked at both, joining them in itself. Only human sacrifices might be offered to it to propitiate disaster. And he was equally afraid not to warn Trevellyan against it. If he offended its god-head . . .

"Come, *makule*," Trevellyan said, impatiently, "tell me what you know about it. It's rather significant that it's dug up the day I return. Here, I've no time now to be bothered. Set it up in the garden, and later . . ."

"More better *no!*" Ka-aina said, emphatically.

Trevellyan laughed loudly, throwing out his chest. "Afraid that . . ."

"I'm scared to tell you," Ka-aina said, speaking rapidly in Hawaiian, "what kind of god it is for fear it will be angry, and I'm afraid not to tell you because . . ." He lifted the god off the desk reluctantly, and setting it carefully on the floor, backed away. "Better let me take this to the sea and put it in the old temple above the Shark cave." There, he had told without saying it in so many words!

"So, it's a Shark god?"

Ka-aina nodded. Trevellyan stuck out his lower lip and thought for a minute. The image squinted at the past and contemplated the future, smiling at both with two cruel, mocking mouths.

"Well?" Trevellyan demanded.

"Without a human sacrifice it cannot be placed anywhere and not bring disaster. If it is placed at Lani-o-akua . . ." he looked uneasily at the idol, "without one . . ."

The Chinaman who had brought in the image slid

out of the door and vanished. Trevellyan let out a great, delighted bellow of mirth and laughed until his face was purple, striking himself on the thigh. Birthwood watched coldly and an uneasy expression grew in Ka-aina's eyes.

"That Chink, gad, it's rich," Trevellyan gasped, choking with delight, "is scared I'll have him knocked on the back of the head when he's not looking, then put a fishhook in his mouth and drag him—" he could not go on. "Here," he kicked the idol contemptuously in the face, "set it up in the walk under the *kukui* trees and let's be done with all this nonsense. There are more important things to be attended to than a lot of superstitious trash."

Ka-aina's brown skin went a sick, ashy gray. Trevellyan was doomed by his impious act. Nothing on earth could save him. Lani-o-akua would be destroyed unless, by some miracle, the god was placated with a fitting sacrifice. Hoisting the heavy idol into his arms, Ka-aina went out, murmuring prayers to pacify it and postpone the day of retribution.

The radiant sky, the warm sunshine seemed unreal. He looked at the quiet trees, camphor and monkey-puzzles, eucalyptus and Norfolk Island pines, breadfruit and *kukui*, Pride of India and Italian cypress. A little breeze ran over them, fluttering the topmost leaves as if they palpitated, apprehensive of the doom waiting to overtake them. A rush of tears blinded the old man's eyes. Familiar sweeps and stately walks, the pools of the garden, the green plunge of the land seaward, time-rusted lava flows, blurred and swirled into the great blue of sea and sky. The weight of the stone image dragged at his arms. Heaving it into a better position, he staggered on. From behind, Trevellyan's voice shouted:

"As soon as you've set it up, Ka-aina, send Patricia to me!"

CHAPTER V

WHEN Ka-aina went for Patricia he found her seated beside her window, staring at the sea. She did not reply when he told her that Trevellyan was waiting for her in the office. Her face was pale and a faint smile hovered about her lips as if, in desperation, she anticipated pitting her will against Trevellyan's. Excitement might ease inner pressure.

"I'll come," she said.

"But everything, *everything*, is finished!" Ka-aina cried, flinging rigid arms out in front of him.

"Have you told Daddy?" the girl cried, leaping to her feet and straightening her body with a single movement which suggested a sword being torn from its scabbard.

"No tell anykind, Patricia, but *auwe, auwe!*" Ka-aina dashed an arm sideways in an extremity of grief and his face, which he had struggled to keep composed, broke.

"I'll tell him, but only if I have to," the girl announced.

"First, I like tell you somekind—" Ka-aina began.

Patricia's eyes leaped to his. Steps sounded.

"Patricia, your father wishes to see you at once,"

Birthwood called from the garden.

She went onto the veranda, debated, then descended the steps. From her action it was evident that she wished to avoid meeting Mrs. Trevellyan. The woman's figure flashed across a doorway, but Patricia's stiffly held head routed her and she fled into the recesses of the house. She would be weeping copiously and continually in her wing of it, Ka-aina thought disdainfully. Birthwood watched Patricia until she vanished around a turn, then taking out a handkerchief wiped his face.

Ka-aina's eyes invaded his and the young man got red. His lower jaw locked into the upper. The Hawaiian tortured his hat between his hands.

"I'm scared to go," he announced, "and more scared not to. If only Mr. Hi-ball had stayed his full time in England, the baby could have been hidden. When he finds out—"

Birthwood signed curtly for him to be silent.

"I'll be wanted shortly without a doubt," he remarked sitting down on the steps. Ka-aina shifted his feet. He studied the young man staring unseeingly before him. David was sound and loyal. He could be depended upon to help.

"I think better us go and wait near the office," Ka-aina suggested. "Maybe Patricia need help."

Birthwood got to his feet. "Christ!" he exclaimed. The smothered word was a supplication for help and support, not only for himself but for all concerned. He stood transfixed by the thoughts streaming through his mind, searing it, then signed Ka-aina to accompany him, and started for the office. Half way he stopped, locked his arms across his chest, and began pacing the lawn. Ka-aina proceeded a hundred yards, then halted.

Trevellyan's voice, with the majestic boom of surf assaulting coral reefs in it, came through the sunshine dominating the garden. Ka-aina braced for the first changed inflection. Roaring in his eardrums prevented him from disentangling words from sentences. Distractingly they all ran into one. He glanced back to assure himself that Birthwood was within call to support him when the need arose.

The young man was leaning against a tree. He appeared quite at ease with his head tilted back against the rough bark, eyes contemplating blue distances showing between strong tree trunks. He created the impression of being in a world of his own, far removed from that of the Trevellyans'. Then Ka-aina saw the rigidity of Birthwood's fingers.

Ka-aina had for Birthwood the large, easy affection characteristic of Polynesians for people living around them. He knew Birthwood to be kind, easy to work for, reliable, and his youth and vigor were props upon which to lean in this emergency which over-taxed his own faculties completely. What would Trevellyan do if he found out? Patricia would not tell him unless she were driven to it. She would plot to escape before Hawke arrived, and she would be counting upon him, Ka-aina, to assist her.

The old man wiped sweat from his face, then jerked as a bellow that seemed super-human in volume and intensity sounded from the office. The waiting men's eyes rushed together. Chinamen raking the lawns grasped their hoes. A second bellow followed, then silence paralyzed the gardens. It ended almost as soon as it began.

"Ka-aina! David! Blast you both, come here! I'll-get-to-the-bottom-of-this-I-tell-you-Patricia!" the savage mutter of words ran into one.

Ka-aina rushed to the doorway. Trevellyan had forced his daughter half way to her knees, and was shaking her with all the violence in his great frame, while he continued to bellow, cursing his Maker, Patricia, the universe. Veins stood out on neck and forehead like purple worms.

"Tell-me-the-name-of-the-bastard-who-seduced-you!" Trevellyan shouted.

"I won't!" Patricia cried, wrenching about trying to break her father's hold. Her hair had shaken loose and lashed around her in glittering waves.

"You won't, eh? You won't! God blast you, you're no better than the mares and cows! I'll find out. Ka-aina! David! Damn everything. Who seduced my daughter?"

He looked up, his face blotched with crimson and gray. Black beard jutted forward like a spade about to be thrust into the earth, black eyes glared fury at the world. His white shirt was drenched with perspiration, his rigid forearms shook like the legs of a horse ridden to the limit.

"What were you doing that such a thing could happen!" he shouted at Ka-aina. "God damn you, you lazy scum of a Kanaka, when I'm through with her I'll kill you!"

Instant by instant his rage mounted. Foam flecks

trembled among the hairs of his beard, sweat streamed down his temples. Ka-aina raised his arm to ward off the blow, and Trevellyan transferred his attention to Birthwood.

"David," he fought for breath. "David—you—blackguard!"

"God . . . damn . . . you!" The words, equally spaced, fell like stones to the floor. Birthwood confronted Trevellyan. "For that I leave by the boat tomorrow!" He tore out of the office.

"Come back, you bloody young fool. Come back, I say. God damn it, I apologize."

"No go, please, Mr. David, no go!" Ka-aina called, imploringly.

Birthwood halted, his eyes hard and angry. He stared at Trevellyan, then re-entered the room. His act was that of a person chained against his will. They were all chained, Ka-aina thought. Chained to Lani-o-akua.

Trevellyan fought to master the anger rending him. "Who's been here, Ka-aina? Who's visited Lani-o-akua since I left."

Ka-aina recited half a dozen names including Hamilton's. Trevellyan watched his daughter, but her expression did not change.

"Which of these men is it?"

"None of them."

"I'm to understand, then, it's some cowboy, some Kanaka," he roared. Taking fresh grasp of her shoulder he jerked her back and forth until she hung limp between his hands. Her face was gray, with sooty shadows about her lips, but her eyes blazed for her temper was as high as Trevellyan's. "I'll-get-it-out-of-you-if-I-have-toknock-every-tooth-out-of-your-head!"

"Mr. Trevellyan!" Birthwood cried, dashing forward.

"Keep-out-of-this-David-I-tell-you!" the panting, grinding voice went on like lava tearing steadily out of a cone.

"Mr. Trevellyan, be careful! Remember your daughter's condition!"

"Condition! What do you mean—condition?" Trevellyan yelled.

"Are you blind? If you manhandle her it'll precipitate events," Birthwood said in a hard voice that contradicted the embarrassment in his eyes.

Trevellyan stared at him, then transferred his attention to his daughter. Patricia stared back, her face a stark defiance. His eyes swept her.

"So-you're-going-to-have-a-baby-are-you?" Trevellyan choked, roaring out a stream of obscenity. "A filthy little bastard! You omitted to mention that. And I spent months in England to find a man worthy of you," he laughed insanely. "And Hawke arrives in three days. Arrh!" He thrust her back and forth.

"Mr. Trevellyan, let Patricia go!" Birthwood commanded.

"Keep-out-of-this-David-keep-out-of-it!" Trevellyan warned hoarsely. "This is between Patricia and me."

Birthwood wrenched one of Trevellyan's hands off Patricia and heaved her to her feet. A spasm contorted her features. Ka-aina spoke to Trevellyan in Hawaiian.

"So that's it, is it? I've about shaken the brat out of you?" Thrusting Birthwood aside, he glared at his daughter, then a great light dawned on his face. "The way's clear! Have your child. In a few hours everything will be over. Do you understand me? Over! No one need ever know. The marriage can be postponed a few weeks. David and Ka-aina's silence is mine as is everyone's here. You'll marry Hawke as planned. Don't try to fight me. If you do, when I find out the name of the man who's ruined you, I'll hunt him down and castrate him!"

Patricia grew livid. Trevellyan shook himself in a relieved, delighted way, then gripped her wrists. She wrenched herself free, reeled and grasped at the desk for support. Ka-aina noted with consternation that she had replaced the ring on her hand. Her face was torn with horror and unbelief.

"I'll do it, I swear I'll do it," Trevellyan cried, his eyes growing cunning as he saw the shaft he had driven in, sinking home. "Listen. If you promise to marry Hawke, I give you my oath that I'll make no further effort to discover the name of your lover. It's the only way you can save him."

Patricia stared at him, stunned. Her thoughts were evident. She knew her father sufficiently to realize that unless she did as he wished, he would put his threat into effect. Even if she succeeded in escaping and getting to Hamilton this evil, old man would hound them to the edges of the earth. Hatred for him, for life, showed in her eyes, then gradually was replaced by cunning, matching Trevellyan's. By promising to marry Hawke she put it beyond her father's power to harm Hamilton. There was a possibility that she might not survive the ordeal ahead. Snatching up her lower lip with one tooth, she stared out of the window. She was plotting some ghastly revenge that appalled her, even as she contemplated it.

"I promise," she announced, then lurched against the desk.

"Carry her to her room, David," Trevellyan roared, "and tell Mrs. Trevellyan to go to her." Then bellowing like a madman, he tore off first one and then the other of his great boots and hurled them into the garden, shattering the window to fragments.

Ka-aina paced the dark garden, listening to voices in consultation. Words stabbed the night like quick, short blows.

"Stop your blasted sniffling or I'll brain you!" Trevellyan's harsh voice ordered. "When the brat's born, bring it to me."

"But, Hi-ball, she won't let me in."

"Who's with her?"

"No one," Mrs. Trevellyan wailed.

"What!"

"I've tried to tell you but you've been so busy getting things ready for Hawke's visit that you didn't listen. The door's been locked since ten this morning and it's nearly midnight. She isn't dead. I heard her moving about, but you must send for a doctor. She'll kill herself," the woman sobbed.

"I couldn't buy his silence. She's young and strong. Kanaka and Chinese women have children without assistance. My girl's as game as they are."

"But this isn't a normal birth. The baby's coming too soon."

There was a silence, then steps with hell and terror in their sound charged down the veranda. Trevellyan pounded on the door.

"Patricia!"

A hoarse, tired voice cried out angrily from within and he recoiled. In the light of the veranda his great shoulders sagged. He looked beside himself. Bending his head he listened, then shouted,

"Ka-aina!"

The old man ran up the steps. From behind the locked door came labored breathing, vague noises, and occasionally a stifled grunt. Trevellyan's blood-shot eyes stared at the world with the uncomprehending hatred of a wounded bull. Determination to hide everything wrestled with fear for his daughter's life.

Ka-aina grasped his belt with shaking hands. Black night was pinned tightly around the earth, torn by half-heard sounds of a woman in agony, fighting alone to bring her child into the world. Once a moan, quickly stifled, crept out through the crack in the door, followed by sounds of desperate straining. Locking his thumbs in his belt, Ka-aina thrust down upon it until it bruised his hip bones. Recalling the expression he had noted in Patricia's eyes before she left the office, he suspected that she was keeping people out with the deliberate intention of dying.

"Break door quick!" he choked, then burst into impassioned Hawaiian.

Trevellyan shouted for his wife. The untidy, cringing figure fled toward them. Grasping the knob, Trevellyan wrenched at it. A smothered, hardly human voice cried out warningly and he desisted, crucified between terror of what might happen if no one went in and of what Patricia might do to herself if someone did.

Ka-aina's nostrils, keen as an animal's, dilated, then froze as they filled with the sickening smell of hot, fresh blood. His eyes leaped to Trevellyan's. There was a pause, followed by the thin, outraged cry of a child forced into the world before its time.

Trevellyan lurched his bulk against the door, bursting it in. His wife threw a wild look of hate about her and followed. Sight of such intensity of feeling in a person so negative was like seeing a corpse coming suddenly and unexpectedly to life. Sitting down, Ka-aina plunged his head between his hands.

He was conscious, in an overwhelming way, of Lani-o-akua. A living presence, a living force was generated by vegetation growing out of soil that had lava underneath it. The vibrations which were created shook people loose inside themselves. He felt as if he were hanging limply inside his own skin, defenceless before the onslaughts of the locality. A sensation bordering on hate stirred in his soul, and he realized that it was the same emotion he had seen in Mrs. Trevellyan's eyes. Lani-o-akua had shaken her to life and in a feeble way she had, for an instant, pitted the tiny fury of her soul against it, then collapsed beneath its force.

He raised his eyes. The tall, dark trees, the millions of spears of grass on the lawn seemed to edge closer like a huge beast warily creeping upon its prey. He heard, as from a distance, voices, steps, the angry, continued crying of the baby. Lani-o-akua was stalking them all.

An infuriated squall from the child made him cringe. Overwhelmingly, he realized his responsibility toward it. Only the previous afternoon he had begged the gods that he might be the custodian of Patricia's child. With the gesture of a person fighting to get above water, he rose to his feet.

"Ka-aina."

Trevellyan stood in the doorway holding a bundle that fought and raged in a minute way. His attitude registered loathing. Ka-aina took the child from him and a tremor went through him when he held the child against his chest.

"Speak of this to no one. See that it never—" Trevellyan whispered the last two words.

Going down the steps, Ka-aina crossed the lawn. When he was out of sight, he turned back the blanket. In the starlight the baby's features were distinct. Despite it's untimely coming the child looked lusty. There was no resemblance to Patricia, but its brown eyes, the odd outward flare of its eyebrows, the small cleft in its chin, marked it as Hamilton's.

He started along the path through the *kukui* grove. An old limb creaked protestingly as another rubbed against it. As he tiptoed past the god he had placed in the clearing that morning, a thought halted him. Laying the baby on the grass, he reached for the knife he wore in his legging and tenderly cut a tuft of still-moist hair from the top of the child's head. Muttering prayers, he approached the image imploring it to safeguard the new life which had come into the world. When his prayers were over, he buried the tuft of floss at the base of the idol and rose to his feet. He was appalled, realizing that he had made the most malignant and destructive of all the gods the guardian of Patricia's child. Would the evil influences emanating from it color the baby's life? There was no choice. Better have that evil force behind it than against it.

Tomorrow he must contrive to see Patricia and, under some pretext, get a lock of her hair in order that he might place her also in the care of the god that looked before and after.

CHAPTER VI

PATRICIA lay in bed staring out of the open window.
Sounds of afternoon came faintly through it; the plain-
tive whistle of a native bird venturing down from the
summit of Haleakala, gardens breathing softly in the
sun, trees stirring as they adjusted themselves to the
approach of evening.

Her mind felt full of ragged rents. Warring emotions
had prolonged premature travail, but already her body,
fashioned perfectly for nature's purposes, felt returning
vitality pricking through it.

She realized that the events of the past thirty-six hours,
divorced from all reality, had put girlhood forever behind her. Her mind sent out feelers, contacting this and
that, and recoiled. She had been cheated of her lover,
cheated of death. With the first pang of childbirth she
had hoped and intended to die, had refused aid with that
end definitely in view.

The horror of the ensuing hours alone blurred everything, making her child unreal. The vile ugliness of it
all. In an effort to escape the memories treading on her
heels, her mind leaped the abyss between past and present. It seemed only yesterday since she had seen Hamil-

81

ton, yet months had elapsed since she had last been in his arms. Even as she thought of him, she felt herself caught in some elemental current, adventurous and magical. She had always been acutely aware of him physically. When he so much as looked at her or touched her, her body throbbed with a force that dissolved bones and will, and sent every atom of her pouring toward him. And he was out of reach forever. If she so much as attempted to see him . . .

She sat up in bed and then, defying her father, relived her time with Hamilton. Nothing, nobody could rob her of that! She recalled the excitement with which she used to greet each dawn, the wild current of life which had surged through her while she dressed, breakfast hurried through in order to reach the trysting place sooner, Ka-aina's maddening deliberation while he saddled, her helplessness to hurry him lest he suspect. And all the time he had known and guarded her secret!

Her mind halted. Sometime during the next day or two she must contrive to give him a note to deliver to Hamilton. She sunk her head in her arms but the twisting roads of memory beckoned, and she lay back on her pillows.

She remembered with exhilaration galloping along the avenue, the turn down a cattle trail, the careful look back. Fragrances of *lantana, ilima, kulu* mixed with the smell of her sweating horse. Cacti huddled on rocky hills, castor oil trees drooped in the sun. She thought of the cautious going among blue boulders piled in a dried gorge, the swift scramble up a bank, the gallop across an opening at the farther end of which Hamilton waited.

Streams of fire coursed through her, recollecting embraces and caresses exchanged under the sky; the delicate sting of quickly given kisses, the savage ecstasy of lips pressed close and long. In her imagination she felt Hamilton's eyes upon her. Through them he embraced her before he reached up to lift her off her horse. The space between them, even before he touched her, throbbed with a powerful essence that aroused in her an abandonment of surrender.

Her mind came to a standstill. She was cold; cold from weakness, weak because she had borne his child.

She had appreciated from the first that the manner of their loving affronted Hamilton without altering the quality of his feeling for her. But the realization that he suffered had not prevented her from insisting that he come. Seeing her daily necessitated endless subterfuge and maneuvering that was in direct opposition to his instincts and principles. He was compelled to rise at four instead of five o'clock. He hurried over the plantation before *lunas* * and laborers were out, grasping all he could of the day's work. While breakfasting, he gave orders to cover it, then set out by secret byways for the scarlet cone, while half the plantation fancied he was riding one section and the other half presumed he was somewhere else.

He had attempted to make it clear to her that love founded on deceit could only have a disastrous end. His wife spent the greater part of her time in America but his code demanded that whether they lived together or apart he owed her fidelity. Having betrayed her, the only thing was to see her, and let her get a divorce on

* *luna*—overseer.

whatever grounds she chose. Patricia had refused to consent to even a temporary separation and when he grew insistent, begged him not to think, not to look ahead, just to be. Some force surging up from the earth beneath them vitalized her, an impulse magical and vast that emanated from the soil, from the ocean teeming with life, a force against which she could not fight. This man was the cry of her being answered, the fulfillment of her need. She would not forgo being with him even for a day.

Hamilton was passionate but the finer side of his nature compelled him to try and make Patricia consent to putting their relations on a permanent basis. He argued that clandestine meetings were certain to be discovered in time. She laughed. He insisted that stolen love was soiled love. She silenced him with kisses. When he met her, he had looked scarcely twenty-eight. After a few weeks he looked his thirty-seven years and more.

She moved fiercely in the bed. His eyes, distracted with anxiety and grief, were engraved upon her mind. Until the past forty-eight hours, she had never experienced grief, beyond the pangs which were largely resentment, when Hamilton finally prevailed upon her to let him go in order that he might be free to return and marry her. Months had elapsed before he carried his point. His face had become gaunt and bleak, and about his mouth was an expression of a man who had betrayed a sacred trust.

She recalled the words he had spoken the last time he saw her:

"I'm going, Pat, because I love you more than honor, family, and friends. I'll get things straightened out as

fast as it's humanly possible. I'll have to sell Waikapu."
His eyes had rested regretfully on the distant acres he
had loved and beautified. "Because of your father it
will be impossible for us to live on Maui. Don't torture
yourself wondering if I'll come back. You love me. To
fail a person who loves you is, in my estimation, the final
sin. Until everything's above board, I shall feel filthy.
To have dragged anyone as young and lovely as you are
into a thing like this—"

"I wasn't dragged, I did the dragging," she had interrupted and he had swept her into his arms, worshipping her honesty.

After an instant, he had stared at the heavy ring he
wore, set with a square-cut ruby. On either side of the
stone the coat of arms of his family was engraved. Removing it, Hamilton had slipped it on to her finger and
kissed it.

Opening the drawer of her bedside table, Patricia got
out the ring and cradled it in the white hollow of her
hand. It made her—no matter what—solidly and forever
his. Slipping it on the fourth finger of her right hand,
she pressed it home. It sealed their love. Nobody could
make her remove it. She felt no remorse or compunction
for the havoc she had brought into Hamilton's life. Her
only sensation was fury, because she had been despoiled
of her lover. She stared out of the window, her face a
frozen storm.

Long, solemn shadows stretched among the trees. The
immediate garden was quiet but she divined, rather than
heard, the rustle of preparation going on around her.
Voices called out, faintly and gaily. Steps passed. Cinders crunched beneath hoofs and boots. Men were riding

in from seashore and mountain bringing ferns and food for the feast which was being prepared. Above the fragrance of the garden, she smelled the sweetness of *maile*, which women were twisting into garlands for the heads and necks of guests. The pungent odor of *palapalai* fern which would cover *luau* tables, caught in her nostrils.

How she had loved, as a child, to go with Ka-aina and the cowboys to gather it from golden-green openings in the forest. While they stuffed it into bags, she basked in the sun, watching the men sling the filled ones onto the pack horses. Then the enchanting rest before starting home while everyone braided wreaths to wear. The gay gallop back, bags bouncing, green fronds waving like minute forests above each horse.

Her ears, alert from Ka-aina's training, distinguished the grate of other bags being dumped on the ground. Bags filled with *opihis* gathered off rocks still wet and salty from the sea. Butter yellow, they were stimulating to the appetite as no other shellfish. Ka-aina had taught her, while still a toddler, to pry them off the rocks and scoop them from the shell with another empty one, and to eat while little waves lapped thrillingly around her legs.

The muted throbbing of ukuleles and guitars, singing, peals of laughter brought tears to her eyes. In a rush the highly colored pageant of Island life rose before her. A life unlike any other which twisted possessive fingers into a person's soul, holding it against the rest of the world. She grasped fully, and for the first time, the imperious beckoning, the hypnotic pull, the mysterious promise of Hawaii. She thought with passionate appreciation of the force of the sun charging land and sea with life. Unsullied, boundless spaces on every side; the stir of creation in water, earth, and air; the arrogant blue of the Pacific; the sound of the trade winds coming over the bulge of the world; savage, silver rain; quick twilights hurrying in from soaring horizons; the hollow sounds of waves breaking against lava promontories; mountains flouting the clouds; the wild leap of green pastures seaward; flowers tearing from their buds in orange, scarlet, blue, and purple.

Breathing hurriedly, she sat up and embraced her knees. Hawke would arrive tomorrow to take her from it all. Hatred of everyone and everything choked her. Life had grasped her, used her to further its own ends, then flung her aside when it had had what it wanted of her. Her mouth grew straight and unlovely. As life had used her, so would she use it!

Cautious footsteps sounded on the walk, crossed the veranda, halted at her door. A tap sounded.

"Come in, Ka-aina."

The anguish in his eyes startled her. He tiptoed toward the bed, holding his hat in his hands.

"Poor girl, poor girl," he said huskily. He swallowed, twisted his features, and whispered, "I got baby. I take care for you."

Patricia nodded. "Who does it look like?" she asked, her eyes fastened on the ceiling.

"Look like father," Ka-aina answered, his face working.

Scarlet blazed into Patricia's cheeks.

"Before I go," she addressed the ceiling, "I'll give you a message to deliver to him when he comes back."

Her face grew bleak.

"No cry, no cry," Ka-aina begged, picking up her hand.

"There is nothing to cry about. Everything is *pau*," * Patricia announced, looking depleted.

Ka-aina's hands shook as he kneaded her fingers between his.

"You all right?" he asked, anxiously.

"That's the hell of it," Patricia replied in a loud, surprising voice. "Not only am I all right, but I'm strong enough to get up and meet Hawke, strong enough to marry him, strong enough to keep my promise so *he* will be safe from Father."

Ka-aina made a quick, protesting movement.

"Hush," he said in Hawaiian. "Hush."

"You must find out when he returns. He mustn't come here."

"I know," Ka-aina replied, batting his eyes like a child fighting tears. "I keep sharp lookout, I listen to all the talk so I find out what ship he's coming on."

Glancing over his shoulder to assure himself that no one was within earshot, he began speaking passionately in Hawaiian, "I had no choice," he insisted, defending his act. "If I had not put the child into the god's care—"

Patricia nodded, tossed out an armful of hair, and waited. Reaching for his knife, Ka-aina cut off a strand. His hands looked flurried as he slipped it into the breast pocket of his dungaree coat.

"It hurts to have to put you into the keeping of such a god," he whispered remorsefully, "but some member of the family will be claimed as a sacrifice. It shall not

* *pau*—ended.

be you or your baby." He wiped his eyes. "If there is no sacrifice, in the end, Lani-o-akua will be destroyed." Patricia caught her breath. After a tense silence her glance met Ka-aina's, then simultaneously they looked out of the window. The sun had set and there was a suggestion of eternal things in the clear, red light burning above the sea. Against it, tree trunks were silhouetted, dark and solid. A twilight, filled with secrecy, was stealing through the garden, dimming it. Loneliness enveloped the locality, making it, for the moment, tragic. A horse neighed, a gust of wind stirred the tree tops, and a peacock screeched in the hills. An electric current of feeling swept Ka-aina's and Patricia's hands together. Their fingers locked. Patricia's eyes swept familiar walks, pools, and lawns.

"A life must be given," she whispered. "Lani-o-akua shall not be destroyed!"

Patricia stood beside the open window, straining to hear the first, vast rustle of a cavalcade of riders coming up the road from Makena. Sunshine like burnished bronze slanted through the garden. Undercurrents of anticipation tensed the air. Her face burned, her throat tightened.

Soon they would all be here; King Kalakaua, Hawke, officers, guests, and sailors. Her father had left at dawn with David, cowboys, and assistants, leading and driving the hundred-odd saddle horses. She had lain in bed listening to the tumultuous departure. Snorts, curses, the dull thud of some animal lashing out with both hind feet against another's ribs. Shrill squeals of protest, retaliating kicks, had filled the thin, sweet morning air. Warning shouts, good-natured laughter, gay sallies as men wrestled to force horses into line and headed for the beach, drifted back, diminishing gradually as they got under way.

Patricia's eyes swooped to her right hand. She had to keep looking at Hamilton's ring to remind herself that only by marrying Hawke could she safeguard Hamilton. What had passed shadowed her like a dreadful cloud. Her eyelids fluttered in her unsmiling face. Nothing mattered, nothing could matter any more. Life had just to be got through with and, if possible, punished. She thought remotely about her child but could not realize the fact of its existence.

Jerking a chair resentfully to the window, she sat down. Her weakness, when she rose to dress, surprised her, for she had felt strong enough in bed. But with her father's indomitable will, she had driven herself to brush her hair and put on a kimono. Her body was sound from an outdoor life. Hawaiian and Chinese women had children and were up and about a few hours later. She was as game as they. Mrs. Trevellyan came at intervals to care for her, brought her food. Not a word was exchanged between them but Patricia scorned to play the weakling and forced herself to eat.

Outside voices made a ceaseless droning murmur, the murmur of the future, of preoccupation with life. All the morning a stream of Hawaiians and Chinese had flowed through the garden. A widespread rustle of people all working for one end, dominated Lani-o-akua. It generated a suffocation in Patricia, made her realize what it meant. Betrothal, ultimate marriage to a man she had never seen, departure from Lani-o-akua, a complete wiping out of the past.

Her long fingers dug into her palms. She glanced at the clock. It was almost three. They should be coming. Suspense intensified her weakened state.

At intervals the afternoon was torn by the squealing of pigs dragged to slaughter, the squawking of fowls, the dull bellowing of fat steers as they fell beneath the knife. In the *kukui* grove hammers sounded, while long low tables were put hurriedly together and spread with fern. She heard the thud of spades digging into soil as underground ovens were enlarged, the crackling and snapping of fires lighted to heat stones. Men with garlanded hats and ringing spurs passed, their arms filled with banana and *ti* leaves, which they dropped on the grass in front of seated women painstakingly wrapping fish, chickens, and other delicacies which were to be steamed underground.

Her eyes went to the clock a second time. Her father and his guests should be arriving! Her hands got cold and the line of her jaw turned white. Rising she pushed the curtains aside and saw natives collecting in the garden and along the road; men moving with large, loafing dignity, sumptuous women in flowing Mother Hubbards, lithe young girls coquetting with striplings bending over guitars and ukuleles with lounging grace; children diving among their elders, their legs looking mischievous and gay. A scattering of white-haired men and women, halting to exchange comments, figures that retained a miraculous appeal and which emanated good-natured interest and tolerance for the antics of a younger generation. In the background hundreds of Chinese coolies, pathetic, scarecrow figures, waited apathetically. Trevellyan's orders compelled everyone to be present when the King and his distinguished guests arrived.

A crowd of young girls with garlands of roses and gardenias hanging from their smooth, round arms was gathering at the gate. They laughed and flirted immoderately with men waiting to take horses as the guests dismounted. The men returned the girls' sallies with badinage. Young and old alike radiated a pagan joy in the consciousness of abundance in store.

It made Patricia feel lonely and apart. Not so long ago she had felt as they did, had embraced life as eagerly, wringing the uttermost from every moment. An elderly cowboy with some horseplay, which brought delighted applause from onlookers, squinted clownishly at the sun, listened, gestured. There was a moment of silence, then an anticipatory flutter ran through the afternoon like an electric shock.

A gathering mutter of approaching hoofs thudding eagerly along the road filled the air. Three horsemen, riding abreast well in advance of the rest, appeared around the bend. The one in the center swept forward. King Kalakaua, riding superbly, mounted on a lathered black horse, galloped up. Older folk prostrated themselves, covering their eyes in the ancient fashion, which forbade a commoner to look at a chief, younger ones cheered and waved.

In appearance the King was arresting; over six feet tall, with the magnificent proportions of Polynesians. His eyes, gentle, kindly, with smooth, subtle lids, swept his subjects with careless affection. From each cheek curly black whiskers stood out in the style affected by Franz Josef of Austria whom Kalakaua greatly admired. His riding breeches of fine dark cloth, London tailored, clasped his strong legs snugly. The coat of a uniform covered with decorations was incongruously open at the neck as the day was warm. A wreath of red roses poised like a rakish crown on his head, another encircled his neck. Reining his horse to its haunches, he received the homage of his subjects with courtly graciousness, but above everything, a person was aware of his affability.

A grizzled Hawaiian, tears streaming from his eyes, seized the horse's bridle, another took hold of the stirrup, and the King dismounted. Men and women pressed forward, kissing his hands, prostrating themselves, presenting gifts and garlands. He stood in their midst, dominating without being forbidding, friendly without being familiar. He was the most travelled ruler of his day; as a king a failure, as a personality a triumph. In the charm of the man one forgot that he had been dined and wined by most of the crowned heads of Europe, that Queen Victoria had been impressed by his polish and bearing, that King Leopold of Belgium, young Prince Wilhelm of Prussia, and the King and Queen of Italy counted him a personal friend. Above all it was the individual who men remarked, admired, and remembered.

With a gay, gracious gesture he signed to Trevellyan and the rider with him to approach, seeming to wrap them with royal approval. Patricia drew the sheer muslin curtains together with a shaking hand. Ears rang, eyes blurred. With an effort she mastered her faculties and looked out. Her father glared about with blood-shot, angry eyes, assuring himself that all was in order. There was a heart-rending quality to the great lumbering figure, suggesting a wounded boar ready to charge blindly in order to ease the rage eating at its vitals. Kalakaua, ever the courtier, announced in a ringing voice:

"Admiral Guy Hilary Hawke, of Her Most Gracious Majesty Queen Victoria's Navy."

Cheers rent the air, flower girls crowded up, horses plunged and snorted. Patricia got a quick, disturbing impression of a tall man with glittering black eyes and white hair that stood out in surprising contrast to the youth of his face and figure. His movements were quick, electric, and controlled. His eyes swept here and there, taking in every detail of the scene. In a perfectly fitting uniform, stiff with gold braid, glittering with medals and decorations, he epitomized man, proud and splendid, forever adventuring over trackless seas. There was about him some quality that stirred the imagination. In spirit he belonged to the goodly company of Drake, Magellan, Columbus, Cook, and Vancouver. His eyes scanned the boundless ocean from the high bridge of a ship, he defended the flag of the British Empire in far-flung corners of the earth. Men rushed to death at his command.

With a sharp movement Patricia rose, turning her back deliberately upon him.

CHAPTER VII

TREMORS ran through Patricia as she stood, white and silent, under the hands of native women robing her for dinner. Her hair, brushed and shining, was carefully arranged in the mode of the day, her feet encased in expensively buckled shoes. Wrists and throat, transparent, faintly veined with blue, were clasped with jewels. Her ivory satin, lace-trimmed dress, ribbed, tucked, bustled, stiffened with whalebone, lay across the bed.

Outside, the evening filled with strange lights and half shadows, lent a portentous significance to the occasion. The sea above the horizon was flamingo red, fading into clear amber. Against the sky the islands of Lanai and Kahoolawe were smudged in black and olive green. A stray gust of wind, like some swift-footed predatory animal, fled over the tree tops briefly disturbing their serenity.

The girl attempted to pick up lost threads of thought that eluded her. Leashed emotions for which there was no outlet injected themselves into the atmosphere. Silence, broken only by Mrs. Trevellyan's vague, contradictory orders that confused the Hawaiian women increasingly, gripped the room.

They glanced at her pinched, harried face and raised their eyebrows. It was known that she lived in terror of her husband, that she was always relegated to the background at such times as these, and they divined her antagonism for Patricia. She palpitated on the outskirts of events, suggesting a bewildered hen blowing helplessly before the wind.

Unnatural quiet fell on the women who, at first, had chatted eagerly and questioned Patricia. She was always friendly with Hawaiians and they felt at ease with her. Rumors had run through Lani-o-akua that the young English admiral with the strange white hair was to marry her. Was it so? Was it possible that Patricia was to live in England and make her bow to Queen Victoria whose picture hung in Trevellyan's drawing room?

Their faculties, keen as those of animals, became aware of treacherous undercurrents washing about them. They began eyeing one another. There was a violent quality to Patricia's silence and they hurried through tasks which ordinarily they would have prolonged for the sheer enjoyment of contemplating beauty; beauty of slim young body clasped in silk and lace, of sparkling gems, and trailing satin caught into enchanting puffs.

When the oldest woman lifted the dress over Patricia's head, she noted the increased fullness of her breasts. Aware of it, an angry red sprang up the girl's neck. Her body had not yet resumed normal proportions. The woman wrestled with hooks and straps while Patricia endured it, an extraordinary expression in her eyes.

Mrs. Trevellyan directed the woman to remove the gown and ordered Patricia to inhale. With a sort of hideous delight she drew the lacings of the corset tighter. After a few minutes of breathing and pulling the girl was reduced to her proper size and the dress was slipped on and fastened.

Patricia's body protested against the unnatural constraint and clamored for its accustomed freedom. Her small round breasts, thrust high above prodding steel, veiled lightly with transparent lace, looked like two creamy apples. Her waist could almost be spanned by a man's circling fingers, slim arms escaped from puffed and gathered sleeves, and the straight lines of her hips were lost in billows of looped satin and cascading lace caught up in the rear by a bustle.

She studied her reflection but after the first instant of satisfied feminine vanity, experienced a sense of complete defeat. Hamilton had never seen her, would never see her dressed like this. With the exception of the first evening, when she had worn a *holoku* of white satin, he had only seen her in muslin and organdie. He could never realize now that she could be the last word in fashion, a woman finished to the minutest detail, comparable to great ladies across the sea. She gloried in the unnatural smallness of her waist that accentuated the swell of her body above and below it. She was of her time and saw nothing grotesque in the distortion of nature.

Satisfaction filled her. Realizing her own loveliness, courage and confidence began to steal back, temporarily dimming the monstrosity of the situation. This was her first bow to society. Beauty, wealth were hers. She knew herself to be desired of men. She knew her own ability to sweep them off their feet.

Mrs. Trevellyan signed to the women to leave. When the whisper of their bare feet died on the veranda, she considered Patricia, creating the impression that she was looking down at her from a height. Bitter lines cut into her mouth, compressed into an expression of virtue mingled with scorn and loathing.

"So the admiral's trollop is tricked out to look like a great lady!" she observed.

Patricia flayed her with a glance.

"I may have been your mother's lady's maid, Hi-ball may have married me to have a nurse for you," the woman's face was distorted with the instinctive antipathy of the weak for the strong, of the unbeautiful for the beautiful, "but I'm a good woman! You—wanton! Dressed up like a virgin, on parade for Kalakaua and British officers to ogle when your breasts are not yet dry!"

Patricia struck her and she staggered against the dresser whimpering and cringing. A red mark sprang out on Mrs. Trevellyan's cheek. Patricia's faculties scattered. For the first time she realized her position fully. Only a spectacular marriage could safeguard her from people who could not discriminate between regal passion and puny purity, between storm-tossed greatness and sheltered littleness. Wealth and position had safeguarded her from question or criticism. Until Hamilton came, her life had been proof against cracks and scratches. She had been permitted a peep at treacherous undercurrents racing forward, she had seen life naked and unashamed. A trumpet had called and she had answered it, but to have to pay unendingly for that response was another matter. Consciousness of security

had made her at heart a coward, for the smirking condemnation in the eyes of the woman facing her put her
soul to rout.

Providing she kept her promise to her father, no
whisper of what had happened would ever reach the
world. With reluctant gratitude her spirit rushed to his
for protection. No one at Lani-o-akua, beyond this
woman and Ka-aina, would ever know the secret of her
past. By marrying Hawke, aristocrat, Admiral in Her
Majesty's Navy, with greater prestige and higher position than any man in Hawaii could boast, she would put
herself forever beyond censorship. Her father was ruthless but he was sound. With a pang of remorse she looked
at Hamilton's ring, then fortified her sense of disloyalty
with the thought that part of her would remain forever
loyal. Hawke was only escape, safety.

A heavy step sounded. Mrs. Trevellyan's eyes, full
of weak, intense venom, slid from Patricia's. Her air of
superior virtue vanished, the only triumphant moment of
her life was over. She glanced at Patricia and went
hastily out of a side door.

Patricia grew rigid when her father halted at the
threshold. It was a terrible moment for them both.
Trevellyan's eyes met hers and glanced aside, like steel
from steel. His face was suffused with color and moist
with sweat. He was in purgatory lest his threat had not
been sufficient to make her fall into line with his plans,
afraid that she might—by refusing to see Hawke at the
last minute, or by her treatment of him when she did—
send all his castles toppling, making him an object of
ridicule in Hawaii. Patricia realized that she might have
been tempted to rebel had it not been for the passage

with Mrs. Trevellyan. It seemed impossible that a person so negative could influence the direction of her life.

The fact that her father had not attempted to see her since the night her child was born, proved that he was afraid of what she might do. The knowledge gave her a sense of power. This time she, and not he, would wield the sceptre at Lani-o-akua. Color flamed into her face.

Trevellyan eyed her; she did not shrink, she did not flinch; she had transgressed in a wholesale way, as he did; she had torn down standards and trampled them underfoot, but she was above the law of afterwards. She had no right to look so beautiful, so unsoiled, so impervious, his eyes said, with reluctant admiration.

"Well?" he questioned.

The word was exchanged, not between father and erring daughter, not between man and woman, but between two human beings. Patricia was overwhelmed. Her father was acknowledging her as an equal! It was unthinkable and moved her profoundly.

She became aware of him in a new way. He was Hi-ball Trevellyan of whom incredible tales were told, Hi-ball Trevellyan who swaggered and swashbuckled through life, he was Hi-ball Trevellyan who, against mighty odds, had snatched a woman of royal family for his wife. Hi-ball Trevellyan whom no obstacle could best. He had built a kingdom in a wilderness, created beauty out of lava and cinders, bent life and people to his will. There was a heroic quality to him, he was part of the history of the Pacific. Suddenly she felt close to him. They were the same sort, splendid outlaws who refused to conform to the standards of the world.

"I'm ready," she said in a ringing voice.

Hi-ball gulped like a baby fighting tears. His eyelids, hot and shiny from lack of sleep and fury, worked fiercely, then steadied into their accustomed glare. "Gad, you're grand!" he roared.

As Patricia walked down the veranda, a strange mental clarity overtook her. She realized what Lani-o-akua stood for, what it was, what it epitomized. Her father! Her father who was like a burst of colors, blue, orange, red, royal purple, all mixed up and spoiled with black. Her father who fed a hundred guests and hundreds of retainers and who had not one friend to love him. Her father, who while he repulsed, attracted by his strength. She looked at him, lumbering arrogantly beside her. His heroically modeled body, his shaggy head, his eyes, black as freshly crusted lava, made him an arresting, thought-provoking figure that stamped itself indelibly on the retina of all who saw him, however briefly. Like Lani-o-akua he possessed a fatal fascination, like Lani-o-akua it was inconceivable that he would ever end.

Glancing at the gardens, pride surged through her. Flaming orange torches tied to the flower-swathed trunks of trees, made gaudy pools of color in the dark. All the people in the world seemed to be strolling across the lawns and streaming along the road. Here it was a lean-flanked British officer, there it was a big Hawaiian sitting on a fountain edge lolling over a guitar, or an old Chinaman with three gray hairs in his beard, smoking a wee pipe with a tiny brass bowl halfway up the stem, so quiet that he commanded attention.

Darkness fighting for supremacy over light, laughter triumphing over silence; rolling of brown eyes and winking of blue; fat, pleasant, loose-coupled older women in flowing *holokus* moving with the stateliness of ships in full sail before the wind; older men with the vigor of horses; young men lithe as jaguars; sailors with rolling gait; girls swaying like saplings in a breeze, all moving gaily toward groves where long, fern-spread tables sent up the aroma of every kind of food.

Sweet potatoes, fish; chickens stewed in the milk of coconuts; *lauluas* of salt meat and fish; bowls of *poi*, faintly lavender and temptingly cool; the pink crystals of salt gathered off dust-reddened rocks near the seashore; glossy seaweed, clean as brine; dried shrimps, brittle as paper and red as garnets; butter yellow *opihis*, scooped from their shells, all sent up an individual and collective fragrance. Young coconuts, stripped of their husks and ready to drink; golden pineapples; ruddy mangoes; freckled hands of bananas; ruby-red mountain apples; stalks of sugar cane, added their scent.

In a grove, beneath rows of torches, men worked with kegs and bottles; barrels of beer to slake the thirst of British tars, barrels of wine for women, *shamshu* for Chinese, square-face gin for Hawaiians. Women with swinging hips carrying liquor to tables, boys showing off, girls uttering cascades of stifled giggles, men singing, shouting *hulas* above ukuleles and guitars. The fragrance characteristic of Hawaiian feasts, a mingled odor of hot food and flowers wilting about warm, human necks, filled the night.

Patricia's arm, which had been loosely linked through her father's, tensed. His eyes swooped down to hers and hers rushed up to his. The sweep of the drama being enacted, impending events to grow out of it, the years marching over Lani-o-akua with resounding tread, swept their spirits together and welded them into one.

"My grand, good gal, my splendid gal!" Trevellyan muttered, blinking tears from his eyes.

With lifted chins they halted at the threshold of the drawing room. Men resplendent in uniform were laughing, drinking, bending over half-caste women—colorful as peacocks or cool and suave as gardenias—imported to Lani-o-akua for the occasion.

Helen MacKaine, as yet a mere girl, remembered by every man who lived during the purple, latter days of the Monarchy, and by sons who replaced them in the more drab forward march of commercialism. Helen, dark, magnetic—divine and damned—who could have boasted that her lovers ranged from missionaries to visiting potentates, whose long hands and rosy fingers wove spells about men's hearts, whose eyes were narcotics, whose body was a fire at which young and old alike warmed themselves or burned themselves to ashes.

"Dearie," blonde, buxom, the bloom of youth dying a valiant death beneath the paint upon her face. A laughing rowdy, a great fellow, who screamed immoderately at race meets, touched men shamelessly for money which she invariably paid back, confounding them, who was never seen without a fan to halt the ravages of easy perspiration ooozing from the pink flesh in which she was steadily being engulfed.

Lehua, cool, creamy, with the lithe, wicked contours of a panther and rice-white, pointed teeth which lured men toward the pomegranate red cavity of her smiling, parted mouth.

The King, his broad chest a blaze of decorations, gay,

affable, commanding, was chatting with a portly officer whose bald head and face were so red that his white moustache looked like froth against it. At the sight of Trevellyan and Patricia, Kalakaua lifted his arm imperiously, silencing the room. With a quick little nod to the officer with whom he had been talking, for Kalakaua was ever the courtier, he started toward the door.

"Aloha! Aloha, my child, aloha! But it is no longer a child we greet, it is an enchantingly beautiful woman."

His black eyes appreciated every detail of the costume that set off the lustre of her youthful loveliness. Without affectation, with the quick, sincere, easy affection of his race, he extended both hands. Patricia made a half curtsey, then felt her fingers taken warmly and strongly into his. An intoxicating sensation of being wrapped in approval, honored, exalted, replaced the feelings of disaster and disgrace which she had experienced during the past seventy-two hours.

She was her father's daughter. Her head went up. Love trapped you, let you in for things! Her eyes rested on Hamilton's ring and a pang pierced her, then she looked at the room. The flower of the British navy, the cream of the manhood of Hawaii were assembled at Lani-o-akua, not because her father had loved a woman greatly and been greatly loved by him, but because he had power! As long as you had the power of gold, of position, you could shape and mould life to your will.

"Patricia!" Her father's voice roused her.

Hawke was at Trevellyan's elbow. He made her think of a lance, lean, tall, erect, with narrow hips and stirring shoulders. Black, level eyes looked from beneath black brows in striking contrast to his thick white hair.

She noted the arrogance of his nose, the proud shape of his head, the pallor of his face under its deep, sea tan. The thought flashed through her mind, "He's a younger son and Dad's bribed him with a huge dower to marry me."

Affronted womanhood, affronted beauty rose in arms. They looked at each other, then Hawke bent formally over her hand. There was a remote, cool quality to his voice when he addressed her but when he raised his head the expression in his eyes had altered. Kalakaua watched them, then glanced at Trevellyan waggishly.

During dinner Patricia caught herself watching Hawke. He had charm, force, quality. The movements of his hands, cadences in his voice, his short, mirthless laughter possessed a magnetism which attracted her against her will. Even when she looked away she was conscious of his slightly bitter, disturbing mouth, smiling formally above his strong chin. His close-set ears, his white hair brushed back from a courageous forehead marked him as a man of will and quick decisions.

She argued that she was taking stock of his points as she would gauge the mettle and temper of an unknown horse. He would marry her for her dowery, she would marry him for position and protection against the tricks and treachery of passion lodged within herself. But even as she argued, instinct warned her that there was not—even now—anything practical in their relations.

In an effort to distract her mind she looked around the room. At the far end of the table her father was inciting his guests to extravagant behavior. At the head Kalakaua was responding to a long-distance toast of Helen MacKaine's. Her body was clasped in vermilion velvet that caught life from her supple limbs, a wreath of roses outlined her head. The King smiled at her indulgently as a father might at an erring, irresistible child whose charming and frantic behavior beckons at ruin. Beside her was Old Man Calhoun, spendthrift, gambler, waster, but a great figure in his own way. A royal liver, prodigal, open-handed, a lover of blue-blooded horses, a prodigious drinker of liquor.

Feeling Hawke's eyes on her Patricia smiled at an officer across the table whose lean, red face was wedged in between two high collar points, then transferred her attention to Lehua, leaning indolently and insolently on an elbow while she chatted with him, suggesting a suave Greek courtesan seducing the general in an enemy's camp. Above the moist, pink expanse of "Dearie's" shoulder, she saw Birthwood's aloof profile. And there was Old Man Calhoun bawling across to a crony, waving a goblet in his mottled, purple hand as he chanted the pedigrees of race horses.

The table, brilliant with candles, heaped with flowers, crowded with dishes, dazzled Patricia. Caviar from Russia, anchovies from Sweden, *pâté de fois gras* from Holland geese, mushrooms from France, candied ginger and coconut from China, plus the plunder of the mountains and the Pacific were crowded together. Rare vintages, brought around the Horn, sparkled, snapped, or glowed like warm amber in long-stemmed glasses that winked slyly above moving hands.

An uproar such as she had never heard filled the night. Some of the guests were drinking, some shouting, some singing. From the garden came wild bursts of sound and the island seemed to be screaming in answer to the protesting clamoring of birds hovering uneasily in the trees. Thrills raced through her. The extravagance of the scene answered an ever-present hunger in her blood. She was electrified by the energy of the scene about her. Impressions beat about her like vast, invisible wings; the thundering shape of Haleakala beneath the stars, lawns swarming with people, gardens drunk with light and color, the majesty of the Pacific breathing quietly against continents sprawled from pole to pole.

She sensed a forward surge of life which took no heed of individuals, felt the pathos of human endeavor blindly groping to contact something behind physical manifestations. There was a quality, touching, wonderful, in the persistent courage of human beings blindly trying to direct destiny, creating discord and destruction while they fancied they ruled the earth. Like her father, like the King, like Old Man Calhoun, drawing steadily toward the end of their splendid and tragic cycles after planting the seed of another distracted generation.

"Your father did not tell me you were so beautiful."

Patricia realized that even while she had been absorbed in the happenings transpiring around her, she had been acutely and antagonistically aware of Hawke. She fixed him with a cool impersonal stare, making a mock of him and his compliment. Color swept into his face and burned the roots of his hair. For an instant a force akin to hatred made their spirits reach impatiently for each other, then she heard herself saying with calculated indifference:

"I'm surprised. As a rule Father advertises merchandise he wants to sell."

"Inferring?" Hawke asked, his glance excluding all women but herself from his world.

She was taken aback, then anger seized her, which was somehow satisfying for it put her safely on the farther side of an abyss. Lowering her lashes she appraised him through them. He had fascination, suggesting as he did, the reckless adventurers of old, and because of a certain challenge that lay in his strange, negative quality. His nearness roused her in a vague, annoying way but the realization that he was not proof against her beauty gave her a sense of advantage over him.

"Being a younger son," Hawke said in a hard, hot voice, "I had to marry money. It's necessary to my career, but since seeing you—" he watched her in an astounded manner that quickened the beating of her heart.

Her skin scorched. She had every reason, every cause to feel antagonistic toward him, and yet some part of her was welling up from an inner depth, impelling her toward him. She fought against the sensation, for she remembered it—the old impulse of the physical. It had trapped her once. Under the circumstances it was an affront. Was it woven into the very fabric of her? Her eyes rushed to Hamilton's ring.

Leaping up Trevellyan planted one foot on his chair and brandishing his glass, shouted,

"The King!"

Guests lurched to their feet. Smiling, urbane, affable, Kalakaua acknowledged the toast. When the applause abated he rose, bowing to left and right, courtly, poised. His eyes, one instant a living black, the next flooded with golden lights, fixed themselves on Patricia and Hawke.

"We also wish to propose a toast," he announced in resonant tones. "We drink to Patricia Trevellyan and Admiral Guy Hilary Hawke." He raised his glass. "May their lives be long and their children many."

Draining his wine he flung the goblet on the floor. There was a shout, then the room rang with the impact of a hundred glasses shattering. Trevellyan heaved his massive frame upward like a man bracing against music mounting toward a stupendous climax. His eyes leaped to Patricia's but the sound recalled to her the memory of her father hurling his top boots through the office window. Blood drained from her face.

Shouts, bellows, bursts of laughter shook the walls and outside, hulas, screams of delight from pursued women, yells of glee from men, or the angry cry of affronted girls mingled in a steadily rising pandemonium. Patricia's head reeled. In a wholesale way her senses were forsaking her. Her body, still weak, streamed and floated away from her, beaten by the concussions of sound about her. She fought to retain consciousness, then felt Hawke's hand laid over hers. The way it was done, as if they were friends of long standing, leagued together to withstand massed attack, left a sudden void in her.

"I beg you," he spoke in low, vibrant tones that commanded while they entreated, "to treat me with the consideration that is yours to give."

She appreciated that he dreaded lest her pallor meant revolt. His dignity drove home the fact that he was, by instinct and inheritance, a gentleman who shrank from

anything that smacked of a scene. All at once she wondered what he thought of herself, her father, Lani-o-
akua.

He rose and faced the table of reeling guests, fine, tall,
distinguished, giving away nothing of what he felt.
Then his commanding voice, which shot curt orders
from the bridge of a man o' war, rang out:

"Your Majesty," he bowed to Kalakaua, "I wish to
propose a toast in return. To my future wife, Patricia
Trevellyan."

With his right hand he raised his glass, with the left
he gathered Patricia's fingers protectingly into his. She
felt as if she, who all her life had been caught in the
flux of great tides, was swept unexpectedly into a sheltered harbor. A shout jarred the rafters. Then she heard
Hawke's flexible, controlled voice asking her to rise.

Her heart gave a queer, half-stifled beat. By turns this
man would be comrade, protector, lover, spirited antag-
onist, with a will higher than her own. She wondered
how he had the power to attract and repel her in so
many different ways. She was aware of the pulse in his
throat, above the confining collar of his uniform, of the
quickened beat of his heart beneath dark cloth and glittering decorations. The space between them throbbed,
dissolving her body and will, sending every atom of her
pouring toward him.

She rose, feeling as if she were being rushed toward a
tremendous climax. Her father's delighted eyes were
upon her, she read the thought in them, "She's run up
against someone she can't boss!" Blood burned her
cheeks, her eyes went up to Hawke's, and fell beneath
his glance. The physical knew its mate, clamored for it.

Inclining her head, she responded to the toast being shouted by her father's guests. Then she heard Hawke saying,

"Now I'll get you out of this."

They went out to the veranda. The night air was like a quick, cool kiss. Hawke steadied her.

"I'm tired," she said.

"Your father told me you'd been ill."

She laughed as Trevellyan might have at his solicitude for her—illness. Torches blazed, people passed like shadows on a screen. The only real thing was Hawke, dark and straight in his uniform. They went to the gate commanding a view of the dim slopes of the island, and leaned upon it. Hawke gazed at her.

"Surely you appreciate, Patricia, that I loved you from the instant I saw you."

"Yes, for I have been loved before."

"It would have been impossible had it not been so."

"I had hoped you wouldn't—love me."

"Unfortunately, I cannot oblige you in that, though I shall endeavor to do so in every other way. I have seen lovely women, Patricia, but you are incredible."

She swallowed. Hawke laid a hand upon her shoulder and the contact sent a shock through her. An instinctive, dominant hunger was tugging at her. She fought against it, trying to save herself from the plunge she craved with every atom of her being.

"Patricia."

"Yes."

"I cannot expect you to love me as I loved you. Instantly. But I want your word, aside from your father's giving of it, that you will marry me. I'll be in the Islands three weeks. At the end of them I hope you will come with me of your own volition. I shall do my uttermost to make you love me—Patricia."

The space about them vibrated with the low voicing of her name. Her eyes met his. There was a confused moment of joy and terror, then his arms had her. Patricia clung back, rapture shaking her. It seemed as though the same exultant blood bounded in their veins and the million cells in their throbbing bodies synchronized with the greater throb of Lani-o-akua. She let her head fall back into the crook of his arm. Hawke's lips met hers. The universe spun with her. She felt the satisfying firmness of his jaw, the sweep of his strong shoulders, the glow of his body through the heavy uniform. Electric pangs of pleasure stung her and she yielded to the satisfying tyranny of his arms.

After an instant, in order to get a longer perspective on the magic surging through her, she leaned back, clasping her hands behind Hawke's neck. Her laced fingers tensed, and Hamilton's ring bruised her flesh. Her skin burned for the traitorous instincts lodged in her, then, as if freeing herself from everything but the future, she tore off the ring and flung it into the darkness.

PART II

DAVID

CHAPTER VIII

DAVID BIRTHWOOD stood thoughtfully beside his bedroom window. The mill was to be closed for good. It was the main source of revenue, but Trevellyan had given the order.

Since Patricia's departure the old man had been restless and listless by turns. Feverish activity alternated with periods of inertia when he prowled about Lani-o-akua like a truculent ghost. His sagging, purplish jowls, visible through his wiry beard, his hot eyes, filled with the long thoughts of the old, his underlip thrust loosely instead of arrogantly forward, attested to the fact that his life was sliding toward its close.

Steps roused him. Trevellyan was coming along the walk like a ship plowing into head seas. Birthwood saw that he had been drinking. He looked this way and that, as if watching for hidden enemies, then halted to address a young Hawaiian hurrying toward the gate. He was adept when it came to wounding and humiliating the pride of natives and he bellowed at the man, demanding an explanation for his presence in the garden.

"You told me to get a bag of *opihis* for your supper," the man retorted.

"But I didn't order you to leave half of them for the Shark God, you yellow livered, superstitious fool!"

"I left them there because of you."

The man's attitude shocked David for it made clear that the Hawaiian no longer feared Trevellyan, for to his way of thinking, he was as good as dead.

"I hear the talk going around Lani-o-akua. You think the Shark God will destroy me. Get the hell out of here. I'll die when I please and it won't be for a long time." He directed a well aimed kick at the man's rear with a colossal top boot. The young fellow tripped and Trevellyan let out a delighted bellow, then wiping the bulging back of his neck with a silk handkerchief, shouted,

"David!"

"I'm here," Birthwood called indignantly.

"Don't come out, I'll join you."

Trevellyan labored up the steps, swung through the door, and dumped into the nearest chair. The room was filled with the rasping sound of his breathing. After an instant he looked around.

"I'm drunk, David, and I'm going to get drunker before the night's over. You've got to drink with me, damn you. Drinking's not much in your line, is it?" He laughed immoderately. "God, how I drank in the old whaling days. Drank to forget and drank to remember. I've seen life with its clothes off, David. It wasn't always pretty but it's been real. Call one of those confounded Chinks. Order whisky. You've got to drink with me—to Lani-o-akua!" He thumped his fist truculently on the arm of the chair.

Trevellyan's eyes fixed speculatively upon him, made

David apprehensive. He was plotting something. After a moment Trevellyan transferred his attention to the window. There was an almost indecent beauty to the sombre and violent sunset burning above the horizon, to the twilight stealthily fingering the garden. A last, slanting ray of light grasped the limbs of trees, dragging them earthwards. Suspense enveloped everything, making the dark slopes of the island lunge outrageously against the sullen afterglow.

Trevellyan slumped, a huge, untidy figure in the chair, his head supported on his fist. The gross, old man was a blot on the earth but for some reason profoundly moving. He appeared to be dispassionately considering his life, which had worked to a climax and stopped with a crash. And the silence had shattered him. Going to the door David shouted Trevellyan's order.

"Whisky and two glasses, Chong!"

Trevellyan favored Birthwood with an evil leer, then lurching to the window, stared at the gardens, silent and absorbed. It was obvious that the coarse, vulgar old man loved Lani-o-akua with all the vehemence of his soiled and splendid soul.

The distant mutter of an unusually heavy surf created the feeling that ominous hosts were marshalling against him. Trevellyan moved restively, hoisting his sagging figure higher. The cook appeared, set the bottle and glasses on the table, and waited, darting a look at Trevellyan as if he longed to make him suffer as he had made others suffer. Divining the secret hatred in his servant's heart, Trevellyan laughed.

"Big night, Chong. Bring dinner here!" He looked about David's room and his eyes seemed to strip the pictures off the wall and dash them on the floor.

"Mrs. Trevellyan?" David ventured, hot with resentment at the old man's headlong invasion of his privacy.

"Let her eat alone and weep," Trevellyan filled a tumbler with whisky and tossed half its contents down. "Some women get their fun out of crying. Gad, she's wept enough to float a squadron of men o' war. Poor bitch. I'm a nasty fellow to hitch up with, as you'll find out before I've done with you this evening. The ship's foundering. Look at my hands, David," he thrust them out, dry and blotched with purple. "They're a dead man's hands but they've got to steer the ship into another port before I sign off." He studied Birthwood. "Lani-o-akua's got to be put into safe keeping. My grand, beloved place, my kingdom in the wilderness. I love it, beyond everything I love it," he broke off, breathing heavily; then seeing the cook, wheeled, "Rattle your confounded stumps and bring dinner, Chong!"

The man leaped as if he had been electrified and Trevellyan reached for his glass.

"Blast you, David, don't stand there like a stick. Carouse with me! I've sung a song that people will remember after I'm dead. There's never been a dull note in it, it's been fine chords crashing grandly since the start. Sing it with me! Lani-o-akua, Heaven of the Gods, Lani-o-akua—"

Picking up the second glass he held it out. David took it.

"I tell ye, lad!" Trevellyan roared, "it's hell to get old and know that somewhere you took the wrong turn. There's a gate we all must go through if we're to be happy. Some think happiness is love, others power,

others fun, but real happiness has nothing to do with
health, wealth, or any physical thing. It has to do with
our souls."

David was confounded.

"The secret's here. The thing is to contact it. Con-
sciously or unconsciously we all want to do so. We can
all find the formula if we want to *enough*. But for one
reason or another we don't get round to it. Then in a
sort of frenzied apology to God, we rush out and build
something beautiful. As I built Lani-o-akua."

Birthwood looked at Trevellyan silently.

"That's how the great deeds of the earth get done.
They are apologies, David, bribes. Lani-o-akua is my
bribe to God to try and buy forgiveness for failing the
divine something He planted in all of us."

Picking up his glass Trevellyan drank from it.

"Lani-o-akua is my excuse for living, but God won't
take excuses. If I don't go through the gate before I die,
I'll have to keep on hunting for it afterwards." He glared
at the dark. "My time's getting short. I'll probably be
back here," indicating the gardens with his thumb he
chuckled, "wandering round trying to get to God. It's
useless running away from Him. You can't run far
enough. He waits, perhaps a million years, knowing
you've got to come at last. But at least if I haven't
touched that beauty, I've made it, David, so I'd be for-
given for trying to play hookey. Lani-o-akua's my ladder
to God."

David stirred, moved by the divine wisdom lodged in
so carnal a man.

"I've got one thing more to do, put the beauty I've
created into safe hands; first, because I love it, second,

because I may need it after I am dead." He leered at Birthwood, then drank from his glass. "Now, for your part in this. You'll probably fight it."

"What do you want me to do?" Birthwood asked.

"Down your drink before I tell you," Trevellyan advised boisterously, but he watched Birthwood as if he were not quite sure he could compel him to do what he wanted.

Birthwood's pulses hurried. The room seemed filled with unexpected possibilities for good and evil which must be watched.

"Have you any sort of affection for this place?" Trevellyan asked, brandishing a lordly arm at the dark.

Birthwood nodded.

"Why?"

"God knows I've had to watch things here that leave a sort of slime on your soul but—"

"But?" Trevellyan prodded him.

"There's magnetism in the very soil."

Trevellyan gave a ghastly grin.

"Well, lad, Patricia's gone. That was the finest piece of business I ever did. A real mating. I knew my gal. Hawke's the same mettle. Gad," he laughed reminiscently, "I nearly burst a blood vessel in the office that morning. But it all worked out fine." He studied the carpet, a deep purple suffusing his jowls, then the color subsided leaving his skin a dirty gray. Birthwood suspected he was thinking of Patricia's child. Reaching for his glass Trevellyan drained it. "Now to get down to business. I'm getting old and garrulous." He laughed without mirth and sat slouched in thought.

Birthwood waited.

"Lani-o-akua was mortgaged to the hilt for Patricia's dowery but with time and careful management it can be put back on a paying basis. Cane growing here is too expensive. Cattle will net the best results in the long run. You're the man for the job." Trevellyan heaved his body upward like a beast struggling to get out of a bog. "I've willed it to you—on one condition."

Birthwood was floored. Rising, he walked to the window. The garden was absorbed in itself. His eyes misted unaccountably. He had deliberately stood aloof from life, but felt clutched by a resistless current sweeping him toward the unknown.

"Patricia?" he said over his shoulder.

"Hawke is her world. She'll never come back. Said so to me and suggested that I deed Lani-o-akua to you. You've got to take it."

Birthwood stared at the throbbing night. It seemed impossible that he could be the destined owner of Lani-o-akua, which he had grown to love against his will. Elation wrestled with the realization of the responsibility that would be his in the years unrolling ahead. He fancied he could hear the clicking of eternity's machinery at work on all sides. Then he heard himself ask,

"And the condition?"

Trevellyan made no answer. The stillness of the room was broken by a reiterated sound, like pain made audible. Trevellyan was gasping like a man being smothered. Birthwood rushed to support him.

"Take your hands off me, blast you," Trevellyan muttered thickly. "Lani-o-akua is yours. My will's made out and witnessed. Take care of it, love it as I've loved it. If you don't, I'll hound you when I'm dead."

A premonition of the weighted future filled Birthwood.

"I won't take it," he said.

An extraordinary, detached grin distorted Trevellyan's features.

"You can't get out of it. You're part of the Plan."

"What plan?"

"God's, you fool."

"It should be Patricia's or her—child's."

"The little bastard's dead," Trevellyan shouted. "Ka-aina! Fetch Ka-aina. I've got to talk to him. God damn it, Ruth will be here tomorrow. You or Ka-aina have got to go to Makena and meet her."

"Ruth?"

"My poor bitch's child. I sent for her. Months ago. You have to marry her."

"I damn well won't. I'll have no part in your filthy made-marriages."

Trevellyan laughed in a suffocated way.

"You've got to. Everything's got to be hurried up. Things must be shipshape before I check out."

A glow like heated iron showed beneath Trevellyan's skin. His pores appeared to be tearing apart. David put out his hand and Trevellyan grasped it, his blood-shot eyes rolling upward. The thought came to Birthwood that flesh was wrestling with spirit and spirit with flesh. The spark of divine force in Trevellyan, directed into the wrong channels by the flesh, was re-asserting itself, taking possession of and mastering the body which had housed and betrayed it.

"David, David, don't fail me. You're of my blood

though not directly of my line," Trevellyan choked, got his head up, and stared dully about him. "You, Ka-aina, my girl Ruth have got to— Oh, Lani-o-akua . . . Lani-o-akua!" His voice broke.

Struggling to his feet he lurched toward the door and reaching it, braced against the jamb, signing at the dark as if he were frantically beckoning to the place he loved.

"Lani-o-akua," he muttered thickly, edging out of the door like a wounded animal dragging back to its lair, "Lani-o-akua, my ladder to God. . . ."

His head dropped on his chest, but he wrenched it up, his eyes tearing at the black curtain hiding the trees and contours he worshipped with his savage and suffering soul. His body stiffened, arched backwards. Birthwood sprang to support him, but Trevellyan crashed before he reached him.

"Mr. Trevellyan, you've drunk too much."

"Drunk too much, hell, I'm blowing up," the old man gasped.

Convulsions racked him. He lashed about the floor as if battling an invisible enemy that was trying to throttle him. Birthwood attempted to hoist him into a chair, but, again, he arched backwards, flinging out his arms as if beating off an opponent. Sweat drenched David and he shouted for Ka-aina.

Footsteps tore up the walk. Ka-aina rushed across the veranda and halted in the door. His horror-filled eyes swooped to Trevellyan, bellowing dully and thrashing about the floor. After an instant Ka-aina plunged his face between his hands and uttered a long, thin wail:

"*Auwe, auwe*, Mr. Hi-ball and the Shark God fight!"

Licking up the tears trickling down his cheeks, Ka-aina unfastened the door of Typhoon's loose-box. She was the fleetest of the thoroughbreds. He must get a doctor and the nearest one was in Wailuku, thirty miles away. It seemed impossible that Trevellyan could be dying, unbelievable that he could ever cease to be.

The mare was restive and apprehensive, snorting, sidestepping, hindering him with the girthing and bridling. He soothed her in a choked voice, led her out of the stable, and with a single movement had the saddle clamped between his legs and was racing down the avenue.

Dying! Hi-ball Trevellyan was dying! He struck the spurs into the mare's ribs and the dusty road echoed to the beat of her flying hoofs. Ka-aina, his face broken with horror and grief, stared ahead. Back in the place of gods Trevellyan lay paralyzed, only his eyes living. And tomorrow his second daughter was to arrive.

He jerked the mare down the rocky trail leading through the cacti. Against stars, burning with passionless serenity, was the long shape of the blowhole where Patricia and Walter Hamilton used to meet. And back in Kanaio the child, born of their love, slept on a *lauhala* mat, unconscious of events thundering on their way.

He snatched the mare back into her stride when she stumbled over a loose fragment of lava. Ahead, lights showed at the feet of the West Maui mountains, heaped with the silvery, white clouds of the Trade wind. Cacti moved rhythmically on either hand with the lift and forward surge of the mare's stride. A sense of uneasiness pursued Ka-aina as he rode. He looked up at the armies of stars swinging overhead and spurred the mare on. Fierce motion eased the horror riding at his heels, but the sound of his horse's hoofs violated the peace of the night.

What is ahead. . . . What is ahead. . . . What is ahead, they seemed to say, but there was no answer to their question. Turgid thoughts shaped slowly in his mind. Of his own volition he had promised the gods of Lani-o-akua to guard Patricia's child, and Trevellyan had commanded him to make away with it. Between the two, days and nights were purgatory. He had avoided Trevellyan as much as possible lest the old man ask him if the child had been destroyed, but Trevellyan had never referred to it, as though he had made up his mind that it did not exist. He was overwhelmed by the responsibility he had assumed. Who was he to appoint himself an instrument of destiny?

He steadied the mare down a level stretch of dusty path and eased her as they approached a turn that vanished behind massed cacti, swimming eerily in the starlight. Hoof beats doubled in his ears and he fought to maintain hold of himself. He must get a doctor . . . get a doctor. . . .

A dark figure on horseback swept around the bend. A cry sprang to his lips which was never uttered, for breast to breast, his horse and the other horse and rider crashed into the dust. The animals floundered and heaved to their feet. Ka-aina lay inert. A shadowy figure whose outlines grabbed at his heart was standing over him. Hamilton.

Involuntarily, his hand went to the pocket of his dungaree coat, a pocket which was never unbuttoned.

"Ka-aina!" Seizing him Hamilton jerked him to his

feet. "Patricia! Is all I've heard true? Speak and end this hell!"

"*Auwe*, here. She give letter for you," he fumbled at the fastening of the pocket.

Thrusting a finger under the flap, Hamilton ripped the pocket open and the note fluttered to the ground.

"Strike a match," Hamilton commanded hoarsely.

With shaking fingers Ka-aina extracted a package of fine sulphur matches from his breeches and detaching one struck it on his legging. The flame sputtered and winked out. Smothering an oath Hamilton snatched the package and striking one, ignited the lot, and dropped them. Swooping on the folded bit of paper, Hamilton knelt in the dust and read hurriedly.

The dark was stabbed by the labored breathing of the horses and by minute, tearing sounds of fresh matches catching fire. Hamilton's face was the color of ashes when he finished reading and he crushed the paper in his hand.

"Where is my child? At least I shall have that."

Getting to his feet he looked distractedly about him. Ka-aina saw he was overcome by something in the letter, and shivered involuntarily. Patricia had evidently been sufficiently honest to revolt this first lover, who had fancied madly that he could expect fidelity from her.

"Where is it, *makule?*" Hamilton asked, seizing Ka-aina's arm and shaking it.

"I don't know," Ka-aina answered, wondering why Patricia had thought it necessary to mention the child. His mind darted around looking for an exit. It would be simpler to give him the child but it belonged to the Shark God and Lani-o-akua.

"Don't lie, you must know," Hamilton said fiercely.

"I don't," Ka-aina insisted in Hawaiian.

"I'll see Trevellyan."

"No can," Ka-aina cried, bursting into Hawaiian. He fought to steady his voice, dashing tears angrily off his cheeks. A blank expression crept into Hamilton's face as he listened, as if Ka-aina's horror were communicating itself to him. "He cannot speak. I have to go to Wailuku for a doctor," he finished, thinking of the miles stretching between him and the winking lights which were his destination.

Hamilton stood sunk in thought.

"If Trevellyan can't talk, there's no object in my going to Lani-o-akua at present," Hamilton remarked, his eyes fastened on the southwestern slope of Haleakala, splendid in the starlight. He stood, a lonely, confounded figure passing fingers dully through his hair.

Ka-aina looked away. It was indecent for him, for anyone, to witness Hamilton suffering. He realized that Hamilton was dominated by Patricia, who had come into his life, seized it, made it briefly a thing of glory, then smashed it to pieces.

"My child," Hamilton began.

Ka-aina took a hurdle. "It came too soon. It is dead."

Rousing himself from his despair, Hamilton started for his horse. Gathering up the reins he turned the stirrup for his foot. The night seemed to wait for his voice, crying out in rebellion for the impossible end of the physical love which had tricked and betrayed him. But he did not speak. His horse tossed its head and he checked it harshly. Ka-aina waited, fearful that Hamilton might change his mind about going to Lani-o-akua.

"There is no object in your riding to Wailuku for a doctor," Hamilton announced, in a dazed voice. "I'm going back. I'll send a boy for one. You're needed at Lani-o-akua."

Snatching up Hamilton's hand, Ka-aina kissed it as he would have kissed a chief's.

"You're a good man," he cried.

Hamilton's laugh, harsh and bitter, sounded doubly terrible in the night.

CHAPTER IX

DAVID walked to the door. Silence that sent the hair crawling on his scalp brooded over Lani-o-akua. He glanced at the clock ticking on the dresser. A little after two. Ka-aina could not possibly get back with the doctor before daylight, and the boat bringing Ruth would anchor about four.

For the time being he was chained to Lani-o-akua. It would be caddish to desert Trevellyan in his present condition. Had not Trevellyan sent for him, he would have probably spent his entire life on his mother's farm on the outskirts of an obscure English village. Smothered excitement pierced him realizing that Lani-o-akua was his if . . .

Feeling a summons from the bed, he turned. Trevellyan lay breathing noisily, his face flushed a dull red. The expression in his eyes sent a chill through David. They said he was done for, but not done with life. There were details that must be finished.

Reluctantly David went over. The bloodshot, burning eyes, glaring from the ghastly, wooden face, moved significantly toward the clock. Ruth must be met, his look said. For instance, slyly the eyes said it, someone must break the news of her father's condition to her.

David's heart pounded. It was grisly, this prisoning of the spirit in paralyzed flesh. Trevellyan's eyes, fierce and entreating, held his. It was unthinkable that this man, even when robbed of speech and movement, imposed his will on everyone around him, suggesting that beyond being himself, he was an instrument of some immense scheme. An amused, evil leer lighted the depths of Trevellyan's eyes, subtly reminding David of what was expected of him.

He must fetch someone and go to Makena. He started for the door feeling Trevellyan's gaze following him and prodding him. A star shone through a tree, but it was not a friendly star. It made him feel as if he were trying to evade some responsibility. The dark was filled with the ghostly sounds of sleeping vegetation, like passing feet tiptoeing into silence. He stamped angrily into the living room.

"Mrs. Trevellyan?"

An untidy heap of clothes huddled in a chair was injected with sudden life.

"I won't go to him. He looks as if he'd like to tear everything and everyone to pieces," the woman cried.

"But someone responsible must be near," David exclaimed, exasperation tearing him. "Ka-aina's away and all the servants have vanished. I've got to go to Makena to meet your daughter." He wondered if Trevellyan had acquainted his wife with his plans.

Mrs. Trevellyan's pale eyes stared down her nose.

"As Ruth's arriving, I don't have to stay," she announced. "Saddle a horse for me."

"I don't understand. You want to ride down with me

and meet your daughter?"

"No!" the woman cried. "I'm going. Don't you understand? I'm going away from Lani-o-akua. I won't wait
for Hi-ball to die. I'm scared of him alive, but I'd be
more scared of him dead," she shuddered and glanced
around uneasily.

"But your daughter cannot stay here alone," he protested.

"She'll have to. Hi-ball took her from me when she
was a baby. She's just a name to me. She'll be enough
like her father not to care for me. I won't stay here.
You can't make me. If I did, I'd go crazy."

Scrambling to her feet she looked about, her neck
jerking.

"I'd be terrified to be here after Hi-ball dies." Her
meager form shook. "His spirit can never rest. It'll
wander around Lani-o-akua. You stay. Ruth stay. Everyone can stay, but I won't. I tell you, I won't. I'm going
now—tonight—while he's helpless to prevent me." She
started for the door.

"Wait, at least, until the next boat," David begged.
"It isn't right for your daughter to be here alone. After
all—"

"She's the child of my body, but everything here is
Hi-ball's. Despite the fact that I bore her, Ruth no more
belongs to me than the trees, mill, or gardens. Everything here is Hi-ball's. You, me—but he can't move or
speak so I'm going away." She laughed as though unbalanced. "If you're wise you'll clear out, too. While
you can. He may get better, then he'll stop you."

A cold hand seemed to fall on David's shoulder, as he
realized that by staying, he pledged himself to an act,

big with incalculable consequences.

"Give me some money. I won't need much. Just sufficient to get away from Lani-o-akua. Hi-ball doesn't need me, he never needed me, he just used me. He was always kind in his own way, but I've always been afraid of him. I was afraid of Patricia, even when she was a baby. I'll be afraid of Ruth. I don't belong with people like the Trevellyans. They're too strong for me. I come of common stock and can't stand up against these dreadful aristocrats!"

Compassion swept David. As if guessing it, Mrs. Trevellyan sidled up and clutched his arm with her skinny fingers. He looked down, and she started crying weakly.

"Help me to get away while I can," she implored.

"Very well. I'll give you sufficient funds to get you to England. When you're settled, write and I'll mail you a check every month. I'm sure Mr. Trevellyan would wish it."

The woman bundled off. David called out and a scared-looking Chinaman appeared.

"I've got to go to the office. Stay with Mr. Hi-ball until I come back."

The expression in the man's eyes made it clear that he intended to slide into the dark.

"You needn't go into his room. Sit outside the door," David ordered shortly.

The man looked relieved and went down the veranda. David started for the office. He was in it to the neck! Why did people feel called upon to do things they detested? Decency and honor compelled him to stay, intelligence urged him to leave.

Galloping hoofs roused him. Ka-aina could not possibly get back before daylight. He hurried down the walk. A lathered horse slid to its haunches and a figure propelled itself out of the saddle.

"Ka-aina!"

When the man told him of meeting Hamilton, David muttered, "God!"

Ka-aina watched the mare easing herself from leg to leg. When she started for the watering-trough, he leaped to stop her. David looked at the towering trees. Gray loneliness and fear of the future was on him.

"One of us has to go to Makena," he announced.

"More better you. I stop with Mr. Hi-ball."

"Saddle a horse for me and one for Mrs. Trevellyan. She's leaving for England." He waited to see how Ka-aina would take the news.

"More better go," he grunted.

David returned to his room. Hi-ball's eyes were fixed impatiently on the door. Carefully framing each word with his lips David told Trevellyan of the arrangements he had made. The old man's eyes glinted with ribald amusement, mocking the serious young man. David straightened up, his face burning.

Ka-aina appeared, and after one shocked look at Trevellyan's face, dead as all deadness, sat down in a chair, deliberately sinking himself into one of the trances common to Polynesians, as if detaching himself from his immediate surroundings, and submerging himself into the universe.

"I'm going," David announced, glancing at the clock. Ka-aina nodded.

At the corrals he saw Mrs. Trevellyan waiting with

two of the servants, loaded with bags and bundles. From
her manner it was evident that she was mad to get away.
She indicated her belongings and David stamped into
the stable annoyed at the thought of having to saddle a
packhorse. Of course she needed clothes, and Ruth
would have things to bring up. When a horse was ready,
he led it out and assisted the men to pack it.

A cold, lonely breeze came down from Haleakala.
Stars blazed above bending tree-tops. He assisted Mrs.
Trevellyan to her horse. She was in a frozen panic to be
gone, which communicated itself to her horse. Ordering
one of the Chinamen to hold it, he mounted and taking
the lead rope of the pack horse went through the gate.
Mrs. Trevellyan averted her head as they passed the
long, dim shape of the house. In one wing two lighted
windows glowed like red eyes.

They rode in silence, the horses picking their way
carefully down the rocky trail. The hour was pregnant
with the future. The dark fall of the island to the sea
weighted David. On the gray expanse of the channel,
the light of the steamer showed like a dim ruby creeping
steadily toward the curve of Makena. When it anchored,
David thought grimly, he would be saddled with another
Trevellyan.

Light began to increase in the east. The outlines of
the island assumed solidity. Stars changed from gold to
silver. Edges of clouds grew pink. David studied the
land about him, solemn in the growing light. Contours
swung with a rhythm in which the beautiful and unbeautiful merged. Long slopes seemed to have a candid
glory in themselves, flaunting *kukui* groves, cane fields,
pastures, uncaring that they were marred by lava wastes.

Roadsides melting past had a definite significance, cacti huddled on hill tops appeared to be consulting together. Chaotic half-thoughts crowded his mind. By nature he was reserved, remote, and unapproachable, and it dismayed him to find himself embroiled in the frank savagery of events which had poured over Lani-o-akua, dragging him in their wake. He looked back to assure himself that Mrs. Trevellyan was all right. She sat in her saddle, crying silently, suggesting a helpless creature in a snare. He too, would be trapped unless he was on his guard every minute, he thought hotly.

Turning off the cattle trail he headed along a casual road following the careless curve of the shore. Monkeypod trees, like vast umbrellas, leaned over the polished water. Coconut groves crowded down black beaches of volcanic sand. Here and there native houses showed behind sturdy stone walls. He heard the distant splash of the anchor going down, and saw the ship's lights reflected in the water.

Turning into a corral, used for shipping cattle, David dismounted and assisted Mrs. Trevellyan to the ground. Her bad teeth, her thin hair, her nose pink from weeping vexed him. In all probability, he thought thankfully, her daughter would be a poor thing. Perhaps, like her mother, she would be overwhelmed by Lani-o-akua. He recalled his own awe when he first saw the island from the ship. Excitement ran through his mind. If Ruth left, Trevellyan would probably will the place to him anyway.

He busied himself unloading the packhorse and carried the bundles across the hard-packed, fragrant beach. Waves uncurled in lead and silver. A solitary whaleboat was sliding away from the dark flank of the ship. Walking to her possessions Mrs. Trevellyan seated herself upon them. An air of quiet triumph enveloped her, as if she had slyly succeeded in some secret venture. She pleated the folds of her skirt while she watched the boat approaching. Her hair was dragged unbecomingly from her face, but her eyes, reddened from weeping, looked ahead, a feverish glitter in their depths. She was freed of Lani-o-akua forever, they said.

Fishing in his pocket David brought out a roll of bills and gave it to her.

"I'll write as soon as I'm located," she whispered, as if fearing that she might be overheard. "I won't need much, David, I'll get a quiet, little place and—live!"

Faint color showed in her dry cheeks.

"You know, I feel almost gay," she confessed. "I've never drawn a free breath since I landed here." She looked at the island and the trees massing Lani-o-akua.

The animosity in her face astonished David. A hail coming across the water roused him. Mrs. Trevellyan got jauntily to her feet. David was routed. Here she was, approaching fifty, gaunt, dry, ineffectual and yet, just by escaping from Lani-o-akua, she had the air of a girl stepping into life. A chill stole about his heart.

"Take my advice and clear out, David," Mrs. Trevellyan advised, as the boat beached with a hiss upon the sand. Hawaiian sailors leaped into the foam and thrust it high and dry. Lifted oars flashed like tall, wet wings.

The portly purser seized a slight girl and running beyond the breaking water set her on the land. Her small feet landed lightly on the beach. She looked dazed by her outlandish manner of arrival, and hesitated, a slight, incongruously elegant figure in a dress of dull red cashmere, tightly basqued above, bustled, and flounced below.

David glanced at Mrs. Trevellyan, but her manner announced that she intended to have nothing whatever to do with her daughter. Signing to one of the boatmen, she indicated her luggage and hurried across the moist sand. A sailor swung her into the boat. She arranged herself and stared back, a lean, triumphant figure defying Lani-o-akua.

David strode resentfully forward and the girl turned. Her glossy, brown hair framed her face like two neatly folded wings. An absurd and delightful little hat perched on her head. Then she laughed, a clear peal of youthful merriment that flew into the pure morning air like the whirr of a bird's wings. The sound affected David oddly. How long would she laugh like that after being at Lani-o-akua? He approached with outstretched hand.

"I'm David Birthwood," he announced stiffly.

The girl looked at him expectantly, then smiled, and took his hand.

"My father?"

David told her. She looked grave and considered her surroundings. A man carried her bags up the beach and David directed him to take them to the corrals.

"Who is that woman leaving here?" the girl asked.

"Your mother," David replied, his face scarlet.

The girl looked amazed, started to speak, then closed her lips.

"We have a long way to go. Shall we start?" David asked.

The girl nodded, and they walked off side by side.

Sand seeped into her slippers, buttoned crosswise on slim, arched insteps. Bending down she tried to scoop it out with her finger. David hesitated, flushed, and picking her up carried her to the corral. Setting her carefully on the stone wall, he busied himself girthing up the horses. A hail from the beach roused him. A sailor was gesturing, indicating a black leather trunk he had set above high water mark. David shouted back in Hawaiian.

"How does my trunk get up?" the girl asked.

"A bullock wagon will be sent down."

"I can't ride," the girl laughed. "I'll have to wait for it, too."

"Won't you try?" David asked, a line between his brows. "It'll be long past noon before a wagon can get here."

She nodded and he lifted her onto her horse. Sensing an inexperienced rider, the animal moved restlessly and Ruth clutched David about the neck.

"Take me down," she said breathlessly.

He obeyed and looked helplessly about him. The girl laughed, her eyes resting expectantly upon him.

"Could you take me in front of you?"

He debated, then rolling his coat into a pad, tied it in front of his saddle. It was impossible to leave her waiting in the corrals, or to take her to a native house. He divined in her a sudden sinking. She looked afraid of the strange, fierce island. Absurdly defenceless. There was a quality in her like a swift, clear rivulet. Mounting, he reached down and swung her up before him. She slipped her arm under his, and leaned confidently against him. Herding the spare horses out of the gate, he headed them home.

When they emerged from the monkey-pods and coconut groves, Ruth sat up and looked thoughtfully at the
great dome of Haleakala.

"It's beautiful, isn't it?" she announced, her eyes seeking his.

An electric current ran through the day, making it
boundless. David was aware of an intense pride in the
island. An illusion of splendor filled him. He looked at
volcanic rocks, heaped in wild disorder, at tilted hills
like blunt teeth fastened in the sky, at the arrogant blue
of the ocean. His nostrils quivered to the elusive fragrance of *lantana* and *ilima* mingling with the stimulating
reek of his sweating horse.

"Yes, it's beautiful," he agreed.

The horses plodded up the steep trail. The sun grew
hot. Perspiration dampened the girl's face, close to his
own. Once she dozed and her head fell into the hollow
of his neck, and he stiffened as if Trevellyan's eyes were
on him. Subconsciously aware of the rigidity of his body,
Ruth woke. David's intuition warned him that she was on
the verge of tears. In her eyes was longing for familiar
surroundings, and he spoke hurriedly to distract her mind.

"Have you ever seen your father to remember?" he
asked.

"Yes," she said, smiling brightly, "he came to see me
when he was in England last year, and told me he'd send
for me after Patricia was married, as he had plans for me."

David's face grew aloof.

"This island's like nothing else in the world," Ruth
remarked. "After England, it's like being transported to
Mars."

David nodded. The voices of the earth, the sound of

horses' hoofs on broken lava, the mysterious whispers of the Pacific, the sigh of wind passing over Haleakala wove an irresistible spell. He could not go, he thought, no matter what happened, he could not go. He could not tear himself from this land of flame and color. Lani-o-akua had seduced him!

His young face grew bleak. Life in a village had smothered him. If he rejected Trevellyan's offer, he would have to return to England, or wander around the world, but he knew that nothing could ever wipe out the memory of Lani-o-akua. No other place could ever satisfy the hunger which would persist in his soul.

He straightened in the saddle, and Ruth glanced at him questioningly, but he did not notice it. His eyes rested thoughtfully on the island. The shadows lying on Haleakala whispered to the clouds gathering over it, trees murmured to the violent soil out of which they grew, sunlight penetrated the depths of the sea, charging it with warmth and life. He felt unified with the spaces about him. They could be his, were his, if—

"Is this Lani-o-akua?" Ruth asked, her lips shaping shyly about the syllables.

They were approaching the mill, still rumbling monotonously. He had forgotten to give the order which would silence it forever.

"Yes," David said.

Ruth was limp, hot, and tired, but smiled valiantly when they dismounted. For a moment she seemed daunted by the tall, strange trees about them. Her fingers clutched David's hastily, and the pupils of her eyes dilated.

"This place is like its name—completely unreal," she

whispered.

"It was to me—when I arrived," he agreed, a trifle curtly.

The girl glanced at him, but said nothing. They walked through the garden and she studied the length of the house, still keeping hold of his hand. When they went up the steps, she halted.

"Is Father very—" she could not go on.

"He can't speak or move, but there's nothing that will shock you."

She glanced at him with quick gratitude. Cadences in his voice wrapped her with protection. She looked slightly apprehensive, but smiled. There was something about her that was brave and sound. Lani-o-akua was no place for a girl of this calibre, David thought indignantly, and his fingers tightened about hers.

"I like it. It sort of scares me, but I like it," she said, breathlessly.

At the door of Trevellyan's room, David took hold of her arm.

"What is it?" she asked, quickly.

"Would you prefer to go in alone?"

"No, please come with me."

Her spirit went to his with a quick little rush. He was bewildered by a sense of responsibility toward this fresh, young creature and bent over her with a protective air. They crossed the threshold together. Ruth's hands flew to David's arm, and clutched it. Trevellyan's eyes were fixed upon the door. Releasing David, Ruth walked to the bed and pressed dutiful lips to Trevellyan's cheek. He smiled faintly with his eyes. She waited at the bedside, her dark head held high, then looked at

David, silently asking his advice as to what should be her next move. Conscious of Trevellyan's eyes upon him, David could not speak or move.

Ruth waited, then settling her shoulders, dusted a burnt match off the table, and straightened the bedding. Ka-aina beamed at her from the corner where he sat, and she nodded shyly. There was a warm, homelike quality to her which made the room brighter because she was there.

After a silence she smiled brightly at David, and drawing a chair up to the bed, sat down and took hold of her father's hand. Laughingly, she told him of how she had had to ride up from Makena. She sparkled and glowed, her brown eyes danced and a flush deepened the color in her cheeks. She gazed at David, confident and friendly. David burned, feeling Trevellyan's eyes, filled with satanic glee, fastened upon him.

CHAPTER X

KA-AINA sat on a rock in the corral listening to castor
oil seeds popping in the sun. There was a glorious
langour in the air, as if the sun were overcome by its
own power. Multitudes of bees, working ceaselessly in
the warm shade of shrouded gardens, flies buzzing under
the ragged, sticky leaves of an old fig seemed the full
voice of life, discussing the future. The atmosphere of
the day was hostile to thought, but his forehead was fur-
rowed and his face solemn. No child, and Ruth and
David had been married four years.

He glanced at the sun. It was past one, Ruth would
be coming for her ride shortly. Going into the stable
he saddled a horse and led it into the corral.

He had taught Ruth to ride. The first year after she
arrived David had been too busy with the re-organization
of Lani-o-akua to spare time, except on Sundays, to go
out with her. She was not a born horsewoman, but had
learned to mount without jabbing an animal in the ribs
with her foot, to take up the reins before leaving the
ground, and to come down lightly in the saddle. At first
she had been timid, but hid it by laughing and sparkling
at mistakes.

She had a misleadingly delicate frame, inherited from her meager mother, but translated into terms of beauty. Her cheek bones appeared high because her eyes were set in deep sockets. Her face, instead of rounding into a soft curve at the chin, developed unexpected strength. That line, steel-fine and clear, was of the stuff of which Trevellyan had been made.

She had never evinced any horror for her father's condition, had assumed the brunt of the nursing as a matter of course, setting out to adjust herself to Lani-o-akua. Her presence brought warmth and comfort to the house, but Ka-aina suspected that David had gone through some difficult, if not terrible hours before youth, propinquity, and Lani-o-akua vanquished him. From the start it had been clear that Ruth loved him, and the shadow of his silence showed in her eyes, but an imperceptible tightening at the corners of her mouth proved she was pitting her will against his. In some deep way father and daughter were leagued together to bring about David's surrender, despite the fact that Trevellyan never recovered his speech.

David spoke finally. When Ruth went with him to tell Trevellyan, his eyes, which had been filled with impatience, relaxed and the old mocking light welled into them. Despite the ghastly punishment that was his, he had triumphed.

Ka-aina contemplated his hands, veined, dry as paper. He had passed the crest of the hill and was following the path that sagged to the finish, but he could not see the end. Even Trevellyan's victory was not really won. After Ruth and David, who would inherit Lani-o-akua? Who would quiver to the scent of gardens in the rain,

or listen to the measured thunder of the sea? David and
Ruth both loved the place but created the feeling that
they were alien stewards watching over it. For whom?

A delicate breeze travelled by, stirring the weeds
growing around the corral. Voices of hidden things
were about him. The future knew and was trying to
tell him. He was on the edge of knowledge, but unable
to hear.

He guessed Ruth felt the lack of a child. Children
completed things. It was preposterous that Trevellyan
had no son to inherit the acres he loved. If Patricia
had been a boy, she would not have gone, leaving Lani-
o-akua desolate. Perhaps, a thoughtful expression filled
Ka-aina's eyes, the gods had intentionally withheld offspring from Ruth and David. He straightened up, secret
resolution growing in his face.

Approaching footsteps roused him. Ruth was crossing
the road. She moved lightly, but there was a hint of a
mince in the exact way she placed her feet, toes pointing slightly outward, which brought a faint, reminiscent
smile to Ka-aina's lips. During the four years she had
been at Lani-o-akua, the transition from girlhood to
womanhood had been completed without her being
aware of it. In her, father and mother mingled incongruously. At times she was vivid and resolute, but as
often inadequate and negative. Some quality in her remained definitely English, a reserve, a remoteness.
Chinese answered in lowered voices when she gave
orders, Hawaiians never forgot to remove their hats in
her presence.

She entered the corral, holding up her skirts carefully.
Ka-aina helped her into the saddle, and she breathed in

the warm air, sensuously, as though there was a flaw in the armor of her mother through which Trevellyan peeped. Watching her, Ka-aina wondered if David was not conscious, at times, of a lack in her, difficult to define. In spite of her flashes of high spirits, the note she struck in life was mild, sweet, and insistent like the reiterated pressing of a chord to the point of monotony. He wondered, without curiosity, if in embraces she ever forgot herself wholly or if, as a wife, she only dutifully and faintly echoed the warmth of her husband.

And yet, oddly enough, the last volcanic activity of the island fascinated her. The first time he had taken her riding among the lava flows she had asked avidly about them, as if the sight of unleashed nature released a suppressed violence in her, inherited from Trevellyan, over which her mother had superimposed herself. And when she was expert enough to ride alone, she invariably wandered among the sombre flows, or basked on the little beaches between them.

"Which side you ride today?" Ka-aina asked, as was his custom.

"Oh, the same way," she laughed, waving toward the steep cone, showing a purple mound on the coast. Ka-aina nodded and watched her start down the rocky trail past the long-silent mill.

When she was out of sight, he went to the garden and halted in the secluded *kukui* grove where the double-faced god kept watch over past and future. Removing his hat he waited before it, a growing suffocation constricting his lungs. Something prodded him, something enormous. Eyes and figure grew tense. Taking the wreath from the crown of his hat, he placed it at the foot of the idol. A breeze ran over the tree-tops, sending shadows wavering across the stone, which seemed to nod slightly. Tip-toeing away, Ka-aina mounted his horse and rode toward Kanaio, his body radiating resolution.

Ruth rode slowly, contemplating the landscape with wide, eager eyes. From the first, she had accepted everything, enjoyed everything about this strange new life with a naïveté which had been largely responsible for attracting David to her. She had listened, entranced, to the jargon, compounded of words filched from a dozen languages, in which he had taught her to issue orders. She discovered that in Hawaii, commands were made into requests, implying that those who served, granted favors to the served. It gave piquancy to life, contrasted with the servility she had been accustomed to receive from English servants, making her feel that at any moment solemn Orientals might be transformed into jewel-encrusted potentates, or Hawaiians, in faded dungarees, into warriors crowned with towering red-feather helmets, carrying polished wooden spears twelve feet in length.

Her childhood and girlhood, spent in a high, narrow house with a prim, bony sister of Trevellyan's, was left behind like a discarded cloak. Like most girls, leading uneventful lives, she dreamed of a home, husband, and children, but she had never expected to play the rôle of a landed lady in an exotic island estate. It tickled her fancy, and she wrote voluminous accounts of her daily doings to girls she had known in Highfield, girls with whom she had never been particularly intimate, but who afforded the necessary outlet for youthful enthusiasms.

She depicted her wedding, held beside the bedside of her speechless father, in detail, making herself appear the heroine of a novel; spent six pages of fine, close writing describing her dress and lingerie, bought with money David had given her, and another two in an account of the mammoth four-poster, gift from King Kalakaua to her father, in which she and David slept.

She had never been beset by the hordes of doubts and fears attendant upon becoming a bride and matron, such as the girls of her time felt requisite to proper womanhood. A strong leaning toward adventure, an eager curiosity about the unknown, bequeathed by her father, made her accept love and marriage, as she accepted the strange island foods served to her daily. She had crawled into the royal bed in a high-necked, long-sleeved nightgown on the night of her wedding and awakened unruffled in mind the next morning. It was all part of the adventure in which she had been launched by Trevellyan when he wrote his sister to send her to Hawaii, an adventure in which she was heartily in accord.

Until Trevellyan came to see her, she had had no intimation that her life would be different from those of the girls she knew, but after he left, a vague hope that the future might have more to offer than marriage to a village curate, began to possess her. When she met David, his clean good looks, his youth, his uprightness attracted her. Lani-o-akua did the rest.

She enjoyed her rôle of a wife; ordered her household admirably; glowed to the vision of herself in ruffled dimities, gathering armfuls of flowers; waited, freshly dressed at the gate when David rode home in the evening; sewed daintily under a becoming rose-shaded lamp after dinner. When an occasional guest stopped in, she entertained prettily and if she inwardly wished that more people came to see them, she never voiced it.

In her mind she fixed upon a many windowed room, adjoining theirs, as the nursery, mentally re-papering it in blue. The fact that it remained empty became an affront as months and then years went by. She was of her time, and liked to imagine herself and David bending over a cot in which a small replica of them both, slept rosily. Of course it was to be a boy, who would inherit the acres her husband managed so ably which afforded a glamorous setting for herself.

She had hinted, more than once, shyly and prettily, that she should get to know the wives of some of the plantation and ranch managers, in order to better acquaint herself with the mysteries of wifehood and motherhood, and divined in David a puzzling reluctance or resistance. When she accused him of it, he had been taken aback because he had not been as successful as he imagined in concealing his feelings. "There are things connected with this place I'd rather you didn't know, unbeautiful things which shouldn't touch anyone like you," he had said stiffly. Vanity flattered, she had pressed him no further. That there was mystery attached to the royal rogue who had been her father, added glamour.

Guiding her horse along the faint trail leading over the lava, she headed for a beach of white sand where she always rested before starting the long climb back to Lani-o-akua. The solitude of the crude spaces about her enhanced the fragility of her womanhood. A bit of a girl living on sweeping acres, was the way she liked to think about herself. She was too engrossed with her own life to be aware of the past throbbing about her. She had known, dimly, of her father's passion for Lani-o-akua, despite the fact that he had been unable to voice it. It had showed in his eyes, forever straining toward the open windows and in his choice of his resting place. She had liked nursing him because of the worshipping expression her activities aroused in David's and Ka-aina's eyes.

With the sentimentality of the day she wanted a son, largely because it would have completed her rôle of a dutiful daughter. On sunny afternoons she could have taken the child to the mausoleum, and watched it playing innocently in the shadow of its grandfather's tomb.

Being alone so much had developed in her the gift of watching herself as she would have an actor on a stage. She was one and all the heroines then in vogue, and extracted a double enjoyment from life by living it and observing it at the same time. She dressed with meticulous care, when she went out to pick flowers, in muslins that emphasized her slightness. She relished every lift of her arm swooping over gaudy beds of flowers. Its slenderness enthralled her, and when she pictured it weighted with a child, her face wore a charming and foolish expression as though she contemplated things too rare for common eyes to see.

She spurred her horse, and it hopped off the flow on to the beach. Dismounting, she tied it to a *kiawe* and stretched on the warm sand. Through lashes, lowered to exclude the dazzle of the restless Pacific, she gazed at waves with crests of emerald and amber, crisping toward the shore. Laying her cheek on her arm she smiled, pleased with the mental picture of herself on the beach. How much more complete it would have been if the golden-headed heir of Lani-o-akua had been cuddled beside her!

Sighing, she closed her eyes and dozed off. How long she had been sleeping she did not know, but suddenly she was fully awake. She sat up, wondering what had roused her. She was accustomed to the wild life of the island, pigs rooting in *kiawe* groves, goats nipping at the scant herbage growing along the edges of lava flows, sleek steers lumbering down to drink at brackish pools among the rocks. The beach was empty, then she heard low smothered sobbing that sent wild rushes of goose-flesh over her.

Running toward the spot from which the sound came, she climbed the flow and started across it, her eyes sweeping its broken surface. A child was sitting in the trail some distance away. She called out, and it looked up, then broke into redoubled wails. She hurried toward it and it attempted to run from her, howling dismally. She was disconcerted, but overtook it, and saw it was a boy of four or five. Despite his deeply tanned skin she knew it was white. Gathering him against her she kissed him. After some sobbing and choking the child stared at her, a line between his brows. The small face, for all that it was blotched a dreadful red from crying, was beautiful.

"You darling!" Ruth murmured, her heart beating queerly.

The slopes surrounding them appeared devoid of human life. She looked at the ranges in the west and at the tawny blue dome of Haleakala. It was unthinkable that a child of this age could have wandered such a distance. The nearest white habitation was fully thirty miles away. Could it have been purposefully abandoned? Animation swept her, visioning herself riding in to Lani-o-akua with a child in front of her. Here was drama if you chose!

"You angel, did you drop from Heaven in answer to my prayer?" she cried, convinced in the stress of the moment that she had fallen asleep praying for a child.

The boy gazed at her blankly, sucking in his lower lip and catching his breath with a sob. He looked bewildered and affronted. She spoke again, and he frowned as if he could not understand, then murmured in Hawaiian. She addressed him in the few, faulty words at her command, and he regarded her with grave, puzzled eyes.

When she reached Lani-o-akua she was hot, tired, and a trifle irritated. The child wriggled and slipped about like an eel, and his legs wobbled on each side of the horse's shoulders as if they had no bones to stiffen them. The cool avenue revived her and she brightened. As though the stage had been set for her arrival, David was unsaddling in the corral. He glanced up, and his face grew blank. Ruth thrilled at his expression and crooned, "Take him, David, my arm's breaking," as though she were in the habit of riding daily with a son.

David looked what he was, a man dumfounded. Before Ruth concluded her story, the child who had cried afresh at sight of another strange face, slept heavily in his arms. They took him to the house. David studied his features, streaked with dust and tears, then shouted at a coolie who was raking up the lawn, to send Ka-aina to the office the instant he came in.

"But how can Ka-aina know more about him than we do?" Ruth asked.

David opened his lips, recollected, and retorted curtly, "Because he knows the trails," then went a deep red at the inanity of his remark.

Ruth glanced at him puzzled but revelled in the sensation of being the central figure in this drama. Bending over the child, fast asleep on a couch, she touched him gently.

"I wonder who the little mite is, he's handsome, isn't he?"

David nodded, debated, then told her briefly and more bluntly than he intended, whose child he suspected it was and the circumstances of its birth. Ruth's cheeks got pink, but not with embarrassment. Compared to her half-sister's, her life was colorless. Inarticulate jealousy of Patricia, who had drunk recklessly of life, making herself more glamorous by doing so, filled her. Gradually it was replaced by the knowledge that her life would be even more dramatic were she to be the rescuer of her sister's child, brutally abandoned and banished from his rightful heritage in the hour of his birth.

"David," she exclaimed, clasping her hands, "it must be Patricia's son." He muttered something about not knowing whether the child had been a girl or a boy, but Ruth, carried away, did not listen. "It's clear to me now," she announced, "why an heir has been withheld from us. The Lord has appointed us His instruments to right the wrong done this unfortunate child."

"Bosh!" David said, then got scarlet. "I beg your pardon, Ruth. You cannot possibly understand, without having lived through the impossible happenings of those days, why this upsets me so."

Unbearably pressed, he etched, briefly and brutally, fragmentary pictures of Lani-o-akua's past, but despite himself some of the magic of Trevellyan's time crept into his plain words. Ruth's face assumed the shocked expression demanded by convention, but she was determined to keep the child.

Heavens, she argued with herself, a woman—a true woman, she corrected her thought—would even oppose her husband in a matter of this sort, if it was necessary. She had found the boy, without food and water, miles from anywhere. He would have perished had it not been for her. It was like a story, better than any story, for was not hers the leading rôle? Atoms of Trevellyan, in the cells of her body, quickened. She felt singled out, a person of consequence, a force to be reckoned with. Making sure that David was watching, she seated herself on the couch.

"Of course, dear, I appreciate why you hesitate to be responsible for this boy, not knowing who his father was. Still, with the right influences—" breaking off modestly, she gazed at her husband, then touched the child's forehead.

David looked stubborn. Sinking disappointment filled Ruth. He was barely aware of her, his mind was focussed on the past in which she had had no share. Then, slowly, triumph permeated her. Wasn't one always reading about a woman's influence, her white hands shaping lives, directing destiny? What if for a quarter of a century Lani-o-akua had been an ample-bosomed wanton, clad in scarlet satin and diamonds? She would pit her might against the past which had ignored her, she would dominate and shape the future. Lani-o-akua would have to take account of her as it had taken account of the rest of the Trevellyans.

"Of course, I'll be largely guided by you in this matter, David, but there are times when a woman's intuition is preferable to a man's judgement. I wish to be present when you interview Ka-aina. After all, if it hadn't been for my finding him, this poor child would have perished in those lava wastes."

David snorted.

"I'll bet anything, knowing you invariably ride in the vicinity of Puu-olai, Ka-aina shadowed you and left the child nearby for you to find." He looked at the boy, sleeping with the clumsy, yet graceful abandon of very young things. "I wish he were older and not so infernally afraid of white people. When I woke him, a while back, and tried to make him talk, he looked ready to rush off and hide in the bushes."

"Poor atom," Ruth murmured, though the child was well-grown. "After all, if he does prove to be Patricia's, have you or I, anyone, the right to forbid him to be here?"

David rubbed troubled fingers through his hair.

"Don't forget, I wish to be present when you question Ka-aina."

"Oh, for God's sake, Ruth!"

"Of course, if you prefer to see him alone—" Ruth made her lips move stiffly.

"My only reason for wishing to do so is to spare you side lights on your family which aren't edifying."

"Simply because a thing's ugly, a real woman doesn't

shrink from it," Ruth announced, enjoying the flush of exhilaration that some people feel when uttering lofty statements, which they imagine are particularly applicable to themselves.

"Be present then," David said shortly.

She looked at him mildly and reproachfully, then bent over the sleeping child, touching it with light, dusting movements, as if removing, among other things, men's unwarranted ill-humors.

When Ka-aina was interviewed the next morning, Ruth was there. Her presence irritated David. He glimpsed, for the first time, the iron in her, for all that she looked soft and malleable. Trevellyan seemed to look out, mockingly, from behind Ruth's limpid eyes. She wore a dress of the Burgundy red that she fancied, a creamy flower at her breast. One arm was placed protectingly about the boy whose confidence she had partly won with delicacies and cajolery. He leaned indifferently against her, his eyes fixed upon Ka-aina.

The man's attitude puzzled David. The fact that he had not turned up for orders the previous evening, implied that he had wanted time to concoct a story, yet when David saw him riding past the gate before breakfast and hailed him, he appeared quite unconcerned. Securing his horse to the hitching rail, he came toward the house like anyone whose mind is occupied with his duties. Spying the child with Ruth he exclaimed:

"Ha! Kid stop here. Which place you find? Run away yesterday. I look every side. *Lapu-wale!*" * The child shrank against Ruth from the anger in the man's

---

* *lapu-wale*—untidy, dirty, careless, a term of condemnation.

voice and his eyes filled with tears. "Yesterday I little more crazy. Look, look, no can find. I tell to Lewai take care the race horses and look some more. All time this *keiki* run away. No use!"

"Is the child Patricia's?" David asked, a cold ring in his voice.

"Patricia baby!" Ka-aina looked aghast. "This boy," he shrugged, dismissing the child as little consequence, "belong white preacher who stop little time in Kaupo. Mother, father got consumption. First mother die and after by and by father die too. I sorry and take the baby. You know, Hawaiian style."

"I'm not fool enough to swallow that," David exclaimed. "Trevellyan gave Patricia's child to you the night it was born."

"But when Old Man give me baby he tell to me, 'Ka-aina, see it never grows up, never sets foot in Lani-o-akua.'" Ka-aina spoke in Hawaiian, but carefully and slowly in order that Ruth might understand. "Do you think, just because Mr. Hi-ball is dead that I would dare to disobey him? But no need make like Mr. Hi-ball tell me. As you recall the baby came too soon. It was a weak, small girl and died two days after my wife and I took it. I was glad," Ka-aina paused and wiped his face, "because I did not want to kill a baby."

Ruth began sobbing.

"You were warned," David reminded her, wondering why he had never given Patricia's child, or its whereabouts, further thought. Probably because he had taken it for granted that Trevellyan would make provision of some sort for it. But events had landslided too fast for the old man toward the end, and this thread had

slipped unnoticed from his fingers. Or possibly Trevellyan had been so assured of Ka-aina's fidelity in obeying
instructions, that he had given no further thought to
the matter. Common sense convinced him that Ka-aina
was lying and yet . . . What did it matter one way or
the other? What did anything matter? Life went its
appointed course.

"Oh, David," Ruth cried, drawing the boy to her,
"let's keep him. It's not right to allow a white child to
grow up without education."

The child regarded her soberly. Nothing of Patricia,
nothing of Trevellyan in the wide eyes, tranquil forehead, and loving mouth. Yet something about his face
haunted David, like one glimpsed in a crowd and never
quite forgotten.

"I shall go to Kaupo," David announced, looking at
Ka-aina, "and make inquiries about the preacher whose
child you claim he is."

Ka-aina shrugged, intimating it was agreeable.

"It isn't to be expected, Ruth, that you can understand why I want to know for sure whether or not
the child is Patricia's."

"Are you afraid he may show traits proving he's a
Trevellyan?"

David did not answer.

"Are Trevellyans such dreadful creatures?" she
laughed archly. "You married one."

Ka-aina smiled, and David grimaced, convinced that
girl and man were leagued together against him in their
determination to keep the boy at Lani-o-akua.

"Can't you trust me to shape a child's character?"
Ruth asked. "If he proves to be Patricia's child, he's my

nephew, and I'm more responsible than you are for his future." Triumph filled her as she finished. The possible relationship gave her prior right over David in this matter. "Ka-aina," she asked authoritatively, "what is his name?"

"Jackie."

"Why Jackie?" David demanded quickly.

"Jackie *haole* name," Ka-aina replied composedly.

David was dashed. He had hoped that the name might serve as a clue to its father, but saw the Ka-aina was telling the truth. Jack was a common enough name among whites. He stared at the proud bright sea showing through gaps in the trees, then ground his heel on the veranda. After all, perhaps it would be better to let the dead past bury its indecent dead, decently.

CHAPTER XI

WHEN Jackie had been with them four years, Ruth begged David to adopt him legally. Although Jackie showed no traits which proved him a Trevellyan, David was certain he must be Patricia's child. To set his mind at rest on the subject, shortly after the boy was found, he took time off from his work to visit the obscure district of Kaupo and made inquiries. They were half-hearted ones for he knew, with exasperation, that Polynesians, when questioned, always give the replies they fancy are wanted. And in this instance, Ka-aina—if he were lying about the child's identity—would have instructed the people in Kaupo what answers to give.

Yes, an Australian Evangelist and his wife had resided in the district some five or six years before. They had come to the Islands in search of health and to spread their particular brand of religion. There had been a boy. When the Browns died within a few weeks of each other, the child had been cared for by Lewai, a Hawaiian preacher, who had later been transferred to Kona. When Lewai left, Kawila, the *kahuna*, had had the baby for a bit, but when he moved to Molokai he had left the child with someone. Probably Ka-aina. It was known that Ka-aina had a large family and liked children.

David wondered if Ka-aina had really taken the Evangelist's son and, Hawaiian fashion, as a return courtesy, presented Patricia's infant to the *kahuna*. He wondered, a trifle disturbed, if Patricia's child would grow up in some lonely, forgotten valley, unaware who he was, ignorant of his heritage across the wind-whipped channel between Maui and Molokai.

Private questioning of the old man brought no further enlightenment. Assurances that if Jackie was Patricia's son, it would make no difference to his remaining at Lani-o-akua, did not make him change his story. He displayed the impassiveness of a questioned child, seemed amazed that David could doubt—had the infant not died—that he would dare disobey Trevellyan. Knowing Ka-aina's kindness it seemed unthinkable that he would kill a child, but knowing also that infanticide had been a common practice among the Hawaiians of an older day, especially where girls were concerned, and recognizing the terror Trevellyan inspired, it was possible that the child might have been exposed or even buried alive, according to the ancient custom.

On the other hand Ka-aina had been devoted to Patricia and would feel a deep affection for her child whose stigma of unlawful birth would carry no weight with a Hawaiian. He might have been tempted to disregard Trevellyan's ultimatum, then as the child grew older, wished to be freed of the responsibility of rearing a boy too remarkable to be the offspring of a pair of wandering Evangelists. Sufficient time had elapsed between Jackie's birth and subsequent finding, to enable the old fellow to have patiently schemed how to get him to Lani-o-akua without betraying or involving Patricia. Possibly, with a cunning of which he hardly seemed capable, Ka-aina had plotted a line of action and carried it through to secure for the child the inheritance which belonged to him. Suspecting that Ruth was probably barren might even have made him feel that the gods wished the child restored to Lani-o-akua. Anticipating possible difficulties where David was concerned, he might have taken advantage of the fact that a white boy had been left destitute in Kaupo about the time Patricia's baby was born, and foisted off Patricia's son as the child of the Brown's, trusting to the fact that the other had been passed from hand to hand so often that tracing it would be difficult.

For a while he wanted to run the matter to earth, meditated writing to the authorities on Molokai to search the island and locate the *kahuna* to see if there was a white child in his brood. The realization of what it would mean to Patricia in her position, were an illegitimate child to be discovered, deterred him. After all, he might be the voluntary custodian of Lani-o-akua, but he was not the arbiter of Trevellyan morals or responsible for their illegal children.

For a while it was almost distasteful for David to have Jackie around, but as time went on he grew fond of him. He was a plump, hardy little fellow of average intelligence, sturdy physique, and marked good humor. At seven he lost his baby beauty. At eight he was transformed into a graceful, aristocratic youngster with an indefinite air of distinction. His eyes were fine, dark, intelligent; his ears set close to a well-modelled, well-

carried head; his lashes were too long; his mouth almost
too sensitive, but the strength of his cleft chin saved his
face from any hint of weakness. He had a lively, wholesome interest in horses, lassoes, and guns, and rode daily
with Ka-aina.

By watching them together, when they did not realize
they were being observed, David attempted to find out
if there was a noticeable bond, but he had to own that
their fondness for each other appeared to be only the
usual liking between *paniolos* and children on Island
ranches. The boy had been too young and too confused
by strange surroundings to be coherent when David attempted to question him. He had always lived with Ka-
aina and Mele, Jackie insisted. But when David asked
if Ka-aina had left him in the lava flow for Ruth to find,
or if he had wandered there himself, the child looked
frightened, and David abandoned fruitless efforts to
probe into the past.

Ruth, of course, spoiled him, but his nature seemed
impervious to harm which might have resulted from
indulgence. He accepted the love with which Ruth tried
to smother him as he accepted food, the comfort of
sunshine, and other good things. Boy-like he was inclined
to be off-hand when she grew too demonstrative, and
David saw that the allegiance Jackie accorded her was
much of the same caliber he had for all living things.
He was devoted to Ruth in a blunt, boyish fashion, but
equally fond of Ka-aina, the cook, and the other men on
the ranch. He was happy, healthy, a good fellow with
everyone. Then one day David realized that Jackie was
unlike other children, in that he did not love, he liked.
He was fond of people and things, but childhood's herit-

age of love was unknown to him. The knowledge bothered David and made him apprehensive of the future.

David had never succeeded in fully ridding himself of the shadow which had fallen on him when he came to Lani-o-akua. He loved the place, was happy enough in his marriage, but, subconsciously, he was always expecting something to pounce on him, something that lurked in secret valleys on days before rain, and whose presence crouched behind the horizon when it was unusually clear. When he was busy with his work, sorting steers for market, or laying out a fence line, he felt overtaken by a sense of unreality; subtly and irrevocably involved in a great plan, and yet as remote from it as a sleepwalker.

It had been impossible to free himself from the memory of Trevellyan's last words, the cry of his soul to find its way home; words muttered in a drunken delirium holding staggering truths which had set David thinking along new lines. There was a definite power behind life that should be contacted, a door through which everyone must go. But humanity in its dim beginnings had lost the key and strayed away. At times he sensed a mighty pulsing in the universe which his soul wanted to answer, to become part of, but body and intelligence got between, preventing the union.

It was best, having no children of their own, to adopt Jackie legally since the child was the logical person to inherit Lani-o-akua, but David was possessed by an unpleasant conviction that he was meddling in business which was not his concern. He had debated the matter, weighed it from every angle, then resigned himself to the step, thinking that it was one of a succession of steps he had taken since coming to Lani-o-akua.

When Trevellyan's will was opened, he discovered that Lani-o-akua had been left to him unconditionally. It was characteristic of Trevellyan to adopt a course of action, then browbeat people into doing as he specifically wished. His responsibility toward his daughters did not matter as long as Lani-o-akua was placed in safe keeping. He had written Patricia to ask if she wished the will contested. After months of indifferent silence, she replied that her dowry was sufficient to keep her in luxury for the rest of her life, and the will must stand.

Instead of being relieved by her reply, David had been depressed. The responsibility of Lani-o-akua had been shunted on to him for good. Ruth was not the type of woman from whom to seek help in intangible matters. He guessed, were he ever tempted to make her the sharer of shadowy things, which at times possessed him to the exclusion of the concrete world, that she would be perplexed and distressed if not actually impatient. In his imagination he could hear her: "Why, David, I wouldn't have thought that a practical, intelligent man like you would plague yourself so, etc., etc."

He looked out of the office door. Her words of that morning still echoed in his ears, "And, David, you might as well go to Wailuku tomorrow and get the papers made out. I suppose you'll have to see a lawyer or something." She had uttered them with a suggestion of feminine helplessness which failed to conceal the iron in her, bequeathed by Trevellyan.

He studied the spur scratches on the floor. The matter might as well be attended to immediately as later. The trees waiting in the garden looked as if they expected it of him. He felt grim, thinking of himself as a pawn in the game of Lani-o-akua. Owner of the estate—he? Slave and servant rather.

Mounting his horse David left the tree-shaded court house. The papers making Jackie his legally adopted son crackled in his pocket. He started down the main street of the little town. It was one of those days that set pulses tingling. The island had a rich smell. The blue battalions of the Pacific glittered and swaggered as they swung shoreward. Clouds heaped majestically above the West Maui mountains. A mirage of romance pervaded the common light of noon. Rivulets sparkled at the roadsides, houses listened attentively to the whispering of gardens drunk with light and color. His horse reached for the bit, shying playfully when some laborer stepped out of the cane fields encircling the nest of houses, masquerading as a township.

Riding along in the sunshine David wished that he knew some member of his own sex with whom he could talk freely, but living at Lani-o-akua had cut him off from sustained human friendships. He had taken an irrevocable step by adopting Jackie. The sheriff, a stout, good-natured half-white had been uninterested, had not even bothered to look up birth records in Kaupo to verify the boy's parentage, until David pressed him to do so. The entry was found, confirming the birth of a son to Algernon and Angela Brown, Evangelists.

David watched sunshine running along the crest behind his horse's ears. Cane whispered and rustled on either side of the road. Air moved like a lady slowly waving a plumed fan. If he only had a friend with whom he might discuss the intangible things forever eating at the edges of his mind! By talking them over they might be cleared up, got out of the way.

He checked his horse impatiently when it attempted to swing into a wide trail leading off the main road. Norfolk Island pines, cypress and mangoes loomed like dark islands above the pale green cane marking the home-site of Waikapu plantation. He glanced at it thinking regretfully that had he not lived isolated at Lani-o-akua, he would have known the plantation and ranch owners on the island, and felt at liberty to drop in at any one of a number of estates for lunch and a chat.

A well-dressed, well-mounted man with iron gray hair rode out of a field and stopped before crossing the road. His features were familiar and unfamiliar in one. Then David's mind clicked. Walter Hamilton! In the same instant recognition leaped into the other man's eyes, but mingled with it was a quick twinge of pain.

"Birthwood," he said, a slow painful color creeping toward his ears.

"Hamilton," David replied, spurring closer and thrusting out his hand.

They exchanged greetings. Hamilton seemed to be wrestling with some impulse that fought natural instincts of hospitality. David was perplexed. To him, this chance meeting with the one man who had visited Lani-o-akua whom he remembered with respect, was delightful. It was like a direct answer to his hunger for a friend. He hoped frankly, as a boy hopes, that he would be invited to lunch. It was not yet one o'clock. But perhaps Hamilton had already eaten and was setting off again. Then the invitation came, as though wrenched from Hamilton's lips against his will.

"Eaten yet?"

"No."

"Come and have a bite with me."

"I'd like to. Thanks."

They rode up the road slowly. David glanced, covertly, at Hamilton. There was a bleakness about his face hardly justified by the eight or nine years which had passed since he had last seen him, and a mechanical quality in his words and actions, as if the spirit animating his body had withdrawn to remote regions. Arriving at the garden, which leaped gaily down to the road in a succession of flowered terraces, they dismounted.

A Chinaman appeared on the veranda.

"Set another place," Hamilton ordered, and the man nodded. "Jim in yet?"

"Already come," the man answered.

"Like to wash up?" Hamilton asked, when they were in doors.

"Please," David answered.

Hamilton directed him to a room at the end of the passage. "Lunch will be served shortly," he said. "I'll join you in the *lanai* presently."

While David removed the dust from his face and head, excitement permeated him. It seemed adventurous to be lunching with a man of his own kind. He looked at the pleasant room, at the flowered wall paper, and four poster covered with a Hawaiian quilt, intricately stitched in the breadfruit pattern. He recalled that Hamilton had been married, and wondered what sort of woman his wife was.

When he was brushed up, he felt singularly happy

and carefree. Going to the veranda, he looked around
and enjoyed the sweep of the island toward Haleakala.
The trees marking Lani-o-akua stood out boldly on the
southern slope of the mountain. Footsteps came down
the hall and he turned. A boy of fifteen or thereabouts
appeared. He carried himself well, his once-fair skin
was tanned a deep clear brown, and above a smooth
forehead, blond hair went back in gay waves. His wide-
open blue eyes smiled warmly.

"I'm Jim Lord," he said holding out his hand. "Uncle
Walter told me to introduce myself. He had to go to the
office. You live at Lani-o-akua, don't you? How far is it
from here, Mr. Birthwood?"

"About twenty-five miles."

"I'd give anything to see the place. The name fasci-
nates me. I've asked Uncle Walter to take me there
ever so many times, but he hasn't got around to doing
it yet."

From the way the boy's eyes lighted when he uttered his uncle's name it was clear that he worshipped
him. David determined to ask them both for a week-end.
Jim might prove to be a companion for Jackie, despite
the gap in their ages.

"Any week-end you can make it, I'd be delighted to
have you both," he said, watching the warm, young
face.

Jim flushed with delight. The mere thought of asking Hamilton and this lad to be his guests made David
feel like an ordinary human being with bonds in common with his fellows. Ruth would be delighted at the
prospect of entertaining a man of Hamilton's standing.
It would afford an opportunity to use the best glass and

China and to preside effectively at the foot of their always-empty table. Perhaps by asking Hamilton over, it would serve as an opening wedge to other local friendships. Remorse filled him, realizing the lonely life to which Ruth was pledged because of marrying him. But there was no longer any reason why they should continue to isolate themselves. Happenings to be concealed from the world did not take place at Lani-o-akua now. He felt almost jaunty.

"Were you born at Lani-o-akua?" Jim asked, watching him in an interested way.

"No, in England, but I came here a number of years ago and have remained ever since."

"Uncle Walter's got to take me over. It's nice of you to ask us. I don't know why I want to go to Lani-o-akua more than to other ranches on Maui. But it's got such a splendid name."

David nodded.

"I've lived with Uncle Walter nearly seven years. After he and Aunt Sophie were divorced he was ill for a long time and had to take a trip away. He visited us in Boston." The boy hesitated. "Uncle Walter is Mother's brother. I don't get on with Father. He doesn't understand about boys and things as Uncle Walter does. We were always at loggerheads, even when I was small." He paused, flushed at betraying family secrets, but David nodded encouragingly and he went on. "It made Mother unhappy. I guess I'm a rotten son. Father wanted to make a business man of me, wanted Lord and Son, on the door. But I hated figures and finance. It smothered me thinking about business waiting for me at the end of school and college. After a lot of persuasion

Mother got Father to agree to my living with Uncle Walter for a while. She said he was alone, and needed someone with him. Father knew if he kept me in Boston I'd run away. I like Waikapu." The boy gazed around him with shining eyes. "It has a feeling of things coming toward you."

There was a flame-like intensity to the boy. He tingled with life to the fingertips and at the same time looked like a dreamer. His manner was poised, princely, and David suspected that in him was the fabric of adventurers.

"We got here at night," Jim went on. "When I woke up and heard mule teams going past, workmen jabbering in strange tongues, wind rustling the cane—it made goose prickles come out all over me, and every morning it seems like that first one."

David nodded. He knew the damnable enchantment of the Islands.

"You know, Mr. Birthwood, Uncle Walter's the sort of fellow a boy wants to be like when he grows up—" he broke off at the sound of Hamilton's footsteps but his eyes said, "Just look at him!"

They lunched at a table set beside open windows. Hamilton was cordial but David felt a restraint behind it. His host's face had a mask-like quality behind the changing play of expressions that Jim's eager talk evoked. David felt eased simply from sitting at Hamilton's table. There was a fine cleanness about this gray-haired, tanned man whom David knew by repute to be one of the most successful sugar planters on Maui. He wondered, without inquisitiveness, what had estranged him and his wife. Had it not been for Jim's presence, Hamilton would have been as lonely as he felt himself at times. The knowledge made David feel closer to his host. His manner warmed, and he smiled recalling how heavy his spirits had been when he set out in the morning.

"It's after two. I should be getting along," he said regretfully, when their cigars were finished.

"Drop in whenever you come by," Hamilton urged. "We'll be glad to see you."

David felt Jim's reminding eyes upon him.

"I'd like to have you both over some week-end soon. I have a boy younger than Jim, but Jackie will be delighted to show him around the ranch."

Young Lord's eyes leaped to his uncle's.

"Wouldn't that be ripping, Uncle Walter? We aren't going anywhere next Sunday—"

Jim did not finish his sentence. David raised his eyes and was non-plussed by the change in Hamilton's appearance. A dead gray had replaced his tan and horror dilated his pupils. The hand which had been lying carelessly on the table was doubled into a fist, and Hamilton's figure seemed to brace against something. David felt as if he had been struck in the face, as if long association with Lani-o-akua had stamped him as unclean. A torrent of protesting words sprang to his lips that were never uttered for Hamilton was pushing back his chair, his gesture implying that he was putting David at a distance. He had regained possession of himself, was once more the easy host, but his spirit was withdrawn.

"Mighty nice of you, Birthwood. Of course I'll be delighted to accept your invitation sometime. The grinding season ends in seven weeks and after the mill's closed I'll give you a ring. This youngster's keen to go over.

I may send him alone if he can't wait. Don't forget to stop in again."

David rose feeling as if he were being herded from the table and out of the house unjustly. The sensation of well-being, of comradeship, which had possessed him, dropped away. Because of his connection with Lani-o-akua, he did not belong in the every-day world of events and people.

Jim, looking vaguely dashed, went with Hamilton to see David off. His horse had been watered and freshly saddled. David appreciated the detail of hospitality, but blight had descended on him.

"I'll ring up when the grinding's over," Hamilton repeated, reaching up to shake David's hand. He was grateful for the friendly gesture but knew, as far as coming to Lani-o-akua was concerned, the grinding season for Hamilton would never end.

PART III

LYNETTE

CHAPTER XII

"*What's* her name?" Jackie demanded, looking intrigued.

"Lynette."

"That's almost a bird's name, but for birds you say linnet."

Ruth studied the letter in her hand. The second reading affected her precisely as had the first. Amazement, excitement, resentment mingled together. When the cowboy brought the mail to the lunch table, she had instantly noticed two heavy, crested envelopes addressed in a bold, strange hand. Picking them up she had seen with a flutter that one was addressed to herself. Ripping it open she saw the signature. Patricia! Her half sister had never so much as acknowledged her existence, now she announced that she and her husband were passing through Honolulu on a tour of the world and were sending their small daughter, Lynette, to Lani-o-akua for a year. She read the letter again:

"It may seem odd for me to expect you to take Lynette, but David will understand why I wish the child to have some memories of the place. She will give no trouble. Ka-aina can arrange for some Hawaiian woman to come in to feed and dress her. He will, of course, have charge of Lynette during the day. She's inclined to be delicate. A year's change from the rigors of an English climate and the restrictions of English life will be beneficial. We've arranged with the captain of the Inter-Island steamer to take care of her and put her off at Makena. I'm writing David also. Patricia."

Stifling for someone to whom she could confide the news, Ruth had told Jackie that he was to have a cousin for a playmate. She had been irritated that David was, as usual, off for the day. What had Patricia written him? Jackie watched Ruth while he busied himself with food. The suppressed eagerness that an imaginative child feels at the thought of seeing someone from distant lands, charged his movements.

"Will Lynette get here tomorrow?" he asked

"Yes," Ruth replied shortly. Characteristic of Patricia to issue her ultimatum and sail on her imperious way!

"Can I go to Makena to meet her?"

"Of course not. The boat arrives at midnight."

"Please let me go. I've never seen a little *haole* girl. I wish she was a boy. I bet she can't braid lassoes."

"Of course she can't, don't be absurd."

"I'll teach her."

"Be quiet, Jackie. I must think. A room will have to be got ready."

"She can sleep with me."

"Of course she can't."

"Why can't she? It would be better because when I get up—"

"Jackie! Lynette's accustomed to luxury. Her father

is an admiral and—" A hospitable bustle claimed Ruth. She felt invested with importance at the thought of being intrusted with the care of a highborn child. Admiral Hawke was Lord Guy Hilary Hawke now, and Patricia, Lady Hawke. Jackie fidgeted.

"I bet Lynette will like Lani-o-akua better than England. I bet she'll like to see the horses groomed and help me to kill mice."

"For Heaven's sake, Jackie! Children in Lynette's position don't get up at dawn to see horses groomed or kill mice."

"Then she'll be no fun at all."

Ruth gathered up the letter importantly. The pink room would be appropriate. Poor mite. Sent like a package in care of a fat half-white to be put off in the dark at a strange land. It was enough to terrify the child. Patricia certainly lacked in motherly instincts, and was selfishly and completely engrossed in her glittering life! This was the best possible thing that could have happened to Lynette, being where she would be given the proper sort of love and care. Jackie, seeing he was forgotten, omitted to fold his napkin and scampered down the steps.

Ka-aina was waiting for him in the corral. They were going to ride up behind the house and drive in a cow, which had calved during the night. They had looked all the morning for her and finally found her, but she had hidden her calf in the brush and they would have to search for it again. Jackie wished that Lynette was here so that she could go with them. She would like the little, sweet-smelling calf that the mother had licked dry. Maybe she had never seen a very new calf. He gave a skip as he crossed the road, elated by the prospect of initiating a companion into the delights of Lani-o-akua. Seeing Ka-aina seated near the horses, he rushed up.

"Ka-aina, I got one swell kind to tell you," he cried, falling into the common way of talking.

"What kind, Jackie?" the old man asked, raising indulgent eyes.

Plumping himself down on the log beside Ka-aina, Jackie explained. Ka-aina's eyes, which had been smiling, grew serious.

"You speak true, Jackie?"

"Yes. I like her name, don't you? Lynette. It sounds like a bird. How would you say it in Hawaiian? Lineki?"

Ka-aina made no answer. An awed expression crept into his face, and he got dazedly to his feet.

"Lineki . . . Lineki," he muttered, like a man in a trance. "Come, we go."

"To get the calf?"

"First I go look the *akua* by the pool."

"Why?"

"I think sure, this time the *keiki o* * Lani-o-akua come," he announced solemnly, placing a hand on the boy's shoulder.

"I wish she was a boy, but it can't be helped. Ask the *akua* if she'll be fun."

Ka-aina nodded absentmindedly, and they started for the pool. Jackie frisked beside him. When they got to the rock, Ka-aina stopped and stared at it. Jackie stole a look at him. He was impatient to hear the god's verdict, but hesitated to disturb Ka-aina for there was a

* *keiki o*—child of.

remembering expression on his face.

"What does the *akua* say?" he ventured finally, in a whisper.

"*Kulikuli*," * Ka-aina commanded, and began muttering in rapid undertones, whether to the god or to himself, Jackie did not know. Unsteadily the old man removed the wreath from his hat, and placed it on the stone.

"Many years before I come ask this *akua* some-kind. Small bird come down. Linnet bird. I no understand. Linnet no Hawaii bird. Linnet belong England. Now I understand. That linnet I seeing not a bird. That linnet spirit of the little child of Lani-o-akua, who comes tomorrow night."

"I can hardly wait to see her. Is this," he touched the rock reverently, "Lynette's *akua*?" Ka-aina nodded. "I bet she'll be glad when she finds out she has an *akua*. But my *akua* is better. It has two faces. Can I give Lynette one? If she's very nice I'll swap *akuas* with her."

"No speak this kind, Jackie," Ka-aina reproved. "*Akuas* no belong mans. Mans belong *akuas*."

Riding to Makena David felt oppressed. He wondered if Lynette would have in her make-up any of the lamentable qualities of her mother. This sending of the child to Lani-o-akua was uncalled for, but it was natural for Patricia to wish her daughter to have some memories of the spot where she had spent her own childhood.

A star appeared behind Haleakala, an enlarged globe of luminous gold, then it paled and diminished to proper proportions. He turned into the tree-shaded road fol-

* *kulikuli*—be quiet.

lowing the dim curve of the bay. A sow heaved to her
feet and lumbered off, and a coconut fell with a soft
thud in a nearby grove. The resentment which had filled
him, since knowing they were to have Lynette, dimmed.
It was brutal sending a seven-year-old child to absolute
strangers. He wished that the boat had arrived by daylight, so that he could have brought Jackie. In the interest
of having a companion of about her own age, Lynette
would have been distracted from the strangeness of her
surroundings.

He reviewed Patricia's letter, which after one dis-
gusted reading, he had handed to Ruth.

"I will be frank with you, David. I cannot be bothered
with Lynette's vagaries. A year in the Islands will do her
good. If she fulfills the promise in her face she'll cause
a furore at court when she grows up. You'll smile when I
tell you the thing I anticipate most is the thought of making a spectacular marriage for Lynette when she grows
up. . . . I know you'll think—these parents! But they
aren't so wrong, David."

He saw the ship's mastlight and heard the anchor go
down. Dismounting, he walked across the beach. A boat
took shape on the dark water, and a voice called out in
Hawaiian. David gave an answering hail. A sailor stood
up and waved a lantern. The bluff bow grounded. The
steersman grabbed Lynette under the arms and swung
her to David.

"Here, the *keiki-wahine*," he shouted.

A feather-light little body landed accurately between
David's hands. He heard a faint, stifled gasp and felt the
mad beating of the child's heart against his fingers. Flinging a horrified backward glance at the sea, the child

clutched his neck with both arms, and buried her face against it. Wading beyond the wash of the waves, he started to set her down, but the frantic hold of her arms tightened.

"There, there," David consoled, "you're ashore."

"Don't put me down. I'm scared. The water's so black," the child gasped.

She was surprisingly small and light for her age and David transferred her to his right arm. She perched on it like a bird poised for flight, but retained her hold of him, as if she were not quite sure that he could be depended upon to keep his word.

Her features were indistinct in the starlight, but David sensed an elfin quality in her, and her slightness seemed to melt into him through the arm about his neck. The sailor in the bows held up the lantern, while two of his mates carried her trunk up the beach. David glanced up and Lynette down, and he thought she smiled. But in the depths of her eyes was the aloofness of a soul which had not entirely adjusted to the earth.

When he set her astride of the saddle, she shrank slightly. He tied a pillow over the pommel and without putting her on the ground, transferred her to the improvised seat and swung himself up behind. Her silence, as they rode, was suggestive of fear of the unseen island, but he suspected she enjoyed the movement of the horse for after they had ridden for a while, she reached down and timidly touched the animal on the neck. He spoke to her once or twice, but she did not answer. Presently she slept, her limp little form giving to each stride of the horse as it toiled up the long star-lighted slopes of Haleakala. When it grew heated from its exertions,

Lynette opened her eyes.

"What's that nice warm smell like salt? I like it."

David smiled. "It's the horse sweating."

Reaching down she touched the reeking shoulder, then sniffed daintily at her fingers. Her smile was luminous. Sitting up she stared around, her sensitive nostrils quivering to the scents of the island; *kiawe, ilima, lantana,* and from above the clean odor of thousands of sleeping trees, growing strongly out of rich soil. A suggestion of eagerness enveloped her, then with a long sigh she sagged against David and slept.

The sun was high when Lynette awakened. A slight noise at her bedside made her turn from the window which opened upon glimpses of a garden that stirred her. A tanned boy was waiting, one hand resting on the coverlet.

"Hello, Lynette."

"Who are you?"

"I'm Jackie. Didn't your mother tell you about me?"

Lynette shook her head.

"I like your name."

"Why?" Lynette asked, sitting up.

"Because it's a bird's. Only for birds you say linnet."

Lynette was interested.

"There are linnets in England," she announced and they smiled shyly at each other, then were at a loss how to go on. Jackie scraped his toes on the floor and, observing that he was barefoot, Lynette looked with increased interest at him.

"Where are your shoes?"

"I only wear them on Sundays and if I'm good, I can

take them off after lunch."

Lynette did not answer.

"Do you like to play with boys?" Jackie asked, after a silence.

"I've never played with anyone."

"Can you ride and swim?"

Lynette shook her head.

"Ka-aina and I will teach you."

Lynette tossed her silky, black hair as though wind were blowing through it. Her raspberry lips, sensitive and delicately shaped, parted breathlessly.

"Can I ride a big horse like the one I was carried on last night?"

"You bet. And I'll show you how to braid lassoes."

Footsteps silenced them. Ruth entered with a warm bustle.

"Jackie, I told you not to wake Lynette," she reproved.

"I wanted to see what she was like. Do you," he consulted Lynette gravely, "want to go to sleep again?"

"I want to get up and see the garden."

She stared, fascinated with the tall, unfamiliar trees, wrapped in sunlight that had a distinct smell. Seating herself on the edge of the bed, Ruth picked up one of Lynette's hands. The child regarded her with veiled hostility, and drew her fingers away.

"Are you my governess or a new nurse?"

Ruth laughed, but looked annoyed, then explained that she was mistress of Lani-o-akua. Lynette listened in a sort of detachment.

"Jackie, tell Melé to bring Lynette's breakfast. When you've eaten it, dear, you must rest again. After today Melé, a Hawaiian woman, will take care of you."

"Ka-aina and I will take care of Lynette," Jackie protested. "Melé only feeds and dresses her."

"That will do, Jackie. Do as I tell you."

He left the room, but once out of sight raced down the veranda. The large, placid woman, engaged by Ka-aina to be Lynette's body servant, was seated in the kitchen drinking heavily-sweetened coffee out of a thick white cup.

"Lynette's *maikai*, * Melé," Jackie cried.

"I too much glad, Jackie."

"Get her *kaukau* † quickly. Will Lynette always eat in bed, Melé? Do *haole* girls have to? Won't she ever eat with me?"

"Sure, after today, eat with you," the woman assured him, getting slowly to her feet.

She placed a glass of milk on a tray beside a bowl of oatmeal.

"Oh, not porridge!" Jackie exclaimed. "Give her something nice." Reaching for a bowl full of mangoes, he selected the two largest and ripest, and placed them in a corner of the tray. "I want Lynette to like Lani-o-akua," he explained.

"Sha! You *pupuli?*" ‡ the woman laughed. "Everybody like Lani-o-akua."

Jackie looked relieved.

"I'll get some *lichi* nuts," he cried, making for the door.

"Hey!" Melé called. "Miss Ruth speak what kind Lynette eat. Oatmeal, milk, toast, one egg. S'pose Miss

* *maikai*—good, nice.
† *kaukau*—food.
‡ *pupuli*—crazy.

Ruth speak some kind—" Melé rolled her eyes roguishly. Reaching out of the window, she plucked a flaming hibiscus blossom and placed it beside the mangoes. "There, you think that look more good?" she asked, uttering cascades of smothered chuckles.

Jackie considered the effect critically, then slow scarlet spread over his face. He should have made Lynette a *lei!* He must get one. Ka-aina always had a new one on his hat every morning. He watched Melé start down the veranda like a laden freighter, then scampered for the stable, surveying his kingdom as he went, to assure himself that it would appear as splendid to Lynette as it did to him.

"I wonder if English trees are as high as Lani-o-akua ones?" he thought, as he crossed the road. Seeing Ka-aina walking restlessly around the corrals, he shouted:

"Lynette's fine. I want a *lei* for her. Give me the one off your hat."

"Already I make plenty *lei* for Lineki," Ka-aina said. "Come, I show you."

Giving an eager skip Jackie grasped the old cowboy's hand. Going into a loose-box Ka-aina pointed at a long, gleaming piece of banana bark, transparently green and silver, still moist from the young trunk from which it had been stripped. Inside it lay strings of white jasmine, carefully threaded end to end, resembling carved ivory and pearls.

"I fix last night," Ka-aina said, placing the wreaths in their green bed in Jackie's hands. The boy inhaled the fragrance of the tiny blossoms eagerly.

"Can I take these to her?" Jackie asked.

"Sure, you give," Ka-aina replied with the generosity

of his race, "but I think better Lineki give her *akua* one *lei*."

"I'll tell her," Jackie said, starting triumphantly and carefully toward the house. Passing the *kukui* grove he put the wreaths on the grass, plucked a rose from a nearby bush, and going to the Shark God laid the flower before it.

"*Akua*, make Lynette love Lani-o-akua," he whispered.

Ruth's voice calling for him hurried him housewards.

"Jackie," she said from the steps, "Lynette's an odd little thing. You must be patient with her. She only spoke to me the once while you were there. Since then she's only watched me in the oddest fashion."

"She talked lots before you came," Jackie countered.

"Probably it's her training. English children are brought up to believe they should be seen and not heard."

"Has she finished eating? I want her to come and play."

"She must rest until noon after her long trip."

"Oh, Mother, she wants to get up. I want to give her these leis. Ka-aina made them last night. By lunch they'll be dead."

"I'll take them to her."

"Ka-aina said *I* could! Oh, there she is," he finished, his face lighting.

Ruth turned, incredulously. Lynette, fully dressed, moving as daintily as a bird on a dewy lawn, was coming along the veranda, her enchanted eyes fixed on the garden. Jackie hurried to meet her.

"Here's something for you, Lynette."

Lynette gazed at the flowers and her eyes opened and opened, then a smile transfigured her face.

"Are these for me?" she asked breathlessly.

"Yes. You wear them like this." With clumsy, boyish eagerness Jackie placed them about her neck.

"Did you string them?"

"No, Ka-aina did."

Lynette looked bewildered.

"There he is," Jackie announced, signing at the old man who was approaching slowly. His face was working with emotion, his eyes blurred with tears. Lynette caught her breath, then went forward and held out her hand.

"Thank you, Ka-aina," she murmured.

Ka-aina kissed the small fingers, covering his eyes as he would have done in the presence of a chief. When he straightened up, Lynette slid her fingers confidently into his dry, old hand.

"Lineki, Lineki," he muttered, "*Aloha, aloha nui loa.* I too much glad at last you come."

Jackie scampered about delightedly.

"Come on," he cried, "Ka-aina and I will show you the new calf and the race horses. Then we'll go to the mill and the mausoleum and the pool, and, of course," he added with hasty contrition, "we must see the *akuas.*"

"What are *akuas?*" Lynette asked, her free hand caressing the wreaths about her neck.

"Gods," Jackie replied promptly.

"Gods?" Lynette asked, looking enraptured.

"Haven't you gods in England?"

The child shook her head.

"Well, we have at Lani-o-akua. I have a god and you

have one, too."

"Have I a god?" Lynette asked, as if it were impossible to credit such a marvel.

"Yes, it's been waiting years and years for you to come to Lani-o-akua."

Lynette's eyes opened until they seemed to hold all the wonder of the world. Ruth spoke quickly, chiding Jackie, but Lynette did not hear. Lifting her radiant face to Ka-aina's, she ran down the steps.

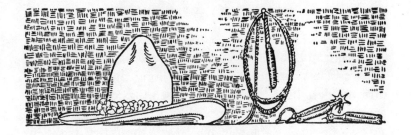

CHAPTER XIII

With her hand tucked trustingly into Ka-aina's, Lynette made the rounds of Lani-o-akua; bent over the little, calf lying in a corner of the sunny corral, looked at the sleek beauty of the thoroughbreds, gazed at the gaping windows and rusty machinery in the mill, stared at the mausoleum. Jackie, radiating importance, raced ahead.

"This is one of my secret places," he announced, diving into a weed grown hollow under the shadow of Trevellyan's tomb. "I found this yesterday." Pridefully he exhibited a parrokeet's tail feather. "And Ka-aina gave me this fish hook. It's made of a man's bone. Look through this." He held out a triangle of red glass.

Lynette took it and held it to one eye. The world assumed sultry hues, trees looked gigantic, the landscape mysterious. Removing it, she regarded it with parted lips, then transformed her attention to Jackie, who had honored her by trusting her with the treasure.

"Can I look through it again tomorrow?"

"You bet. Every day. Now, Ka-aina, let's show Lynette the *akuas*."

"*Akuas* are gods, aren't they?" Lynette asked expectantly.

Ka-aina nodded, and touched Lynette's hair with gentle fingers. They retraced their way along the hill, Lynette uttering delighted little shrieks when pigs dodged among the weeds or peacocks ran with swift gliding movements across openings. Jackie leaped along the dusty path, his bare feet spurning the ground. Lynette observed them intently.

"Wait," she commanded, disengaging her fingers from Ka-aina's.

Sitting down, she began hurriedly removing her shoes and stockings. Jackie watched with a pleased expression. When they were off she stood up and ventured forward. Little vibratory messages from the earth ran through her toes, up her legs.

"Hide them," she ordered, "or she will make me put them on again."

Ka-aina smiled. "Miss Ruth no care. In Hawaii *keiki* no wear shoe."

"What's *keiki?*" Lynette demanded.

"Kids, like us," Jackie explained.

Lynette beamed. Ka-aina collected the discarded shoes and stockings, and they went on. After they had walked for a while he indicated Lynette's feet. "No sore?" he asked.

She shook her head and dug her toes into the dust. Some inner part of her was expanding. Trees seemed taller, sunlight brighter, the sky a deeper blue.

"Come on, Lynette," Jackie urged, "and see your *akua*. Mine has two faces."

"Two faces!" Lynette murmured.

They climbed the hill slowly. The warmth of the

earth under her bare feet filled Lynette with delicious
languor which changed to swift pleasure when she
stepped into a damp hollow. Jackie raced ahead and
waited impatiently. Ka-aina assisted Lynette up the
bank. She saw the sheet of water, reflecting the images
of trees, and recoiled.

"Don't you like it?" Jackie asked.

"Water scares me. When I'm near it I can't breathe."

"How do you keep clean?"

"I don't mind it in basins and tubs."

"It's the same stuff that is in pools and the sea."

"But lots of it scares me."

"When you learn to swim you won't be afraid. Come,
Lynette, and look at your *akua*."

Lynette followed him gingerly along the flower-
banked pathway, holding tightly to Ka-aina's hand.

"No scare, Lineki, I take care," he said.

She edged away from the pool, and he swung her
upon his arm. Jackie parted the dense ferns and exhibited
the rock. Lynette studied it silently, pressing against the
old man. Jackie patted the stone and smiled.

"May I touch it?" Lynette asked.

"First give one *lei*," Ka-aina said, removing a string
of jasmine.

Protest leaped into Lynette's eyes, then her hand,
which had flown up to intercept Ka-aina's, dropped
down.

"You give, Lineki, then all time this *akua* take care
of you."

She felt vaguely pleased, and leaning forward placed
the wreath on the rock, then jerked back.

"No scare, Lineki, this *akua* belong you."

Lynette touched the stone timidly. It was damp and sweet with moss, and her nostrils quivered.

"I like its smell," she said, then frowned at the pool, "but I wish my *akua* wasn't here."

"Because of the water?" Jackie asked. "If you want, I'll change gods with you." His eyes defied Ka-aina. "Mine's in the garden and has no water near it. Let's show Lynette my *akua*, Ka-aina."

"One minute." The old man set Lynette on the ground. "I like make somekind. Good kind, Lineki. Ka-aina know. I like one small piece of hair for give the *akua*. Then anytime you trouble, he take care."

The child nodded. Drawing the knife from his legging, he separated a glossy spiral from its mates and cut it off carefully. Lynette wriggled and laughed when the cold blade of the knife touched her neck. Her eyes were those of a child learning a new game. Ka-aina murmured over the lock, scooped out a tiny hole at the foot of the rock, and covered the hair with earth.

Jackie started ahead, impatient to exhibit his god.

"Put me down," the little girl ordered when she and Ka-aina reached the bottom of the hill. "I want to feel the dirt with my feet again."

"Good no more shoe, eh?" Ka-aina asked.

A cry of delight escaped from her lips when she felt the cold stone walk against the soles of her feet.

"Oh, Lynette, it's fun having you at Lani-o-akua," Jackie cried.

"What's that word you keep saying?"

"Lani-o-akua's the name of this place." Jackie made a lordly gesture that gathered the landscape to them. "Say it, Lynette. Lani-o-akua."

She repeated the syllables carefully. Lani-o-akua. She liked to say it, to feel it run solemnly around her lips. Lani-o-akua.

"That's the way," Jackie announced.

"What does it mean?"

"Heaven of the Gods."

Lynette was overcome. She gazed at the trees. Heaven of the Gods. Heaven of the Gods. How full of wonder, how beautiful. It made everything seem sacred.

Jackie entered the *kukui* grove and beckoned. When she saw the image she froze.

"How horrible! And it's got the same ugly face on the other side!" she finished, as if that were the crowning outrage.

"It isn't ugly," Jackie broke in hotly. "Shark Gods have to look like sharks. He'll be mad with you if—"

"If I what?" Lynette asked, tremulously.

"Lineki, give *lei* quick," Ka-aina urged, but the tone of his voice made the words a command.

He removed a wreath hastily, and she suffered the act without verbal protest, but her eyes dilated.

"You give, Lineki."

She obeyed. Stepping backwards quickly she groped for Ka-aina's hand.

"No *pilikea*, Lineki," he assured her, then began talking under his breath.

"What's he doing?" Lynette asked, unsteadily.

"Praying, so the god won't hurt you because you said he was ugly."

"But he is," she insisted.

"His face is like a shark's because—"

"What are sharks, Jackie?"

"Big fish that live in the sea and eat people."

Uttering a stifled scream, Lynette tore her fingers out of Ka-aina's and fled.

"No use talk this kind to Lineki," Ka-aina scolded, when he overtook the little girl and had her gathered in his arms. "Lineki no understand. No cry, Lineki. Ka-aina take care. Every day us three fellas give *akua* nice *lei*, then no *pilikea*. I think better go look calf again. You like, Lineki?"

Catching her breath, she nodded.

"Yes, let's go and see the little calf," she whispered, glancing apprehensively at the *kukui* grove.

Hoisting her upon his arm, Ka-aina started for the corrals.

At lunch Ruth vetoed Jackie's statement that he and Ka-aina would take Lynette riding.

"Not today, Jackie. Lynette must rest."

Lynette directed a rebellious look at her, but did not attempt to dispute the order. She *was* a governess or nurse. She stopped you from doing things you wanted. Neatly she cleaned the last scrap of food off her plate and waited.

"Now, dear, I'll take you to your room." Ruth rose. "Have a nice sleep, and you can play for a while after supper."

"Oh, Mother, let Lynette sleep in the garden. There's a fine, shady place under the camphor tree. Ka-aina and I will sit by her till she wakes up."

Lynette's eyes lighted.

"Oh, please may I? I've never slept outside."

"Not today, dear."

"Why not today?" Jackie demanded. "It's warm, and Ka-aina can put his raincoat on the grass for her to lie on."

"That will do, Jackie."

"You're mean to make Lynette go to her room. She wants to sleep in the garden. It's more fun."

Ruth opened her lips, but the tense, silent animosity in Lynette's eyes silenced her.

"Very well," Ruth conceded, "I'll take out a blanket and pillow." She smiled brightly at the small girl.

When Lynette was established to her satisfaction, Ruth returned to the house. As the doorway engulfed her, Lynette leaned up stealthily on her elbow.

"More better lie down, Lineki," Ka-aina advised. "S'pose Miss Ruth see, she take you inside."

"Yes, lie down," Jackie urged.

She obeyed, but signed to the boy to come closer.

"I want to lie on Ka-aina's—" she paused, unable to recollect the word Jackie had used, "on that thing of his you said at lunch I could lie on."

Jackie laughed. "Lynette wants your raincoat, Ka-aina."

"It's rubber and will be cold," Jackie said when Ka-aina returned with it and spread the garment carefully on the grass.

"I'll like it. I don't want anything like England any more. Only Lani-o-akua things."

"Don't you like England?" Jackie asked, hopefully.

"No, I hate it. I never had a calf to play with there, and there were no *akuas*. And no one gave me flowers to hang round my neck." She touched the wilting garlands tenderly.

Jackie glowed.

"I like everything here," Lynette said dreamily. "The trees and the smell of the sun, and you and Ka-aina. But I don't like her much. She's a governess."

"Oh, Lynette," Jackie cried, "it seems like you've always been here. And we haven't even begun to show you anything yet."

Lynette sighed rapturously. It was a heaven for people as well as gods!

"Hold my hand, Ka-aina," she commanded, "then I won't be afraid if I go to sleep that I'll wake up in England."

When she woke long shadows lay across the lawn. As a matter of habit she started to shiver, then realized that the sun had lost none of its warmth. A sea of cloth of gold went away to meet the sky, and horsemen with wide straw hats and ringing spurs were riding in, and dismounting in the corrals.

"Who are all those people?" she asked, sitting up.

"The cowboys. Let's go. They'll want to see you. Na-lua-hini has an accordion. I'll ask him to play it for you."

Lynette was not quite sure what an accordion was, but jumped up to learn. Ka-aina picked up the raincoat, and gathered her hand into his.

As they neared the corrals Lynette's eyes shone, but when they went through the gate she shrank against Ka-aina. The enclosure was crowded with sweat-stained horses, men were swinging off saddles while they laughed and chatted in outdoor voices that rolled out new, rich sounding words. Ka-aina addressed them in

Hawaiian, and delighted surprise spread over their faces. "Patricia *keiki!*" they exclaimed, and swarmed up. Lynette didn't know what it was all about, but felt wrapped in approval and fun. An old fellow with roguish eyes and a vast paunch picked up her hand and kissed it. She looked pleased, and the other men followed suit. Then with a fine boom of mirth, the fat one removed a wilted garland from his hat and placed it about her neck.

"Little dead but no can help. What for Ka-aina no tell to us you coming, Lineki? S'pose I know, sure I make swell *lei* for you. Never mind, I make tomorrow. What kind *lei* you like? Rose *lei*, or maybe *paanini?*"

Lynette knew what roses were, they grew in England. *Paaninis*, whatever they were, belonged to Lani-o-akua and were therefore preferable.

"I want a *paanini lei*," she said shyly.

Shouts of delighted mirth filled the corral. Na-lua-hini slapped his vast leg and everyone laughed.

"Na-lua-hini's fooling," Jackie explained. "*Paanini* is cactus and full of prickles."

Lynette jumped up and down. Life at Lani-o-akua was wonderful. In England great brown men did not joke and tease you. An elfin expression flitted over her face.

"I want a *paanini lei*, Na-lua-hini, a big one and I'll watch you make it."

Roars of approval greeted this supreme piece of wit.

"You swell kid," Na-lua-hini assured her. "I make anykind *lei* for you. Maybe rooster *lei*, maybe one *lei* of fine stones."

Lynette laughed, carried away by pictures of strug-

gling chickens hanging around her neck, or stones too
heavy to lift.

"Here," Na-lua-hini said, "I take you for little *holoholo*." Without waiting for her answer he snatched her
into the crook of his arm, heaved into the saddle and
with extravagant flappings of his legs, headed his horse
out of the gate and galloped down the avenue.

Half closing her eyes, Lynette clung to his neck.
Wind streamed blissfully against her face, through her
hair. Trees flashed past, the brown road raced toward
them and melted away on both sides.

"There." The man jerked his horse to its haunches.
"Tomorrow I take you again."

"Oh, will you, Na-lua-hini? Fast like that?"

"Bet-you-my-life," he assured her.

They rode into the corral, and Ka-aina reached for
her. She transferred the happy hold of her arms to his
neck.

"Like it, Lynette?" Jackie asked.

"Bet . . . you . . . my . . . life," she answered, uttering the words with studied care.

Na-lua-hini struck himself gleefully on the thigh.

"You swell kid, learn quick like anything."

Lynette beamed at the praise.

She watched him ripping girths out of rings and pulling off the saddle.

"Now I get accordion and play for you," he informed
her.

Rapture ran through Lynette. The corral was filled
with nice-smelling dust, horses were rolling and drinking from the water trough, men putting away their gear

in the stable. A pig scampered through a corner, scaring the horses. Men shouted, laughed, and waved their arms. The commotion delighted her. If it would only go on forever.

"Now I get accordion," Na-lua-hini announced.

Lynette was afraid that the other men might go, and she wanted them all to stay there. They were bits of Lani-o-akua. To her relief, they seemed in no hurry to go home, but climbed on to the fence or squatted on their hams, lighting cigarettes, talking, and laughing. Ka-aina seated her on a log, and she edged close. He tousled her hair. Jackie leaned his elbows through a rail and smiled at her. Her eyes drank up the scene; a horse was rolling and grunting with pleasure, jerking its legs toward its stomach and tossing up dust; tall waiting trees were beginning to have a look of evening; the sea stood up like a bright wall, shutting out England.

Na-lua-hini returned clasping something under one arm. He deposited his bulk on the log near Lynette, and she looked at the worn, octagon-shaped mystery he carried. She ventured to explore it with a forefinger. Na-lua-hini moved, and it stretched out like a live thing. She jerked back, snapping her hands behind her, and everyone laughed. Arranging himself, Na-lua-hini slid his hands under the end straps and began playing, pulling the instrument back and forth like an elastic box. Lynette did not venture to breathe.

Clearing his throat lustily, Na-lua-hini rolled his eyes at her, then his big voice boomed out words that stimulated Lynette so much that she was hardly able to sit still. She watched him absorbedly. As though catching something wistful in her eyes, Na-lua-hini stopped.

"Here, Swell Fella, you *kokua* * me."

Lynette flashed him an inquiring look. Taking her between his fat knees, he fitted her hands under the straps on the ends of the instrument, placed his large ones over hers then, miraculously, her hands and arms moved, pumping with Na-lua-hini's in rhythm and unison.

"Now sing like this," he ordered.

> *"Mele ana e!*
> *Mele ana hoi!*
> *Mele ana ka wahine,*
> *Lomi-lomi ia!"*

Lynette screwed back her head to watch his lips. Words danced and jumped off them, words that were gay, roguish, glad, and merry all in one. He sang the verse a second time, more slowly, and she imitated him in her high, clear treble.

Men, seated on the rails, beat their spurred heels deliriously against the fence, the squatting ones thumped one another on their backs.

"*Maikai*,† Lineki, *maikai!* Swell! You smart kid. Sing one more time."

They all sang, including Jackie and Ka-aina. Chanting, laughing, and swaying while horses went down paths shaking themselves, and the little pig watched with bright eyes from the weeds. Bubbles of joy rose and burst inside Lynette, and she began dancing and jumping between Na-lua-hini's knees.

* *kokua*—help.
† *maikai*—good.

"Mele ana e!
Mele ana hoi e!
Mele ana ka wahine,

With an excited cry, she clapped her hand over Na-lua-hini's mouth and finished the line her own way.

"Lani-o-akua ia!"

A shout which seemed to lift her to the clouds answered her.

"Keiki o Lani-o-akua! *Keiki o* Lani-o-akua!" the men cried sliding off the rails and getting to their feet. Tearing wilted wreaths from their hats, they loaded her with them. The atoms of her body sang. It must go on for ever and ever! Pressing against Na-lua-hini, she signed imperatively for him to play again. His elbows began obediently pumping up and down, while the accordion expanded and contracted like her heart.

Riding down the avenue, David saw her, cheeks flaming, hair flying against the worn accordion, tilted rakishly between Na-lua-hini's spread knees. Lynette recognized him vaguely, like a person seen in a dream. Then some secret part of her, instinctively started to close up at sight of a grown person of her own kind. But after an instant, she forgot to be awed for magic walked through the afternoon.

"Sing too," she called.

"Like Lani-o-akua, Lynette?" David asked from his horse.

She clasped her fingers tightly, as though she were keeping rapture safely inside her, then said,

"Bet . . . you . . . my . . . life!"

CHAPTER XIV

DURING the subsequent weeks, Lynette seemed like a wanderer who had returned, rather than a visitor at Lani-o-akua. She was off with Jackie at five every morning to see the thoroughbreds groomed. She sat on the top rails of corrals while men roped and branded, learned to braid, and swing miniature lassoes under Ka-aina's instruction, conferred in pidgin English with the Chinese gardeners while they raked up the lawns.

She never seemed to tire, never seemed to have sufficient of Lani-o-akua. When they were not riding, she and Jackie played the absorbed games of childhood around the mill and mausoleum. Barelegged and bareheaded, she came in late for bath and supper, then, clad in a kimono and straw sandals, rushed out for a last hug of the calf, a brief chat with some cowboy who rode in late, a final scamper through the garden, before she was captured and carried off to bed.

On several occasions when the full moon sailed through peacock-blue, star-scattered heavens, she stole out with Jackie. Like all growing boys, he had, until Lynette's arrival, slept without waking until dawn. The first time empty beds were discovered, Ruth, thoroughly alarmed, had dispatched David to find the young truants. He discovered them in the mill, whose empty rooms and rusty machinery fascinated them. Another night he located them playing near the mausoleum, still as mice in the moonlight. On a third occasion he caught them riding bareback in the avenue.

When the fourth disappearance took place, Ruth instructed David to find Lynette, and bring her in for a scolding. She was undeniably the instigator of these nocturnal prowlings. There was no knowing what might happen if they continued going off. They might get lost or hurt.

"And you've got to reprove her, David, I won't. The child's attitude toward me is hostile, though I've done everything possible to win her confidence."

David nodded. He saw that, to Lynette, Ruth would always be the "governess" who smacked of England, and the life she had spurned. Tramping through the gardens, mellow with moonlight, he realized that Lynette would never have dared to attempt such a thing in England. The virus of Lani-o-akua had entered her veins.

He went to the mausoleum, a blanched shape among the trees, through the mill, up to the pool. Failing to locate the children in any of the spots where they usually played, he headed for the cowboy's quarters. The night was too beautiful for Polynesians to sleep, however hard they had worked, or might have to work the next day.

As he neared the trees surrounding the huddle of houses below the mill, music reached his ears. Advancing to the edge of the grove, he came to a standstill. Lynette was leaning against Ka-aina's knee, her face luminous in the moonlight, as she listened to Na-lua-hini and his mates singing to the accompaniment of the ancient accordion and resounding guitars.

It seemed inconceivable that such a being could have sprung from people like Patricia and Hawke. Lynette's personality was elusive, her soul inaccessible. Her swift sense of fun, her moments of dreaminess were eloquent of a soul in complete accord with its environment. David never saw Ka-aina swing her into a saddle, that he was not aware of her spirit quivering with freedom. When she gazed at trees, some inner part of her winged its way upward to poise lightly among their swaying, sun-gilded tops. Recalling how Patricia had stated in her letter, that the thing she anticipated with the greatest pleasure was the thought of arranging a brilliant marriage for Lynette, his heart contracted. Flying feet would be restrained to a walk, elfin laughter curbed, will-o'-the-wisp nature pruned until it conformed with old-world standards of what was proper and fit.

Watching her in the circle of singing men, he appreciated that there had never been any of the aloofness which a person might have expected in her dealings with these people of an alien race. They were fragments of Lani-o-akua, therefore precious and beloved.

Despite the happiness relaxing her limbs, a lawless air enveloped her. In a dim, baby way she knew her days at Lani-o-akua were numbered. Unknowingly she was jealous of every instant to be spent in this place of unfettered color, warmth, and beauty before she was snatched back to the restricted life and blighting cold of England. Determination to enjoy every possible moment of Lani-o-akua—which in sleep was wasted—was behind her stealing out at night.

The indifference of the careless figures about her to the demands of a work-a-day world, struck an answering chord in her. Her lifted face was like a cup spilling over with joy, but her tiny jaw was locked against anyone who might attempt to wrest from her a jot of this extra dividend of happiness. He smiled. In her was combined fairy and pirate.

Then, with a shock, he recognized in her expression the same extravagant love of her surroundings that he had seen in Trevellyan. A disquieting impression stole through him. Through Lynette, Hi-ball was loving and looking at Lani-o-akua again! The supposition affected him profoundly.

He hesitated, then retraced his steps to the house. Ruth was waiting impatiently on the veranda looking, for some reason, like her mother. He wanted to tell her his thought.

"Where are the children?" she asked irritably.

"I couldn't find them. It's warm as day. They won't come to any harm and when they're tired, they'll go back to bed."

"Oh, David!" she exclaimed, "Lynette's—"

"We mustn't interfere with her," he said quietly.

"What do you mean?"

He hesitated, then walked indoors without answering.

"Lynette, Ka-aina's going to take us to Makena today," Jackie whispered as they tip-toed along the veranda next morning. She nodded, glanced warily at Ruth's room, and went quickly down the steps. An electric current ran up her legs when her bare soles touched the wet grass.

They crossed the dusty road and entered the corrals, filled with men saddling horses. They called out to her and Lynette's face lighted. Going to Ka-aina, she took hold of his belt.

"Let me ride Nani," she begged.

"What for all time you steal my horse?" he asked teasingly, throwing a rope over the mare's neck.

Lynette looked at him without replying. He knew! Nani stepped like a fine lady, her coat flashed like wet gold, her ears were little alert birds sitting on the lifted curve of her neck. Ka-aina tousled her head, then got his saddle. He placed a blanket on the mare, fitting it to her back with quick, patting movements. Jackie smiled re-assuringly at her while he busied himself with his own mount. Ka-aina made a gesture of placing his saddle on Nani, then with a wide grin seized hers and fastened it on. Lynette smiled. It was a game that he played every day, but she was always afraid it might not end the right way.

Slipping his hands under her arms, Ka-aina tossed her up. Her toes found the stirrups, and she took up the reins.

"Ha! Look fine, Lineki, Nani swell horse," one of the men called, and she sat in silent rapture.

"Already you eat?" Ka-aina asked.

Jackie shook his head.

"Then more better *kaukau* with us."

Lynette smiled the far-away smile of complete peace. Beyond everything, she loved to eat in the long shed with the cowboys. The cavalcade left the corral. The roll of Hawaiian words, horses snorting, hoofs knocking against loose pieces of lava, filled the morning with a brave song. When they reached the long shelter with its wooden tables, thick white cups of steaming coffee, and platters of flapjacks, a muscle in the vicinity of her heart cramped. "Lani-o-akua!" she thought, "the best place in the world."

Na-lua-hini lifted her to the ground, and fastened Nani to a tree. Horses jostled one another, skinny dogs slipped between moving legs, and waited hopefully about the table. A fat Chinaman in a soiled apron came out of the cookhouse calling to the men to hurry and eat, because he had to slave in a hot kitchen all day while they loafed in the hills. Good naturedly the men returned his banter as they lifted their legs over the benches, and began helping themselves prodigiously, pouring tablespoons of rich-smelling, brown sugar into their coffee, reaching for fat pieces of salt meat, dipping their fingers into *poi* bowls, heaping flapjacks on their plates.

The naked backs of Lynette's legs tingled when they felt the smooth, wooden bench. Around her, men ate and laughed, dogs fought suddenly over bones tossed aside, the cook continually refilled cups. Windless, vast, the blue day went to meet the amethyst sea of early morning, lapping the shores of the island. Above the trees, hills climbed toward the summit of Haleakala which the sun was edging with quick gold.

Ka-aina reminded her constantly to eat, but she was absorbed in taking in everything around her; the way Moku always pushed his hat on the back of his head when he was eating, making you hold your breath for fear it would slide off; how Kimo drank coffee with rushing noises; and the streak of grease that would shine on Na-lua-hini's chin, no matter how many times he wiped it away with the back of his hand.

"Here's a fine piece of salt beef, Lynette," Jackie said, transferring a dripping morsel to her plate.

Lynette's slim fingers tightened upon it. In England people did not take the best bits of food off their plates and give them to you, nor could you take it up in your hands. Then she forgot to bite it because a hen with a rooster pursuing her, collided with the water trough causing a commotion among the horses.

The meal ended all too soon, but the adventure of going to Makena was ahead. The long, hot ride was freighted with interest; a *wiliwili* tree, covered with red beans, a gaunt sow with sagging belly grunting ill-humoredly at her offspring, cacti huddled like people on hill tops, horses picking their way down the rough trail. Ahead was the sea, which seen from a safe distance, always made her think of a wall, shutting out England. Behind it her mother and father moved, and there were governesses and nurses and days which were all rules. Rooms with high, narrow windows covered with close, dark curtains that shut in, instead of excluded, the gray cold lurking outside. In an excess of loathing, she spurred closer to her companions.

They reached the beach. A mullet flashed into the air, and dropped back into the translucent water.

"Oo, the dear, little fish. I bet it's having fun," Lynette cried.

"It's trying to get away from big fish that want to eat it," Jackie, the small realist replied.

Lynette tensed in her saddle. They jogged into a co-conut grove, and Jackie dismounted.

"Come on, Lynette, we're going to the Shark Cave."
He pointed at the red hill. At its base waves shook their
manes and pranced around it.

Alarm began to fill Lynette. Off Nani, she was closer
to the water—water that always made her feel empty
and breathless. Taking her hand, Ka-aina set off along a
trail skirting the base of the cone. Red, cindery slopes
shook in the sun and below, the sea tore its blue into
white against rough lava capes. An eel flew through the
air like a short dart, hurtling itself from a shallow brackish pool, where it had been basking, into the safety of
deep water.

Ka-aina stopped at a big rock with rough, pointed
shells sticking to it. Taking out his legging knife, he
pried a handful loose, scooped the yellow mass out of
one, and gave it to Lynette. She put it into her mouth.
It tasted salty and crunched pleasantly between her
teeth. Jackie and Ka-aina began filling their neckerchiefs
with them.

"Let me get some," Lynette cried, scrambling up the
rock. Ka-aina showed her how to edge the blade under
the shells, and pry them off with a quick movement before they clamped down. She was entranced.

"No *kaukua*, too many now," Ka-aina cautioned.
"After by and by we get coconuts for lunch."

Lynette drew a blissful breath, then recalled that before eating, she would have to go into the water. Suddenly, the hot day got cold, the red hill looked forbidding, but Jackie was leaping along the trail calling
her attention to everything. She kept close to Ka-aina
because the restless water swelled against the lava ledges

and dropped back, whispering about strange things.

"*Malama*,* Jackie, *malama*. No go too close," Ka-aina called.

Jackie nodded, and scrambled over a ledge jutting above the sea. Ka-aina picked Lynette up and carried her to the edge.

"What are we going to see?" she asked, trying to remember something that crouched in the back of her mind like a black spider.

"The Shark Cave," Jackie reminded.

"Long time before Jackie *akua* stop this place," Ka-aina said, pointing at the remains of a *heiau*.†

Lynette shivered.

"Look, look," Jackie said excitedly, "hundreds and hundreds of sharks, Lynette. Well, six or seven," he finished meeting Ka-aina's eyes.

Against her will Lynette peered over. Water, the color of aquamarine, swirled under the ledge and went with sucking noises out of sight. Then she saw dark, shadowy shapes drifting and gliding in and out of the submerged cave, half swimming, half lazing in the great lift and fall of the Pacific.

"Big fellows, aren't they?" Jackie said proudly.

Lynette nodded, her eyes fever bright. The shapes drifted, sank, rose, vanished, and re-appeared. One rolled over slowly, exposing the dead white of its belly. It was close enough to the surface for Lynette to see its eyes, set on either side of a blunt nose, and the cruel wedge-shaped mouth. Something tugged and pulled unbearably in her head. She knew. The fish looked like

* *Malama*—"take care."
† *heiau*—temple.

Jackie's god that she loathed. She hid her face against
Ka-aina's neck, and shuddered.

She walked on the inside of the path going back in
order to get away from the water; awful water where
big fish chased little ones to eat them, and sharks with
the faces of gods waited to eat people!

When they got back to the coconut grove, Jackie
went behind a tree and began pulling off his clothes.
Ka-aina unbuttoned Lynette's dress, and she felt small
and cold.

"Gosh, it'll be fine, there are no rollers today," Jackie
gloated, coming up, naked except for a bit of red cloth
tied around his waist and pulled through his legs.

"What's that red thing you're wearing?" Lynette
asked.

"A *malo*."

"Make me one, Ka-aina, with your handkerchief," she
begged.

"Girl no need *malo*," Ka-aina laughed.

"But I want to look like Jackie."

"You rascal kid," the old man laughed, tousling her
head. He pulled off the last of her garments, and air
that was like soft hands touched her body. She shook
herself delightedly. Jackie dived into the water like a
flying eel, reappeared, shook water out of his eyes, and
began digging into the sea with his brown arms.

"It's bully. Come on."

"I'm scared—"

"There's nothing to be scared of."

"Sharks!"

"They never come here," Jackie assured her.

Ka-aina walked to the edge of the water where waves

left wet arcs on the sand, and slid swiftly back into the sea. Jackie splashed and shouted. Ka-aina waded out, sand swirling about his boots like coffee dregs. Perhaps it was nice, Lynette thought dubiously. Jackie was having fun, Ka-aina wouldn't take her where sharks were. He lowered her gently, and she scrambled up his shoulder.

"No scare, Lineki, I hold."

She needn't be afraid, Jackie was beside her, Ka-aina said he would keep hold of her. He dipped her in slowly. Water ran up her legs like cold hands dragging her down. She screamed frantically, then everything went black.

When Lynette opened her eyes, Jackie and Ka-aina were sitting beside her, worried expressions on their faces. Ka-aina's hand was on hers, and she grabbed it.

"What kind *pilikea*, Lineki?" he asked tenderly.

"Yes, what did happen? A person couldn't be *that* scared of water." Jackie exclaimed.

"When I felt it coming up me, I couldn't breathe."

"No talk this kind any more," Ka-aina reproved. "I put dress on, then we eat nice *opihi* and coconut."

Lynette drew a relieved breath. Everything was Lani-o-akua again! Jackie went up a leaning tree with Ka-aina's knife between his teeth. When he reached the top, he cut among the leaves, and green nuts came bouncing down. Ka-aina showed her how to husk them, pounding the end that came off the tree on a stone until the fibre became soft. Then, bit by bit, he stripped the white threads away until the nut was bare. With gentle bumpings of the pointed end on a rock, he kept turning the nut around until the top cracked off like a cap. He lifted the fragrant water to Lynette's lips, and she drank thirstily. When she had enough Jackie and Ka-aina finished it. They ate *opihis*, husked more coconuts, and for desert had the jelly-like slippery meat out of the nuts.

A band of goats wandered through the grove, followed by a forlorn looking kid.

"Oh, the dear, little thing, I want it," Lynette cried.

"Mother *maké*.* S'pose you like can take home."

"Oh, Ka-aina!"

Jumping up, Jackie took the rope off his saddle and lassoed the kid. When the noose tightened about its neck, it bleated, but stopped when Jackie picked it up. When he gave it to Lynette to hold, she was so happy she was speechless. Ka-aina smiled and picked a tuft of *pua-leli*.† The kid ate its leaves with quick little chews, and looked around for more.

"Tonight I give milk," Ka-aina promised. Knotting the lasso about the kid's neck, he gave Lynette the rope to hold. Her eyelids quivered. Bliss beyond anything that England had to give!

"Now I think better *moemoe* Lineki. I go mend one fence. S'pose you scare, Jackie can stop."

"I'm not lonely, I have my goat," Lynette murmured, proudly running her hand over the kid's rusty coat.

Picking up the kid, Ka-aina placed it beside her. After a struggle, it relaxed and cuddled against her. She laid an arm across it, dimly conscious of Ka-aina and Jackie going toward the horses.

* maké—"*dead.*"
† milkweed.

When she woke she gazed at the dozing kid and sat up carefully, so as not to disturb it. The afternoon was breathless. An irresistible impulse to rid herself of her clothes seized her. Slipping out of them, she sat contentedly waiting for the kid to wake up. How sweet it was! She hung over it. A coconut frond fell with a rushing sound, and the kid leaped up. Lynette laughed and pounced upon it, making loving sounds against its neck. It no longer feared her and flicked an ear, then began sniffing for weeds.

"I'll find *pua-leli* for you," Lynette said, drugged with joy.

They wandered through the grove. Cool streaks of emerald showed here and there in the sea, where shoals of snowy sand from other beaches shifted with the currents. Waves broke with silver rushes among black rocks and piled lava. The kid investigated weeds, nipping at some, and disdaining others. Lynette watched absorbed. It was nice standing in the sun, naked. She looked at the long slopes rising toward Lani-o-akua. Its enchantment was upon everything, making the afternoon magical.

Despair pierced her which was replaced by a rush of resolution. When her mother wrote, commanding Uncle David to send her back to England, she would run away. Fortified by the thought, she fell upon the kid hugging it so hard that it snorted. She laughed and wandered on, her skin chanting a saga of freedom.

Hoofs crunching sand attracted her attention. She turned eagerly. Jackie and Ka-aina were coming back! But a strange horse and rider had halted by the trail leading to Lani-o-akua. The person was not a boy nor yet was he a man. He stood between both, his hair shining in the strong light. Lynette smiled, and he dismounted.

"Where on earth did you drop from?" he asked in an amazed voice.

Lynette looked at him thoughtfully. "Are you a prince?" she asked.

"Not by a long shot. Why?"

"In stories princes always have blue eyes and golden hair."

He laughed. "Well, you're going to have a terrible burn if you run around undressed much longer. Where are your clothes? I'll help you to put them on."

"Carry my goat," Lynette commanded, when he finished tying his horse to a tree. Tucking the kid under his arm, the young man started for the coconut grove, Lynette walking beside him.

When they reached her clothes, the young man tied the kid to a tree and picked them up. Shaking the sand out of her waist, he buttoned it on, held up her little pants, and she stepped into them deftly. After he fastened them to the waist, she held aside her hair so he could put her dress over her head easily. When the operation was concluded, she drew the kid into her lap.

"You don't feed it enough," the young man said, passing his long fingers over its thin shoulder.

"Ka-aina says its mother is dead. Jackie roped it for me. Tonight Ka-aina's going to give it milk."

Her companion nodded with warm, smiling eyes.

"Do you live around here?" he asked.

"At Lani-o-akua," Lynette replied, her face lighting.

Interest leaped into the blue eyes fixed upon her.

"What's your name?"

"Lynette."

"What's yours?" she asked, after a silence.

"Jim Lord."

Hostility filled Lynette's eyes.

"Do you live in England?" she asked, suspiciously.

"No, Lynette. Why?"

"Lords live in England. My father is one."

"I'm not a lord, Lynette."

"You look like a prince. I like you, but I don't like your name."

"If your father's a lord, what are you doing at Lani-o-akua?"

"Mother sent me to Uncle David for a year, but I'm not going back to England!" Her small face wore a look of determination.

"Don't you like England?"

"I only like Lani-o-akua."

He stared at the sand.

"When I left Wai-kapu this morning, I intended to go to Lani-o-akua. For some reason Uncle Walter doesn't seem to want to go there, though Mr. Birthwood invited us."

"Mr. Birthwood is Uncle David."

"I know. Uncle Walter doesn't know I'm here. I was just beginning to feel sorry about sneaking away, when I saw you."

"And my goat," Lynette reminded.

"And your goat." He rubbed the little creature behind the ear, and it began sucking his finger. Lynette looked disconsolate.

"It wants its dead mother!"

"Poor little brute. Wait." Leaping up, he started for his horse, and took a small tin out of the saddlebags.

"What's that?"

"Milk."

"Milk pulls out of cows."

"People pull it out of cows, and put it in cans," he said, laughing. Taking out a pocket knife, he punctured the tin and poured the contents into the shell of a coconut. The kid began sniffing.

"How did you have it, Lord Jim?"

"I often ride about the West Maui mountains and take along a small kit for making coffee."

"Let me feed it," Lynette begged, embracing the kid's neck with one arm and forcing its nose into the milk. It struggled and blew bubbles, then one knee hit the shell and slopped half the milk over Lynette's dress. Jim snatched the shell away.

"You'll drown it. Give it to me."

Soaking a corner of his handkerchief in the milk, he stuffed it into the kid's mouth and it began sucking. Wetting his middle finger, he let the kid taste it, then sank his hand into the milk. The kid nosed about, found the tip and sucked greedily. Lynette watched spellbound. When the last drop was gone, she grasped Jim's arm and rubbed her head against it. To her, because of the incident, he was hallowed.

"I like you, Lord Jim. You can hold it." She laid her hand on the kid. "When we get to Lani-o-akua, you show Ka-aina how to feed it."

"You're beautiful, Lynette," Jim announced, impulsively placing his arm around her slight neck. She smiled, and he kissed the cool hollow of her temple.

"I wish Jackie and Ka-aina would come so we could go," she said, fitting herself into the curve of Jim's arm.

"Where did they go?"

"To fix a fence."

"Weren't you afraid to be left alone?"

Lynette shook her head dreamily. The afternoon was beginning to die at the edge of the sea. Clouds waited above the horizon, like folded white wings. Wind breathed in the green tops of old coconut trees, and cattle wandered along the beach.

"I'm glad you're going to Lani-o-akua with us," Lynette said.

He bent his cheek to her hair. Sliding her hand into the crook of his arm, she looked up, then they stared at the beautiful loneliness of the sea.

"I hear Jackie and Ka-aina coming," Lynette said, after a long, close silence. "Now, we can go."

A tremor went through her companion.

"Are you cold, Lord Jim?"

He shook his head. His lips were smiling, but his eyes reminded her of Uncle David's which always looked far-away. The nice sound of horses coming closer, filled the grove. Jackie waved, started to gallop forward, then, seeing Jim Lord, stopped.

"Lord Jim's going to Lani-o-akua with us. He fed my goat milk out of a tin," she said, rising.

Ka-aina dismounted.

"Aloha. Which place you come?" he asked, smiling.

"Wai-kapu. Walter Hamilton is my uncle."

"Nice man," Ka-aina remarked but his voice had altered.

Lynette felt the jar. Ka-aina wasn't glad to see Lord Jim any more, and Jackie was put out. She felt bewildered. The sun was plunging toward the sea, spilling wild lights on the clouds, and the water looked so hard and bright that it seemed to clang, like struck iron.

"Carry my goat, Lord Jim," she cried, unsteadily. "I want to go to Lani-o-akua."

He did not move and looked as if, all at once, he wanted to leave.

"Carry my goat," she repeated, and when he did not move, she burst into tears.

He was on his knees instantly, and swept her into his arms.

"What's the matter, Lynette?"

"I don't know," she wailed, ducking her head into his neck.

"No cry, Lineki," Ka-aina said. "I think little tired. Too hot. Come too far. Better all fella go home. Here, I carry goat, Lineki. *Haole*, you carry Lineki. I think good you come. Lani-o-akua fine place. I think very late for supper. Maybe Miss Ruth *hu-hu*," he laughed. "This boy, Jackie, he seeing one small, wild bull and like to rope. Sure nuff he catch and tie up. By golly, Jackie, you swell *paniolo*, this time. I proud on you."

The tight knot inside Lynette let go. Jackie was smiling because Ka-aina had praised him, Lord Jim was looking at him admiringly. Ka-aina carried the kid. Lynette released her breath, and gazed adoringly at the old man. Ka-aina always made everything seem like Lani-o-akua.

CHAPTER XV

HAMILTON stood on the veranda, staring at shadows lying across Haleakala. Behind the solemn shape of the mountain, a full moon, like a huge silver bubble, sailed in the amethyst afterglow. Wind sighed among the tall Norfolk Island pines and rustled the cane fields surrounding the house like a restless sea. He listened for the sound of a horse's hoofs, but the road was silent.

When Jim had telephoned the previous night, saying he was at Lani-o-akua and wanted to stay, Hamilton, taken unawares, had an impulse to tell him to come home, then nerves snapped into line, and he said that he might remain. Jim knew he was at liberty to roam as he pleased through the West Maui mountains when his work with his tutor was over, but he also knew, though it had never been said in words, that his uncle did not wish to go to Lani-o-akua, or to have him go. Whenever Jim suggested that they take advantage of Birthwood's invitation, Hamilton put him off. It was difficult to justify his repulsion for the place without at least partially divulging the secret which still ate at him like a cancer.

The cook announced dinner, and he went in. Jim had stated that he would leave for home about four, but possibly Birthwood had persuaded him to remain and ride back by moonlight. Hamilton thought of the night he had spent at Lani-o-akua. The locality had been partly responsible for the one dishonorable act of his life, and now he was faced with the knowledge that it had lured Jim into his first deceit.

Against his will he recalled the months following his discovery of Patricia's unfaithfulness. Morning after morning he had marshalled his men to work, veins burning, the machinery of his mind held up. He had made the rounds of the plantation, fields blurring and spinning before his eyes. In a frozen way he had been glad that his wife was away on one of the prolonged trips that proved their incompatibility. As soon as he could command his faculties sufficiently, he wrote, confessing infidelity. And his wife obtained a divorce and maintenance.

He stared at his plate. Submerged in the egotism of despair he had moved among people in an unpeopled world of his own. There had been unbalanced periods when he plotted fantastically to wreck Patricia's life as she had wrecked his; he would follow her, kill her, blazon to the world that . . . Then the tired mind ceased to function.

When he had opened his eyes into consciousness, after weeks of brain fever, a trip away was advised. He agreed lethargically. Life was a flat, gray sea without horizons. But he wondered, with secret terror, if his will had been strong enough to seal his lips in delirium. He was reassured by watching people's eyes; conjecture, wonder was in them, but no surety as to what had shipwrecked him at the apex of life.

He spent six months with his sister in Boston. Dulled

as he was it did not take him long to see the grim antagonism between his brother-in-law and his small son, which caused the boy's mother anxiety and sorrow. Father's and son's souls, as well as natures, were in direct opposition. Barton Lord was material, Jim at heart a joyous vagabond. Because his uncle came from far off glamorous islands, Jim attached himself to him, and confessed that when he was fifteen he intended to run away and see the world. His spare moments were spent poring over atlases, pouncing on scattered islands, studying the noble shapes of continents, his eyes filled with the brave dreams of youth.

Barton Lord finally agreed to let Jim accompany his uncle home, knowing that if he attempted to keep him in Boston he would run away. Hamilton scratched at the table cloth. Jim had been with him nine years. From a boy of eight he was verging on manhood. The rhythmic jog of an approaching horse brought Hamilton to his feet.

"Have a good time, old man?" Hamilton called from the steps.

"Bully, Uncle Walter, but I feel a rotter sneaking off as I did." Gripping Hamilton's arm, Jim looked at him. "But you understand. Remember when I was a kid how names like Raratonga and Zamboanga used to make me feel? Well, the name Lani-o-akua did the same thing. Pulled me."

Hamilton nodded.

"I knew, for some reason, you weren't keen about my going over. Lots of times when I've been riding, I thought I'd slip off and see the place, then was ashamed to cheat because you're so splendid."

Hamilton winced.

"Sit down and eat, Jim."

Pulling out a chair Jim obeyed. "I was just on the point of turning back as I reached Makena when I saw a little girl on the beach with a kid. She hadn't anything on, and looked like a sea sprite. I got off and talked to her—"

"And?" Hamilton prompted.

"I dressed her because I was afraid she'd get sunburned. Then Jackie and Ka-aina came. I'd made up my mind it was shoddy to sneak to Lani-o-akua, but Lynette insisted on my going with them." He plunged into an account of his visit.

"Now, old chap, for a few details which you've omitted," Hamilton said, smiling. "What is little Lynette's other name? She sounds delightful. If she weren't such a baby, I'd be inclined to fancy you'd fallen in love with her."

"That's the funny part, Uncle Walter. Lynette's only a kid, but I loved her from the moment I saw her, the way you love high mountains and the sea, and at the same time she makes you feel like very early mornings do. If you met her, you'd understand what I mean."

Suddenly Jim laughed in a reminiscent way.

"When I told Lynette my name was Lord, she looked as if she would like to kill me."

"Why, Jim?"

"Her father's a lord, and she doesn't want to have to go back to England. She hates the cold and restrictions as I hated Boston."

An electric current, like a quick warning, ran through Hamilton.

"Lynette's other name, Jim?"

"Her father's is Lord Hawke, her mother, Lady Patricia, used to live at Lani-o-akua."

Hamilton had half expected it, but faced with the reality, felt as if he had walked into a wall, and broken himself against it. All the blood in his body crowded into his heart, suffocating him. Rising, he walked out of the room.

Gripping the veranda railing, he stared at the stars. Invisible tides ebbed and flowed around him. The black void of the night seemed an abyss about to engulf him, which was followed by a sensation of hurtling through space. The familiar contours of the Island no longer seemed friendly and close, the soul had gone out of it leaving it waste and desolate, peopled with ghosts that the years could not lay.

Gradually he recovered himself, but blood stung in his veins as if it had been mixed with corroding acids. Which course would be wisest to follow? To say nothing, or lay down all the cards? Perhaps if he told Jim why he hated Lani-o-akua, he would not go there again. He must send him away, where he would be safe from the influence of the locality and contact with even infant Trevellyans. It was significant that Jim—whom he loved as a son—had been finally tempted to go to Lani-o-akua by Patricia's small daughter.

He returned to the table. Jim sat, stunned and uncomprehending.

"Old man," he said, managing his voice carefully, "I'm going to tell you something that I've never told anyone."

The room throbbed with the mighty pulses of the

past. Jim waited, his eyes fixed on his uncle.

"For God's sake, Jim, forget Lynette. I loved her mother."

The boy looked amazed, then remarked.

"No one could be worse off for knowing Lynette."

"Perhaps," Hamilton retorted, and a thought came which made him clench his hand under the table. Perhaps Lynette was his daughter! No, such a supposition was improbable. Patricia would never risk her position with Hawke, and Hawke's world, by presumably adopting a baby whose origin might leak out in time. She would forsake a child as she had forsaken her lover.

"I know the futility of trying to live other peoples' lives for them, Jim. Each individual is entitled to his own experience, but Lani-o-akua and Trevellyans are not ordinary experiences. I know. Because I spent twenty-four hours in that locality and met Patricia Trevellyan, my whole life's been blasted. I won't go into details about what happened, but it bowled me over when you phoned last night saying you were there. I'll get your father to consent to send you around the world. After you've seen other places you'll forget Lani-o-akua, but if you stay on Maui, you won't."

"I'm keen to travel, but if you bundle me out of here, won't it look as if I'd got into a dirty mess?"

Hamilton meditated.

"I'd like to stay through the summer. I'm to play in the Inter-Island polo match in August."

"There's no reason for your leaving before September."

"I hope—"

"What do you hope, Jim?"

"That I'll be like you when I grow up."

"God forbid."

The boy looked at him thoughtfully, and Hamilton plunged into a rough outline of the countries he wanted Jim to visit. He listened, his face glowing. In a year, Hamilton thought, Jim would have completely forgotten Lynette. He was verging on manhood. He would meet other girls. After all, perhaps he had gone off at half-cock, but, he reflected, in a crisis it was always better to lay down all the cards. Nothing had been lost, and possibly much gained.

"Uncle Walter."

"Yes, Jim?"

"You wouldn't mind if I went back once before I go, would you? You see, I sort of promised Lynette I'd go back and see her again."

Hamilton placed his hand on the boy's shoulder.

"Of course I'll mind infernally, but of course you'll go, Jim."

David stood at the office door watching Lynette flitting down the avenue, bending swiftly and lightly to kiss each tree and boulder that she passed. She was unconscious that she was being watched. Her legs looked touchingly youthful when she stooped over, and her hair seemed to sing when she straightened up. Bare feet pressed the earth with passionate affection and when she glanced up at sunshine, slanting like long, dusty searchlights among the branches, a gay, flashing look of expectancy filled her face. Even Trevellyan had never loved Lani-o-akua as Lynette loved it!

He could not imagine the place without her. It would

be a crime to tear her away. He computed the time. Six, almost seven months had gone. When Patricia wrote recalling Lynette, it would be his lot to inform the child. He stamped down the steps. Seeing him, Lynette waved.

"Uncle David," she cried, scampering up to him, "I found a peacock's nest by the big pool with eggs in it. I want to show them to you."

Twining her fingers possessively about his, she tugged at his arm. They strolled up the hill. Studying Lynette in her scant frock, David wondered if any child brought up in the rigid discipline of an English nursery had ever had her mode of life so completely altered. Despite Ruth's unsleeping vigilance and attempts to mould the girl's behaviour along the lines she thought were necessary to one born in Lynette's station, she managed to eat with the cowboys, swim in water troughs if she were hot, slip out at night to prowl in the gardens, and leave garlands before strange stones that she believed were gods. The lustre of perfect health, combined with perfect happiness, lent a visible radiance to her person.

"If we go very quietly, Uncle David, maybe we'll see the mother peacock sitting on her nest. I wish Jackie and Ka-aina would come back from roping wild cattle, I want to show them the eggs too."

"Did you mind being left, Lynette? You're too small for that kind of riding."

"I didn't mind. I had Lani-o-akua." Her face glowed.

A little, tanned dryad, she slipped through the underbrush, then walked along the edge of the pool.

"There she is, isn't she pretty?" Lynette pointed into a thicket of ferns. "Do you think if I touched her, very gently, she'd fly away?"

"I'm afraid so."

"But I wouldn't hurt her, I just want to stroke her because I love her." Smiling, she tiptoed toward the nest. Uttering a shriek the pea-hen flew away. Falling on her knees Lynette crooned over the eggs.

"Would it hurt if I touched one?"

"No, Lynette."

With a rapturous intake of breath she laid a forefinger on the nearest egg. "It's still warm from the mother pea-hen!" she whispered, her face lighted with marvel.

She hung over the nest, embodying the very essence of the loveliness about her; she was the whisper of tiny leaves, the echo of the sea, the warm airs wandering about the garden. Then she turned sharply, as if her attention had been arrested by something. Her body tensed furtively, and her eyes widened.

"What is it, dear?" David asked.

Her gesture brushed him aside.

"I'm listenin', Uncle David."

"To the peeping of the pea-chicks in their shells?" he teased.

She smiled fleetingly, but the absorption of her face did not alter. She had a quality to her more disturbing than beauty, suggesting as she did, that she was linked to invisible realms.

"Often when Jackie and Ka-aina are gone and I'm alone—" she glanced up shyly, then seemed to think better of what she had intended saying. For some reason David felt bothered. Her attitude, face lifted, lips parted in a half smile, created the illusion that she was gazing at someone he could not see. A thought that brought moisture out on his skin, slid through his mind, but Lynette's untroubled face and serene interest made him dismiss it. Straightening up, she walked to the brink of the pool.

"Look at my Blue Country," she said in a far-away voice. "I used to be scared of water so Jackie made up a game. He said that in there," she pointed at the reflection, "is another Lani-o-akua. We pretend that when Mother comes to take me away I'll hide there and only you, Ka-aina, and Jackie will know where I've gone. And then, sometimes, when Mother and governesses weren't around, I'd come out and talk to you."

David was complimented at being included among the chosen few, but felt uneasy.

"Your Blue Country is lovely, but you mustn't forget it's only pretend. If you tried to reach it you'd drown."

"I know, but if I did go in and couldn't get out, I'd be *here!*" she said, triumphantly.

"Lynette!"

"I'm listening, Uncle David."

Part of her was obediently attentive, but her attention was focussed upon some object which had no connection with the words she uttered. Watching her, he felt as if he were running a race with confusion. There was a hint of impatience in her face, as if she wanted to be rid of him while she tried to distract his mind from what really engrossed her.

"Promise me you'll never try to get away—"

"Through the Blue Country?" she asked, when he hesitated.

"Yes."

"I won't. I know, really, it's water, but when Mother

sends for me I'm going to run away."

"And it'll be my job to bring you back."

"Do you want me to go away to England?" Lynette asked, flinging the word from her.

"Of course not, but it'll be my damn duty to make you go."

With a visible effort the child detached her mind from the object of its concentration. "Poor Uncle David," she murmured. Her eyes travelled over the tree tops. "I'm going to stay at Lani-o-akua. Mother can't make me go." Her lips quivered.

David took hold of her hands. He realized, despite her extreme youth, that a strength, almost appalling, was housed in the slight vessel of her body.

"Lynette—"

She did not reply, but looked around like one who has lost something precious, then freeing herself from his hold walked off. David followed her with his eyes. When she reached the downhill path she began running as if escaping from horror, or in pursuit of a treasure. He listened. Her footsteps headed through the gardens for the corrals. Horsemen were coming in, bullock carts bumping along the avenue.

He turned. For the time being Lynette was safe, but he must consult with Ka-aina. When the time came for her to return to England, she must never be left alone. A little breeze, so chill that it made him shiver, passed by. His mind searched back through the minutes since he had come to the pool, and he wondered where he had got the impression that Lynette had been conscious of a presence he could not see. Truly he had lived at Lani-o-akua too long. Was it affecting his reason?

CHAPTER XVI

"Hold it tighter, Lynette," Jackie ordered, as he rubbed his lasso with a piece of fat.

Lynette wrinkled the bridge of her nose. She was honored at being permitted to assist in the greasing of the new rope, but disliked the smell of tallow. Glancing up Jackie saw the aversion in her face.

"Don't be a weak *haole*." *

Tears filled Lynette's eyes. Seeing them, Jackie dropped the rope and hurried to her.

"You're not a weak *haole*, I was only teasing."

Lynette dug the tears out of her eyes with her wrist and took fresh hold of the rawhide. Jackie worked in happy silence, forcing grease into the weave of the rope, and Lynette's eyes examined rusted wheels and rotted leather straps hanging from the machinery in the mill. Castor oil bushes drooped in the sun, trees twisted their roots like gnarled fingers through cracks in the concrete, lizards whisked over the walls. Sunshine and peace brooded over the island and spread splendor on

* term of contempt used by Island children to whom the Hawaiian cowboys who take care of them in early childhood are the supreme heroes.

233

the sea that slept carelessly under the blue arch of the sky. Doves cooed, and a parrokeet whistled three shining notes, then darted for the summit of Haleakala.

Lynette's eyelids fluttered down like a drugged person's, and she inhaled greedily as if drawing Lani-o-akua into her. Her soul seemed to follow the curves of the land, and her hold of the rope slackened. Jackie looked up impatiently, then recognizing the far-away mood, he smiled indulgently.

"Lynette!" he reminded.

"I'm sorry, Jackie," she said, coming back with a guilty start. "I was thinking about Lani-o-akua and forgot I was helping you."

Jackie smiled a quick, understanding smile and looked around proudly. "You love it fearfully, don't you?"

Lynette nodded, her slight body expanding to make room for the acres she worshipped. Jackie regarded her in a satisfied manner, then asked forlornly,

"What'll we do when your Mother—"

"I won't go, Jackie, she can't make me!"

"You sort of scare me when you look like that, Lynette," the boy said. "You remind me of Kahoolawe." He gestured at the long red island, bleeding dust into the sea.

"I feel like Kahoolawe, all sore and spoiled, when I think about England."

"They shan't take you away," Jackie declared grabbing her hand fiercely with his hard, boyish one. "We'll run away."

"Where?"

He thought intensely. "We could go to Kahoolawe. Lewai wouldn't care if we stole his canoe. No one lives there, and we wouldn't be found."

Lynette considered the desolate island doubtfully.

"I couldn't help much. I can't paddle a canoe."

"I can do it alone," Jackie insisted.

"I'd be sad there," Lynette said slowly. "Kahoolawe looks like I used to feel before I came here." She dissolved in tears. "But I could *see* Lani-o-akua from there!"

"Don't cry, Lynette, don't let's think of horrible, unhappy things that are a long time away. Your Mother may have forgotten about you. Sit in the window and I'll finish oiling my rope, then we'll swim in the water trough, and go for a ride." Picking up the end of the lasso, he thrust it into her hand. "Pull hard, Lynette. Pretend I'm a wild bull."

Lynette's face brightened and she started for the window, then, a few paces from it, stopped.

"Climb up," Jackie urged. "Is it too high? I'll boost you."

Lynette looked at him reprovingly.

"He's standing in front of it," she protested.

Jackie stared at her. "No one's there."

Lynette looked unbelieving.

"Don't look like that," Jackie ordered, then his face lighted. "Oh, you're pretending!"

"I'm not. It's the old man," she whispered.

"What old man?"

"The old *haole* man who watches us while we play."

Jackie looked indignant.

"There's no old *haole* man here, Lynette."

"Don't talk so loud, he can hear you." She gestured at the window, looking embarrassed.

"No one's there, Lynette. You're crazy."

"But I see him!"

"You can't because—"

"But, Jackie, I do!" she cried, bursting into tears.

Jackie, upset as he was, stamped his foot, then seeing her distracted eyes, went to her.

"Why are you crying?"

"I don't know. Something's tugging in my head." The boy breathed unsteadily.

"He's going away," Lynette whispered.

Seeing her desolate face, Jackie took hold of her arm.

"What's he like, Lynette?"

"He's old and big and wears black boots and breeches."

"Maybe it's an *akua!* Let's ask Ka-aina."

"He wouldn't like it," Lynette announced.

"How do you know? Does he talk to you?"

Lynette shook her head.

"He doesn't say words, he talks—the other way," she explained, looking warm and shy.

Jackie coiled up his lasso.

"I don't understand. Let's go riding."

"Yes, let's."

"Maybe I can rope Nani like Ka-aina does." The boy made a pass with the loop as though snaking an imaginary horse's head. Lynette laughed, a gay, shrill peal that flew into the warm air like bird notes.

Lynette did not refer to their companion again and in the press of days, crowded with healthy interests and activities, Jackie forgot about him. Then one evening when Ka-aina was with them on the steps after supper,

Lynette whispered triumphantly,

"There he is, coming up the walk."

"Who?" Jackie asked, absorbed in finishing a whip-cracker.

"The old man."

Jackie glanced at the twilight-filled garden, drenched and sweet from recent rain.

"Oh, Lynette, there's no one," he protested.

Her face grew secret and closed, then she grasped his arm. "Look, there, near the *kukui* grove."

Jackie spoke to Ka-aina in Hawaiian, and the old man's face went a dead gray. Dropping on one knee he took hold of Lynette's arms with shaking hands.

"What kind you talk, Lineki. Tell Ka-aina straight."

The child looked at him gravely.

"I told Jackie the old *haole* man was coming."

"Wait, I no understand," Ka-aina said, controlling his voice with difficulty.

Lynette contemplated the garden serenely.

"He's there, on the lawn."

Horror crept along Ka-aina's limbs, paralyzing them.

"He's going out of the garden. Shall I run and stop him?"

"More better no! Maybe *hu-hu* if you make like that."

"He likes me—"

Ka-aina swallowed. "More better this time you two fellas go *moemoe*." *

"Is he an *akua*?" Jackie asked, gathering up the sisal fibre with which he had been working.

"Maybe," Ka-aina answered, glancing warily over his shoulder.

* *moemoe*—sleep.

"If he's an *akua,* why does only Lynette see him?"

Ka-aina pondered, then replied carefully in Hawaiian,
"Only those who are close to the gods can see across
into their country."

Jackie looked at Lynette, awed. From habit Ka-aina's
hands busied themselves arranging the folds of her kimono. After a moment, as if the words had been
wrenched off his lips against his will, he asked,

"No scare, Lineki?"

The child looked amazed.

"Sure, no need scare, this *maikai.*"

When the house engulfed the children's figures, Ka-
aina sat down limply. His limbs shook. Rumor had it that
Trevellyan's spirit roamed Lani-o-akua on nights when
the moon was in *ku.** For years he had lived in terror lest
he encounter the old man at some unexpected moment,
but time had slid by with never a hint or whisper across
the gulf, dividing the dead from the living.

And now Lynette saw him in daylight! Ka-aina knew
no one would talk to Jackie or Lynette about Trevellyan, yet her description, repeated in Hawaiian by
Jackie, left no doubt as to who it must be. He must talk
to David.

When he reached the lighted parlor windows, he
stood quietly. A shaded lamp lighted David's and Ruth's
profiles. He fought with himself, debating whether or
not he should broach the matter; then, unable to face
the responsibility alone, made up his mind to speak.
After all, David was not like the majority of white men
who would have pooh-poohed the thing as impossible.

---

* period of the moon when Polynesians believe supernatural forces
are in the ascendancy.

He waited. His voice must sound natural. Ruth must not guess that anything unusual was a-foot, or she would want to be in it.

A breeze shook the flowers, and he tensed feeling like a creature making its way cautiously along a perilous trail in the dark. Summoning his voice he said,

"Mr. David."

"Yes?" David replied, raising his eyes from his book.

"Somekind I like talk."

"Go to the office, I'll be along directly, Ka-aina."

He waited in the comforting light until David rose, then hurried to the office. Setting a match to the desk lamp, he stepped back. The familiar room steadied him, then he shuddered, recalling the passages of life which had taken place within its walls.

David came briskly up the steps.

"What is it, *makule?*" he asked, then noting Ka-aina's face, he frowned. "What on earth has happened?"

Ka-aina told his tale.

"But Great God!" David exclaimed in Hawaiian, pressing his fist against the desk. "Such a thing is impossible. Someone's been talking to the children about Trevellyan."

"You think Kanaka or Chinese talk this kind? All man scare Mr. Hi-ball now, just like before. No, sure Lineki see Old Man."

"There are no such things as ghosts."

Ka-aina's eyes locked David's. "You know everykind?" he asked.

David walked to the door. After an intense silence in which the night seemed to participate, he turned. He felt physically upset and completely confounded. Ka-aina could have no object in inventing such a story.

"But if no one's told her about Trevellyan, how on earth can she possibly know what he looks like?"

"Lineki is close to the gods," Ka-aina explained.

"Wait! I must think."

Tiny splitting noises filled his brain. He had recognized from the moment he had met her that Lynette was an exalted soul, close to the divine. When he did not speak, Ka-aina said earnestly:

"Lineki loves Lani-o-akua as greatly as Mr. Hi-ball did. Her love is the bridge for him to come over and reach Lani-o-akua again."

David had never loved greatly, but was sufficiently intelligent to appreciate the power of love in working so-called miracles. Dog's love for man and the answering love meeting it constituted a marvel, leaping the abyss between the dumb, and those endowed with the power of speech. Some unseen essence which both possessed, threw out invisible messages, unifying them and it into a whole. Might not a love as extravagant and selfless as Lynette's and Trevellyan's for Lani-o-akua meet and merge? Might it not fuse invisible attributes in them? It was plain that Ka-aina did not doubt that it was possible, accepted it, not as a common happening, but one in accord with nature's laws.

From years of association with Polynesians, David knew that primitive people were more acutely aware, more attuned to forces working behind and through nature. Crippling concepts of the universe did not hamper their minds. In them, as in children and animals, the subconscious was alert. The trance-like withdrawals, characteristic of Polynesians, a sort of obliteration or sub-merging of self into the whole, hinted that they were well-versed in the art of seeing and feeling life as a vast unit, both within and outside the perceptions of the physical senses.

From observation, he knew that primitive peoples appeared to have the gift of listening with their minds, giving heedful attention to nature's vast whispers, which enabled them to have a mystic communication with her varied manifestations. Wind streaming through trees, the joy of water leaping down precipices, the breathing of the sea had meaning for them. Ears undulled by the noises of civilization heard vital whispers. Might not other senses, unblunted by unnatural conditions of living, grasp intangible things? Might not their eyes, or the eyes of a child like Lynette, who was indisputably an almost perfect creation, see forms too fine and shadowy for less highly developed natures to discern? As an artist detects color and shadings of color in landscapes, unseen to the average eye, might not . . . David jerked up his mind, wondering if living so long at Lani-o-akua had made him believe that it might be possible for the living to see the dead.

Reason, logic, commonsense refuted the likelihood, but he'd had inklings at times that the universe was trying to transmit some message which—from lack of development in himself, perhaps—could not get through. He grew cold, his mind confused by the cold insistence of habits of thinking of which people such as Ka-aina were free. He heard the distant roll of the ocean, dew-drops sliding down leaves, the minute rustlings of sleeping vegetation. Voices everywhere, whispering some subtle language which he could not translate. Behind the visible he sensed an invisible world. Where one began and the other ended, how far one permeated into the other, no one knew.

"We'll talk further about this tomorrow, Ka-aina. I cannot think."

Ka-aina shifted his feet, torn between action and inaction, suggesting a person listening for orders which are not issued, then patience and unquestioning wisdom spread over his face.

"The breadfruit of the gods is not ripe," he announced, the words sounding like rocks dropped into a deep pond.

"I don't understand, *makule*."

"When the Ancient Ones and the Great Ones are ready, and not until then, will be known what this all portends," Ka-aina said in Hawaiian. "To pluck fruit from a tree before it is ripe is folly, and until events ripen man is ignorant of where or to what they lead. To attempt to know things before you are ripe to understand them, is folly, leading to interference which conflicts with the purposes of the gods. I felt that you should know that Lineki's eyes see what we cannot, because she is closer to Them than we are, but—"

"I understand," David broke in. "Lynette is not afraid and we, through ignorance, must not alarm her, but I do not wish her to be left alone from now on, if for no other reason—" He related the incident at the pool, which haunted him. "Now go and sleep. If we stay here too long talking, Ruth will come."

"Yes. She cannot understand. This is only for us two."

David's dry lips tightened. Extinguishing the light he

retraced his way to the house. He paused to ease the suffocation in his heart, then made his way toward Lynette's room. If Ruth came in search of him, he could say he was assuring himself that the children were in bed. He must be alone.

His hand closed on the doorknob. Suppose Lynette had slipped out. His mind recoiled from the thought that a being as exquisite as she, might have a rendez-vous with Trevellyan. Then he was ashamed. Trevellyan had created beauty and could not himself be entirely un-beautiful.

Opening the door he waited until his eyes adjusted to the dark. Making his way to the bed, he looked down. Like a flower cast by a careless hand, Lynette lay sleeping in the beautiful abandon of childhood. Repose so perfect stamped her features that his throat ached, knowing that when she left Lani-o-akua, she would never sleep nor look like that again. Her attitude, her expression were eloquent of her complete accord with her surroundings. According to accepted ways of thinking, a person seeing manifestations of the unseen world was appalled, but Ka-aina had insisted that Lynette evinced no fear and now the serenity of her face confirmed it. He noted the complete relaxation of her body, no rigidity of the muscles, no twitching, nothing to indicate that the child was in an abnormal or over-strung state.

That she was more highly developed than most, was undeniable; it was evident in her worship of the beautiful, in her capacity for love. To David recurred the memory of her coming down the avenue, kissing rocks and trees, and that, coupled with Ka-aina's assertion that her love for Lani-o-akua was the bridge for Trevellyan to come over and reach it again, shook him to the soul.

He recalled Trevellyan's wild, thought-provoking words, his assertion that he would come back to Lani-o-akua to try and find the gate he had failed to go through, the gate that led to God. The passion of his soiled and suffering soul for the locality had the divine, limitless fibre of Lynette's love, differently manifested.

Love was the most powerful, the most beautiful force in the world, wiping out self and thereby creating a greater self. Might not love, by its sheer luminosity of insight, if it were great enough, light up the misleading forms which the senses created, making them transparent to things beyond? Love, such as Lynette had for Lani-o-akua, transcended individuality, destroying the prison of self, putting her in touch with things beyond the perception of touch, smell, taste, sight, and hearing.

Lynette half smiled in her sleep, and he stood quite still, as if in a sacred presence. His head ached, he was incapable of wrestling further with the situation confronting him. Perhaps it was all a fantastic dream, perhaps living at Lani-o-akua was pushing him, all of them, toward madness. If he did not sleep, reason would snap. Going to the veranda he stared at the universe that seemed to withhold jealously her profoundest secrets, as though deeming mankind unworthy to share them.

In the morning he woke filled with unrest. From somewhere in the garden, a laugh, whose piercing sweetness seemed to mock him, reached his ears. Lynette, who would never laugh like that again when she was taken from Lani-o-akua! He went out to the veranda. She was squatting on the stone walk, rolling *kukui* nuts down its slope. When she saw him, she ran toward him, light as thistle fluff in the wind.

"Can I ride Makani today?" she cried, taking possessive hold of his arm.

"He's pretty big for a little girl like you."

"But he's so beautiful. Ka-aina said if you said so, I could."

"Very well, sweetheart."

In order to observe Lynette, David told Ka-aina and the children to ride with him. He watched her, as Ka-aina did. She poised light and sure on the bay gelding, chatting, laughing, then became lost in the green and blue beauty of the earth. Swift, intent, her body drank in sun and wind. When she turned her head, she created the illusion that she was listening to music too fine for human ears. But there was nothing disturbing about her. She radiated health, was interested in the mending of a water trough, in a broken fence which a wild bull had charged through.

Bouncing in the saddle she challenged Jackie to a race. He flushed, and his eyes looked as though a lamp had been turned up inside him. Through Lynette he had at last inherited childhood's rightful kingdom of love.

"Gosh, Lynette, you're fun. Sure, I'll race you. Want a head start?"

She cried out in disdain, and he dashed off. She pursued him, her bare heels thumping her horse's ribs. Ka-aina's eyes met David's.

"I know you think I *punipuni*.* You wait, you see I tell you straight. Lineki no like other fellas, but long

* *punipuni*—lied.

time before-all man like Lineki."

David gestured sharply. The old man's words stabbed, implying how far mankind had strayed from its divine heritage. He felt himself to be on the brink of some event which might shake his conceptions of the world into pieces. And yet it was an ordinary day; he was riding with an old Hawaiian and two children, islands drowsed in the sea, clouds drifted overhead, the world revolved on its axis.

Lynette and Jackie cantered back.

"I beat," Lynette cried, her face crimson with pride and exertion.

"Lynette's a real *paniolo*, Dad," Jackie laughed. "You'll have to give me a new horse so I can beat her next time."

David nodded mechanically, but his mind strained. The day went its appointed way like its predecessors. When they got back to Lani-o-akua, he rode up to Ka-aina.

"What you told me seems impossible. Lynette appears entirely normal. Sound minds do not see apparitions."

"I did not tell you Lineki was not normal," Ka-aina remarked in Hawaiian. "In time you will see that I have not been lying. Be with her all you can and—" He gestured significantly.

When David heard the children at supper, he went out to the veranda and jerking a chair back, sat down.

"Uncle David, give Nigger to Jackie tomorrow and we'll race again. I bet Makani wins, don't you?" Lynette cried, her face glowing.

David smiled. Melé came out with fresh relays of

milk and the children joked with her, as if she were their own age. He studied Lynette covertly. She was a trifle plumper than when she first came to Lani-o-akua and her fair skin was tanned a light brown. Her eyes had the clarity of childhood, but the wisdom of the ages was in them, the innocence of youth, and the dispassionate contemplation of eternity. He moved uneasily. Pushing back her chair, she scrambled upon his lap.

"Can I use your Sunday bridle tomorrow, the one with the tassels on it?"

He nodded, following the play of expression on her face while she talked to Jackie and Melé. Occasionally, or did he imagine it, she paused briefly as if giving attention to some happening about her and he wondered if, with the improvement of her physical being, there had been a quickening of other faculties as well.

"Come, Lynette, let's play by the pool till bedtime," Jackie suggested, crumpling up his napkin with a quick glance at Melé.

"Fold up, you *kolohi keiki*, I see!" Gleefully the woman grabbed for him, but sliding out of his chair, Jackie raced around the table, Melé panting in pursuit.

Lynette bounced on David's knee.

"Isn't Lani-o-akua fun, Uncle David?" she cried, throwing her napkin on the floor. Melé shouted in mock fury and darted for it, but leaning down Lynette flung it over the railing.

"Lineki, I lick you!" The woman tried to control her laughter.

"Go on, Melé, lick her. She's a bad girl!" Jackie shouted.

Flinging her arms about David's neck, Lynette buried

her face against him. Melé, her loose flesh shaking with mirth, attempted to drag her away, rolling her eyes at Jackie and David. Flinging a backward glance over her shoulder, Lynette beat an excited tattoo with her heels against David's leg, then suddenly became still.

"He's waiting to speak to you, Uncle David," she announced. Her words shattered the evening like smashed glass. David realized the whole situation was upon him and tried to postpone the moment.

"Who wants me, Lynette?" he asked without looking around, sparring for time in which to collect himself.

"The old man," Lynette answered.

Jackie started to speak, but David signed for him to be silent. Melé looked blank, and David addressed her in Hawaiian. She shrank back. David collected his faculties. His mind must register correctly!

"Ask him what he wants, Lynette."

"What do you want, *makule?*"

David fancied he heard a faint but audible sigh coming from below the railing. Lynette looked up, a bewildered expression in her eyes.

"Why doesn't he speak to you? I wish I had black boots that go high up your legs like he has. Will you buy me some, Uncle David?"

David's mind clenched. He realized that he was face to face with something enormous, on the brink of a shadowy borderline that lurked beyond the world of actualities. He was aware of Melé's horrified expression and of Jackie's interested eyes. He must act fast and coolly, keep his head.

"*Makule,* speak to us," Lynette commanded, impatiently, "don't just look. What do you want?"

David turned slowly. The garden was empty, but he had a horrid sensation that someone was there, watching them. Lynette leaned over the railing. It was the terrific truth! Lynette saw Trevellyan, was accepting his presence without question. He shivered.

"Are you cold, Uncle David?"

He nodded. Lynette's face, save for a slightly puzzled expression, was serene.

"Silly old man not to tell you what he wants," she remarked.

David breathed with difficulty. He had an upsetting impression that Trevellyan was anxious to be rid of him, of them all, in order to be alone with Lynette. His equilibrium tottered.

"No one's there, Lynette," Jackie chided, scowling.

"The old man is."

Uttering a stifled cry, Melé vanished. Lynette looked after her, non-plussed.

"Why did Melé run away, Uncle David?"

"Because you're talking to an *akua* she can't see," Jackie answered. "I wish my *akua* walked around."

"Your *akua* is half-fish. He would have to swim," Lynette laughed. "My *akua's* an old man. I wonder how he gets out of his rock. He's goin' away. Let's run up to the pool and watch him crawl back into his stone."

Jackie was enchanted. "Let's! You always think of nice things to do."

"Trot off to bed, kids, you've ridden all day," David ordered. "You can go to the pool some other evening."

Lynette's face fell and Jackie looked dashed.

"Oh, Daddy—" he began, then stopped. The youthful

pair exchanged quick glances. David saw the agreement in their eyes to slip out after everyone was asleep. Some inner part of him recoiled at the thought that an exquisite little soul like Lynette reached out to contact Trevellyan. Trevellyan who was half-rascal, half-hooligan; Trevellyan, who in his youth liked to pick quarrels with sailors and fight with longshoremen; Trevellyan, who had the vision of beauty in his soul and a cancer of evil in his heart.

"Uncle David, are you sick?" Lynette asked.

"No, Lynette, I'm tired. Run along and tell Melé I want to see her."

Pressing her fragrant little mouth to David's cheek, Lynette slid off his lap. David watched her and Jackie race down the veranda. His brain ached. He tried to realize that he had been an actual spectator when another human being addressed an invisible presence. When Melé had been interviewed and instructed, she controlled her tears and wiped her eyes on the train of her cotton *holoku*.

"No good Lineki have dead man for *akua*," she protested unsteadily.

"It's all right," David assured her. "Lynette's love is the bridge for the old man to get back here," he said, using Ka-aina's words automatically. It was the only explanation.

When the woman left, David sat inert. Dinner was ready, Ruth would come in search of him. He gripped the arms of the chair. He must get hold of himself. Nothing would be gained by telling her. Footsteps made him look up.

"David, you look ill!" Ruth exclaimed. "What's the matter?"

Going to the railing he leaned heavily upon it, debating. He controlled his face with difficulty. "I had no intention of speaking of this to anyone, Ruth, but the necessity of confiding in someone has overruled my judgment." He plunged into an account of what had taken place.

Ruth looked unconvinced and a little scornful.

"Lynette's a fanciful child. A person of your intelligence knows there are no such things as ghosts."

"To discredit ghosts is a sop to man's mighty intellect," David retorted harshly, "—but since time immemorial there have been records and traditions of ghosts. Man is too much of an egotist to believe that physical death is the end of him. He believes, wants to believe, or tries to believe that there are other worlds. Why cannot an ego swoop down on its old haunts occasionally?"

Ruth compressed her lips and then smiled.

David took fresh hold of the railing. "I'm beginning to wonder if the average person isn't like a blind man, tapping his way forward with a cane, believing in only what he touches at the moment, which alone exists for him. You cannot deny that Lynette's more highly organized than any of us. There may be revelations to a higher consciousness which a lower one is blind to."

Ruth gave a faint, lady-like snort.

"People have created a world, circumscribed by their own limitations, Ruth, just as creatures of more limited consciousness perceive the world within still narrower limits. No doubt our perceptions and conceptions are higher than those of a slug, but it would be a bold materialist who would dare to assert that the universe is revealed to us in all its dimensions. The consciousness of the average human being is bounded by height, breadth, and length, but the soul of man has never been bound by what may be called physical forms of consciousness. It's conceivable, isn't it, that in different stages of consciousness a person may conceive more of the world gaining knowledge which can never be translated through the medium of the five senses?"

"You're thinking aloud not talking," Ruth interrupted. "Your mind's become affected from living here too long. Come and eat something. You look as if you'd been talking to ghosts!" And she laughed.

"I sat by while another human being did."

"Stuff and nonsense. I always suspected that Lynette was a little off, and now I'm convinced of it. The absurd little creature has picked up these fancies from the Hawaiians. I knew no good would come of allowing her to run wild the way she has. From now on I'll see to it that she's kept within reasonable limits. Too much freedom—"

"I wish Lynette left alone," David interrupted. "We must not interfere in this matter. Lynette, perhaps because of her perfection, is a plank, or link, between this visible and the invisible world. She is the most exquisite—"

"If she were older, I'd suspect you of being in love with her," Ruth announced acidly.

A bitter retort sprang to David's lips, but he checked it. Ruth marched toward the dining-room with the triumphant air of a person who has scored a bull's eye. David followed silently.

CHAPTER XVII

DAVID leaned on his desk waiting for the mail. Each one brought Lynette's departure closer. Observing the child closely and constantly, as he had during the past months, he was convinced, beyond argument or doubt, that nothing was wrong with her. She was indisputably a being apart and, because of the extra dimension of her love, was freed of the prison of self, thereby finding a greater self which had no limitations. The conviction invested her with a hallowed quality that mixed his love with reverence.

Footsteps sounded, and he straightened up. The cowboy spilled letters and papers from his leather saddlebag and a heavy creamy envelope slid out. David stiffened. Lynette's summons! When the man left he opened Patricia's letter. He scanned it; a governess would arrive in two weeks. The bright day dimmed. He listened to the rushing, pouring sound of wind, like the voice of eternity speaking across time, then went to the door.

How could he tell Lynette? How would she take it? He looked at freshly watered flower beds, then at the insolent beauty of trees soaking in sunlight. Ruth tripped down the steps carrying a basket and shears.

"Patricia has written for Lynette," he announced.

"When does she have to go?"

"A Miss Mansfield arrives in two weeks."

"Poor little girl," Ruth remarked, snipping off a spray of orange lilies, but David fancied that she was not entirely displeased.

"It's monstrous to tear that child from everything she loves. If it were possible, I'd keep her."

"Don't take it so to heart, David. After all, it would be wrong to let Lynette waste her life here."

"Has yours been wasted?" David demanded.

"Why, David!" Ruth exclaimed.

"Lynette will never be happy away from Lani-o-akua."

"She'll forget it in a year, David. Children's memories are short," Ruth asserted, snipping off a second lily.

"Children's memories reach back into eternity," David retorted.

"For a sane, sensible man you have the most peculiar notions." Ruth laid the second spray of lilies beside its mates and stooped for a third. Her attitude gave David a curious turn. Telling Lynette would be like cutting at the roots of her life.

"Would you like me to break the news to her, David?"

"No!" he almost shouted.

"I don't know what's got into you. You do behave in the strangest manner now."

"I'm sorry, Ruth."

She snipped off another flower.

"For God's sake, don't keep cutting lilies while I'm talking. Can't you realize that I feel like a damned executioner?"

"You're making mountains out of molehills. Lynette

will be upset, of course. She's an unrestrained little creature, but think of her prospects. I wish I'd been the daughter of a lord."

Some fleeting expression in David's eyes made her catch her breath.

"I suppose I am, but Father treated me shabbily, you must admit, sending me away as he did, never publicly acknowledging me. But that's life," she sighed in a martyred way. "The ones constituted to make the most of advantages don't get the opportunity, while Lynette, who'd rather run wild like a little Hawaiian, doesn't appreciate her good fortune."

David flung off and crossed the road. Hearing voices in the mill, he headed toward it. Ka-aina was seated on a broken piece of masonry watching Lynette and Jackie playing. Lynette received her doom in white-lipped silence, then caught her breath.

"I can't go, I can't go!" she whispered, without tears.

"It's wicked of you, Daddy, to make her go!" Jackie burst out. "I hate you!"

"Jack!"

"Well, why must she? Write and tell her damn mother we won't give her back."

Lynette grabbed Jackie's hand, and their eyes met in a meaning glance. David wondered what they were plotting, and Ka-aina looked away. Dropping on one knee David took Lynette's free hand. The child closed her eyes.

"I won't go!" she insisted.

"You'll have to, dear. Cry and you'll feel better."

"I can't. I'm all burning and dry inside."

"We're going away for a while," Jackie announced

with childish dignity. David stepped back. He had no right to intrude on their grief, simply because they were children. Perhaps if Lynette was alone with Jackie she would cry. He watched them go out of the mill and wander across the pasture lying between it and the mausoleum hill.

"Ka-aina—"

The man turned.

"Follow the children."

"Better no this time, Mr. David."

"Perhaps you're right, but after this they must never be allowed out of sight."

"No make anykind for two-three days, but after—I, too, much scare."

David ground his heel into the earth.

White-faced and silent Jackie and Lynette sat in the shadow of the mausoleum. Behind them, cypresses and eucalyptus moved, and lingering raindrops from a morning shower fell to the earth. Sighing, Jackie edged closer to Lynette. With little jerks Lynette's eyes moved over the wind-ruffled sea, followed trees, mantling the hillsides, then rested with a sort of awful despair on an opening with horses grazing across it.

"Oh, Jackie, I love it so," she said in a hard, breathless voice.

"Don't cry, Lynette. Everything seems to stop when you do—" He dug his bare heel into the earth. "We must run away quickly."

"To Kahoolawe?"

He nodded.

"When?"

"Tonight."

Lynette looked around wildly, then with a stifled cry flung herself onto the grass.

"I want to stay here." She clutched at the turf. "I want to smell it, feel it—"

Jackie grew pale around the nostrils.

"If we don't go, they'll take you to England. You can see Lani-o-akua from Kahoolawe, and when your mother's forgotten about you, maybe Daddy will let us come back."

Lynette sat up and her face became still.

"My *akua's* watching us. Do you think he'll tell where we've gone?"

"Of course not. Maybe he'll help us to get away."

"I wish we didn't have to go tonight. Uncle David said the governess," she hurled the word from her, "won't get here for two weeks."

"I know, but Daddy and Ka-aina will watch us when the time gets near for you to go. They won't think about us running away now. If you don't want to go to England, Lynette, we'll have to go tonight."

"I guess you're right, Jackie, but I feel as if pieces were being torn from inside me when I even think about having to leave."

Jackie burst into tears.

"Don't talk like that, don't look like that. I think you love Lani-o-akua more than me, more than anything."

"Don't you?" Lynette asked, amazed.

"No, I love you more than Lani-o-akua or anything."

She looked as if such a thing was not to be credited, then dug her head against his arm. "I'm sorry, Jackie, but I can't help it. I love Lani-o-akua best."

He nodded understandingly, and his fingers blundered across her cheek.

"It doesn't matter, Lynette darling." He stared at Kahoolawe sprawled in the glittering channel. "It looks far," he said, "but if we start before the wind gets up, it won't be hard paddling. I'll steal food and hide it in the stable so we can get it tonight."

Lynette nodded.

"We better go back, Jackie, or they'll start wondering where we are."

They rose and followed the path leading along the crest of the hill. Once Lynette halted and glanced back.

"What are you looking at?" Jackie asked.

"My *akua*."

"We better put some leis on his stone. Wait—I have an idea. I'll give you to my *akua*."

"I don't like him."

"Never mind, he's a strong *akua*."

"What'll I have to do?"

"I'll cut off a piece of your hair and tell him he's got to be your *akua*, too, and you must give him something and maybe you better kiss him."

Lynette froze, then an awful resolution filled her eyes.

"Yes, I'll kiss him. I'll do anything that'll help me to stay here."

They turned into the avenue holding forlornly to each other's hands. As they neared the garden, Lynette's face lighted.

"There's Lord Jim, talking to Uncle David."

Jackie scowled.

"Why do you look like that? Don't you like him?"

"No, because you like him lots, but it doesn't matter,

because we're going where he won't be." His eyes rested on Jim's long figure, leaning against his sweating horse.

"I've come to say goodbye, Lynette," Jim said, striding forward.

"Do you have to go away, too?" Lynette asked, dully.

"Yes, Lynette, but I shall come back here some day to see you."

Lynette's face quivered, but she controlled it.

"Where are you going?"

"Oh, to Africa, India, Ceylon, England."

Lynette took her hands from his.

"I guess I'll leave out England," he laughed. "Don't forget me. I'll write to you sometimes."

"I've never had a letter from anyone. Do you want to say goodbye to my goat?"

"Of course." Smiling he picked her up, but Jackie scowled and she asked to be put down.

He set her on her feet and placed an arm about her.

"Are you going to stay for dinner?" she asked.

"I don't think I'd better—" Unable to fight the impulse Jim kissed her swiftly on the lips. She looked pleased and touched, then her eyes went to the hills. She caught her breath, swallowed, and rushed off, Jackie at her heels. Jim rose dumfounded, and David told him briefly

"Poor little kid," Jim said compassionately.

David moved as if stripping himself of a distasteful garment. "It seems impossible that a child can suffer so," he exclaimed. "The next two weeks will be ghastly. God only knows what Lynette may attempt."

"I don't envy you your job. You must feel like a hangman."

"I do!" He studied the slim young fellow, then said

impulsively, "Stay to dinner, won't you? It'll be no end
of a help. You, no one, can imagine how I dread what's
ahead, but I know you've an inkling of how much it hurts
to have to send Lynette away."

"I cannot imagine Lani-o-akua without her. I can't
picture her in a nursery."

"I've been wanting infernally to have someone to talk
to, Jim. There are things which have been bothering me,
things that most people aren't constituted to understand.
I hope," David smiled bleakly, "that you won't think I'm
cracked when I tell you—about Lynette."

"I'd believe anything about her. She has an extra something that stumps you, and at the same time makes you feel
sort of humble and half-finished when you're near her."

"You've hit it exactly. Phone your uncle and tell him
you're staying for dinner and the night. If I don't talk to
someone—"

When Jackie and Lynette saw the moving whiteness
of moonlight on sleeping grass and its intense glitter on
the sea, a strange exhilaration filled them which tingled
the hair on their scalps. Lynette held Jackie's hand tightly
as they tip-toed past the house. The boy drew her into the
kukui grove, snatching a rose off a bush as he passed.

"I want to give you to my *akua*."

"Maybe *she's* watching." Lynette glanced at Ruth's
room. "We better not waste time."

"It's not wasting time to ask an *akua* to help you."

Lynette shivered, pushed through the moist ferns, and
waited beside the black Polynesian god. Muttering in
Hawaiian, Jackie hurriedly cut off a lock of her hair and
buried it.

"You're smart as Ka-aina."

Jackie looked delighted. "I'm not sure if I said the right words, but give him the rose and kiss him to make sure."

Shutting her eyes, Lynette bent and touched shrinking lips to the cold stone, then fell back into the ferns. Jackie swooped on her, a suffocation at his heart.

"What's the matter?"

Lynette shuddered. "I feel like I did when Ka-aina dipped me in the sea." Sitting up she looked around vaguely.

"We must hurry and go. This is our only chance."

Lynette followed him unsteadily. At the steps she halted. Her face was devoid of emotion, but a dry sob wrenched her.

"Hurry, darling," Jackie urged.

"I'm saying goodbye."

She gazed at flower-banked reservoirs, at familiar lawns, at the stark whiteness of the mill, and the sombre island which was their destination.

"He's watching us."

"Who—Daddy?"

"No, my *akua*." She choked and rushed down the steps.

"What is it?" Jackie asked as they hurried toward the stable.

"He looked frightened and angry and sorry. He told me that if I went away he had to go too."

"Did he say so?" Jackie asked puzzled.

"Not with words. He talks—the other way."

Jackie nodded and dashing into the stable began saddling. Lynette wandered along the loose-boxes, and fell on her goat in a passion of despair. When she unwound her reluctant arms, the animal wandered off flicking its ears. Jackie pushed her clumsily onto her horse.

"Oh, Jackie, my home, my home!"

The horses were restless and uneasy, sensing untoward things in the night. The boy vaulted into his saddle.

"Come, Lynette, we must get away before they start looking for us. I hope Lord Jim talks to Daddy for a long time. They went to the office. Daddy told Mother he wanted to show Lord Jim some books, but really he wanted to talk with him alone."

"We can't go! My *auka's* standing in the gate," Lynette whispered. Jackie frowned. His horse plunged and shied out sidewise as he started through the gate and Lynette's mount reared, then sat on its haunches and balked.

"Lick Makani, make him go!"

"He can't go, my *auka's* holding the bridle—"

"Tell him to let go. If he doesn't I'll *hit where he is!*" Jackie cried fiercely.

Lynette gasped. "You mustn't hit an *auka! Makule,* let go!"

The horse plunged, ducked, and dashed through the gate. Jackie flung an uneasy glance backward. When they passed the mill, he checked his animal.

"I want to listen and hear if anyone's coming."

They waited, for the ghost of an instant, two desperate, youthful runaways leagued against a world of grown-ups. Satisfied that no one was following, Jackie released the breath in his aching lungs. Passing the mill and trees they emerged into moonlight so brilliant that it blanched the island, flooding hills and hollows with a tremendous white light.

"Don't keep hanging back, Lynette. Look at Kahoolawe. It'll be fun living there."

She nodded in a desolate way.

"They'll begin looking to see if we're in bed," Jackie said, and Lynette spurred up.

They reached the shore, finally, and rode into the whispering coconut grove.

"It's there," Jackie said in a relieved voice, pointing at the slender, dark shape of a canoe. "I was scared Lewai might have taken it and gone fishing." Dismounting, he unsaddled the horses and turned them loose. Lynette watched them heading up the long slope toward Lani-o-akua. "We've got to take the saddles in the canoe or they'll know where we've gone," Jackie said, removing the coconut leaves covering the boat.

"I forgot the water and food," he announced when the saddles were stowed away, "but I'll get coconuts."

He worked frenziedly until a dozen or more green nuts were collected. "Now help me, Lynette, like this." Stepping inside the outrigger, he took hold of the crosspiece and by inches dragged and worked the craft toward the water. "Shove harder, Lynette. It's heavy."

When a small wave broke over his instep, he sighed with relief. Lynette's hands dropped from the crosspiece and she gazed back at Lani-o-akua, her eyes heavy with longing.

"You're wishing to go back," Jackie stormed, "but if you do, you'll have to go to England. Are the paddles in?"

"Yes."

Waiting for a wave Jackie gave a last push and the boat rode free. He attended to the last details of launching, and signed for Lynette to get in. She leaped and fell headlong into the dugout to avoid touching the sea. Jackie picked up a paddle and standing in the stern, selected his course. Unrest filled him, born of the moonlight and their unknown destination. Lynette crouched in the bottom, staring at the play of gold and lead on the water. Aided by a light, land wind the canoe slid away.

For a while the boy paddled silently and Lynette huddled against the saddles. Water whispered stealthily along the sides of the boat, uncanny things seemed to pass in the air, brushing by like the ghosts of ghosts. Desolation settled on Jackie, but he kept his eyes resolutely on Kahoolawe, a dark blot under the moon. The silence of night spread over the world, broken only by the murmur of water all around. Jackie glanced back.

"There's *wa-naau*." He indicated the dim whiteness of the false dawn beginning to show behind Haleakala. "They're probably hunting everywhere for us now."

Lynette shuddered.

"Eat a coconut," Jackie advised.

"There's no rock to bump it."

He tossed her his legging knife. "I got young ones. They're soft enough to cut and have plenty of water."

Lynette occupied herself by husking the coconut. Light increased in the east, the moon changed from gold to silver. A breeze sprang up, sending little shivers scurrying over the water.

"When will we get to Kahoolawe?"

"Not for a time, Lynette. I can't make the canoe go very well, but we'll reach there before night."

Lynette nodded, but her longing eyes were fastened on the dark groves of trees, marking Lani-o-akua.

"Don't keep looking back. You make me sad."

Lynette dissolved into tears.

Dropping the paddle into the bottom of the canoe, Jackie crept forward and locked her in his arms.

"I feel as if I were dead, Jackie!"

"If you want, I'll go back." He looked wistfully at the peaceful reaches of the island behind them, "but if we do, you know what will happen."

"I know. Go on to Kahoolawe."

He resumed his paddling. With daylight the wind freshened, and the sea began breaking into caps. It was only the usual mild trade wind sea, but sufficiently alarming. The boy tried manfully to conceal his uneasiness. Ahead and on all sides rolled water bluer than the bluest cornflower that ever grew. Waves with glittering, metallic crests rose, arched, and grayed with a backward sweep into blue again. Jackie and Lynette had looked down on such a sea many times from Lani-o-akua, but seen from a distance it resembled an indigo sky, sprayed with pale stars. They had not heard the faint hissing of millions of breaking caps which were formidable seen from a canoe whose gunwales were only a few inches above the water.

Jackie paddled, watching the smash of spray on the shiny backs of tossing waves. Every so often one, greater than its fellows, reared into the air and with a roar rushed forward. Lynette watched him trying to force the canoe out of the course of wind and sea toward Kahoolawe, whose gaunt cliffs were beginning to slide past.

"I wish Ka-aina was with us," she said in a small voice.

"Me, too," Jackie answered. Back and arms ached, and he had to rest repeatedly. He watched the island and was worried, realizing that they were going by it. Ahead and far to the right, Lanai lay like a humped, purple whale in the sea. The wind would drive them between the two islands. He remembered Ka-aina had said that in the old times Hawaiians made trips from New Zealand to Tahiti, and from Tahiti to Hawaii. Then Tahiti would be the next island. He counted the coconuts and wished he'd brought more. He glanced at Lynette. She was sitting in a disconsolate heap, her eyes fixed on the dimming mass of Haleakala. He redoubled his efforts, working until his face was crimson in a last futile effort to head the canoe toward Kahoolawe.

"I can't make it go there, Lynette." He signed at the island. "Maybe we shouldn't have tried to come." He looked at the southwest where the wind was driving them. Empty, blue wastes of water heaved under the sun.

"Lewai's canoe is strong, isn't it?" Lynette asked, bothered by the trouble in Jackie's face.

"Yes."

"It won't sink, will it?"

"Don't be scared, Lynette. Our *akuas* will take care of us. My *akua* is yours too, now, and he's a fish god so he can make the sea still and when we get near an island—"

"What island?"

"Tahiti."

"Is it far away?"

Jackie nodded, his eyes full of tears.

Lynette shivered. Water talked to the wind and sky as it rose, sank, shifted, driving them toward the southwest with a lift and a surge.

Laying down his paddle, Jackie went to her and they sat close, their eyes fixed on red Kahoolawe which was falling astern. In the east Haleakala stood up like a great cloud. A wave threw a sheet of spray over the canoe, drenching them and filling the bottom of the dug-out with water. A stifled cry broke from Lynette's lips. Jackie bailed with an empty coconut then resumed his seat beside her. The sun blazed, lacquering the shifting blue of the sea with bronze.

"Lynette, you're afraid," the boy accused.

She nodded. Jackie blinked. He was not actively frightened, as an adult would have been, but felt cut adrift from every familiar landmark of his brief life. Placing an arm about her, he edged closer for comfort and felt more content and secure than when he had been at the helm. Silence, broken only by the hissing of millions of foaming crests, encompassed them. An occasional cross sea tilted the canoe, but the steadying outrigger prevented it from rolling as a boat would have done. Feeling the rigidity of his companion, Jackie persuaded her to look up, and the whiteness of her face shocked him.

"Don't be scared. We're all right. Maybe Ka-aina will come after us."

"I wish he would, Jackie. Is that a sail behind us?"

Jackie watched. "It's only a bigger wave."

"I'm hot and thirsty, Jackie."

"I'll fix us a coconut to drink, then we can lie down and put our faces under the saddles to get out of the sun." He commenced stripping a nut, and Lynette looked on.

"When Ka-aina comes he won't give us back, will he?" she asked.

"Of course not. We'll tell him why we ran away. I'm sure he'll be along soon. They'll hunt, and he'll find out Lewai's canoe is gone, and get another and come after us."

"Are you sure he will, Jackie?"

The boy nodded.

"But what if Uncle David comes with him?" Lynette

said, doubtfully.

"Let's pray to our *akuas* to have only Ka-aina come."

"You pray, I don't know how to."

Jackie bent his head.

"Now the praying's over, Lynette, let's go to sleep. When we wake up, I bet we see Ka-aina sailing up. He can make this old canoe go right. I'll fix the saddles like this. Now lie down and stick your head underneath and I'll lie by you. Put your face on my arm so it won't get wet. There . . . now we'll go to sleep."

CHAPTER XVIII

"BEFORE we turn in, Jim, I'll have a look and make sure that the kids are in bed," David rose and turned out the lamp in the office.

He felt eased from his talk, though it had been with a boy many years his junior. There was something sound and wholesome about Jim. He had listened while David discussed the subject which had hold of his mind, evincing no doubt of his veracity. More than once, while David related the incident when he had first realized that Lynette saw Trevellyan, he had felt as if no normal person could possibly believe him. The weeks and months which had passed since the evening had taken something from his consternation, but had not entirely removed depths in the fact that appalled. At moments while he and Jim sat in the office, he had presented a front of defeat. During their conversation he realized how often and how passionately his mind returned to the subject. Awake or asleep it possessed his thoughts to the exclusion of everything else.

They went down the steps and through the garden. The mystery of the island rose from the ground and breathed from the vegetation. Ahead, where the land

spilled to the sea, lay a vast dimness charged with moonlight, which seemed to come and take hold of Jim and
David against their wills.

"Just an instant, Jim, I'll have a look and make sure the
kids are in bed, then show you your room," David said,
as they reached the house.

"Righto. I'll wait here."

Walking along the veranda, a sensation of uneasiness
crept over David. The day, long and troubled, had left
its mark on him and peopled the night with threatening
spectres. In all probability the children were sleeping,
worn out with emotion. Entering, he saw Jackie's empty
bed. He had been so relieved at being able—for the first
time—to discuss the situation thoroughly that he had not
realized how time had gone by. But it was absurd to be
alarmed. Possibly Jackie was sleeping with Lynette for
comfort. He hurried to her room.

"They're gone, Jim," he announced. "I'm uneasy.
There's no telling what Lynette may attempt. I'll rouse
the men, and locate Ka-aina. He may have some inkling—"

Shouting for the cook, David sent him speeding to the
men's quarters. Hearing his raised voice, Ruth appeared.

"What's the matter?"

"The children have gone." .

"They've been gone before."

"Yes, but now they're desperate."

"They must be around somewhere. There's no cause to
feel alarmed. If you'd allowed them to be punished—"

David dashed down the steps. Of a sudden the still
night was filled with menace that seemed part of the
moonlight and sleeping earth.

"*Auwe, auwe!* This no good!" Ka-aina cried when

David roused him. "I think sure no make anykind till little more time to go away."

"Have you any idea where they may be?" David asked, cold with anxiety.

"Better look every place. Lineki little more crazy because she must go away. What for Patricia take? I see s'pose *keiki* saddles stop." He slid through the door into the stable and called back, "Gone!"

They consulted, assembled the men, and dispatched them on foot and on horseback. Gardens and hills echoed to voices calling out in the moonlight. Roused dogs barked. The silence of the night was filled by turmoil that seemed to spread out in widening waves.

By noon the great pool and all the reservoirs had been dragged, caves searched, lava flows combed. David was livid, Jim tense.

"It's impossible for them to have vanished like this," David raged. "The men have covered every foot of country for miles around. Of course we'll locate them in a few hours, but in the meantime I'm in hell."

Jim uttered a curious, smothered sound that made David turn sharply.

"What's the matter?"

"If anything happens to Lynette, I'll bust. I loved that kid from the moment I saw her."

The thought leaped to David, for the first time, that perhaps when Lynette grew up this splendid stripling might solve life's riddle for her. Jim's affection, or worship, for Lynette would survive the gap in their ages. His first meeting with her at Makena had a poignant quality which would make it impossible for him ever to entirely forget her, and the thoroughness with which he had suc-

cumbed to her spell, hinted that Jim loved her more
deeply than he realized. Perhaps, for Lynette and Jim,
splendid things lurked in the offing. The supposition that
comfort, happiness, and protection might eventually be
Lynette's, consoled David briefly, then was swept aside
by the gravity of the immediate situation.

He phoned sugar planters and ranch owners, enlisting
their aid. About one o'clock Ka-aina came running in,
his face gray under its tan.

"Just now Nigger and Makani come home. I look see
and tracks go to Makena. Maybe *keikis* steal canoe and
go away."

"Christ!" David said.

"More better go Makena quick. Maybe try and go to
Kahoolawe, but Jackie no very smart for paddle canoe
yet."

"Get horses, Ka-aina."

"One minute. I make somekind."

The old man hurried toward the *kukui* grove and
pushed through the high ferns, then a long, wavering cry
tore the afternoon.

"What in God's name—" David ran across the lawn,
Jim at his heels.

Reaching the grove they saw Ka-aina clutching something in his hand.

"Lineki hair!" he cried, his face distorted with grief
and terror. He displayed the black, silky curl, covered
with fine dust, and pointed at the shallow hole in which it
had been hurriedly buried. "No good, no good make this
kind. Gods of the water are not for her!"

He stood paralyzed, while a hard, brittle wind shook
the tree tops, then started for the stables on a run. They

rode the horses mercilessly over the rough miles to the sea, glittering and empty under the afternoon sun. Lurching and swaying, the lathered beasts surged to the water trough and for once were not dragged away. Those known to have canoes were enlisted to aid in the search and, shortly, a small armada of slender boats spread out, fan-wise, dotting the sea.

David, Jim, Lewai, and Ka-aina manned the largest. Paddles dipped and flashed, arms and shoulders were tense, faces strained. Silence came down from the clouds to fight with the wide hissing whisper of the sea. Mountains and islands looked withdrawn as if making it evident that they had had no part in the catastrophe. The direction of the wind and send of the sea were carefully estimated and the approximate drift of a canoe, inexpertly manned, computed.

"If anything happens to Lynette, if anything happens to Lynette," Jim kept repeating, under his breath, until David looked angrily at him. The boy's despair was an affront because it was focussed entirely on one of the runaways.

"There's Jackie to be thought of, too," David reminded, but Jim did not appear to hear.

He knelt in the bows, blue eyes sweeping the heaving Pacific, his fine long figure, charged with youth and force, silhouetted against the future in some subtle way and magnified to heroic proportions by the water. The sun fell toward the west. The canoe dipped and lifted. Paddles flashed, vanished, and flashed again. David worked mechanically, but with the passage of minutes his face grew old and, the last of youth was wiped from his eyes. Just as the sun was dipping toward the sea, a black speck lifted briefly against the reddening west.

Jim turned, and David and Ka-aina looked at each other. Lewai gave a shout. The canoe was a couple of miles ahead, drifting aimlessly, sagging into hollows, lifting on swells, seen, and lost the next instant. In silence they paddled to overtake it, David forcing his tired, gritty eyes to search the highly colored, shifting expanse ahead.

Thoughts streamed through his mind and he fancied that he heard all the years which had gone into the making of Lani-o-akua crashing into space. Wind and sun seemed wrapped tightly about him, and water screamed and called in his head. Fragmentary pictures of Lynette flitted before him, her face, the passion of freedom that always enveloped the bare backs of her legs, the quick turn of her head to catch sounds too faint for other ears, her eyes filled and brimming with Lani-o-akua, hair dancing in lordly winds sweeping down from Haleakala. He must send her from it all!

Dusk stole over the sea, killing its blue. Jim stood up in the bows and uttered a great cry,

"The canoe's empty!"

David felt as if he had been smashed in the face with a club, and Ka-aina's shoulders crumpled, then he squared them and dug his paddle viciously into the sea. David's eyes, bleak and hard, swept the slender black shape ahead. It was guiltless of small figures, working frantically to escape. This, this then, was the end of it all!

"Maybe," Ka-aina choked, tears coursing down his battered cheeks, "maybe *akuas* think better this way?"

In the middle of the canoe, two saddles were heaped, the pommels resembling turtles' heads against the afterglow. Leaping overboard, Jim swam through the shifting sea, grasped the outrigger, and heaved himself aboard. Then his voice came like a clarion,

"They're sleeping!"

Like a bird swooping to protect its young, he bent and lifted Lynette while Jackie's touselled head heaved into view. Half a dozen brisk strokes brought the pursuing canoe abreast. Lynette struggled like a mad thing to break from the hold of Jim's arms.

"Lynette, Lynette," he said.

"I don't want you," she sobbed, her eyes sweeping the figures in the boat, then seeing Ka-aina she reached out her slim arms. "Ka-aina! I want to go to Ka-aina!" she cried.

"Give, give!" he commanded.

Lynette thrust Jim from her, casting a wild, frightened look at the sea, then scrambled into the old Hawaiian's arms. The realization came to David that there was, and would always be, only one thing on earth for Lynette— Lani-o-akua and the things of Lani-o-akua.

"Lineki, Lineki, child of my heart," Ka-aina murmured, wiping his wet cheek against her hair.

Jackie smiled in a pleased, dazed way.

"I told you, Lynette, that Ka-aina would come."

She nodded, and clung fiercely to the old man's neck.

"No scare, Lineki, no scare. Everykind all right. I take care."

At the last words her eyes flew to his, then she crumpled against his breast.

PART IV

THE GATE

CHAPTER XIX

LYNETTE sat listlessly in a high-backed chair. Outside a gusty wind swirled dead leaves against the house. Her limbs felt weighted and her temples bound. She shrank with all the sensitiveness of sixteen, from contemplating the pending interview with her mother. It seemed as if a crowd of invisible and violent forces were stirring in her, like armed men assembling for battle. What did this unexpected visit mean? Her mother was on the eve of a year's cruise around the world and it was unheard-of for her to leave London at such a time.

At Christmas and for a fortnight in summer her parents visited the manor. She was never at ease with them and always felt relieved when they left. For her father she had admiration which never quite succeeded in becoming love, but for her mother, only antagonism because she had torn her from Lani-o-akua.

For nine years she had lived with Miss Mansfield. The woman was well-born and intelligent. At first the utter desolation of her small charge confounded her, making her more lenient than she might otherwise have been, and their status continued to be that of friends, rather than pupil and instructress.

In the winter Miss Mansfield rode to hounds with Lynette, and because the woman had been at Lani-o-akua, Lynette was fonder of her than might have been expected. When Patricia's note had arrived, announcing she would follow on the heels of it, both pupil and teacher had been perplexed and apprehensive.

Rising, Lynette went to the window and drew aside the heavy hangings. The icy road was empty, bare branches were silhouetted against a leaden sky, faintly washed with pale lemon in the west, where a winter sunset was dying with untimely haste behind low dark hills. Lynette felt akin to the trees, bereft of beauty, frozen. Since she had been taken from Lani-o-akua, she had never felt really warm. Damp cold that had crouched for centuries in corners and cupboards of the vast old manor would not be ousted by quick, insufficient summers that ran hurriedly to their end. Central heating, recently installed, was a myth that left halls tepid, and plunged you into the agonizing discomfort of rooms, intentionally left out of the heating system lest bodies become weakened and unhealthy from the supposed luxury.

The inarticulate, unreasoning impatience of youth swept Lynette. These folk, among whom she had been born and must, perforce, for the time being stay—but to whom she would never belong in spirit—seemed to glory in discomfort, and wear it as a mark of distinction. Her sense of beauty recoiled from purple ears, blotched wrists, and mottled fingers. When men and women assembled for hunts, rubbing their hands and extolling the weather, she wanted to laugh aloud. Beneath their suits and habits there were unsightly woolens encasing bodies and limbs; garments that became grotesque when you hurriedly dis-

robed, garments worn as a protection against the very
discomfort of insufficiently heated rooms of which these
people made a fetish. Her own skin, fine and sensitive,
pricked and crawled under Scotland's finest weaving,
irritated, smothered, clamoring to be free, to breathe.

She regarded her surroundings with childish animosity;
heavy rugs, panelled oak walls, velvet hangings, crystal
chandeliers reflecting light from an inadequate fire, burning under a marble mantel. It did not deceive her by its
suggestion of warmth. She knew. When you touched the
mantel it was barely warm, when you stood by the fire,
above your knees there was no heat. She was tired of moving cautiously lest air like chilly fingers thrust slyly
around wrists and ankles, mocking the protection afforded by uncomfortable garments encasing you like an
unsightly skin. Doorhandles were so cold you winced
when you had to touch them, beds heated by warming
pans had chilly places around the edges that bit at you unexpectedly when you moved. Perhaps there were three
days in summer when you dared to stretch and feel all
your body, and then you could not be sure that your skin
might not be tormented by an unforseen chill lurking in
some unexpected quarter. Her flesh had not been warmed
through once during the nine years since she had left
Lani-o-akua, and a sort of dead cold slept in her bones
that nothing could thaw out.

When people exclaimed at the warmth her face became
secret and closed. They did not know warmth, who had
never been at Lani-o-akua. When some landscape, or
the beauty of a sunset was remarked, she was still. They
did not know beauty, who had never seen the beauty of
Lani-o-akua which summoned humans to fall down and

worship at its feet. They had never watched a sunset, who had not seen the falling sun clanging against the proud, blue Pacific that wore islands, like blossoms, on its breast! Her still face flushed, and the impression she always created, of being encased in wax, dropped away. A pale radiance emanated from her slight body and her eyes, which were the key to and the veil of her soul, brimmed. Then force, like an electric current, ran through her and she projected her mind across seas and continents, surrendering her soul to the spell of Lani-o-akua. Her nostrils remembered the reek of well-greased lassos, flowers dying around straw hats. Her ears heard laughing voices calling out resounding words and singing roguish songs. Her eyes saw dawns breaking behind the rich foliage of tropic trees, and islands materializing out of the sea, as on the first day of creation. "Oh God, help me, help me to get back!" she whispered. Shadowy figures moved like ghosts in her mind; Ka-aina, Jackie, Nalua-hini, Chinamen eternally raking lawns. It was characteristic that it was not individuals, but the whole, that she wanted.

Footsteps came down the hall. Her face lost its passionate expression and became a mask in which only the eyes lived. She wondered if her mother had arrived without her hearing wheels on the ice-encrusted drive. The great brass knob turned, and Miss Mansfield entered. Her bony, but not entirely displeasing, typical English figure, was assembled inside a tight, blue dress of heavy cloth, like a regiment drawn up to withstand attack. From the way she held herself, Lynette knew she was apprehensive, perhaps wondering if she had failed to satisfy Patricia in the preparation of her daughter to take her place in the glittering London world. Lynette smiled. Her début, two years away, would never take place. One way or another, before then, she would contrive . . .

"Word has come, Lynette, that your mother will not arrive until after dinner." Miss Mansfield appeared on the verge of adding more, then checked herself.

They ate in the high, impossibly cold dining-room, while wind whimpered and prowled around the house. Lynette was irritated by the maids' careful, lowered voices, and when they vanished, she turned.

"Why do English servants always whisper as if something indecent had just happened in the house? At Lani-o-akua everyone joked with you while they worked."

Miss Mansfield's color heightened, but she looked faintly amused. Lynette occupied herself with food, then, conscious that she was being observed, suffocation filled her. Something vital was afoot. When the maids took away the meat course, she looked up.

"Do you know something you're not telling me?"

Patches of red appeared in Miss Mansfield's thin, wind-bitten cheeks. "I've been instructed not to inform you of the reason for your mother's visit."

"Whatever Mother's planning, is just planning, because I'm going back."

The woman's face lost its thoughtful expression and compassion made it briefly beautiful. "Dear child, you haven't the means to accomplish the trip to Lani-o-akua for one thing and for another—"

"Lord Jim will help me when he gets here. In his last letter—"

"I shouldn't have permitted you to correspond with him, Lynette, but when he first wrote, you were such a tragic, forlorn little object that it seemed brutal to deny you the comfort of occasionally hearing from someone connected with Lani-o-akua."

"He wasn't really, he was only there twice, but he understands how I feel about it, how I love it. No one at Lani-o-akua has ever written to me, and hearing from Lord Jim was next best. I've liked getting letters from far-away, beautiful places where he's been. They seemed like stepping stones back to Lani-o-akua."

"Is he," Miss Mansfield's hands, those of an unfulfilled woman, fast drying up, moved nervously, "in love with you, Lynette?"

"Of course Lord Jim's not in love with me. I love him because he's beautiful, the same kind of feeling you have, well, for trees and islands and great clouds. You know, as if something inside you rushed to meet them. If he hadn't been at Lani-o-akua with us," her voice sank to a whisper, "I wouldn't have read or answered his letters."

"I've been worried for fear you might care for each other and, under the circumstances—" Miss Mansfield broke off, flustered.

"What do you mean?" Lynette asked

Miss Mansfield took a mental hurdle.

"Your mother stated that I was not to inform you of her reason for this visit, but I feel you should be warned, or at least partially prepared. A Danish prince, whose name your mother did not disclose, has approached your parents regarding you." The woman broke off, moistening her dry lips with her tongue.

"Go on."

"It seems he saw you riding in the hunt last week when he motored by and asked who you were. He wishes to meet you with the object of marrying you."

"Me!" Lynette exclaimed, her face incredulous.

"It appears he was so impressed by your appearance that he called on your parents and they, naturally, appreciated the honor of having a man of his rank—"

"Is he coming with Mother?"

"I don't know."

Wheels crunching gravel and ice startled them. Lynette rose. She always felt breathless at the prospect of seeing her mother, and was eager to postpone the moment.

"I'll wait upstairs until she sends for me. It was nice of you to warn me. I won't give you away, Miss Mansfield. Mother thinks because she is strong that she can make everyone do exactly as she wants. But she can't make me because, you see, when I had to go away from Lani-o-akua, Ka-aina told me that God promised that I would come back."

"Now send Lynette down," Patricia said.

Miss Mansfield inclined her head. Despite her effort to appear unmoved, it was obvious she was deeply shocked. Patricia smiled sardonically. The prerogative of ancient virgins! When the door closed on Miss Mansfield's spare figure, she relaxed.

Her beauty had increased rather than diminished, and she possessed an unthinking composure which arrested attention and left a person vaguely uncomfortable, the composure of a woman whose every ambition has been fulfilled. Her hand went to the dull gold knot of hair, coiled on her neck, and her long fingers touched it lightly, then fell back and rested on the wide arm of the chair. She was impatient to see Lynette, anxious to assure herself that the girl, seen under close and critical inspection, would be as breath-taking as glimpsed on a horse.

She had been astounded the previous afternoon when she was informed that Prince Axel was calling and wanted to see her on a private and pressing matter. They had met at court, danced a few times. He was unforgettable. The extraordinary pallor of his skin suggested that he had lived in dark cellars or under water of great depth. He was tall, but his strength did not suggest the healthy vigor of an out-of-doors man. You pictured him bending over cushion-piled couches and reclining feminine forms and yet, actually, he was internationally famed as a sportsman. He was also socially prominent in all the capitals of Europe. His fortune was fabulous. Sufficiently close to the royal family of Denmark, yet not in direct line for the throne, he was at liberty, technically, to marry as he chose. Yet he had never married. Undoubtedly he had mistresses. He was forty or thereabouts. His advent in any capital was an occasion for lavish entertainment. Matrons had dangled daughters before him, unsuccessfully, for twenty years.

Patricia glowed. When he had been ushered into her private drawing-room, she had been struck afresh by his coloring, or lack of it. Despite the fact that he was recently returned from India, his skin retained its dead whiteness and his ash-blond hair, smartly brushed back from the temples, gave the impression that he was entirely hairless.

The interview had been brief, courtly, and to the point. He had seen Lynette, made inquiries to find out who she was, and desired to meet her with the object of marrying her if she proved as lovely as she had looked on a horse. Patricia's color had mounted. It seemed incredible that with a world of women to choose from, his fancy should have lighted on her daughter for whom she had always planned a brilliant match. She had intended to manage a young Earl or Duke, but it went with the rest of her life that, without so much as raising a finger, a prince should come and ask for Lynette.

While they talked she attempted to estimate his character. Some untoward quality lurked behind his pale eyes, whose coldness remotely shocked her, but he was rich, highly born, a remarkable match for any girl. She had concealed her satisfaction, stated that Lynette, as yet, was only sixteen. In two years she would be presented. Then she waited.

"Is there anything to prevent my meeting her?" Axel had asked. "Have you any objection to our being betrothed until she is of age?"

Patricia appeared to give the matter deep consideration. It was evident that Axel was completely obsessed by his glimpse of Lynette. "I can arrange, I think, for you to see her, but I will have to consult with my husband, of course."

"Do not make me wait too long. I have been unable to sleep or eat for the past forty-eight hours."

Instinct told Patricia that Hawke would not be in favor of this match though he would, of course, appreciate its worldly advantages. To have their daughter affianced to a prince before she was out of the nursery would be an achievement. She broached the subject that evening while she and Hawke were driving to a banquet. Hawke protested that Lynette was too young to be betrothed. Sixteen! Patricia had remarked dryly, that other girls had been married and mothers at sixteen. Hawke

was silenced, then announced bluntly that he disliked the
Dane. Patricia asked for reason. "Actually, I know nothing to his discredit, but I've an idea the beggar's not
savory, despite the fact that he's managed to keep his
reputation intact." "A man can't live to be forty and remain a saint," Patricia had retorted. Hawke glanced at her
and took her hand. The fire lighted between them at Lani-
o-akua had burned through the years with undiminished
force. Her hot blood flamed when she looked at his profile, the lift of his chin. Black eyes and blue swept together and fused. It ended by Hawke consenting to allow
Axel to see Lynette. Patricia had been elated, but received
a severe jolt when Hawke announced, from some depth,
baldly as one of his sailors might have, that to him the
whole business stunk.

She shifted in her chair. What detained Lynette? Axel
was waiting in the library consumed with impatience. A
suspicion that Miss Mansfield might be warning her of
what was in store for her, made Patricia sit erect. To a
woman of Miss Mansfield's type it would be nothing
short of indecent to think of consigning a young girl to
a man of Axel's kind. Hearing approaching footsteps,
Patricia sank with studied negligence against the back of
her chair.

Lynette entered. They greeted each other formally,
and Patricia told Lynette to sit down, but she was swept
away by the girl's appearance. In a blue frock that just
missed being gray, hollowed slightly at the neck and
frilled with white lawn, with full sleeves to the elbow,
which allowed her slim arms to escape, Lynette looked as
alluring as the thin blue behind a high mountain. At once
entrancing and unattainable. Her large, blue eyes were

grave and aloof and, from the moment she came in, they never moved from her mother's face.

Despite her quietness, Patricia suspected Lynette was on the defensive. She must approach her subject carefully. There was never any telling what this silent girl might do. While appearing to give her entire attention to what her mother was saying, Patricia suspected that Lynette's mind was focussed on something else. Was she meditating rebellion, or did she appreciate the advantages of such a match?

There was something wild and sweet about her, something un-English. Her mouth, dewy and unfinished, matched her dreamy eyes, but the strength of her chin, delicate and deft, gave lie to the suggestion of extreme, helpless youth which enveloped her like a cloak. She had an air of being able to vanish in an instant, she would remain virginal even after she was married, and that quality would inflame a man like Axel. Her withdrawn air hinted at a sort of spiritual valor that nothing could affect. Once, while Patricia was speaking, Lynette smiled fleetingly. Patricia was irritated. Lynette possessed some attribute that put her forever out of reach. When she moved, even slightly, the elusive sweetness of rain-drowned flowers enveloped her. She sat on a stool, close to the fire, spreading her white hands to it. Outside, a speculative wind fingered the corners of the house, and Lynette lifted her head as if listening for a voice she longed to hear.

What did this child know that she never put into words? What occupied her mind to the exclusion of everything else? Her eyes seemed to swim under their long lashes, but their depths were serene as if something within her was always intact. Sunshine was in her eyes and sun-drenched landscapes, strong and still. Patricia wondered, and wondered what brought the thought, if Lynette was thinking of Lani-o-akua. It was not likely. She had never once referred to it, nor spoken the name since she had been taken from it. That she had been impossibly affected at the time, and for months afterwards, Patricia knew.

"What a lovely thing she is," the woman thought. "Quite incredible."

She weighed the cool, delicate figure brooding over the flames. Lynette was as impenetrable as an African jungle, profound as the sea. When Patricia finished talking, Lynette rose and stood over the fire.

"It suits me to oblige you about this," she said quietly.

Patricia could not credit her ears, much less comprehend the significance of the remark. Lynette suggested an alabaster lamp, lighted by a nebulous flame. Reluctance at the thought of consigning a creature of such rare and remarkable calibre to a man like Axel, swept Patricia. He would shatter the lamp rather than be denied knowledge of the fire that lighted it, then ambition prodded her.

"What, exactly, do you mean?" she asked.

Lynette glanced at her, her expression implying that, for her, her mother did not exist. It was a challenge. Patricia's nostrils dilated, and her figure tensed.

"I mean exactly what I said; that it suits me to oblige you about this," Lynette repeated. "I'll wait in my room until you send for me."

She walked slowly toward the door, giving her mother ample opportunity to reprove her if she chose. When the door closed on her slim, erect figure, Patricia rose and paced the room, then flinging herself upon the divan,

she called out sharply,
"Prince Axel!"

Going to her room, Lynette curled up in a low chair,
pulled close to the fire. Her face was flame white in the
semi-darkness. For the first time a definite channel of
escape presented itself. Her mind thrust forward like a
warrior's sword, hacking its way through enemies. The
prince, her mother had said, was fabulously rich. Men
gave costly gifts to women they wanted to marry. Young
girls did not wear expensive jewelry so she might be able
to manage to sell some of it without it being missed, and
obtain money to return to Lani-o-akua. Her skin burned,
then she threw up her head and looked at the future as
Trevellyan had looked at the land of Lani-o-akua. Anything, anything, she would do anything to get back!
Someday, somehow, she would manage to send the cost
of the gems back to Prince Axel, and write and explain
why she had done such an unheard-of thing.

Because her parents would be absent, her own actions
would be less hampered. Miss Mansfield would not, of
course, help her, but she would write to Lord Jim asking him to come to England immediately. There were
twelve months in which to make arrangements. A flame-
like intensity enveloped her as she stared back through
the black cold of England toward the everlasting summer of Hawaii.

Going to a small desk, she unlocked a drawer and extracted a mass of letters, tied with a narrow leather thong.
Ka-aina had cut it off his saddle the day she left, to tie
up a bundle of treasures Jackie had given her in an effort
to express his undying devotion, and she had kept it as

something hallowed, using it to bind Jim's letters as another girl would have used a ribbon.

At first she had been desolate because no one at Lani-o-akua ever wrote, but as she grew older she guessed that if any letters had come, her mother would have ordered Miss Mansfield to intercept them. Untying the thong she glanced through the letters. Dear Lord Jim. She had never appreciated how she clung to him with her mind. He was the sole link to the past in which she eternally lived and moved, her only means of help. His last letter, from Japan, stated that before she was eighteen, he would arrive in England. Her face burned. She would write tomorrow and tell him to come at once. Tremulous eagerness filled her as if escape were upon her. Lord Jim understood what Lani-o-akua meant to her, how hunger for it grew instead of diminishing, because there was nothing here with which to satisfy it. He would come as fast as possible.

He had sent her strange, delightful gifts at intervals; a scarlet and white *pareo* from Tahiti, slender, silver bangles that some Javanese dancer had worn, ear ornaments from the Gold Coast, a nose ring that had been part of the regalia of some ebony chief, coral from Ceylon, and recently an immense, red fish made of tough cloth-like paper which the Japanese flew from poles to announce a son's birthday. Enraptured, she had flown it from her bedroom window. Its great round mouth was braced open by cross-sticks of bamboo, so that the wind blew inside it, making the sixteen-foot monster wave as if swimming in air instead of water. How brave and gay it had looked, dipping and leaping, a great red and pink shape floating incongruously above formal Eng-

lish gardens and proper English hills. Maids and gardeners
had collected under her window shocked lest some
passerby might see it. Miss Mansfield had been notified
and advised Lynette to take it in, but when she felt particularly rebellious she flew it, laughing when the servants
averted their faces in order not to see the heathen thing
as they passed.

She glanced at the clock. She had been in her room
half an hour. What were her mother and the prince doing? Perhaps he had decided he did not want her, or
her mother had felt she was too young. Terror filled
her. She locked up the letters, and hid the key. It would
be easy, she thought desperately, to be nice to this unknown man who, indirectly, was giving Lani-o-akua
back to her. Her mother was apprehensive that she
might offend him, had made it clear that he was a person
of consequence, and that his singling her out was an
honor. Well, she would be nice to him—if only she could
get to see him! Of a sudden, he seemed a friend, someone
close and dear.

Faint, reviving warmth crept through her. Her mother
was not likely to let such a chance slip through her
fingers. Of course she would meet him, of course her
mother would consent to her being betrothed. You never
knew about life, she thought with a gust of rapture. Today had been just a day like all the others since she left
Lani-o-akua and then, without warning, affairs began to
happen which would make it possible for her to get
back. A tap sounded on the door, and she erased all expression from her face.

"Your mother wants you, Lynette."

Lynette noticed that her governess looked upset.

"What's the matter? Has Mother been scolding you about the fish?"

"What fish?" asked the woman, looking bewildered.

"My red one."

"Oh, my dear, no! How can you think about such things?"

"I like it and don't want it taken away."

"What a child you are, Lynette! It's nothing short of desecration to think of affiancing a baby like you to a man like Prince Axel. He must be over forty and besides—"

"But I'm glad about it."

"Glad, Lynette?"

"Something that's been tied in a tight knot inside me ever since I came away, has let go." Lynette looked at the woman, smiled slightly, and went down the hall.

At the door of the drawing room, she halted. Voices reached her, a man's and a woman's. Prince Axel was inside. She would meet him, make herself like him, but she must be careful to conceal the joy in her mind. She entered sedately, but her pulses were tingling.

The room was in semi-darkness, except for the fire and shaded candles. Her mother was seated on the divan, and a tall man stood on the hearth, one arm leaning on the mantle. His height put him above the candles and his face was indistinct, but his long body looked satirical and something about it suggested power, mystery, and cunning. Lynette felt aversion for him, and yet interest in him as well. She must remember and keep remembering that only through him . . . Patricia signed for her to come nearer and she fancied she heard the man catch his breath.

"So this is the beautiful baby, the fairy princess I saw," the man remarked half playfully, straightening up.

She lifted her eyes and heard him, this time distinctly, swallow a breath. From being immobile his whole bearing became injected with elasticity and anticipation.

"Lynette, give Prince Axel your hand," Patricia commanded.

The man stepped forward. Lynette felt as if her body were a glass box in which her thoughts, feelings, and desires were ranged for his inspection. His eyes seemed to rout out secrets from every corner of her self and scatter them on the ground. A tremor passed through her. Then she realized that he was looking at her as if he could never look enough. Greed was in his eyes and a sort of esthetic delight and perplexity. She started at the coldness of the fingers that closed about hers. Bending, the prince pressed his lips to her hand, and a chill shot up her arm as if it had been plunged into water, but she reminded herself she must act, for only by acting . . .

Patricia made a place on the couch, and Lynette sat down. Her knees felt wobbly, but she kept her chin up. The prince resumed his position on the hearth. As her eyes became accustomed to the light, she saw his features distinctly. They seemed perplexingly familiar. Coffee was brought and served. She wished the prince would sit down so she could see him better.

He talked to her mother, addressing her occasionally, and each time he looked at her, her heart fluttered. Lacing her fingers tightly, she gazed past his legs into the fire. Whenever possible she stole a look at him and a pain came into her head trying to recall where she had seen him, or someone like him. His features blurred from the turmoil in her mind, but she knew instinctively that he was deeply affected by her.

In order to give herself courage she projected her mind back to Lani-o-akua. Warmth drugged her and her body seemed to melt and float away. Then she realized that the prince was addressing her directly, and tensed.

"How is a man to wait two years for anything as incredibly lovely as you are, Lynette?"

"Two years isn't long," she said, trying to make her voice sound natural, but when the words were out, she swallowed.

"Not when you're as young as you are," said the prince laughing. Coming over he seated himself on the couch beside her.

His face numbed her brain. Where had she seen the chill horror of those features before? His eyes, the dead gray of pebbles, were almost without pupils, like the blind eyes in a sculptured head. His person suggested unknown violences. He was handsome in an evil way, she thought childishly, and fury against her mother swept her. She sat there, deliberately planning to marry her to such a man, simply because he embodied worldly position, rank, and power. All her mother cared for was . . . things. She was beautiful, you couldn't deny that, and there was something exciting and wholesale about her, like avalanches and volcanoes which were, at once, gorgeous and destructive.

Lynette listened to arrangements being made, in which she was vitally involved, but which did not affect her. They were just . . . plans. Things entirely outside of her. She and the prince were to be privately affianced.

When her parents returned the betrothal would be made public. In the meantime the prince would call once a week. Of course, Miss Mansfield would be present during his visits. Lynette noticed that her mother smiled in a still way as she said it, like a person tormenting a caged tiger. The prince agreed like a person under a spell. Under *her* spell, Lynette thought breathlessly. He looked as if he wanted to eat her. She shivered and her body became limp at the prospect of having to see him again. Self-contempt swept her. Nothing was so terrible that it couldn't be done to get back to Lani-o-akua. It was silly to be so repelled. He was, in his peculiar way, good looking. His pallor was revolting, but his features were chiselled like a statue's. It was his eyes that she hated, his eyes that appeared to see nothing. She must remember he was rich, great, that he liked her, and if she pleased him he would give her presents that . . .

She forced herself to be agreeable. He talked, lightly and playfully, as a person would talk to a very small child, promising to take her to see his yacht when her mother returned, speaking of beautiful distant places where he'd been, where some day *they* would go.

"And now, Prince Axel, your extremely ancient bride-to-be must retire," Patricia said, mockingly.

"When may I see you again, Lynette?" he asked.

"We'll arrange that later, Prince Axel," Patricia broke in. "Say goodnight, Lynette."

"With your consent I'll put the seal of betrothal on her," Axel said, in a formal voice. Thrusting his hand into his pocket, he drew out a small box and opened it. Firelight leaped greedily into a diamond that almost seemed to crackle it was so bright. Patricia made a smothered, protesting sound.

"Lynette's far too young to wear a stone of that size."

Desperation swept Lynette. There it was . . . freedom! Escape! She must contrive to get it before her mother made it impossible. She glanced swiftly at the prince. He was watching her, watching to see if she would take it. The top of her head felt as if it were going to blow off. Involuntarily, she reached out her hand.

"*So?*" the prince said. "You would like to wear it, Lynette?"

"It's . . . beautiful. It's like the morning star when it comes up behind . . ." she was so frightened that everything went blank for an instant. She had been going to say "Haleakala" and then her mother would have known why she wanted the stone, why she was willing to become Axel's fiancée, just so she could see the great, silver-white morning star blazing when *wa-naau* came up like a ghost to tell Lani-o-akua a new day was soon to be born.

Silence filled the room. There were, Lynette knew, different kinds of silences, and this one was charged with dynamite. They all sat perfectly still, as if afraid if any one of them moved so much as a fraction, the room would explode. The prince stared at her like a man standing in front of a locked door that has suddenly flown open to let him in. He glanced at her, then at the stone in his hand. A slow red came into his face, making it alive and he folded his lips inwards as if he were trying not to bite. Lynette felt suddenly tired, as if hypnotized.

Prince Axel was thinking that she could be won with gems, and he was glad and angry about it. He had imagined, perhaps, that she was different, felt that she, the

real Lynette, lived in a far-off place where nothing and
no one could reach her to possess her. As she did . . .
at Lani-o-akua. Safe and still. Beyond reach. The undying passion that thralled her, ridding her of consciousness
of self, clutched her, and a force outside herself, greater
and more powerful than anything she had ever experienced, began rushing through her. Light filled her mind,
and she completely transcended the prison of her own
body, and was absorbed into something boundless. An
unreal sensation possessed her of blissful union, of being
whole. Her being seemed to expand and expand. Then she
was back in the room, dazed, but calm. The prince would
speak first, and she knew the exact words he would say
before he uttered them.

"So, Lynette, you like . . . gems?"

Hope was in his voice, mixed with ruthless contempt,
the contempt of a collector who has been deceived by
some seemingly priceless work of art, which has proved,
on closer inspection, to be an imitation.

"I love beauty," she said, breathlessly. "That diamond
is like dew-drops and fire. It makes me feel as they do, as
if—"

"Go on," he urged, bending closer.

"As if something inside me wants to rush toward them
and be part of them, part of their beauty."

"You are unbelievable, matchless, perfect! When I
look at you I feel the same way."

She was shocked, but the force outside of herself which
had become part of her, steadied her. She smiled and
Axel caught his breath.

"Of course you must wear it," he exclaimed, seizing
her hand.

"Axel, her father will not permit Lynette—"

The prince glanced at Patricia, and his expression implied that he had no more time for her because he and Lynette were in a world which she might not enter. Scarlet blazed in Patricia's cheeks and her head flew up like a flag fighting a rough wind.

"You told me, Lady Patricia, that you would uphold me."

"That will do, Prince Axel!"

They looked at each other as if they were enemies, then Patricia seemed to fold a cloak tightly about herself. Lynette got a quick impression that her mother had been going to fight for her against herself, then from habit had surrendered to the things that loomed large in her mind . . . power, rank, and wealth. Perhaps her mother had a self that she hid or had killed, a self that had been born at Lani-o-akua, but that living or life had killed. The room was still again with a different kind of stillness, a silence which waited impatiently to end.

Axel looked at Lynette's hand, that he still held, and she gazed at the ring which was like the silver morning star lighting her back to Lani-o-akua. Her arm was icy from contact with Axel's flesh, dank as a fish's. With a supreme effort she lifted her third finger, and he slipped the ring home, his fingertips following her smooth skin greedily. When it was in place he raised her hand and kissed it. Patricia moved angrily, and Axel's eyes mocked her, as if saying, "This thing's beyond you, now. It's between me and your daughter."

He rose to his feet, winner, and gravely possessed himself of both Lynette's hands.

"May I kiss you?" he asked with formal courtesy to

which his pale eyes gave lie.

Lynette nodded, feeling as if she were tied into a deep dream, and Axel murmuring under his breath in Danish. The strange, lisping syllables reminded her of fins cutting water. She moved like an animal trying to get free of thongs. That face, coming down to hers, those lips seeking her— She knew! This man's face was like a shark's, like that of the Shark God at Lani-o-akua. She swayed, and he caught her, pressing his mouth on her parted one. Her head fell back into the crook of his arm, her eyes dulled, her body contracted as if wasted by sickness. She felt as she had when Ka-aina dipped her into the sea! Axel's embrace had the chilly, possessive quality of bottomless water. She drew air into her lungs like a drowning person, but in the back of her mind thoughts beat like little hammers. "I mustn't scream! I mustn't scream! I kissed the Shark God the night Jackie and I ran away, and I'll kiss Prince Axel so I can get back."

She was dimly aware of her mother rising swiftly to her feet. Her face was chalk-white, blue shadows lay by her nose. In her eyes was a look of remembering against her will. She started to speak, then sat down suddenly, like a person confronted by the spectre of herself. Transcendent understanding, an enlarging and clearing of the mind, seized Lynette. She saw her mother, completely and distinctly, for the first time. Her mother, who seemed cold, was hot, hotter than fire. Passionate, consumed by passion. She fancied that the passion which rode her was lashing her daughter into this man's arms before her eyes. Complete detachment, that of a man on a high, safe peak, looking down at a distracted world, filled Lynette. She had all people fooled, because she loved no human being!

Her love was greater, it went beyond devotion to individuals and things; it embraced rocks, trees, dreams, sunsets, wind, animals, the rustle of day coming up over the world. It put her beyond things and people in a great, safe place which was always blue.

Her face was transfigured, unearthly. How had she attained that peace which she had first experienced at Lani-o-akua, that joyous peace which ranged beyond concrete things? It was hers, even while the prince still had his arms about her and her mother sat looking on. Secret beauty lay on her like dew on grass. She smiled, and Axel reluctantly released her. Her mother looked as if she could not move, and Lynette gazed at the diamond on her left hand. Aeons, the forces of the universe, sunlight imprisoned in green things, water, fire, the weight of the earth, pressure had done their parts to make it, and man had contributed his mite to the whole, shaping it and placing it, a stepping stone of light and beauty, to take her back to Lani-o-akua.

CHAPTER XX

THRUSTING aside the pay sheet on which he was working, David stared out of the window at the solemn fall of the island to the sea. His eyes, his body, even his hair felt alert. Like most persons living close to nature, he sensed distinctive individualities impregnating certain days. When he rose in the morning, he had grasped an unusual quality in the atmosphere which had increased instead of diminishing as the hours wore on. He was accustomed to the feeling of wonder-in-waiting, attendant on any unusually fine dawn, but this sensation was different, a sort of invisible, stately processional marching toward a definite end. Trees, stones, blades of grass, particles of soil, insects, human beings, and animals seemed to contribute their aggregates to the collective soul of the locality of which he had been overwhelmingly conscious all day.

He straightened up, attempting to ease the sense of suffocation which filled him. Vaguely, and at the same time vividly, a vast organism was stirring which was actually behind the visible world, but which made itself felt through the varied phenomena of nature. The feeling of some great, impending event made him restive. The afternoon was so still it shouted for attention. A flood of gold and blue light rained on the earth. Trees stood proudly in the sunshine and their shadows looked holy.

He re-applied himself to his work, but the out-of-doors tapped at his mind incessantly. His pencil flagged, his mind sent out feelers trying to translate the message in the day. He traced down the list of ranch workers, noting their time and the amount of money coming to them after their supplies from the ranch store had been subtracted. Jackie was inclined to be careless about book keeping. He smiled at some ridiculous drawing on the margin of a page that the boy had sketched absent-mindedly.

It seemed impossible that Jackie was eighteen. He was an arresting-looking youngster, with dark brilliant eyes which looked wet and hot at the same time. A lazy dignity, a grace almost Polynesian, marked his movements. He still wondered about Jackie's identity, watching for traits which might mark him a Trevellyan. At times a hinted resemblance to someone he had seen tormented David, then for months and years it was absent. He wondered, as he corrected an entry, if he would ever know for certain.

Jackie should be sent, for a couple of years at least, to a mainland college. Like most Island boys he had been educated by tutors. His mind, while not brilliant, had flares which hinted that it was not yet fully awakened. Never having had companions of his own age and kind, Jackie did not appear to miss them, but David felt responsible about the matter and had, on a couple of occasions, invited a neighboring rancher's son over for a week-end. Jackie had been polite, but after the first hour, plainly bored.

Looking up, David allowed his mind to wander over the past which had built up to the present. Trevellyan, Ruth, Jackie, Lynette. What of her? They had never had a word about her since the day she had been carried, a tiny, frozen white ghost, onto the ship, a ghost whose eyes stabbed his memory. In his imagination he heard her laughing in the garden as she had laughed as a child. How gossamer-like she had been, how finished in perfection, like little gold leaves on treetops, like the spray on tiny waves. Lynette . . . her name was like a breeze!

"Uncle David."

How perfectly his ears remembered the cadences in her voice, as if the words had been actually uttered!

"Uncle David."

He flung around.

"Lynette!"

He recognized her instantly though she had been a child when she left, and was now a young girl. The same pure forehead, the same expression in her eyes, the radiant happiness of a mind fixed beyond self. For an instant he could not move, then he rose unsteadily.

"Uncle David, I'm back, I'm back!"

Running to him, she melted into his arms. David held her thinking that nothing was ever ended, everything only begun. Her eyes were drugged with sunshine and joy, her face had the clean, fulfilled look of land, after rain has fallen upon it.

"Your mother—"

"Mother doesn't know I'm here." Seating herself on the edge of the desk, she related what had happened, speaking briefly of the long trip across two oceans and a continent, and David thought she was like a homing pigeon in her singleness of purpose. Listening to the account of her life, of her trip, made him realize that, since the day she had left Lani-o-akua, she had been starting back.

"Your mother will be terribly angry when she—"

"Probably she knows by now, but she can't make me go back. I'll never leave Lani-o-akua again."

"Nothing can be done until we hear from her, Lynette. Be happy and enjoy yourself while you can."

She nodded. "Let's go outside."

Twining her fingers through his, she drew him to the steps and gazed about her. The distant ocean's roar, mynah birds chattering in the trees, the shriek of a peacock reached them. Lynette's nostrils quivered to remembered scents and her body relaxed and expanded, becoming a part of her surroundings. David saw that it was not people who made Lani-o-akua precious to Lynette; it was, and had always been, the total. As yet she had not asked after any individual, but stood, quivering to the soul of the locality, an integral part of it. Odd for one so young to be so detached, but she had been like that even as a child. Her affection for people was in proportion to their relation to the whole. From the hills behind the house came sounds of horsemen returning, and she recollected herself.

"I want to see them coming into the corrals. Tell Aunt Ruth I'll be in after a while."

David watched her cross the lawn. Not an air stirred in the garden, but the whole place was mysteriously alive and seemed to gather closely about her. He found Ruth sewing by her bedroom window. Her small frame had become a trifle meager and settled, but her face was still charmingly colored, perhaps reflecting the rich warmth of the burgundy-colored dress she had on. A white rose was pinned where the bodice crossed in front in a high, careful fold. Her hair, glossy from a hundred brush strokes night and morning, was guiltless of gray, her skin creamy, her hands finished with small, neat nails.

"What brings you looking for me at this time of day, David?" she asked, laying down her sewing.

"Lynette's back."

"What do you mean?"

"She's here. She walked in on me a few minutes ago . . . just like that!"

"Does her mother—"

He repeated Lynette's tale. Ruth listened without comment until he finished, then remarked:

"Lynette would behave in such a manner. Fancy a girl in her senses running away at the thought of being married to a prince! Did she tell him he looked like a Shark God?" she asked with a laugh that had a slight edge to it.

"She didn't say."

"What does she intend to do?"

"Remain here."

"Her mother will never permit it."

"Nothing can be done until we hear, or Patricia comes."

Ruth almost leaped in her seat, if a being so ladylike and contained could be said to leap. "What makes you think she might, David?"

"You don't know Patricia. I do."

Ruth laid her sewing aside. "It seems absurd that two sisters, two half-sisters," she corrected herself, "should never have met. I suppose a mother would come after a daughter who ran away as Lynette did, but it's hardly possible that Prince Axel will still want her." An expression in David's eyes arrested her notice. "Is Lynette still as lovely as she was as a child?"

"More so, if it's possible."

Ruth meditated.

"I shouldn't be surprised," David said in a flat voice, "if Prince Axel turns up also. From what Lynette told me, I don't relish meeting him. And it will seem almost like having a ghost for a guest to have Patricia back here."

Ruth touched her knee with thoughtful fingers.

"How much older than I am is Patricia?"

"I don't know exactly. Several years."

"It will be interesting to meet her," Ruth remarked, looking pleased, but her expression hinted, "It will be good for Patricia to meet and realize her little, unknown sister, the uncrowned queen of Lani-o-akua."

David moved restively. Despite the fact that he loved Ruth there were times when she jarred; although he was too loyal to admit it, she smacked of her mother who, at best, had been futile. Ruth was not futile, but she was negative, occupying herself with trifles and missing the great things completely. She looked pleased, probably because she was younger than Patricia, or possibly because she might entertain a prince, while Lynette was at the corrals and new designs were being woven into the great loom that held the terrific pattern of the years.

"There'll be no sending Jackie to college until Lynette goes," she announced, taking up her sewing and

shortening the thread in her needle. "Of course Patricia
has destined Lynette for someone like Prince Axel, otherwise it would be rather lovely if Jackie and Lynette—"

Protest leaped into David's eyes, but he controlled it.

"Seemingly that would be the solution for Lynette's remaining here but—"

"Of course Patricia would never permit it. We aren't
of high enough station. She'll be along, knowing we have
a boy." Ruth assumed an air of affronted motherhood.

David moved as if throwing Ruth and everything away
in order to devote his mind to the present. "Lynette said
she'd be in presently to see you."

"Where is she?"

"At the corrals."

"She would greet a lot of Kanakas before seeing me,"
Ruth sniffed.

"Lynette didn't come back to see any of us."

"What do you mean?"

"It's the place she loves."

"People make places."

"Sometimes places make people."

"I don't follow you."

"Environment often lends lustre to otherwise ordinary
individuals. Lani-o-akua—"

"You always refer to this place as if you were talking
of a living thing," Ruth remarked, impatiently.

"It's a living entity."

Ruth took a careful stitch with the air of dismissing
the vagaries of a child. "At times, when you talk
strangely, as you do now, I realize you've been at Lani-
o-akua a very long time."

"Aeons," David replied. "And I know you're thinking that it's affected my mind a little."

"Well, hasn't it?" Ruth asked.

During dinner David watched Jackie and Lynette carefully. Jackie's manner was eager and shy. His face glowed, and his eyes swam when they looked at her. Quiet triumph enveloped Lynette, the triumph of a tree which has successfully retained its hold of the earth after a hurricane has passed over it. She was so still, even when she spoke, that it was startling. They were an oddly touching pair, suggesting young demi-gods who had forgotten, or did not care, whether they were human or divine.

David saw that there would be no love-making, or thought of love for some time. They had slipped back to their old footing and he reflected, comfortingly, that human beings, beyond everything, were creatures of habit. Untoward developments and complications were further safeguarded by Lynette's attitude of being removed from the material objects and Jackie, because of years of unbroken association with Polynesians, retained an almost childlike quality, that intensified some sides of his character, while subduing others. There were times when it was difficult to realize that Jackie was an adult instead of a boy. His manner of speaking and thinking, while it missed being childish, was childlike in its very simplicity and lack of self-consciousness. It enhanced his charm, and gave him a poignant appeal.

"Lynette, Ka-aina said if you want, we can go to Makena tomorrow," Jackie announced.

"Would he mind if we didn't . . . yet? I want to stay

here and soak it all in."

"Of course he won't. He'll be glad just to walk around with us. He's getting old. He misses sometimes when he throws a lasso, now."

"Does he! He didn't look any different to me."

"His hair is quite white. Didn't you notice it?"

"No, Jackie. You see—" She broke off as if it were unnecessary to explain.

"What, Lynette?"

She started to reply then said, "Wait! I'm listening."

"To things passing by, like you used to?" the boy asked, after a silence.

She nodded.

"I wonder if you'll see your *akua* again?" Jackie smiled teasingly. "Do you remember, Lynette?"

"Of course. Have you never seen him?"

"Never. Maybe you only thought you saw him."

Lynette shook her head. "No, I remember everything, his black eyes and his beard and his boots. Let's find Ka-aina, and go to the pool and sit by my *akua* stone. Maybe he'll come out. I'd like to see him. I want everything that belongs to Lani-o-akua."

Ruth's eyes met David's, and his skin burned. Her expression implied that Lynette's mind was not entirely sound. Jackie leaned toward the girl.

"Do you want Ka-aina very much? I'd like to have you alone. There are millions of things I want to ask you; all you've done since you went to England."

"I don't want to talk about it here."

"Oh, Lynette!" Jackie threw a joyous arm about her shoulders. "You're just the same. It seems as if you've never been away."

"I never went really, Jackie. Just my body went."

"It seemed like that to me, too. I used to pretend you were here. Sometimes when no one was round, I talked to you."

"How beautiful, Jackie, how dear of you."

David stared at the tablecloth. That explained Jackie's indifference to companionship. Throughout the years he had had an invisible companion who fulfilled every need. It was shocking to realize how little the physical mattered.

"Why didn't you ever write to me, Jackie?"

The boy looked thoughtful. "I tried to a few times, but that wasn't the way. I couldn't reach you on paper. When I wanted you so much I ached, I'd sit very still and think and think about you till I filled myself with you. Then you seemed right here as if I could touch and see you."

"Oh, Jackie! I know I came to Lani-o-akua. It wasn't just pretend. When I almost burst with wanting to be here, I'd shut my mind and keep out everything around me and think of Lani-o-akua. After thinking and thinking, I *was* here. The only times I couldn't get here was when Mother and people were at the manor. They got in the way."

"I was awfully glad, but not very surprised when I saw you today, Lynette," Jackie said. "The only surprising part was you weren't little any more."

"Was I little when I rode and talked to you while I wasn't here?" Lynette asked.

"Yes. I forgot I was growing up. I've always felt just as I did when we were together."

David meditated. That accounted for Jackie's child-like quality. It was a state of mind, not limited intellect or development.

"Would you mind, Uncle David, if we went out?" Lynette asked. "I'm not hungry. I'm full-up to the chin with happiness."

Ruth started to speak, but David's eyes stopped her.

"Yes, Lynette, you both may go. If you get hungry before bedtime you know where the safe is."

She kissed him lightly and swiftly, then took hold of Jackie's arm. He watched them walk into the garden. When their footsteps died away, Ruth straightened imperceptibly, and the strange, sweet silence which filled the room snapped, restoring it to usual.

"I see you intend to let Lynette run wild again."

"She's so perfect, I don't mean only outwardly, that it's wrong for anyone to dictate what she shall do."

"Like everyone else, you're completely under her spell. I'm fond of Lynette. She's my niece, but she always behaves as if I didn't exist."

David made no comment.

"It's irritating. For instance, instead of asking my permission, as she should have, to go out, she asked yours. Wouldn't it annoy you if Lynette was oblivious to you as a person?"

"I suppose it would, Ruth. But after all, you and I, in fact everyone, for Lynette, is incidental. Watching her, I'm inclined to believe that the great secret of life is hers. She places people in their right relation to—"

"David, you've been reading those ponderous, perplexing books in your office that you bought after she left, and are quoting from them. Anyone with sense knows that people, for people, are the most important thing in life."

"It's because people have permitted people to be the most important—"

"Spare me, David. Your harangues make my head ache. Do you suppose," Ruth brightened, "that Patricia will come alone or with Prince Axel?"

"It's impossible to tell. Lynette left England almost four months ago. Her mother was probably informed at once when she vanished, and will undoubtedly suspect she came here. Patricia's had ample time by now, wherever she was, to be well on her way. We should have word from her any day now."

"I shall have to see that things are set right before she arrives," Ruth announced, looking important.

Lynette pushed back her warm, wild hair. Despite the silence she was aware of minute noises around the pool that gleamed like polished metal in the twilight.

"I'd forgotten it was so big," she whispered.

"Let's go to the bench and talk," Jackie suggested.

Lynette nodded, but she did not want to talk. A sensation of being far away, but close to the heart of everything, possessed her. When they reached the seat, under moist ferns grown high about the stone that was her *akua*, she laid her hand on it, then smiling quickly and sweetly, recollecting the old rite, took the flowers from about her neck and placed them upon it. Jackie nodded approval, and drew her down on the seat.

The smell of wet earth was everywhere. Lynette took a succession of deep breaths. "Oh, Jackie, it's so beautiful.

I want to kiss everything." Catching a spray of fern she brushed it with her lips.

"That makes me think of the way you used to kiss stones," Jackie said. "If we did nothing, but sit here forever and ever—" Emotion choked him.

"I know the feeling inside you. I've had it too, Jackie. When I held the diamond the Shark Prince gave me, my mind opened out until it held everything. After I got in bed I kept thinking and feeling the ring with my finger. I thought how it was made, how everything I love was in it, green things, light, water, fire, the earth pressing it until it was harder than rocks. I had to kiss the prince to get it and when he kissed me I drowned, but nothing mattered. I was willing to do anything to get here."

Jackie nodded. "God promised you'd come back. I always remembered that."

"Me too. The only part that worried me was how to get away. After I had the diamond I wasn't scared any more, but I was afraid I wouldn't do things right, so I wrote to Lord Jim to come and help me."

"Lord Jim!"

"Yes. He always wrote and sent me things. I wanted to bring a big, red paper fish he gave me, but it was too clumsy. Mother left orders that I was to see the prince once a week. I couldn't bear it. After the second time I began planning how to get away. He used to eat me with his eyes. I decided to get away without waiting for Lord Jim to come. It scared me, but I'd think about Lani-o-akua and be brave."

"Tell me everything, how you sold the diamond, and—"

"I don't want to think or talk about it now, Jackie."

"You needn't, Lynette. Tell me some other time. To-night let's—"

"Be in Lani-o-akua?" the girl asked.

"Yes."

They sat close together in the twilight which was hurrying into night.

"There's the Blue Country." Jackie pointed at the pool. "Only it's purple now."

"How beautiful it is, how deep."

"Like you, Lynette."

She smiled. Tired steps that dragged slightly came up the hill.

"Ka-aina," Lynette said. "Oh, Jackie, I feel as if I'd never been away, as if everything were back where it used to be."

"Me, too."

Lynette watched the opposite side of the pool expectantly and when Ka-aina appeared, beckoned. "We're here, *makule*, by the *akua* stone. Now if only my *akua* would come," she mourned, when Ka-aina was seated on her other side, "then I'd have everything."

Ka-aina kneaded her hand silently with rough, stiff fingers. "Good, good that you come back."

"You know, Lynette," Jackie broke in, "*Akuas* and those kind of things get all mixed up in your mind when you grow up. White people say there is only one God and Hawaiians—"

"Got God and *akuas*, too," Ka-aina insisted.

"I'm sure they are *akuas*, too, anyway here." Lynette looked with soft, thoughtful eyes at her surroundings. "I wish my old man would come. Why doesn't he, Ka-aina? I'd like to see him again."

"This kind little hard for tell, *keiki*—time easy, because *keikis* have just come from the gods—"

"Wait," Lynette commanded, "I feel my *akua* now." She waited expectantly, vaguely aware of the sudden rigidity of Ka-aina's figure. After a tense silence she asked, impatiently, "Why can't I *see* him?"

No one replied and after some moments, Lynette announced forlornly, "He's gone."

Ka-aina looked at her hand and gave it a consoling pressure. Lynette's mind swept up trees, gardens, hills, mill, mausoleum. Then a thought, swift as a naked runner, came to her for the first time.

"Who made it?" she asked.

"Made what, Lynette?" Jackie demanded.

"Lani-o-akua. Who planted all these trees, built this pool, and all the rest? I never thought about it before."

"Your grandfather."

"My grandfather?" Lynette cried, opening her eyes. "Tell me about him. Quickly."

"Ka-aina knows better than I do. Tell Lynette, *makule*."

The Hawaiian stirred like an old hound reluctantly roused from its dozing on a hearth. He inspected the seam of his riding breeches, then looked up. "S'pose you like, Lineki, I tell."

Stars climbed to the zenith while Ka-aina talked. Lynette and Jackie sat still as mice while the old man's words summoned up hosts of the past; hosts whose tread echoed resoundingly, mounting with the years. Shadowy figures passed in review filling the gardens like clicking machinery that the constantly whirling earth kept winding up.

Instead of dimming, time intensified the old man's memories. Trevellyan lived again, distinct to the listening pair as their hands. His oaths, his rages, his love for Lani-o-akua filled the night. He drove hounded Chinamen, rode to Makena to meet men-o'-war, played poker with King Kalakaua. Ghosts laid by the years rose from their graves to live again and, by the very simplicity of his words, Ka-aina put the rhythm of life into his tale.

As he talked Lynette's expression altered. From being attentive it became thoughtful, then tense, and passionate. Queer, stifled beats ran through her heart which angered her for they interfered with her hearing Ka-aina properly. She wanted every sound around her, however minute, silenced.

"What's the matter, Lynette?" Jackie asked.

"Be quiet, Jackie, I want to, I must, hear it all!"

Spectres of a buried generation crowded about the pool, always dominated by an enormous figure in thigh boots. Lynette heard the whine of Trevellyan's whip biting at bending backs, and flying arms plying shovels desperately to hasten the laying of paved walks and the digging of pools. Great boots stamped in to barracks where exhausted Chinamen slept, oaths ripped the dawn, figures, jerked from bunks by limp black queues, bumped the ground.

She felt in her being the passion which had been Trevellyan's for Lani-o-akua that bore the stamp of his merciless and beautifying hand. But when Ka-aina voiced the Hawaiian belief that no security would ever be Lani-o-akua's until a human sacrifice was given to appease the anger of offended gods, her fingers dug into Jackie's arm and her face, a dim, white blot in the dark, flew up like a flag of truce.

"It must not be destroyed!" she cried.

"No, maybe no," Ka-aina said, wiping moisture off his forehead.

"Don't mind so, Lynette," Jackie said, putting a consoling arm about her. "Maybe it won't happen till after we are dead."

She stared at him condemningly, then sat frozen in her seat. The vast, soft voice of nature murmuring in its sleep awed her into silence. She had an impression that the spirit of Lani-o-akua was waking from a long trance. The soul of the locality, compounded of the million lesser souls animating it, grass, rocks, beasts, trees, and people, was rousing itself to face some climax. The peace which had filled her during the afternoon was slipping toward a cliff that ended in darkness.

"Grandfather," she spoke in stifled tones, "should have killed someone to make Lani-o-akua safe."

"Lots of Chinamen died because he worked them too hard," Jackie said, cheeringly. "Probably that'll be enough."

Lynette looked doubtful. After a silence she asked Ka-aina to tell the rest. He went on with reservations where Patricia figured. When he detailed Trevellyan's last days, how his eyes tried to get out of his body to see again every inch of Lani-o-akua, Lynette grabbed his hand.

"I felt like Grandfather did while I was in England. As if I'd burst if I couldn't get to it. I love Lani-o-akua the way he did."

"Yes," Ka-aina said, solemnly.

Lynette looked him in the eyes. "Was my *akua*, Grandfather?"

"Of course not, Lynette," Jackie broke in. "Your grandfather's in the Mausoleum. Even a ghost couldn't get out. The walls are a foot thick and the door's padlocked from outside."

Ka-aina watched Lynette in a deep, strange way.

"*Akuas* aren't ghosts. They are gods," Jackie explained. "See the difference?"

"I wish I could have known Grandfather," Lynette said, slowly. "He must have been grand, raging around, scaring everyone, and always thinking about Lani-o-akua and loving it. I like him. I bet I wouldn't have been scared of him. Wouldn't it be fun if he was alive now? He'd come bellowing up the path and tell us to go to bed, and I bet we'd go. He'd crack his whip and pretend he was going to lick us and, when we ran down, we'd hear him laughing all the way down the hill."

"Yes, sure, Old Man make like that," Ka-aina agreed, "and sure he too much like you fellas."

"He'd like Lynette best," Jackie asserted.

Ka-aina nodded, and the garden stirred to a ghostly breeze as if whispering assent.

"If I could have only seen him once," Lynette said, regretfully.

"But you can, Lynette."

"He's dead, Jackie."

"I'll get the key of the mausoleum out of the office tomorrow and take you inside."

"But he's in his coffin and only bones."

"No. I saw him once. His coffin has a glass top so you

can look in. He's pickled in some kind of fluid."

"No make this kind," Ka-aina protested, jerking out of the doze into which he had been peacefully sliding.

Lynette's excited eyes stole carefully to Jackie's and his fused hers in a silent promise.

CHAPTER XXI

"Wait till I tie the horses, Lynette."

The girl paused before the picket gate leading to the mausoleum hill. Awe filled her at the thought of seeing the man who had been responsible for creating Lani-o-akua. Her eyes took careful note of everything, like those of a person about to embark on a strange sea.

"Why are there no clouds today, Jackie?" she asked.

The boy noted the dazed appearance of distant islands, the peculiar color of the sea, the absence of movement in the air.

"A *kona's* coming," he announced.

"I wish one would. I love storms. They let loose tight feelings inside you."

"If a big *kona* comes, it'll delay your mother's ship," Jackie said, fastening the gate.

"I hope it does. I want a little time like we had before. I've been gone from England four months and she may get here any time."

"Maybe she won't come."

"She will, and the prince'll come with her."

"I won't let them take you away."

Lynette pressed her cheek against his shoulder. With

clasped hands they walked toward the mausoleum. Secrets of the earth crouched among ragged, old eucalyptus and slender cypresses standing like exclamation points, emphasizing the beauty of the spot.

"I like Grandfather for building this place so he could watch over Lani-o-akua after he was dead," Lynette said, gazing around her. Sunshine, familiar smells, the tang of the Pacific bred bravery, but her whole soul was a-quiver. She felt close to something breath-taking and sombre, unlike anything she had experienced at Lani-o-akua. Jackie glanced at her.

"Would you rather not see him, Lynette?"

"I want to."

Jackie fitted the great key into the lock and setting his shoulder to the heavy iron door, pushed it inwards. It grated harshly on the stone floor, and Lynette recoiled from the sound. Heat, light, vitality radiated from the earth, but air, like a cold breath suddenly expelled, came out of the vault. Jackie entered, his footsteps making a hollow sound. Driving her teeth into her lip, Lynette followed.

After a moment her eyes adjusted to the gloom. In the center of the high chamber, on an oblong slab of black marble, was a mammoth coffin of ebony with tarnished silver handles. It looked impressive and dreadfully alone, despite the fact that a smaller casket, on another marble slab, was beside it. Jackie began unscrewing the lid.

Lynette laced her fingers tightly. Something was fluttering inside her.

"Who's in the other coffin, Jackie?"

"I guess his wife. You can't look at her because she's

done up tight. But underneath this lid there's plate glass over your grandfather."

"Isn't he your grandfather, too?"

"I guess he is, but he seems only yours."

Lynette nodded. She felt that way, too, as if the old man of whom Ka-aina had spoken the previous evening, belonged to her exclusively.

"He's a fine looking old fellow." Jackie indicated the coffin. "This top is heavy. Give me a hand while I slide it off."

Lynette took hold of the small end and they lowered it carefully and placed it against the slab.

"I've never seen a dead person, Jackie."

"He doesn't look dead, Lynette, just as if he were asleep."

She relaxed. Her eyes went hesitatingly, then eagerly over the long coffin, then rested on the grim, straight form inside. For an instant she stared in silence, then made a strangled sound.

"That's my *akua!*"

"It couldn't be!"

"It is!"

Leaning over, she studied Trevellyan's features. The nose was bold with wide nostrils and the black beard heavily streaked with gray. There was nobility to Trevellyan's face in its terrific repose. The ears, flat against the skull, were finely shaped and unmistakably aristocratic. The whole expression was fierce and relentless, creating the impression that at any instant the eyes might fly open and he might rise, shaking off the fluid in which he was immersed, as a dog shakes water off its coat.

"He looks as if he felt angry because he had to die,"

Lynette whispered.

"Why are you so white?"

"I can't think, Jackie, my head's bursting. What does it all mean? How did he get out? I know he wants me to do something for him . . . something I *must* do!"

"Oh, Lynette, I shouldn't have brought you here," Jackie exclaimed, his arm flying about her shoulders protectingly.

"I'm not scared, Jackie, but I'm bursting because of not knowing and understanding—"

A foreboding of tragedy treading on their heels upon Lani-o-akua stole over them both, chilling them. Sunlight rained on the earth, and islands lay rigid in the sea which was so still that it seemed to be holding its breath. Lynette started unsteadily for the door, and Jackie hurried after her. Reaching the terrace, Lynette sank on to the grass, and Jackie dropped on one knee beside her.

"Lynette—"

"I didn't mind seeing him. I saw him all the time when I was here before. I'm trying to think hard so I can understand. You said last night that ghosts weren't *akuas*, but Grandfather was the *akua* I used to see."

"It's hard, Lynette," Jackie said heavily.

"Do you suppose all dead people are sort of *akuas* because they don't have to stay inside their bodies any more?"

"Maybe."

"Then if dead people are a kind of *akua* they could go anywhere."

"I guess so, Lynette."

"Now I'm beginning to understand. Grandfather loved Lani-o-akua so much he couldn't stay away from it even after he was dead, and because I love it the same way—"

"I hate to think of your seeing a ghost."

"But ghosts are only little *akuas*," Lynette insisted.

Jackie kissed her cold cheek fiercely.

"You look sort of sick, Lynette. Ka-aina said we shouldn't do this."

"I'm not sick, but I feel tired. I'm glad I saw him again, but I wish I could see him the way I used to."

"I'll close up, and we'll go for a ride."

Lynette waited, running tense fingers through the warm, dry grass. She listened to Jackie moving around inside the mausoleum. She felt worn out and listless and at the same time vibrantly alive in a new way.

"I can't lift up the lid," Jackie said, coming to the door. "Shall I leave it for today?"

"Yes, he won't mind."

Jackie started to speak and desisted. Coming out, he drew Lynette to her feet. They started toward the horses in silence. Despite the intense clarity of the morning the atmosphere was filled with hard, hot vibrations. The universe seemed cleared for combat. Mountains looked like blue steel, flaunting their solidity, challenging the sky. The ocean drew the strong, straight sword of the horizon across it, forbidding it to move.

A sudden, secret joy mingled with excitement—incomprehensible to anyone except nature worshippers —swept Jackie and Lynette. Their fingers locked, and the life in their hands mingled like fluid. Their eyes met and their flesh got hot and cold.

"Golly, Lynette, a *kona's* coming all right, and it's going to be a whopper."

Lynette was too moved to manage her voice. Looking

at the diamond-clear distances, she had a distinct impression that all nature was waiting to take up arms in her defence. It seemed that if she should so much as lift a finger to command it, the sky would swoop down upon the sea, mountains hurl themselves upon the plains.

"Let's go on a high hill and sit still, Jackie."

"Yes, let's."

Riding to a grass-covered cone above the last army of trees, they dismounted. About them was the astounding silence of lava flows, the smell of grass and sunlight, and off in the distance the august presence of islands thrusting from the sea. They derived a deep comfort from the solitude of the spot, aware that in lonely places lingered secret memories of the ancient earth. Every so often the horses stopped grazing to throw up their head, and stare uneasily at the blue immensity of sky and water filling the south.

In a way impossible to analyze in words, Lynette felt a distinct telepathy with the universe. It was whispering to her, encouraging and consoling her, promising her something beautiful and unknown that left her breathless. Earth, sky, and water were united in one message which had been coming to her through the ages. She moved cautiously, her body feeling emptied and filled.

"You look so strange, Lynette."

She smiled. Her face, half-dazed and half-proud, disturbed him. It suggested that she, deliberately and in the full consciousness of what she was doing, was slowly detaching herself from everything earthly.

"I can't explain how I feel. Yesterday I felt as I used to here, but today—"

"What about today, Lynette?" Jackie asked anxiously.

"I feel sad and brave, happy and frightened all in one."

"It's because a *kona's* coming and everything looks waiting and strange."

"Maybe. I'm glad I got here yesterday and Lani-o-akua was the way it used to be. Oh, Jackie, I used to want it so badly that I burned! And I wanted," she spoke like a person defrauded, "to have a while here before things started happening."

"Perhaps you will. Your mother may not come for ever so long."

"Even if she doesn't, it's too late. Things have started happening already," Lynette said, forlornly.

"What things?"

"The kind you can't see. Don't you feel them moving past us?"

Jackie nodded in a disconsolate fashion. An immense dull jar from the ocean shook the day. Ranks of rollers, coming from the south, were deliberately and majestically depositing billions of watery tons against the Island which seemed to quiver and recoil, then brace itself for battle. Lynette caught her breath and Jackie seized her hand.

"I've never heard the sea make such a sudden, great noise. Look at the white water along all the islands." He pointed at Kahoolawe, Molokai, and Lanai.

Lynette felt like a person frozen in a dream, watching a cherished possession being taken away.

"When we came up here, Jackie, I didn't want to go back to the house, but now I do. I want today to be like the ones we used to have. Maybe if we go to lunch and do all the usual things this tight, frightening feeling will leave me. I want to get it out of me. I can't breathe and feel as if cloths were wrapped around me."

"I feel like that too. Look at the horses. They're watching for things to start happening."

Lynette shivered and gazed at the sea. Breakers that reached across the sky were following on the heels of each other with wide, even spaces between. The second line broke against the islands and just as the atmosphere was recovering from the concussion, a third line burst with a muffled, tearing roar.

"What makes the ocean like that, Jackie?"

"There's been a hurricane in the south Pacific and this is the tag end of it."

"Will it come here?"

"Hurricanes don't reach Hawaii."

"How do you know?"

"I learned from geography books."

Lynette looked consoled, but not convinced.

"There are things in your eyes, Lynette, that frighten me. Do you know something you're not telling me?"

"No, Jackie, but everything's trying to tell me something and I can't understand. I wanted to come up here and sit still so I could hear better, but it's no use."

"You seem farther away from me, Lynette, than when you were in England. Let's, let's pretend it's before again."

"Let's."

"We'll eat lunch, then find Ka-aina, and watch the cowboys come in like the first night you were here and—"

"And make Na-lua-hini play his accordion and—"

"Tonight we'll sneak out and—"

"And Aunt Ruth will send Uncle David to find us, and he'll pretend he can't like he used to."

Leaping on their horses, they raced down the hill with an air of having eluded foes which were pursuing them. When they reached the stable Lynette's cheeks were flaming unnaturally.

"I feel all right now, Jackie; do you?"

"Fine. Keep pretending fast. Let's give our *akuas* leis before we go to lunch and ask them to help us."

"My *akua's* Grandfather so he'll help extra hard. But I'd rather not go with you to give the Shark God his lei. He seems the prince to me and the prince him. It's all mixed-up in my mind. I feel sick remembering you gave me to the Shark God the night we ran away—"

David and Ruth were at the table when Lynette and Jackie went in.

"You've heard from Mother, Uncle David!" Lynette announced, seeing his face.

"Yes, dear."

"When will she get here?"

"Tomorrow."

"I told you, Jackie, I wasn't going to have my time that I've wanted so fearfully. Is the Shark Prince coming too, Uncle David?"

"Yes, Lynette."

Her legs went all weak and funny, and she sat down. "Help me to pretend, Jackie."

"I will. You're scared but you're brave too, Lynette."

"Yes, they can't make me go, but it frightens me when things are hard and ugly."

"Perhaps," Ruth chose her words meticulously, "your mother intends to visit for a while. I'm sure when she realizes how much Lani-o-akua means to you she'll consent to your remaining with us."

"She won't, and I'll hate having her and the prince at Lani-o-akua, spoiling it." She looked at the gardens remorsefully.

Ruth pursed her lips, and Jackie placed his arm along Lynette's shoulders with a clumsy and touching gesture. Lynette laid down her fork.

"Uncle David, I'm too full of feelings to eat. May I be excused?"

"Yes, dear."

"I have an idea," Jackie said, "that I'll tell you when we are outside."

When they were seated on the lawn near the gate, he looked at her, his eyes warm and shy.

"If you marry me, Lynette, they can't take you from me. If you're my wife—" His voice shook absurdly.

"It's funny. Everyone wants to marry me."

"Everyone?" Jackie asked indignantly. "Who besides the prince?"

"Lord Jim. He's always loved me, even when I was a kid."

"Did he tell you so?" Jackie demanded.

"No, but I knew, though I lied to Miss Mansfield about it, and in his last letter before I left—"

"I don't want to hear about it."

"Don't be angry, Jackie. I don't want to marry anyone."

"Not even me?" the boy asked, flushing.

"No, but I'll marry you to stay here."

He looked dashed and relieved.

"I wish you wanted to."

"I don't, not much anyway, though I love you lots,"

she added, noting the hurt in his eyes. "Maybe it's because we are cousins, and they aren't supposed to marry."

"They do sometimes, and before white men came to Hawaii, Hawaiians thought it was all right for brothers and sisters to marry if they were of royal family, so it can't be very bad for cousins."

Lynette dug her fingers abstractedly into the earth. The ferocity of the sunshine was menacing, shadows looked treacherous, and the jarring of the ocean against the islands bewildered her. The afternoon was collecting itself like a race horse about to leap forward. Her fingers touched a hard object and closed on it. A long puff of wind came out of the south and died away, leaving a vacuum behind.

"Darling, listen," Jackie said, in a stifled voice. "I can't tell you how much I love you. I never thought about marrying you till just now at lunch—"

"You're a darling, of course I'll marry you, Jackie," Lynette said, gravely and gently.

"We'll go tonight and when your mother and the Shark Prince come tomorrow, it'll be too late for them to do anything except be angry."

"It doesn't look as if they could get here with the sea's raging like that," Lynette observed hopefully.

"But you better marry me anyway because if they don't come tomorrow, they will soon. We'll ride to Wailuku and find a priest and make him marry us, then we'll come back."

"All right. It feels like the night we ran away, doesn't it?"

"Yes." Jackie covered her hand with his. "What are you holding?"

"Something I felt in the earth while you were talking."
She opened her hand. "It's a ring!"

The heavy gold was tarnished, but a large square cut
ruby shone through the encrusting earth.

"It's red as blood," Lynette murmured.

"It can be your engagement and wedding ring," Jackie
said in a business-like manner. "Maybe *akuas* put it there
long ago and Lani-o-akua's been keeping it till today."

"How beautiful."

"Put it on." She obeyed. "It's too big, it's a man's ring,
Lynette. Maybe it belonged to your grandfather. I'll
wrap it with string so it won't slip off." Groping in his
pocket Jackie brought out a wad of twine, bound the
ring where it was narrowest, and re-fitted it to Lynette's
finger.

"That's better. I'll show it to Uncle David at dinner.
Shall we tell him we're going to get married? I'd like to.
I love Uncle David. He's kind and always understands."

Jackie thought. "I don't think we'd better. You can
never tell about grown-ups."

"But if we're going to marry, we're grown-ups too."

"I suppose we are, Lynette, but I don't feel like one,
do you?"

"No." The afternoon was terrifyingly beautiful,
ridges and valleys in the West Maui mountains and in distant islands were so distinct that they looked unreal. A
long, hot puff of air came from the south like a vast
breath being expelled. It was followed by quiet, broken
only by the troubled roaring of the sea. The sound filled
Lynette with despair. Her eyelids fluttered down, then
flew up as a second gust of hot, dry wind streamed
against her face. The clarity of the afternoon was be-

ginning to be obscured by a transparent haze, and the sunshine coming through it had a curious, crude quality that made even stones look violent. The universe was preparing deliberately for upheaval. Lynette's teeth worked on her lower lip.

"I feel like when we were in Lewai's canoe and it wouldn't go right."

"Don't be afraid. I'll take care of you."

"But everything looks funny, Jackie."

"It's only the *kona* getting nearer."

She sighed as if his words held little comfort, holding her breath for the next puff of wind. It came, after a little, stronger and more sustained than its predecessor. The afternoon was being steadily injected with electrical force generated by wind tearing over the bulge of the earth and coming up against quiet air. It pushed against it, recoiled, desisted briefly, then attacked again. The atoms of Lynette's body shook. Wind surging forward, then dying, then streaming forward again, created the illusion that the universe was panting.

"I feel as if the world were going to burst!" Lynette whispered. "Let's walk round and look at everything." She blinked tears out of her eyes.

With each passing minute the wind increased and the intervals of quiet got shorter. Trees bent, bushes shook themselves, grass ran before the blasts, quivered, stopped, and started off when the next draft of air began sucking forward.

"Let's go to the pool. It'll be quieter there, Jackie."

The sound of gathering wind, coming through the trees, suffocated her. The afternoon was assuming titanic proportions; distances propelling themselves outward and growing hazy, mountains swelling, horizons mounting higher and higher.

"Oh, Jackie, do you suppose it's the end of the world?"

"Don't be silly."

"I'm not, but everything inside me is pulling into pieces."

"*Konas* are oftener harder than this. The wind hasn't begun to blow yet. I thought you loved storms."

"I do, but this one is different."

"Yes, Lynette."

She went up the path and paused a panting, stormy figure at the brink of the pool.

"There's our Blue Country, Jackie." She pointed to the water, reflecting sky and trees. A gust of wind leaped the tree tops and scurried over the surface wiping out the mirrored reflections. "It's—gone!" she cried, despairingly.

"Lynette, don't, don't look like that. It's only because your mother and that damned Shark Prince are coming that everything is frightening. After they've gone it'll seem like Lani-o-akua again."

"Are you sure?"

"Of course."

"You don't look as if you thought it would. You look like I feel inside."

"Lynette, I feel terrible."

"Let's find Ka-aina. We'll make him tell us about *konas* before we were born, worse than this one will be."

"This is just beginning so how can you tell it's going to be so awful?"

"I know. Look at the sky. There isn't a cloud, but you can almost see the wind racing over the mountains. And it's getting stronger every minute. Listen to it ripping over things, as if the world were splitting to pieces."

They found Ka-aina dozing on the feed bags. He roused himself when they sat down beside him. Lynette clutched his arm.

"You scare, Lineki?"

"Yes."

"What kind you scare?"

"The wind."

Ka-aina looked into her eyes. "Don't be afraid," he said, in Hawaiian. "Wind is God's soul talking to the earth."

Lynette dug her head against the dusty sleeve of his faded *palaka*.

"Dear Ka-aina, when I'm with you everything seems all right, even Mother's coming doesn't matter."

"Patricia come?"

"Tomorrow," Lynette replied.

"And that damned *haole* who looks like the Shark God and who wants to marry Lynette is coming with her," Jackie finished.

"The Breadfruit of the Gods is ripe!" Ka-aina muttered.

Wind roared overhead with a gathering sound. Intelligence, older than the earth, was rushing out of spaces beyond the stars to other spaces even more remote. Lynette possessed herself of Ka-aina's hand. He covered hers with his free one and stared at the afternoon, which was steadily gathering impetus and projecting itself into Lynette's consciousness, trying to transmit some urgent message. She glanced at Jackie and he got to his feet as if he had been prodded and walked to the door.

"The boys are riding in, Lynette, and everything's ex-

citing. The trees look angry and frightened, and the sea's
a smother of foam."

"Come with us, Ka-aina," Lynette begged.

He rose and she folded her arm over his.

"I think sure Patricia no can come. Tonight gods will
walk on land and sea. But maybe can come, the Breadfruit of the Gods is ripe."

"What does that mean?" Lynette asked. "You've said
it twice."

He explained. An awed expression filled her eyes.
Jackie glanced at her, but she was looking at Ka-aina.

"What are you thinking about, *makule?*"

"The old do not think, they wait," he answered, sitting down on an empty box.

Corrals were filling, men unsaddling hurriedly, con-
jecturing, commenting. Lynette listened, her heart ham-
mering so hard that it suffocated her. This was no
ordinary *kona;* it was a runaway hurricane which had
escaped from the south Pacific and was racing through
latitudes where hurricanes were not supposed to come.
Was it possible that after so many years the old prophecy
about Lani-o-akua—

Seeing the expression on Lynette's face, the speaker
desisted leaving the rest of his remark to be snatched up
by his companions' minds. But Lynette, more highly organized and sensitive than all of them, got his thought.

"Jackie, Pilipo's wondering if that horrible thing Ka-
aina told us last night is coming true!"

"What thing?"

"That Lani-o-akua will be destroyed unless a sacrifice
is given—" she could not finish.

Jackie placed a consoling arm about her shoulders and

looked into her blanched face.

"Remember, Lynette, and keep remembering what Ka-aina said; that the wind is God's spirit." He looked up with awe-filled eyes. "He's passing over Lani-o-akua."

CHAPTER XXII

GLANCING at his watch, David started for the dining room. The roaring of wind, shaking the night, made thinking difficult. He listened to darkness tearing past. If the velocity of the gale kept increasing there would be no limit to the damage done by morning. In a few hours rain, thunder, and lightning would add themselves to the convulsion. The wind was electrifying everything. His skin was dry and burning, his hair stiff and harsh. He both dreaded and resented the advent of Patricia and the prince, and wondered how it would end.

Ruth looked up from her soup. "Where are the children?" she asked.

"I don't know."

"This is the worst wind I've ever heard. I'm anxious about Patricia and the prince coming from Honolulu in such a gale. Do you suppose it'll get much worse?"

"It's impossible to tell."

"Have you completed arrangements for meeting them at Makena?"

David nodded.

"Do you suppose the boat'll have to dock at Kahului instead of coming to Makena? If it does they won't arrive until noon. It would be too annoying. I've planned the nicest breakfast."

Enormous rending sounds shook the atmosphere.

"What is that noise?" Ruth asked, laying down her spoon.

"Wind."

"Wind?"

"It's rising," David said, jerking out his chair.

"It's too annoying the way Jack and Lynette disregard meals. How a person is expected to keep servants!" Ruth sipped her soup with a martyred air.

David did not bother to mention that at Lani-o-akua servants remained indefinitely. After several minutes Ruth turned to the Chinese boy with the air of a general commanding armies. "Find Miss Lynette and Mr. Jackie, Ching, and tell them to come to dinner at once."

He went out. Lynette, escorted by Jackie, appeared shortly. David realized with a shock that in twenty-four hours Jackie had emerged from adolescence to manhood. His warm dreamy eyes were direct and brilliant, the dimple in his chin had become a cleft.

"It's long after the dinner hour," Ruth remarked.

"I know, Mother," Jackie replied looking at her from under his slender, flaring eyebrows. Then he scowled. Ruth had ordered his and Lynette's places put out on opposite sides of the table, so it wouldn't look lop-sided, she told herself, but in reality because she knew that Patricia and certainly the prince would prefer it.

"Ching, put my place by Lynette's," he ordered.

"Aren't you together enough without having to sit side by side?" Ruth asked irritably.

"Lynette's been gone for years and only got back yes-terday."

Lynette took hold of his arm.

"I forgot. You were never really gone, were you?"

"No, Jackie. You just couldn't see me."

"Never mind this time, Ching," Jackie said to the Chinaman who was hovering uneasily about the table, "but after tomorrow—" breaking off he smiled and flushed to the roots of his hair.

The quality of his smile puzzled David. In it, triumph and adoration mingled and both were spiced with the impishness of a boy who is planning to, or has outwitted, his elders.

The room was filled with the roar of wind that sounded as if it were shaking the earth into fragments. Lynette listened to it, turning her head slightly.

"I love it. I wish I could spread out wings and fly be-fore it."

"You look as if you could go without wings, Lynette," Jackie said.

Smiling her aloof little smile, she laid her hand on the table. "Uncle David, we found this ring in the dirt near the front gate. Did it belong to Grandfather?"

David examined it. It seemed dimly familiar, but he could not recall ever having seen Trevellyan wear it.

"That's not the Trevellyan coat of arms," he said, after a silence. A mental image of a tense, white hand wearing it kept flitting through his mind. Then the picture soldi-fied. It had been on Patricia's hand, clenching the edge of the desk in the office, the morning Trevellyan came home with the news of Hawke's arrival.

"I recall having seen your mother wear it once," he said, wondering why the loss of so valuable a gem had never been mentioned. Lynette started to remove the ring.

"Don't," Jackie ordered.

Lynette looked rebellious, then her face grew warm and soft.

"Let me see it. Why, it's a pigeon blood ruby!" Ruth exclaimed. "Why don't you want Lynette to take it off, Jack? If you only found it this afternoon there can be no particular sentiment attached to it."

"It's—" the boy began indignantly, then finished lamely, "because *akuas* kept it till Lynette came back and it might be bad luck to take it off."

"Rubbish. You're too old to believe in *akuas*. There are no such things," Ruth said, flatly.

"Ka-aina says—" Lynette began.

"Ka-aina's an ignorant, superstitious old Hawaiian."

A succession of shattering, splitting noises, roars, muffled detonations shook the night. Ruth started and Lynette shrank back in her chair.

"Don't be scared, just keep remembering, Lynette."

"I am."

"What, if I may ask, is it you want Lynette to remember, Jackie?" Ruth asked.

"It's senseless telling you, Mother. It's just something Ka-aina told us this afternoon that you couldn't understand."

"That's good. Your own mother unable to understand something a Kanaka told you."

"But you couldn't. It was beautiful, but it would only sound silly to you."

"Then probably it is." Ruth made the words final. "There's to be no going out of doors tonight. With your mother and the prince arriving in the morning I can't allow you to run the risk of being struck by falling trees. If anything happened to Lynette—"

"I'm sorry, Mother, we've got to go out," Jackie said.

"David!" Ruth flung around like a person who has reached the limit of endurance. "You're largely responsible for this, for my own son defying me. If you'd allowed the children to be punished for running off at night—" She looked ready to burst into tears, then finished stiffly. "It's your duty, David, to insist that both Jack and Lynette remain in the house tonight. After all, we're responsible—"

"You aren't, I came here myself." Lynette resembled a lamp whose wick was being slowly and steadily turned higher and higher.

"That is aside from the matter, Lynette. Now you are here I couldn't face either your mother or Prince Axel—"

Lynette's eyes silenced her. Dull roars, smothered explosions in the atmosphere jarred the night until it reeled. Ruth grasped the arms of her chair. David sat frozen, not by the convulsions outside, but because of an impression that all of them, the house, dishes, table, Lani-o-akua were avalanching down a long incline toward chaos. His perceptions, heightened to an unnatural point, took heed of each detail. He saw Lynette's long lashes droop and quiver, saw the expression on Jackie's face, seen only on men's faces when threatened by danger, a lifting out of self or shaking off a self. Then he heard Lynette whisper,

"After dinner, Jackie, let's tell Uncle David."

Jackie signed fiercely at her to be still.

"But, Jackie, I'd like to."

"You mustn't!"

They faced each other, their spirits clashing. David's eyes moved swiftly from one pale, strained young face to the other. Jackie looked at Lynette, chin thrust forward, lips set in a hard line. Lynette returned his stare indignantly, and their crossing glances clicked like swords. For a fleeting moment and for the only time in her life Lynette resembled Patricia. Nausea hit the pit of David's stomach. Where had he lived through a scene similar to this? In another life, another world?

Then his mind crumpled. Good God! He knew! He remembered! Patricia and Walter Hamilton had worn the identical expressions when they had been seated at this very table, confronting each other on a night long ago. He recalled the passage which had precipitated the deadlock. Patricia had ordered him to have Typhoon saddled for Hamilton at dawn, and he had refused angrily to accept her mount. His mind reassembled, noted, recognized; first, Jackie's odd, flaring eyebrows, then his straight nose, last the cleft in his chin. He was Walter Hamilton's and Patricia's son, and Lynette's half brother!

The night was gathering momentum, plunging, staggering under the wind that was splitting the atmosphere to shreds. His mind seemed on fire, his brain filled with tearing noises. He plunged his head into his hand, then lifted it to look again. There was no mistake. None. Jackie's features shouted his parentage!

"Uncle David, are you sick?" Lynette asked.

David could not answer. Pressing his fist against the table he braced against the back of his chair. Ruth hurried to him and laid her hands on his shoulders, but he threw them off,

"For Christ's sake, let me get out of this, or my brain will burst!"

"What can we do?" Lynette panted, taking tight hold of her horse's bridle, and bracing against a tree which partially broke the blast of the hurricane.

The world overhead was filled with the angry muttering and hurrying of wind which had lost its steady southerly direction and was coming from every quarter of the globe.

"I guess we'll have to go back and pretend we got married. That priest," Jackie glanced at a lighted window behind a lashing oleander, "was nice. He looked sorry when he told us he couldn't marry us without a license. I should have thought about getting one, but everything's happened so fast since you got back . . . yesterday!"

"Don't be sad, Jackie. Tomorrow while everyone's busy being angry, you go and get one. I'll stay with Ka-aina."

"You better hide, Lynette."

"But I feel safe with him."

"He's so old now, he's slow and tired. If you were in a jam and I wasn't round, he might go to sleep while he was thinking of a way out to help you."

"That makes me sad."

"Why, Lynette?"

"It's like something being finished."

Jackie took hold of his stirrup in a business-like way as if counteracting the effect of Lynette's words and his defeat in getting married. Galloping in the wind from Lani-o-akua had been exhilarating. The hurricane had still been high overhead, the world filled with supernatural beauty. The horses had fought for their heads and raced forward. But now the wind seemed foiled, clouds were becoming titanically involved with one another, and savage rain smoked against the earth.

"We might as well start back, Lynette."

They galloped along the road, which dodged and jumped when lightning ripped the sky. Thunder roared, and the sea screamed and lashed at the island. They rode crouched over their horses' necks, trying to shelter their faces. Jackie set the pace, husbanding the animals' strength to meet the miles lying between Wailuku and Lani-o-akua. He eased the gallop to a canter when the road began mounting the low hills below Waikapu. Before they were well among them, Lynette lifted her face from the stinging, wet mane of her horse.

"Are you tired?" the boy asked.

She nodded. Sheltering his face under his crooked arm, Jackie tried to make out where they were. Lightning ripped the sky, showing the swinging ridges behind Waikapu. On a small rise to the right, Norfolk Island pines lurched and swayed like the masts of square-rigged ships, shorn of sails and rigging, lifting disconsolate spars to the storm. Grabbing Lynette's horse by the bit, Jackie waited for the next flash. It came, blinding him, but he got a glimpse of a flickering road ducking into fields of lashing cane.

As if sensing rest and shelter the animals charged through the torn, wet dark until they almost ran into a hitching-rail at the bottom of a tortured garden.

"Where are we?" Lynette asked, sliding off her horse.

"At Waikapu."

"That's where Lord Jim used to live!"

"Yes. Someone's up. There's a light in the house."

"I want to get back to Lani-o-akua before Mother and the Shark Prince come."

"Their ship'll be delayed by this storm. It can't be much after two. If we rest an hour, we can be there by dawn."

Running through the beaten garden, they charged up the steps. Jackie recovered his breath and was about to pound on the door, when it opened.

"Are you Mr. Hamilton?" he asked, looking at the tall, gray-haired man in a bathrobe.

"Yes."

"May we come in?"

"Of course." Stepping back he held the door open, his kind tired eyes friendly and astonished.

Lynette stole a shy glance at him. This was Lord Jim's uncle who hadn't wanted him to go to Lani-o-akua.

"I'm Jackie Birthwood," the boy announced.

Lynette saw, or fancied she saw, the man wince.

"I've met your father."

"When?"

"He stopped here for lunch once, years ago."

"Can I put the horses in the stable . . . because of the trees?"

"I'll wake up one of the servants."

"I'll do it. I'm wet anyway." Seeing Lynette, Jackie recollected himself. "Mr. Hamilton," he began gravely, then a devil popped into his eyes, "this is . . . my wife."

Lynette felt vaguely pleased. Smart Jackie. If they had to pretend they were married it might as well be from the start.

"I'm happy to meet you, Mrs. Birthwood. Come indoors while your husband puts up the horses. Hadn't you
better change into something dry?"

"I'll only get wet again. We'll have to go back to
Lani-o-akua soon."

"Very well. Sit down while I point out the stables."

Lynette sank into the nearest chair. Her wet dress
was heavy, her body felt like lead. Leaning her head
against the high back of the chair, she closed her eyes
and listened to Jackie being directed. "I'll be back in a
minute, darling," he called, and she opened them again.
Jackie and Mr. Hamilton were on the steps. Their shoulders were the same width and for some reason looked
identical. Jackie ran down the walk and Mr. Hamilton
stared after him, then came in. Going to the sideboard,
he poured out some wine.

"This will warm you."

She accepted it. His eyebrows, the shape of his face,
the dent in his chin were like Jackie's! Like Jackie's
would be when he was old. Her mind was tired and
heavy. Leaning her head against the back of the chair, she
waited. Jackie's returning steps roused her.

"Feel better, darling?"

"Yes. I'll be ready to go on in a few minutes."

"Don't hurry. You don't mind our staying for a bit, do
you, Mr. Hamilton? We rode from Lani-o-akua to
Wailuku tonight. I guess I might as well tell you why
we're galloping around in this storm." Seating himself
on the arm of Lynette's chair, he possessed himself of
her hand. Lynette saw Mr. Hamilton's eyes widen as
they lighted on the big ring on her fourth finger. He got
a dead white, then redder than the ruby, then white again.

Jackie was stroking the top of her head and didn't notice. "You see, Mr. Hamilton, Lynette—"

"Lynette!" Mr. Hamilton exclaimed in a smothered voice.

"Yes, this is Lynette. Didn't Lord Jim tell you about her? I liked and hated him before," he laughed in an embarrassed manner, "because he liked Lynette so much, but we had fun together."

Mr. Hamilton's face looked as if it were carved out of gray wood that was very old and dry. Jackie played with the ring.

"Lynette's mother is coming tomorrow, and we ran away and got married so she couldn't take Lynette to England again."

Mr. Hamilton's gray face got red, and the cords on his neck stood out like stiff ropes. Lynette felt frightened. Some monstrous thing was in the room with them. Jackie told their story with pauses and explanations.

"Drink your wine, Lynette. You're shaking."

She nodded, her mind seething like yeast.

He took her empty glass. "Now you'll feel better. Could I have some, too, Mr. Hamilton?"

"Of course. I intended to offer you some."

They went to the sideboard. Light from a center lamp winked in the cut glass decanters and fell on their faces. Feature for feature, limb for limb, they were cast in the identical mould, the only difference between them, the difference of their years. For some reason Lynette wanted to cry. It was like looking at ghosts! Mr. Hamilton poured out two glasses of wine.

"Here's luck, Jack," he said, his voice strange and dry.

"Thanks," Jackie answered, looking pleased. He peered

into the mirror at Lynette, then glanced quickly at the man beside him. Slowly, he put down his glass.

"Mr. Hamilton—"

"Yes?"

"Look." He pointed at their reflections.

"I see our . . . resemblance."

"You look more like my father than Dad does."

Mr. Hamilton made a sound that was like pain. Lynette wanted to speak, but could not, wanted to cry, but her tears were frozen. The dreadful thing in the room edged closer. Jackie and Mr. Hamilton left the sideboard and sat down. Jackie chatted, but whenever he looked at the older man's face, which was his own, Lynette felt hollow. It bothered her the way Mr. Hamilton's eyes kept following her hand which wore the big ring. He tried to look away, tried not to see it, but always his eyes were drawn back. Finally, grasping the arms of her chair, she leaned forward.

"Why do you watch my ring?" she asked, breathlessly.

"It's . . . beautiful."

"Isn't it?" Jackie said, and told how they had found it. "It's Lynette's wedding ring," he finished.

"I thought it might have belonged to Grandfather, but when I asked Uncle David he said he had seen Mother wear it—"

Mr. Hamilton got to his feet, tightening the cord of his bathrobe as if he intended cutting himself in half.

"Have you ever been to Lani-o-akua?" Jackie asked.

"Once, years ago, for a night."

"When Grandfather was alive?" Lynette inquired eagerly.

Mr. Hamilton nodded.

"I'd like to have known him. Ka-aina told us about him last night. Tell me more, Mr. Hamilton."

"Mr. Trevellyan was away when I was there."

Lynette sighed regretfully. Walking to the sideboard, Mr. Hamilton poured himself a glass of whisky. The back of his neck looked rigid. Lynette thrust into Jackie's arm.

"Let's go," she whispered. "I want to be near Ka-aina."

"You're tired. Put your head against my shoulder. We'll go in a minute. I like Mr. Hamilton, don't you?"

"Yes."

Lynette rose, and Jackie walked to the door with his arm around her. Mr. Hamilton walked on Jackie's other side and swallowed whenever he looked at him.

"Thank you for letting us come in and for being so kind," Jackie said when they reached the door. Mr. Hamilton did not reply, and Lynette glanced up inquiringly.

"I thought when we came in that your hair was gray, but it's quite white, isn't it?"

The expression in his eyes frightened Lynette and she grasped Jackie's arm.

"Let's get back to Lani-o-akua quickly," she whispered. "I want to get back before Mother and the Shark Prince come and spoil it. It's going to be horrible."

"You needn't even see them. When I tell them we're married there'll be no sense in their staying around and they'll go."

Mr. Hamilton opened the door. His breathing sounded thick and hot, like lava rushing out of a cone.

"Are you sick?" Lynette asked.

"No, Lynette."

Her eyes flew to Jackie's. "He looks like Uncle David did when he left the dinner table tonight."

"Yes, he does," Jackie agreed, his dark brows gathering in a puzzled frown. "I sort of hate to leave him, Lynette. Mr. Hamilton, would you like us to stay a while longer?"

He shook his head, but grabbed Jackie's shoulder, looking as if he wanted to say something he simply couldn't. He opened the door and Jackie exclaimed,

"Look! All those trees went down while we were talking, and we never heard them!"

"Everything feels like a dream you're trying to get out of," Lynette said. "I used to dream of being in England when I knew I was really in Lani-o-akua and—"

Jackie nodded. "Please come over to Lani-o-akua soon and see us Mr. Hamilton. I like you."

Again Mr. Hamilton tightened the cord of his bathrobe still further. "Thanks, Jackie. I'll come . . . tomorrow."

CHAPTER XXIII

THE night engulfed Jackie and Lynette. Hamilton closed
the door and leaned against it. When he was able to
command his limbs sufficiently, he started for the living
room. Mists fogged his vision. He collided with the sharp
corner of a table, then seeing the dim shape of a chair,
grasped it.

Jackie was his son! No one seeing them together could
mistake their relationship. And Jackie was Lynette's half
brother! With difficulty he managed to sit down. Because of him and Patricia the happiness of those storm-
ridden children must be murdered. Recalling their wind-
blown, rain-beaten young faces, his mind cramped. Then
habits which were the outgrowth of desolate years re-
asserted themselves. Slowly his mind straightened out and
began to function.

When he had first looked at Jackie, he had wondered
where he had seen him before and concluded that it
must have been at some race meet or polo match. There
was an odd familiarity about the brown eyes, something
warming and likeable to the forceful young face and
well-held head. Then he had transferred his attention to
the girl standing beside him. The wet hair clinging to

her temples made her look defenceless.

When Jackie had spoken her name, he had been shocked, realizing that it was from this exquisite creature he had sent Jim, hoping that he might forget her. Recalling Jim's words, "Meeting her was like waking up on a cloudless morning," he grasped the arms of his chair. Without seeing, without knowing Lynette he had condemned her because she was a Trevellyan. But in spirit she was not a Trevellyan, though she had come to the earth through them. She was foam, young leaves, and the whispers of God that are in little breezes.

With the abortive egotism of human beings he had interfered in matters which were not his concern, meddled in God's business, deeming it wisdom. Jackie's admission of childish jealousy confounded him further. Had he not sent Jim away, this marriage, which could not stand, would probably never have taken place. While relating the reasons of their elopement, Jackie had given fragmentary bits of information about Lynette's life. Her desolation in England, her one solace being Jim's letters and gifts, her effort to hasten Jim's long-contemplated trip to England, and her flight, precipitated by horror of the man to whom her parents had affianced her—which had prevented her from waiting for Jim to arrive.

He crushed his temples between his palms. Had she remained until Jim came, Jim who had never forgotten her and who had roamed the earth waiting for her to grow up, this last complication would never have happened. Tearing out of the chair, he began pacing the floor.

He must leave for Lani-o-akua, and blast the lives of the young pair who were victims of their parents' passions. How would it, how could it end? Incidents of the past hour returned; his unbelief when he saw Jackie's likeness to himself, and the shock when he recognized the ring he had given Patricia on Lynette's hand.

Memories submerged in his subconscious mind rose like an in-flowing tide; his first sight of Patricia in the garden, the urge which had driven him to go away, his horse's lameness which had forced him to return, their evening together, the next day at the pool, the ensuing weeks that seemed, actually, to burn when he met Patricia daily at the red cone. With grief, god-like in its proportions, he faced it all. Why, when instinct had prodded him to go, had circumstances outside himself compelled him to go back? It was unthinkable that the torment of the past nineteen years could be without a purpose.

His mind charged around like a riderless horse. Jackie, Jim, Patricia, himself, Trevellyan seemed victims of some invisible purpose that marched over their bodies . . . to what? With what object, beyond the pitiful human desire to build, had Lani-o-akua been created? Through its magnificent achievement which was like some splendid portal, they had all walked . . . some of them against their wills. How was it possible that a woman as carnal as Patricia could be the mother of a girl as exquisite as Lynette? Purity breathed from her skin, radiated from her person. Behind the tangled and terrible events leading to her advent on earth, there must be a motive!

Flinging himself into the nearest chair, he stared at the floor. He must dress and go to Lani-o-akua, and deliver the death blow to Lynette and Jackie's hopes. Outside, the night lay spent against the earth. The wind had died down, prostrate trees sprawled uncomplainingly across terraces shorn of their mad growth of flowers. It seemed, as he sat there, that nature had attempted, unsuccessfully, to protest at the fate which had been in store for Jackie and Lynette. He had seen that Lynette had been vaguely afraid while she sat beside Jackie resting. She had grasped that there was something untoward in Jackie's likeness to him, and in the avid way he had stared, against his will, at the ring she was wearing. She had fancied that in marrying Jackie she was sealing her future to the locality she worshipped and, instead, the marriage would make it impossible for her to remain.

Getting up, he went to the sideboard and poured himself a drink. The lost pair were hurrying to Lani-o-akua in order to get there before Patricia arrived. Trembling seized him. Though he no longer loved her, the thought of seeing her again was physical pain. He tried to climb above surging thoughts which beset him, and to realize the harvest this wild night had brought. He had found his lost son, and he must wreck his future! He tried to thrust away persistent visions of Jackie bending adoringly over Lynette. And he was as responsible to Lynette as he was to Jackie for he had driven Jim from her. How would they receive the news he must bring? With Jackie's protection wrested from her forever, who would shield Lynette from the mother she hated and the man she loathed?

It all might have been averted if he had not sent Jim away! He saw that the windows were beginning to turn gray. He must order a horse and go. His shoulders sagged. The cook was up and an odor of coffee drifted through the house. Some laborer was coming up the walk to report the damage done by the hurricane. He went toward the door and opened it.

"Uncle Walter—"

"Jim—"

CHAPTER XXIV

"Tired, Lynette?" Jackie asked, leaning over to take her hand.

"No."

"You're so quiet."

"I'm cold and a little scared. I wish we were really married. I'd feel safer."

"Me, too."

Dawn was breaking. Lynette peered at the slopes she loved, magnified and exaggerated by slowly lifting mists. To the right, under the clouds, was a long glimpse of the sea and, streaking toward Makena, the speck of a ship.

"We beat them," Jackie said.

Lynette nodded. As they drew nearer to Lani-o-akua, the prostrate forms of uprooted trees loomed oddly in the pastures.

"Oh, Jackie!" Lynette cried. The sight affected her deeply for the trees of Lani-o-akua had seemed as everlasting as the hills.

"Don't mind, Lynette. They'll grow again. Let's have coffee, and we'll feel better."

Lynette did not answer. She was numb with exhaustion, and the havoc about her sapped her of her last ounce of

358

strength. As they neared the corrals, they were compelled to make detours for the devastation became wholesale. Crashing giants had become involved with lesser trees pulling them earthwards as they fell. They lay across walks and in reservoirs. Roots stuck up like spread hands raised in supplication, limbs were shattered, the air filled with the smell of pulped wood and bleeding sap. Some groves had been entirely obliterated, others left practically unhurt as the hurricane freakishly wreaked its fury where it would. There had been little rain in comparison to the velocity of the wind which had exhausted itself in an electrical blast, then guiltily fled.

"Let's unsaddle here and turn the horses loose," Jackie suggested. "I doubt if we can get much nearer—"

Lynette slid off. Lani-o-akua seemed bereft of life. No one was stirring, no riders saddling up, no birds calling among the trees.

"Where's everyone?" she asked, breathing unsteadily.

"I guess out seeing what damage has been done. Dad had to go to Makena and Ka-aina must be with him or he'd be waiting for us."

"Lani-o-akua has a feeling of being dead," Lynette said, her eyelids quivering. They started for the house. The garden was a shambles. They crawled over some trees and under others toward the comforting smell of coffee drifting from the kitchen. Then Lynette saw the clothes line by the door with pins like little brown birds sitting along it. Her heart caught. It belonged to a well-ordered, beloved world which had been left on the other side of the *kona*.

"Lynette, I want to kiss you before we go in. Everything's going to be all right."

"Dear Jackie."

Their lips met briefly and swiftly. When they walked in, the cook wheeled.

"Son-of-a-pitch! Where you two fella go last night?" he demanded truculently. "This time all man go look which place you stop."

Lynette drew a relieved breath. That accounted for the silence which made Lani-o-akua seem dead.

"We were riding," Jackie answered. "Is Mother awake yet?"

"Miss Ruth go Makena with Mr. David. Too much scare big wind, and because no can find you fellas. What for make this kind? Gar-damn-go-to-Hell clazy *holoholo* last night. Tree fall down, no can see anykind."

Lynette beamed. Cooks only got cross when things were every day. Jackie pulled out two chairs, and the cook slammed two cups on the table and filled them.

"Did Ka-aina go to Makena too?" Lynette asked, pulling the steaming coffee toward her.

"I no know. I no care. Maybe go, maybe look for you. Son-of-a-pitch every kind broke." The cook stared out of the door at the plundered gardens. "I tink one year no nuff for clean up. I tink ten thousand trees bloke. S'pose Mr. Hi-ball see, sure he all same clazy. Run every side with big whip and lick fellas so work more fast."

An excited chill crept through Lynette. The mental picture of her grandfather driving men before him in herds was exhilarating.

"You're smiling. You're happy!" Jackie said heaping sugar into a second cup of coffee.

"I was thinking about Grandfather. I wish he was alive. I bet he'd stand on the garden steps with his whip and tell Mother and the Shark Prince they couldn't have me."

Jackie nodded. "It's fun being here alone, isn't it? I'm glad Mother went too."

Lynette nodded, but her abstracted eyes drifted to the garden. Steps sounded. "Ka-aina!" she cried, joyously.

"Where you *keikis* go last night?" he demanded, his gentle face almost grim.

Lynette felt revived. Cooks and cowboys only got cross when things were normal. In some miraculous, blessed way Ka-aina had, as usual, succeeded in adding the finishing touch that put things back in their old places. She sighed blissfully. Jackie glanced at her questioningly and she nodded.

"We went to Wailuku," he announced.

"What for go Wailuku last night?" Ka-aina wanted to know.

"We got married."

"Good, good made this kind! Now nobody can take Lineki away. Good boy, Jackie, good boy."

He was crying and kissing their hands, and the cook angrily wiping his eyes on his apron and muttering in Chinese. Sitting down in the nearest chair, Ka-aina looked at the pair drinking coffee, then said apologetically in Hawaiian as he indicated the bare table,

"And this is your wedding feast. It should have been a *luau* with people from the eight islands invited."

"What for no tell me?" the cook demanded in mock fury. "You wait. I make swell *kaukau* * quick. I no care s'pose high up *haoles* wait and Miss Ruth too much mad—"

* *kaukau*—food.

"We'll have a real wedding *luau* later on, Chong, when Lynette's mother and the Shark Prince have gone."

"More better eat some good ting now. Good luck!"

"Yes, more better," Ka-aina agreed.

"I'm not hungry. I'm too happy to eat," Lynette breathed. "I wish Grandfather—" Her mind drifted away.

"S'pose you like, Jackie, I tell Mr. David," Ka-aina offered.

"No, I want to tell him myself."

"Maybe more good, but I got somekind to tell Mr. David, too, some old kind things that never yet I tell to anyone."

A cold wave, like the edge of the sea, touched Lynette, and she shivered.

"Are they nice things, Ka-aina?" she asked apprehensively.

"Swell kind, Lineki."

"I'm glad you came. After we got back I was scared that Lani-o-akua was *pau*."

Ka-aina elevated his eyebrows waggishly. "Only some tree broke. After clear up plenty new ones come quick."

"Dear Ka-aina, drink coffee with us," Lynette said, reaching for his hand.

The cook piled the table with food. Lynette grabbed his skinny arm and made him sit down with them. She was tremulous with happiness. Her eyes kept seeking Jackie's, then Ka-aina's, then the old cook's who had rowed at them and loved them, stood for raids on the pantry, and had had the sanctuary of his kitchen violated uncounted times in the past, when she and Jackie left ailing or maimed creatures in boxes behind the great stove. He had threatened them with buckets of scalding water, made passes at them with sticks of firewood, and cared for the animals. This was the Lani-o-akua she had loved, ached for, fought to regain. It was hers once more, anyway for this enchanted hour.

With much horse-play and buffoonery, the cook asked her leave, as lady of the house, if he might be excused in order to resume his duties. Jackie laughed, and Ka-aina looked delighted. She felt as she had the first evening in the corrals; as if the whole world were playing a game with her. If only it could go on for ever and ever.

Finally Jackie rose. "I'm going to get into fresh riding clothes. You better too. Then shall we go up to the pool and wait till they come?"

Lynette nodded.

"Keep a sharp lookout, Ka-aina, and when they come call me," Jackie said, pushing back his chair.

"*Ae.*" Ka-aina said, as if taking orders from his master.

"Maybe this afternoon I'll have a chance to go and get our—"

Lynette sprang out of her chair, and Jackie got scarlet to the ears.

"I nearly let the cat out of the bag," he laughed as they walked along the veranda. "Change quickly, darling," he ordered when he left her at her door.

As they started for the hill, Lynette looked about her. Through overturned trees the sea, save for the mile-white lather of foam along the shore, looked curiously peaceful. The day was so still that it seemed like the first one of creation or the last one of the world. Jackie picked his way among the fallen trees and Lynette followed. The fragrance of soaked earth began rising as the sun cleared

Haleakala. Frightened birds, which had flown away, were beginning to venture back.

"Wait here, Lynette," Jackie ordered as they neared the crest of the hill.

"Why?"

"I'll tell you in a minute."

Thrusting his way through the tangle, he disappeared, then returned shortly, beckoning in a relieved way. Lynette joined him. The pool gleamed like a mirror, reflecting eternity. Only one of the cypresses had fallen. Lynette looked sadly at the hundreds of eucalyptus, piled like prostrate bodies, forming a barricade, over which the wind had had to leap before assaulting the cypresses and pool. They looked humble and proud with their great, dark heads resting limply against the earth. Then for fear her heart might begin to stampede, she looked at the serene blue of the sky reflected in the water. The calm of it, after the destruction of the gardens, sank like balm into her soul. Kneeling down she bathed her face. Jackie dropped on one knee beside her.

"Don't cry, Lynette," he begged.

"I'm not. Why did you want to come first?"

"I was scared the pool might be spoilt or broken."

"Dear Jackie!" She flung her arms about his neck. "Let's sit here and look at our Blue Country."

The warmth of the sun increased and from below came the sound of chopping axes.

"The boys have begun clearing the garden, Lynette. In no time it'll be nice again. We were silly to feel so bad when we got back."

"Yes. This is the only place that seems like Lani-o-akua." Possessing herself of Jackie's hand, Lynette laid her cheek against it. "When I shut my eyes and feel the sun on me it seems like when we were kids," she murmured, then raised her lashes as if afraid that the words might rouse ambushed enemies.

Jackie did not answer.

"You're sad, Jackie, and it makes you look like Mr. Hamilton. It scared me because you are so like him. As if you were his son. I kept thinking about it when I saw you together."

"I like him. I bet he'd be a nice father."

"Not nicer than Uncle David. I love him."

"So do I, but it's funny, Dad never seems like my father nor Mother like a mother. She's always tried to make me feel the way boys ought to feel about their mothers, but I can't. I never loved anyone till you. I just liked."

Lynette edged closer. "That makes me sad. I was like that before I came here, locked up tight inside. But after being at Lani-o-akua I loved everything."

"I hear horses," Jackie broke in.

Lynette started shaking. Jackie listened. "It's the boys coming in. Ka-aina said he'd call—"

They relaxed and gazed at each other like condemned people whose death sentence has been postponed.

"Remember, darling," Jackie said after a long silence, "no matter what, stay out of sight. Don't try to see me after I go down. Whenever I can get away, even if it's only for a few minutes, I'll come to you. If you hear anyone coming, run and hide."

Lynette nodded.

"If I get lonely, I'll go to Grandfather."

"All right. They won't think of your going there."

They listened to mynah birds noisily discussing the

devastation, and gazed at the reflections in the pool. Then a long call, like a wail, broke the silence.

"*Pimai, pimai!*" *

Jackie swallowed, got to his feet, and pulled Lynette up.

"I'm scared, Lynette. There are so many of them. I mustn't give away that we aren't really married. We must be . . . quickly. I'll never feel safe till you're my wife. Just thinking about your mother and the Shark Prince makes me shake." He looked at Lynette's constricted face. "Think about your grandfather while I'm gone and then you'll be brave."

She listened to him pushing through the trees, then scrambled to her feet. She must be near him, keep him in sight. Fallen trees would hide her. Branches snatched at her, trying to stop her, but she eluded them. Terror that left her empty and breathless, that did not even give her time to think, had her in its clutch. She heard voices, axes, saw unreal figures lopping off branches and dragging them away. Already the walk to the gate had been cleared. Jackie spoke to the workmen, and their voices made the day real.

A thought, like the sting of a bee, darted through her head. She might as well try to sneak an offering to the Shark God. A great breadfruit tree had crashed down in front of the *kukui* grove, like a solid green screen. Fruit lay pulped and scattered across the walk. Timorously and reluctantly she worked her way toward the image with a fern leaf in her hand. As she was about to lay it at the base of the idol, she saw them coming.

She did not want to look at them, but could not tear

* *pimai*—come.

her eyes away. David, moving as if he carried a heavy load on his shoulders; Ruth, her face and neck blotched and red from weeping. Behind them, the two she hated, moving in tight-lipped silence.

Jackie, his hands thrust deep in the pockets of his riding breeches, waited at the head of the steps. Defiance, mixed with longing for some promise of support from David and Ruth, showed in his face. Lynette's hand went out unsteadily seeking for support, touched the cold stone god, and she jerked it away as if it had been burnt. A note like the sustained humming of a bee sounded in her head, tangling up her mind. Her mother recoiled on seeing Jackie, then frowned. The prince turned his pallid face to her, asking about him, and she gestured curtly. Jackie did not move aside to let them pass. David addressed him, but the boy did not seem to hear. His being was focussed on the tall figures coming up the steps.

David spoke to the men clearing the garden, and when Patricia and Prince Axel were out of earshot, addressed Jackie. He nodded, and they went into the house. Lynette sank on to the grass, her hands shaking. She'd better go back to the pool. Jackie would come before long to tell her how things were going. When she got to the pool she bathed her burning temples, then stretched limply on the warm stones. She must be careful not to fall asleep because her mother and the Shark Prince might come looking for her. She tried to expand her mind, but it was full of people who prevented the machinery from operating properly.

The morning was filled with the sound of chopping axes and indignant birds scolding at the destruction of their world. Nervousness gripped her, she wanted someone to talk to, wanted to smother her thoughts with words.

Sickening inertia was stealing through her quivering body. She wanted someone fierce and strong to stand with her and Jackie against the rest. Why wasn't her grandfather alive? Why didn't he come to her when she needed him? He could. He was dead, and didn't have a body which he had to stay inside. The sound of someone pushing through the foliage sent her leaping to her feet. She wanted to run toward the sound and from it. Then she saw Jackie, and the sight of him balanced her mind. He came toward her without speaking and took her into his arms.

"They're eating breakfast. Dad knows something so dreadful, Lynette, that it makes him look sick. He wants to see me in the office as soon as he can. I had to come up for a minute. I had the most horrible feeling when I left you—"

"What was it?" Lynette asked, digging her hot forehead against his neck.

"I wanted to tell you when I left, but I couldn't. Oh, Lynette, I felt I'd never see you again. I came back on purpose to make the feeling wrong." He wiped his face.

Lynette clung to him.

"Don't let them get me, Jackie. I wish Grandfather was alive to help us."

"Me, too."

"Maybe I should go down with you. It's dreadful that you are getting it all."

"Darling, I don't want you to come."

"What about Mother and the Shark Prince? What do they say?"

"They're so angry that they can't speak. Your Mother's face gets the funniest expression on it every time she looks at me, as if she'd like to tear me to pieces."

"I wish they'd get things over with," Lynette whispered. "I'm so tired. Waiting is dreadful."

"Yes. Everybody seems to be waiting. Ka-aina's waiting to talk to Dad and he wants to talk to me and the Shark Prince and your mother wants to talk to you. There's a horrible feeling *that they're all scared to begin.* As soon as Ka-aina's finished seeing Dad, I'll tell him to come up here and stay with you."

"Oh, will you!"

"Yes, and when Dad's finished with me, I'll come back."

Lynette nodded.

"I guess they're through breakfast by now. I'd better go down."

He unwound his fingers from Lynette's, then reclasped them, and she walked to the brink of the hill with him.

"You haven't that feeling now, Jackie, have you, that you won't see me again?" she asked, her voice catching.

He shook his head valiantly.

When he was out of sight Lynette sat down slowly on the walk. Breath jammed her lungs until they ached. She looked at the peaceful water, trying to steady her mind. Incessantly chopping axes seemed to be making mincemeat of the world. Perhaps it would be better to go to the mausoleum. Doing something, anything, was better than just sitting and wondering what was happening below in the house, office, and garden. A subtle change took place in her as if she had adjusted to an unseen burden.

She went down the hill, skirting the kitchen. That way she would pass the office and might be able to over-hear what was being said there. Approaching cautiously, she halted, then seeing her mother and the Shark Prince walking toward the guest cottages, she shied like a frightened horse. Their heads were bent, their faces frozen into bitter lines. Each seemed angry with the other, yet united against their wills. When they disappeared in Kalakaua's cottage, she fled across a section of lawn which had been partially cleared of wreckage.

Voices drifted out of the open windows of the office. Ka-aina's and Uncle David's. It would be comforting just to see them. Climbing among the branches of a fallen tree she peeped down. Ka-aina was holding his hat, looking like a person about to lay down his trump card. She could not hear what he was saying, only his voice. For an instant Uncle David grew as rigid as if he had been run through with a spear, then crumpling over the desk, plunged his head into his arms. It was as shocking as seeing a tree fall on a windless day. What could Ka-aina have said to do that to Uncle David who was always strong and still? Ka-aina looked as if he could not believe his eyes, then went forward and laid his hand on Uncle David's bent back. He jerked Ka-aina off as if he could never forgive him for some monstrous thing he had done. Ka-aina looked paralyzed, then screamed out:

"Mr. Hi-ball said he must never grow up, but when you and Miss Ruth had no children, I knew the *akuas* wanted him at Lani-o-akua so I left him in the lava flow for Miss Ruth to find—"

"I always suspected it. Yesterday at lunch, no, at dinner, I saw his likeness to Hamilton and—"

Ka-aina started to speak, but David signed with one arm, silencing him and banishing him forever. All at once Ka-aina looked as weary and old as the earth and as betrayed. He attempted to speak a second time, but David said, in a rasping voice: "Send Jackie here. Don't say anything. I'm the one who's got to tell him. Oh, great God!"

The humming note in Lynette's head which had started when she saw her mother and the Prince enter the garden, and which had never quite stopped, grew louder. Something, it was something dreadful about Jackie. She shook her head, trying to clear out her mind, but the sound was increasing, getting as loud as the wind yesterday, filling the world. She saw Ka-aina leave, and heard Jackie's quick steps hurrying toward the office. With a super-human effort she assembled her faculties. Before anything, Jackie would tell Uncle David about their pretend marriage which soon would be real. The day seemed to hold its breath, and the sound of axes to fill the world. She watched for gladness to come to Uncle David's face when Jackie told him. She ventured closer and waited expectantly.

"There's something I want to tell you, Dad, before you say anything to me."

"Be quick about it, Jackie. I've got something to tell you."

"Don't be angry. Last night Lynette and I got married so her mother—"

Uncle David looked as if his mind was in convulsions. Jack rushed to him.

"Dad—"

"Wait! Wait a minute, Jack!"

Snatching up Uncle David's hand, Jackie held it. The warm, boyish clasp injected David with the necessary courage. Bracing back like a man facing a firing squad, David looked into Jackie's eyes.

"You'll need every ounce of manhood you possess, Jackie, to stand what I've got to tell you."

Jackie grew haggard.

"Is it about . . . Lynette?"

"It concerns . . . both of you. Jack, Lynette's your half-sister."

"My half-sister! *How?*"

"You are Patricia's illegitimate son."

"I don't believe it. That horrible woman couldn't be my mother, *too!*"

"She is."

All the color and roundness had gone out of Jackie's face. "Who . . . who is my father?" he asked, then crimsoned to the hair. "You don't have to tell me. I know."

"Know! How can you possibly know?"

"Last night . . . Dad, we aren't really married. We went to Wailuku, but didn't have a license. On the way back we stopped to rest at Waikapu. Mr. Hamilton—"

Getting to his feet, David gripped Jackie's arm.

"Get hold of yourself, old man."

"But Lynette! I love her, I've loved her since the very first instant I saw her. And now I can't have her. Can't ever marry her!"

It was Jackie speaking, but not his voice any more. It was a man's voice, hard and savage. Something was tearing to pieces inside Lynette's head. A dark curtain came down in jerks before her eyes, and the day tilted on end and began sliding down a long slope. Cold waves from a bottomless ocean began washing around her ankles. The rending noise in her brain grew steadily louder. She must run away . . . somewhere. Jackie was her brother. They couldn't be married. The Shark Prince and her mother would get her.

Lynette half-saw and half-felt her body slide off the log and begin running. Bits of tree-piled lawn opened and shut in front of her. More trees, all lying at angles. Where was she going? She tried to recognize some familiar object, but her surroundings were spinning apart and running together alternately.

She was lost, no one could save or help her. No one! Then she saw the mausoleum. Of course . . . her grandfather. She must get to him. He would come back from being dead, as he had years ago, to be with her. It had not been until the time got near for her to return to England that she had begun to see him. She was in worse danger now.

Her foot caught in a branch and she fell headlong. A wild impulse came to rip at the treacherous thing that delayed her and squandered precious moments, then she was brought up sharply by the impact of an idea. Her grandfather had always wanted her to do something for him. What exactly she could not make out. Well, she'd say, "I'll help you, Grandfather, but you must save me, help me, too." For the first time she became a mental force, independent of physical limitations.

She rose. The violence of uncertainty slipped from her figure. For some reason the shape of the mausoleum seemed distorted. She was not seeing straight. Then she gasped. A big eucalyptus had crashed across it! Mists rose, blurring the landscape she loved, pressing its chaos into her brain. Her movements wavered, imagined voices filled her ears. Then in a passion of determination, she gathered herself, flung down the slope, and landed on the terrace.

She would break in the door, hide beside her grandfather who had loved Lani-o-akua as she did, who would get out of his coffin to help her. He would not let them take her. She tried to brush aside the vapors which confused her.

"Grandfather, Grandfather," she whispered. Her fingers touched the iron door and she thrust against it. It gave unexpectedly. She half-fell into the vault, remembering that Jackie had neglected to lock it the previous morning.

She saw the coffin top against the slab where they had left it because it was too heavy to lift. Then she dug at her eyes. The vault was filled with light. She looked up. The crashing tree had caved in the roof. With a supreme compulsion of will she focussed her eyes. A shriek escaped her lips and she collapsed against the wall. Not only had the tree shattered the roof, but falling concrete had knocked Trevellyan's casket from its base, splintering the plate glass top into fragments. A strange smell of some pungent, fast-drying liquid stung her nostrils and filled the tomb. She saw, with horrified stupefaction, Trevellyan's form sprawled with unseemly abandon on the floor.

If she had seen everyone she had ever known rushing stark naked and howling into the world, she would not have been as shocked. For an instant her senses forsook her. The sombre, inescapable aura of death was about her, and she began crawling across the floor like a mortally wounded animal.

"Grandfather, Grandfather," she whispered, putting out her hand to touch his silk shirt, "come with me!"

She clutched at it, as if by the very force of her grip, she was holding together the acres they both loved. A portion of the material gave and she stared at it. Her eyes fogged. Blindly, she began seeking for the way out. Somewhere far away she was conscious of warm sunlight. They must get to it. Faces flitted across her mind; Jackie's, as she had last seen it, Ka-aina's when Uncle David threw him out, the agony in Mr. Hamilton's eyes when he looked into the mirror with Jackie. The world was done, she and her grandfather must be on their way, quickly.

A dry wind began blowing bewilderingly behind her eyes. Through torn darkness she caught glimpses of the trees and pastures they worshipped which the mad *kona* had destroyed. The chill mists about her were changing to a tossing sea. She began running and turning to make sure that her grandfather was following. She could not see him because a band was tightening about her head, blood pounding against it until her senses reeled. But she felt him, he was there.

She paused for a fleeting instant before crossing the road. Two horsemen were tearing along the avenue. The animals leaped fallen trees, crashed among piled branches, fighting and floundering to get free. She recognized Mr. Hamilton, then cried out,

"Lord Jim!"

Her voice was lost in breaking branches. They went on. She was going *pupule*. Lord Jim wasn't here. He was far away. Yet his face had been real. Her reason began slipping. Everything was *pau*, was avalanching with gathering speed down a long, dark slope that ended in nothing. She sank upon the warm earth and contact with it steadied her. Inertia drugged mind and body, but with a supreme effort she pulled herself free of the numbness which tried to overpower her limbs.

She reached out her hand. Her grandfather was there. Something deep and beautiful passed between them. She saw, from a great distance, her mother pacing the front walk. A tall figure came up the steps, a figure that became transfixed when it encountered her mother's. Mr. Hamilton. They faced each other like ghosts meeting ghosts. She must be off, or they might see her. She struggled up the tangled slope of the hill, fighting trees that attempted to stop her. Perhaps Ka-aina and Jackie were waiting for her. They would be excited and glad when they saw who was with her.

Something strong and compassionate was drawing her forward, something peaceful and vast that annihilated the chaos encompassing her. The band confining her brain burst. Her mind escaped, streamed out, burned up the darkness and confusion around her. "Come, Grandfather," she breathed, and darted on. "There's no more Lani-o-akua, we must go to God—"

She heard, from a great distance, the triumphant insistent singing of a skylark hovering above the water that held the dear image of Lani-o-akua within its magic and inviolate circle, and from farther off a great voice calling. She reached out her hand, started toward it, stumbled over a fallen limb and fell headfirst from the stone coping into the pool.